TRANSLATED INTO OVER 30 LANGUAGES

★ ★ ★

NPR TOP 100 THRILLERS OF ALL TIME

★ ★ ★

WINNER OF THE CWA IAN FLEMING STEEL DAGGER
HONOURING ORIGINAL AND DISTINCTIVE THRILLER WRITING

★ ★ ★

LONGLISTED FOR THE 2008
MAN BOOKER PRIZE FOR FICTION

★ ★ ★

SHORTLISTED FOR THE COSTA FIRST NOVEL AWARD

★ ★ ★

WINNER OF THE GALAXY BOOK AWARD
FOR BEST NEW WRITER

★ ★ ★

WINNER OF THE 2009 BARRY AWARD
FOR BEST FIRST NOVEL

★ ★ ★

WINNER OF THE ANNUAL GRAND PRIX BY JAPAN
ADVENTURE FICTION ASSOCIATION

★ ★ ★

WINNER OF THE 2009 AUDIE AWARD
FOR BEST SUSPENSE NOVEL

★ ★ ★

NAMED AS A BEST DEBUT FINALIST
IN THE UK INDIES CHOICE BOOK AWARDS

★ ★ ★

WINNER OF THE INTERNATIONAL THRILLER
WRITER AWARD FOR BEST FIRST NOVEL

A RICHARD AND JUDY BOOK OF THE DECADE

* * *

SHORTLISTED FOR THE SOUTH BANK SHOW
AWARD LITERARY CATEGORY

* * *

FEATURED IN THE BARNES AND NOBLE LIST OF
TOP TEN FICTION DEBUTS OF 2008

* * *

NAMED ONE OF THE *OBSERVER* REVIEW'S
MOST THRILLING BOOKS OF 2008

* * *

SHORTLISTED FOR THE *LA TIMES* MYSTERY/
THRILLER BOOK OF THE YEAR

* * *

WINNER OF THE *STRAND MAGAZINE* 2008 CRITICS AWARD
FOR BEST FIRST MYSTERY NOVEL

* * *

SHORTLISTED FOR THE THEAKSTON OLD PECULIER
CRIME NOVEL OF THE YEAR

* * *

SHORTLISTED FOR THE CWA JOHN CREASEY NEW BLOOD
DAGGER FOR BEST DEBUT NOVEL

* * *

SHORTLISTED FOR THE DESMOND ELLIOTT PRIZE
FOR FIRST TIME NOVELISTS

* * *

WAVERTON GOOD READ AWARD

* * *

NOMINATED BY AMAZON.CO.UK AS PART OF THEIR NEW AND
EMERGING AUTHORS LIST FOR THE FAVOURITE BOOKS OF 2008

Also by Tom Rob Smith

Agent 6
The Secret Speech

CHILD 44

TOM ROB SMITH

SIMON &
SCHUSTER

London · New York · Sydney · Toronto

A CBS COMPANY

First published in Great Britain by Simon & Schuster UK Ltd, 2008
This edition published by Simon & Schuster UK Ltd, 2011
A CBS COMPANY

Copyright © Tom Rob Smith, 2008, 2009

1 3 5 7 9 10 8 6 4 2

Simon & Schuster UK Ltd
1st Floor, 222 Gray's Inn Road
London WC1X 8HB

www.simonandschuster.co.uk
www.tomrobsmith.com

Simon & Schuster Australia
Sydney

A CIP catalogue record for this book
is available from the British Library

ISBN 978-0-85720-922-1

Extract from *The Uses of Literacy* by Richard Hoggart,
published by Chatto & Windus.
Reprinted by permission of The Random House Group Ltd.

Printed by CPI Cox & Wyman, Reading, Berkshire RG1 8EX

To my parents

Soviet Union
Ukraine
Village of Chervoy

25 January 1933

Since Maria had decided to die, her cat would have to fend for itself. She'd already cared for it far beyond the point where keeping a pet made any sense. Rats and mice had long since been trapped and eaten by the villagers. Domestic animals had disappeared shortly after that. All except for one, this cat, her companion which she'd kept hidden. Why hadn't she killed it? She needed something to live for; something to protect and love – something to survive for. She'd made a promise to continue feeding it up until the day she could no longer feed herself. That day was today. She'd already cut her leather boots into thin strips, boiled them with nettles and beetroot seeds. She'd already dug for earthworms, sucked on bark. This morning in a feverish delirium she'd gnawed the leg of her kitchen stool, chewed and chewed until there were splinters jutting out of her gums. Upon seeing her the cat had run away, hiding under the bed, refusing to show itself even as she'd knelt down, calling its name, trying to coax it out. That had been the moment Maria decided to die, with nothing to eat and nothing to love.

Maria waited until nightfall before opening her front door. She reckoned that under the cover of darkness her cat stood a better chance of reaching the woods unseen. If anyone in the village caught sight of it they'd hunt it. Even this close to her own death, the thought of her cat being killed upset her. She comforted herself with the knowledge that surprise was on its side. In a community where grown men chewed clods of earth in the hope of finding ants or insect eggs, where children picked through horse shit in the hope of finding undigested husks of grain and women fought over the ownership of bones, Maria was sure no one believed that a cat could still be alive.

*

Pavel couldn't believe his eyes. It was awkward, thin, with green eyes and black speckled fur. It was unmistakably a cat. He'd been collecting firewood when he saw the animal dart from Maria Antonovna's house, cross the snow-covered road and head towards the woods. Holding his breath, he glanced around. No one else had spotted it. There was no one else about; no lights at the windows. Wisps of smoke, the only sign of life, rose from less than half the chimney stacks. It was as though his village had been snuffed out by the heavy snowfall, all signs of life extinguished. Much of the snow lay undisturbed: there were hardly any footprints and not a single path had been dug. Days were as quiet as the nights. No one got up to work. None of his friends played, staying in their houses where they lay with their families huddled in beds, rows of enormous sunken eyes staring up at the ceiling. Adults had begun to look like children, children like adults. Most had given up scavenging for food. In these circumstances the appearance of a cat was nothing short of miraculous — the re-emergence of a creature long since considered extinct.

Pavel closed his eyes and tried to remember the last time he'd eaten meat. When he opened his eyes he was salivating. Spit ran down the side of his face in thick streams. He wiped it away with the back of his hand. Excited, he dropped his pile of sticks and ran home. He had to tell his mother, Oksana, the remarkable news.

*

Oksana sat wrapped in a woollen blanket staring at the floor. She remained perfectly still, conserving energy as she devised ways of keeping her family alive, thoughts which occupied her every waking hour and every fretful dream. She was one of the few who'd not given up. She would never give up. Not as long as she had her sons. But determination itself wasn't enough, she had to be careful: a misjudged endeavour could mean exhaustion and exhaustion invariably meant death. Some months ago Nikolai Ivanovich, a neighbour and friend, had embarked on a desperate raid upon a State granary. He had not returned. The next morning Nikolai's wife and Oksana had gone looking for him. They'd found his body by the roadside, lying on his back – a skeletal body with an arched, stretched stomach, his belly pregnant with the uncooked grain he'd swallowed in his dying moments. The wife had wept while Oksana had removed the remaining grain from his pockets, dividing it between them. On their return to the village Nikolai's wife had told everyone the news. Instead of being pitied she'd been envied, all anyone could think about were the handfuls of grain she possessed. Oksana had thought her an honest fool – she'd put them both in danger.

Her recollections were interrupted by the sound of someone running. No one ran unless there was important news. She stood up, fearful. Pavel burst into the room and breathlessly announced:

—*Mother, I saw a cat*.

She stepped forward and gripped her son's hands. She had to be sure he wasn't imagining things: hunger could play tricks. But his face showed no sign of delirium. His eyes were sharp, his expression serious. He was only ten years old and already he was a man. Circumstances demanded that he forgo his childhood. His father was almost certainly dead, if not dead then dead to them. He'd set off towards the city of Kiev in the hope of bringing back food. He'd never returned and Pavel understood, without needing to be told or consoled, that his father would never return. Now Oksana depended upon her son as much as he depended upon her. They were partners and Pavel had sworn aloud that he'd succeed where his father had failed: he'd make sure his family stayed alive.

Oksana touched her son's cheek.

—*Can you catch it?*

He smiled, proud.

—*If I had a bone*.

The pond was frozen. Oksana rooted through the snow to find a rock. Concerned that the sound would attract attention she wrapped the rock in her shawl, muffling the noise as she punctured a small hole in the ice. She put the rock down. Bracing herself for the black, freezing water she reached in, gasping at the cold. With only seconds before her arm became numb she moved quickly. Her hand touched the bottom and clutched nothing but silt. Where was it? Panicking, she leant down, submerging all of her arm, searching left and right, losing all feeling in her hand. Her fingers brushed glass. Relieved, she took hold of the bottle and pulled it out. Her skin had turned shades of blue, as though she'd been punched. That didn't concern her, she'd found what she was looking for – a bottle sealed with tar. She wiped away the layer of silt on the side and peered at the contents. Inside was a collection of small bones.

Returning to the house, she found Pavel had stoked the fire. She warmed the seal over the flames, tar dripping onto the embers in sticky globs. While they waited, Pavel noticed her bluish skin and rubbed her arm, restoring the circulation, ever attentive to her needs. With the tar melted, she tipped the bottle upside down and shook. Several bones snagged on the rim. She pulled them free, offering them to her son. Pavel studied them carefully, scratching the surface, smelling each one. Having made his selection he was ready to leave. She stopped him.

—*Take your brother.*

Pavel thought this a mistake. His younger brother was clumsy and slow. And anyway the cat belonged to him. He'd seen it, he'd catch it. It would be his victory. His mother pressed a second bone into his hand.

—*Take Andrei.*

*

Andrei was nearly eight years old and he loved his older brother very much. Rarely going outside, he spent most of his time in the back room, where the three of them slept, playing with a pack of cards. The cards had been made by his father from sheets of paper sliced into squares and pasted together, a parting gift before he'd set off for Kiev. Andrei was still waiting for him to come home. No one had told Andrei to expect anything different. Whenever he missed his father, which was often, he'd deal the cards out on the floor, sorting them by suits and numbers. He was sure if he could just finish the pack then his father would come back. Isn't that why he'd given him the cards before he'd left? Of course, Andrei preferred playing with his brother but Pavel no longer had time for games. He was always busy helping their mother and only ever played at night just before they got into bed.

5

Pavel entered the room. Andrei smiled, hoping he was ready to play a hand, but his brother crouched down and swept the cards together.

—*Put these away. We're going out. Where are your* laptys?

Understanding the question as an order, Andrei crawled under the bed retrieving his *laptys*: two strips cut from a tractor tyre and a pile of rags which, when bound together with string, served as a pair of makeshift boots. Pavel helped tie them tightly, explaining that tonight they had a chance of eating meat as long as Andrei did exactly as he was told.

—*Is Father coming back?*

—*He isn't coming back.*

—*Is he lost?*

—*Yes, he's lost.*

—*Who's bringing us meat?*

—*We're going to catch it ourselves.*

Andrei knew his brother was a skilful hunter. He'd trapped more rats than any other boy in the village. This was the first time Andrei had been invited to accompany him on such an important mission.

Outside in the snow Andrei paid special care not to fall over. He often stumbled and tripped, for the world appeared blurred to him. The only things he could see clearly were objects he held very close to his face. If someone was able to make out a person in the distance — while all Andrei could see was a blur — he put it down to intelligence or experience or some attribute he'd yet to acquire. Tonight he wouldn't fall over and make a fool of himself. He'd make his brother proud. This was more important to him than the prospect of eating meat.

Pavel paused by the edge of the woods, bending down to examine the cat's tracks in the snow. Andrei considered his skill in finding them remarkable. In awe, he crouched down, watching as his brother touched one of the paw prints. Andrei knew nothing about tracking or hunting.

—*Is this where the cat walked?*

Pavel nodded and looked into the woods.

—*The tracks are faint.*

Copying his brother, Andrei traced his finger around the paw print, asking:

—*What does that mean?*

—*The cat isn't heavy, which means there'll be less food for us. But if it's hungry then it's more likely to go for the bait.*

Andrei tried to absorb this information but his mind drifted.

—*Brother, if you were a playing card what card would you be? Would you be an ace or a king, a spade or a heart?*

Pavel sighed and Andrei, stung by his disapproval, felt tears beginning to form:

—*If I answer do you promise not to talk any more?*

—*I promise.*

—*We won't catch this cat if you talk and scare it away.*

—*I'll be quiet.*

—*I'd be a knave, a knight, the one with a sword. Now you promised – not a word.*

Andrei nodded. Pavel stood up. They entered the woods.

*

They'd walked for a long time – it felt like many hours, although Andrei's sense of time, like his sight, wasn't sharp. With the moonlight and the reflective layer of snow his older brother seemed to have little difficulty following tracks. They were deep into the woods, further than Andrei had ever gone before. He frequently ran in order to keep pace. His legs ached, his stomach ached. He

7

was cold, hungry and although there was no food at home at least his feet didn't hurt. The string binding the rags to the tyre strips had come loose and he could feel snow edging under the soles of his feet. He didn't dare ask his brother to stop and re-tie them. He'd promised — not a word. Soon the snow would melt, the rags would become sodden and his feet would become numb. To take his mind off the discomfort he snapped a twig from a sapling and chewed the bark, grinding it down into a coarse paste which felt rough on his teeth and tongue. People had told him bark paste sated feelings of hunger. He believed them; it was a useful thing to believe.

Suddenly Pavel gestured for him to remain still. Andrei stopped mid-step, his teeth brown with bits of bark. Pavel crouched down. Andrei copied him, searching the forest for whatever his brother had seen. He squinted, trying to bring the trees into focus.

Pavel stared at the cat and the cat seemed to be staring at him with its two small green eyes. What was it thinking? Why wasn't it running away? Hidden in Maria's house, perhaps it hadn't learnt to fear humans yet. Pavel drew his knife, cutting the top of his finger and daubing with blood the chicken bone his mother had given him. He did the same with Andrei's bait, a broken rat skull — using his own blood since he didn't trust his brother not to yelp and startle the cat. Without saying a word the brothers parted, heading in opposite directions. Back at the house Pavel had given Andrei detailed instructions so there was no need to talk. Once they were some distance apart, on either side of the cat, they'd place the bones in the snow. Pavel glanced at his brother, to check that he wasn't mucking up.

Doing precisely as he'd been instructed, Andrei took the length of string from his pocket. Pavel had already tied the end into a noose. All Andrei had to do was position it around the rat's skull.

He did this and then stepped back as far as the string would allow, getting down onto his stomach, crunching and compressing the snow. He lay in wait. Only now, on the ground, did he realize that he could barely see his own bait. It was a blur. Suddenly afraid, he hoped the cat would go towards his brother. Pavel wouldn't make a mistake, he'd catch it and they could go home and eat. Nervous and cold, his hands began to shake. He tried to steady them. He could see something: a black shape moving towards him.

Andrei's breath began to melt the snow in front of his face; cold trickles of water ran towards him and down his clothes. He wanted the cat to go the other way, to his brother's trap, but as the blur got closer there was no denying that the cat had chosen him. Of course, if he caught the cat then Pavel would love him, play cards with him and never get cross again. The prospect pleased him and his mood changed from dread to anticipation. Yes, he'd be the one to catch this cat. He'd kill it. He'd prove himself. What had his brother said? He'd warned against pulling the snare too early. If the cat was startled all would be lost. For this reason and the fact that he couldn't be sure exactly where the cat was standing Andrei decided to wait, just to be sure. He could almost bring the black fur and four legs into focus. He'd wait a little longer, a little longer . . . He heard his brother hiss:

—*Now!*

Andrei panicked. He'd heard that tone many times before. It meant he'd done something wrong. He squinted hard and saw the cat was standing in the middle of his snare. He pulled the string. But too late, the cat had leapt away. The noose missed. Even so, Andrei pulled the lank string towards him, pathetically hoping that somehow there might be a cat on the end of it. An empty noose arrived in his hand and he felt his face go red with shame. Overcome with anger, he was ready to stand up and chase the cat and catch it and strangle it and smash its skull. But he didn't move: he saw that his brother remained flat on the ground. And Andrei, who'd learnt to always follow his brother's lead, did exactly the same. He squinted, straining his eyes to discover that the blurred black outline was now moving towards his brother's trap.

The anger at his little brother's incompetence had given way to excitement at the cat's imprudence. The muscles in Pavel's back went tight. No doubt the cat had tasted blood, and hunger was stronger than caution. He watched as the cat stopped mid-step, one paw in the air, staring straight at him. He held his breath: his fingers clenched around the string and waited, silently urging the cat on.

Please. Please. Please.

The cat sprang forward, opened its mouth and grabbed the bone. Timing it perfectly he tugged the string. The noose caught around the cat's paw, the front leg was snared. Pavel leapt up, yanking the string, tightening the noose. The cat tried to run but the string held fast. He pulled the cat to the ground. Screeching filled the forest, as though a creature far larger was fighting for its life, thrashing in the snow, arching its body, snapping at the string. Pavel was afraid the knot would break. The string was thin, frayed. As he tried to edge closer the cat pulled away, keeping out of reach. He cried out to his brother:

—*Kill it!*

Andrei still hadn't moved, not wishing to make another mistake. But now he was being given instructions. He jumped up, ran forward, immediately tripping and falling face down. Lifting his nose out of the snow, he could see the cat up ahead hissing and spitting and twisting. If the string broke, the cat would be free and his brother would hate him for ever. Pavel shouted, his voice hoarse, frantic:

—*Kill it! Kill it! Kill it!*

Andrei staggered up and without any clear idea of what he was doing bounded forward and threw himself on top of the cat's thrashing body. Perhaps he'd hoped the impact would kill it. But now, lying on the animal, he could feel the cat was alive and wriggling underneath his stomach, scratching at the grain sacks that had been stitched together to make his jacket. Keeping himself flat on the cat to stop it escaping, Andrei looked behind him, his eyes pleading with Pavel to take charge.

—*It's still alive!*

Pavel ran forward and dropped to his knees, reaching under his younger brother's body only to come in contact with the cat's snapping mouth. He was bitten. He jerked his hands out. Ignoring his bleeding finger he clambered to the other side and slid his hands under again, this time arriving at the tail. His fingers began creeping up the cat's back. From this line of attack the animal had no defence.

Andrei remained motionless, feeling the struggle play out underneath him, feeling his brother's hands nearing the cat's head, closer and closer. The cat knew this meant death and began biting at anything – his jacket, the snow – crazed with fear, fear which Andrei could feel as vibrations in his stomach. Imitating his brother Andrei cried out:

—*Kill it! Kill it! Kill it!*

Pavel snapped the animal's neck. Neither of them did anything for a moment, just lying still, breathing deeply. Pavel rested his head on Andrei's back, his hands still tight around the cat's neck.

Finally he pulled his hands out from underneath his brother and stood up. Andrei remained in the snow, not daring to move.

—*You can stand up now.*

He could stand up now. He could stand side by side with his brother. He could stand proud. Andrei hadn't disappointed. He hadn't failed. He reached up, took his brother's hand and got to his feet. Pavel couldn't have caught the cat without him. The string would've broken. The cat would've escaped. Andrei smiled and then laughed, clapping his hands and dancing on the spot. He felt as happy as he'd ever felt in his entire life. They were a team. His brother hugged him and the two of them looked down at their prize: a scrawny dead cat pressed into the snow.

Transporting their prize back to the village unseen was a necessary precaution. People would fight, kill for such a catch, and the screeching might've alerted someone. Pavel refused to leave anything to chance. They'd brought no sack with which to conceal the cat. Improvising, he decided to hide it under a pile of sticks. If they encountered anyone on their way home it would appear as if they'd been collecting firewood and no questions would be asked. He picked the cat out of the snow.

—*I'm going to carry it under a pile of sticks, so no one can see it. But if we were really collecting firewood you'd be carrying sticks too.*

Andrei was impressed by his brother's logic – he would never have thought of that. He set about gathering wood. Since the ground was covered in snow it was difficult finding any loose sticks and he was forced to rake through with his bare hands. After each sweep he rubbed his fingers together, blowing on them. His nose had begun to run, snot collecting on his top lip. He didn't mind though, not tonight, not after their success, and he began to hum a song his father used to sing, sinking his fingers back into the snow.

Experiencing the same shortage of sticks, Pavel had moved away from his younger brother. They would have to separate. Some distance away he saw a fallen tree with branches protruding at all angles. He hurried towards it, placing the cat in the snow so that he was free to snap off all the dead wood from the trunk. There was plenty here, more than enough for both of them, and he glanced around, looking for Andrei. He was about to call out when he swallowed his words. There was a noise. He turned sharply, looking around. The woods were dense, dark. He shut his eyes, concentrating on that sound – a rhythm: the crunch, crunch, crunch of snow. It was getting faster, louder. Adrenaline shot through his body. He opened his eyes. There, in the darkness, was movement: a man, running. He was holding a thick, heavy branch. His strides were wide. He was sprinting straight towards Pavel. He'd heard them kill the cat and now he was going to steal their prize. But Pavel wouldn't let him: he wouldn't let their mother starve. He wouldn't fail as his father had failed. He began kicking snow over the cat, trying to conceal it.

—*We're collecting . . .*

Pavel's voice trailed off as the man burst through the trees, raising the branch. Only now, seeing this man's gaunt face and wild eyes, did Pavel realize that he didn't want the cat. He wanted him.

Pavel's mouth fell open at more or less the same time as the branch arched down, the end slamming against the crown of his head. He didn't feel anything but he was aware that he was no longer standing. He was on one knee. Glancing up, head cocked at an angle, blood streaming into one of his eyes, he watched as the man lifted the branch for a second strike.

*

Andrei stopped humming. Had Pavel called out? He hadn't found that many sticks, certainly not enough for their plan, and he didn't

13

want to be told off, not after he'd done so well. He stood up, pulling his hands out of the snow. He stared into the forest, squinting, unable to see even the nearest of trees as anything more than a blur.

—*Pavel?*

There was no reply. He called again. Was this a game? No, Pavel didn't play games, not any more. Andrei walked in the direction he'd last seen his brother but he couldn't see anything. This was stupid. He wasn't the one who was meant to find Pavel, Pavel was meant to find him. Something was wrong. He called again, louder this time. Why wasn't his brother answering? Andrei wiped his nose on his coarse jacket sleeve and wondered if this was a test. What would his brother do in this situation? He'd follow the tracks in the snow. Andrei dropped his sticks and knelt down, searching the ground on his hands and knees. He found his own footsteps and traced them back to the point where he'd left his brother. Proud of himself he switched to his brother's footsteps. If he stood up he couldn't see the footprints so, crouching down, with his nose only an arm's length from the snow, he carried on, like a dog chasing a smell.

He arrived at a fallen tree, sticks scattered all around, footsteps everywhere – some deep and large. The snow was red. Andrei took a handful, crushing it between his fingers, squeezing it and watching it turn to blood.

—*Pavel!*

He didn't stop shouting until his throat hurt and his voice disappeared. Whimpering, he wanted to tell his brother that he could have his share of the cat. He just wanted him back. But it was no good. His brother had left him. And he was alone.

*

Oksana had hidden a small bag of powdered cornstalks, pigweed and crushed potato peelings behind the bricks of her oven. During inspections she always kept a small fire burning. Collectors sent to check that she wasn't hoarding grain never looked beyond the flames. They mistrusted her – why was she healthy when the others were sick, as though to be alive was a crime. But they couldn't find food in her house, couldn't brand her a *kulak*, a rich peasant. Instead of executing her outright they left her to die. She'd already learnt that she couldn't beat them by force. Some years ago she had organized the village resistance after it was announced that men were on their way to collect the church bell. They wanted to melt it down. She and four other women had locked themselves in the bell tower, ringing it continuously, refusing to let them take it away. Oksana had shouted out that this bell belonged to God. She might have been shot that day but the man in charge of the collection decided to spare the women. After breaking down the door he'd said that his only orders were to collect the bell, explaining that metal was necessary for their country's industrial revolution. In response she'd spat on the ground. When the State began taking the villagers' food, arguing that it belonged to the country and not them, Oksana had learnt her lesson. Instead of strength she feigned obedience, her resistance remaining a secret.

Tonight the family would have a feast. She melted clumps of snow, bringing it to the boil and thickening it with the powdered cornstalks. She added the remaining bones from the bottle. Once cooked, she'd grind the bones down to flour. Of course she was getting ahead of herself. Pavel hadn't succeeded yet. But she felt sure he would. If God had given her hardship he'd also given her a son to help. All the same, if he didn't catch the cat she promised not to become angry. The woods were large, a cat was small, and anyway anger was a waste of energy. Even as she tried to brace herself for disappointment she couldn't help becoming giddy at the prospect of a meat and potato borscht.

Andrei stood in the doorway, his face cut, snow on his jacket, snot and blood running from his nose. His *laptys* had completely come apart and his toes were visible. Oksana ran over.

—*Where's your brother?*

—*He left me.*

Andrei started to cry. He didn't know where his brother was. He didn't understand what had happened. He couldn't explain. He knew his mother was going to hate him. He knew it was going to be his fault even though he'd done everything right, even though it was his brother who'd left him.

Oksana's breath was snatched from her. She brushed Andrei aside and hurried out of the house, looking to the woods. There was no sign of Pavel. Maybe he'd fallen and injured himself. Maybe he needed help. She ran back inside, desperate for answers only to see Andrei standing by the borscht with a spoon in his mouth. Caught red-handed, he looked at his mother sheepishly, a line of potato soup dribbling from his lip. Overcome with anger – anger at her dead husband, her missing son – she ran forward, knocking Andrei to the ground and pushing the wooden spoon down his throat.

—*When I pull this spoon out of your mouth tell me what happened.*

But as soon as she pulled out the spoon all he could do was cough. Enraged, she shoved the spoon back down his throat.

—*You useless, clumsy, stupid boy. Where is my son? Where is he?*

She pulled the spoon out again but he was crying and choking. He couldn't talk. He just kept crying and coughing and so she hit him, pounding her hands on his tiny chest. Only when the borscht was in danger of boiling over did she stop. She stood up, moving the soup off the fire.

Andrei whimpered on the floor. Oksana looked down at him,

her anger melting away. He was so small. He loved his older brother so much. She bent down, picked him up and sat him on a chair. She wrapped her blanket around him and poured him a bowl of borscht, a generous portion far larger than he'd ever had before. She tried to spoon-feed him but he wouldn't open his mouth. He didn't trust her. She offered him the spoon. He stopped crying and began to eat. He finished the borscht. She filled the bowl again. She told him to eat slowly. He ignored her, finishing a second bowl. Very quietly she asked what had happened and listened as he explained the blood in the snow, the dropped sticks, the disappearance and the heavy footprints. She closed her eyes.

—*Your brother is dead. He's been taken for food. Do you understand? Just as you hunted that cat, someone was hunting you. Do you understand?*

Andrei remained silent, staring at his mother's tears. In truth, he didn't understand. He watched at she stood up and left the house. Hearing his mother's voice, he ran to the door.

Oksana was on her knees in the snow, staring up at the full moon.

—*Please, God, give me back my son.*

Only God could bring him home now. It wasn't so much to ask. Did God have such a short memory? She'd risked her life to save his bell. All she wanted in return was her son, her reason to live.

Some of the neighbours appeared at their doors. They stared at Oksana. They listened to her cries. But there was nothing unusual about this kind of grief and people did not watch for long.

TWENTY YEARS LATER

Moscow

11 February 1953

The snowball thumped into the back of Jora's head. Caught by surprise, snow exploded around his ears. Somewhere behind him he could hear his little brother laughing, laughing really loudly – proud of himself, proud of that shot even though it was a fluke, a one-off. Jora brushed the ice off his jacket collar but fragments had already snuck down his back. They were melting, sliding down his skin, leaving snail-trails of freezing water. He tugged his shirt out of his trousers, reaching his hand up as far as he could, scraping at the ice.

Unable to believe his older brother's complacency – busy with his shirt instead of checking on his opponent – Arkady took his time, clumping together the snow, handful on top of handful. Too large and the snowball became a dud shot: difficult to throw, slow in the air and easy to dodge. That had been his mistake for a long time, making them too big. Instead of having a greater impact they could be swatted out of the air and more often than not they disintegrated of their own accord, falling apart and not even reaching his brother. He and Jora played in the snow a lot. Sometimes there were other children but most of the time it was just the two of them. The games would start casually, growing more and more competitive with each hit. Arkady never won in so far as anyone could be said to win. He was always overwhelmed by the speed and power of his brother's throws. The games ended the same way: frustration, surrender, getting annoyed, or worse, crying and storming off. He hated that he was always the loser, and worse, he hated that he got so upset about it. The only reason he kept playing was because he was sure that today would be different, today he'd win. And today was that day. Here was his chance. He edged closer but not too close: he wanted the shot to count. Point-blank didn't count.

Jora saw it coming: a glob of white arcing through the air, not too big, not too small, just like the kind he'd throw. There was nothing he could do. His hands were behind his back. He had to admit his little brother was learning fast.

The snowball struck the tip of his nose, breaking into his eyes, going up his nose, in his mouth. He stepped back, his face encrusted with white. It was a perfect shot — that was the end of the game. He'd been beaten by his little brother, a boy who wasn't even five years old. Yet only now that he'd lost for the first time did he appreciate the importance of winning. His brother was laughing again — making a real show of it, like a snowball in the face was the funniest thing. Well, at least he never gloated like Arkady was doing now; he never laughed that much or squeezed that much satisfaction from his victories. His little brother was a bad loser and an even worse winner. The boy needed to be taught a lesson, cut down to size. He'd won one game, that was all: one fluky, insignificant game, one game out of a hundred: no — one out of a thousand. And now he was pretending that somehow they were even, or worse that he was better than him? Jora crouched down, digging through the snow, all the way to the icy ground below, collecting a handful of frozen mud and grit and stones.

Seeing his older brother making another snowball, Arkady turned and ran. This would be a revenge shot: put together with care and thrown with as much power as his brother could manage. He wasn't going to be at the receiving end of one of those. If he ran he'd be safe. The shot, no matter how well made, no matter how accurate, could only travel so far in the air before it began to lose shape, fall apart. And even if it hit, after a certain distance they were harmless, barely worth throwing at all. If he ran, he could finish on a high. He didn't want his victory overturned, tainted by a succession of quick hits from his brother. No: run and claim success. Finish the game now. He'd be able to enjoy the feeling until at least tomorrow when he'd probably lose again. But that was tomorrow. Today was victory.

He heard his brother shout his name. And he looked back, still running, smiling – sure that he was out of any effective range.

The impact was like a fist in his face. His head flicked round, his feet left the ground and for a second he was floating in the air. When his feet touched the ground again his legs collapsed under him, he fell, crumpled – too dazed to even put his hands out – crashing into the snow. For a moment he just lay there, unable to understand what had happened. There was grit, mud, spit and blood in his mouth. He tentatively pushed a mitten-covered fingertip between his lips. His teeth felt coarse like he'd been force-fed sand. There was a gap. A tooth had been knocked out. Beginning to cry, he spat into the snow, raking through the mess, looking for his missing tooth. For some reason that was all he could think about right now, that was all he cared about. He had to find his tooth. Where was it? But he couldn't find it, not against the white of the snow. It was gone. And it wasn't the pain, it was the anger, outrage at this injustice. Couldn't he win one game? He'd won it fairly. Couldn't his brother give him that?

Jora ran towards his brother. As soon as the clump of mud, grit, ice and stones had left his hand he'd regretted his decision. He'd shouted out his brother's name, wanting him to duck, to avoid the shot. Instead, Arkady had turned around directly into the impact. Instead of helping him, it had seemed like a particularly malicious flourish. As he approached he saw blood on the snow and felt sick. He'd done this. He'd turned their game, a game he enjoyed as much as he enjoyed anything, into something terrible. Why couldn't he have let his brother win? He would've won tomorrow and the day after and the day after. He felt ashamed.

Jora dropped to the snow, putting a hand on his little brother's shoulder. Arkady shook it off, staring up with red, tear-filled eyes and a bloody mouth, looking like a savage animal. He didn't say anything. His whole face was tight with anger. He got to his feet, a little unsteady.

—*Arkady?*

In reply his little brother just opened his mouth and cried out, making an animalistic sound. All Jora could see was a set of dirty teeth. Arkady turned around and ran away.

—*Arkady, wait!*

But Arkady didn't wait – didn't stop, didn't want to hear his brother's apology. He ran as fast as he could, his tongue searching for the newly made gap in his front teeth. Finding it, feeling the gum with the tip of his tongue, he hoped he'd never see his brother again.

14 February

Leo stared up at Apartment Block 18 – a low-rise, squat slab of grey concrete. It was late afternoon, already dark. An entire working day had been lost to a task that was as unpleasant as it was unimportant. According to the militia incident report, a boy aged four years and ten months had been found dead on the railway lines. The boy had been playing on the tracks, at night, last night, and was caught by a passenger train; his body was cut up by the wheels. The driver of the 21.00 to Khabarovsk had communicated at his first stop that he'd caught a glimpse of someone or something on the tracks shortly after leaving Yaroslavskiy Vokzal station. Whether that train had actually hit the boy wasn't yet established. Maybe the driver didn't want to admit to hitting the child. But there was no need to press the issue: it was a tragic accident with no question of blame. The matter should've already been closed.

Ordinarily there was no reason Leo Stepanovich Demidov – an up-and-coming member of the MGB, the State Security force – would have become involved in this kind of incident. What was there for him to do? The loss of a son was heartbreaking for the family and relatives. But, bluntly, it was meaningless at a national level. Careless children, unless they were careless with their tongues, were not State Security concerns. However, this particular situation had become unexpectedly complicated. The parents' grief had taken a peculiar form. It seems they were unable to accept that their son (Leo checked the report – committing the name Arkady Fyodorovich Andreev to memory) had been responsible for his own death. They'd been telling people that he'd been murdered. By whom – they had no idea. For what reason – they had no idea. How could such a thing even be possible – once again, they had no idea. Yet even without a logical, plausible argument they had an emotive power on their side. There was the very real possibility they were convincing other gullible people: neighbours, friends and strangers – whoever might listen.

To aggravate the situation further, the boy's father, Fyodor Andreev, was himself a low-ranking member of the MGB and, as it happened, one of Leo's subordinates. Aside from the fact that he should know better, he was bringing the MGB into disrepute by using the weight of his authority to give credibility to this unfeasible assertion. He'd crossed a line. He'd let his feelings cloud his judgement. Had the circumstances not been mitigating, Leo's task here might well have been this man's arrest. The whole thing was a mess. And Leo had been forced to take temporary leave from a sensitive, genuine assignment in order to straighten the matter out.

Not looking forward to the confrontation with Fyodor, Leo took his time walking up the stairs, contemplating how he had ended up here – policing people's reactions. He'd never intended to join the State Security Department; the career had grown out of his military service. During the Great Patriotic War he'd been recruited for a special-forces unit – OMSBON, the Independent Motor-rifle Brigade for Special Tasks. The third and fourth battalions of this unit had been selected from the Central Institute of Physical Culture, where he'd been a student. Hand-picked for athleticism and physical prowess they were taken to a training camp at Mytishchi, just north of Moscow, where they were taught close combat, weapons training, low-altitude parachuting and the use of explosives. The camp belonged to the NKVD, as the secret police was known before State Security became the MGB. The battalions came under the direct authority of the NKVD, not the military, and the nature of their missions reflected this. Sent behind enemy lines, destroying infrastructure, collecting information, carrying out assassinations – they were clandestine raiders.

Leo had enjoyed the independence of his operations, although he was careful to keep that observation to himself. He liked the fact, or perhaps just the impression, that his fate had been in his hands. He'd flourished. As a result he'd been awarded the Order of Suvorov 2nd Class. His level-headedness, military success, good looks and above all his absolute and sincere belief in his country had resulted in him becoming a poster boy – quite literally – for the Soviet liberation of German-occupied territory. He and a gaggle of soldiers from a patchwork of divisions were photographed surrounding the burning wreck of a German panzer, guns in the air, victory on their faces, dead soldiers at their feet. In the background, smoke rose from smouldering villages. Destruction and death and triumphant smiles – Leo, with his good set of teeth and broad shoulders, was ushered to the front of the photograph. One week later the photograph had made the front page of *Pravda* and Leo was being congratulated by strangers, troops, civilians, people who'd wanted to shake his hand, embrace him, this symbol of victory.

After the war Leo had moved from OMSBON into the NKVD itself. That progression had seemed logical. He hadn't asked any questions: it was a path lain down by his superiors and he'd walked it, head held high. His country could have asked anything of him and he would've readily agreed. He would've run Gulags in the Arctic tundra of the Kolyma region had they asked him. His only ambition was a general one: to serve his country, a country that had defeated Fascism, a country that provided free education and healthcare, that trumpeted the rights of the workers around the world, that paid his father – a munitions worker on an assembly line – a salary comparable to that of a fully qualified doctor. Although his own employment in the State Security force was frequently unpleasant he understood its necessity, the necessity of guarding their revolution from enemies both foreign and domestic, from those who sought to undermine it and those determined to see it fail. To this end Leo would lay down his life. To this end he'd lay down the lives of others.

None of this heroism or military training had any relevance today. Here was no enemy. This was a colleague, a friend, a grief-stricken father. And yet, even so, this was an MGB protocol and this father in mourning was the subject. Leo needed to tread carefully. He couldn't allow himself to be swayed by the same feelings that were blinding Fyodor. This hysteria was putting a good family in danger. If left unchecked the groundless chatter about murder could grow like a weed, spreading through the community, unsettling people, making them question one of the fundamental pillars of their new society:

There is no crime.

Few people believed this absolutely. There were blemishes: this was a society still in transition, not perfect yet. As an MGB officer it was Leo's duty to study the works of Lenin, in fact it was every citizen's duty. He knew that social excesses – crime – would wither away as poverty and want disappeared. They hadn't reached that plateau yet. Things were stolen, drunken disputes became violent: there were the *urki* – the criminal gangs. But people had to believe that they were moving towards a better state of existence. To call this murder, was to take a giant step backwards. Leo had been taught by his superior officer, his mentor Major Janusz Kuzmin, about the trials of 1937 where the accused had been briefed by Stalin that they had:

Lost faith

Enemies of the Party were not merely saboteurs, spies and wreckers of industry, but doubters of the Party line, doubters of the society which awaited them. Applying that rule, Fyodor, Leo's friend and colleague, had indeed become an enemy.

Leo's mission was to quash any unfounded speculation, to guide them back from the brink. Talk of murder had a natural drama which no doubt appealed to certain types of fanciful people. If it came to it he'd be harsh: the boy had made a mistake for which he'd paid with his life. No one else need suffer for his carelessness. Maybe that was too much. He needn't go so far. This could be resolved tactfully. They were upset – that was all. Be patient with them. They weren't thinking straight. Present the facts. He wasn't here to threaten them, at least not immediately: he was here to help them. He was here to restore faith.

Leo knocked and Fyodor opened the door. Leo bowed his head.
—*I'm very sorry for your loss.*

Fyodor stepped back, allowing Leo into the room.

Every seat was taken. The room was crowded, as though a village meeting had been called. There were elderly people, children – it was obvious that the entire family had gathered. In this kind of atmosphere it was easy to imagine how feelings had been whipped up. No doubt they'd encouraged each other to think that there was some mysterious force to blame for their little boy's death. Maybe that made their loss easier to come to terms with. Maybe they felt guilty for not teaching the boy to stay clear of the railway lines. Leo recognized some of the faces around him. They were Fyodor's friends from work. And they were suddenly embarrassed at being caught here. They didn't know what to do, avoiding eye contact, wanting to leave but unable to. Leo turned to Fyodor.

—It might be easier to talk if it was just the two of us?

—Please, this is my family: they want to hear what you have to say.

Leo glanced around — twenty or so sets of eyes were fixed on him. They already knew what he was going to say and they did not like him for it. They were angry that their boy had died and this was their way of expressing that hurt. Leo would simply have to accept that he was the focal point for their anger.

—I can think of nothing worse than the loss of a child. I was your colleague and friend when you and your wife celebrated the birth of your son. I remember congratulating you. And it is with terrible sadness that I find myself consoling you.

A little stiff perhaps but Leo meant it sincerely. It was met with silence. Leo considered his next words carefully.

—I've never experienced the grief that follows the loss of a child. I don't know how it would make me react. Perhaps I would feel the need to blame someone, someone I could hate. But, with a clear head, I can assure you that the cause of Arkady's death is not in dispute. I have brought with me the report, which I can leave with you if you wish. In addition to this I've been sent to answer any questions you might have.

—Arkady was murdered. We want your help in investigating, if not you personally then we would like the MGB to place pressure on the procurator to open a criminal case.

Leo nodded, trying to maintain an air of reconciliation. It was the worst possible beginning to their discussion. The father was adamant: their position entrenched. He was demanding the formal opening of an *ugolovnoye delo*, a criminal case, without which the militia wouldn't investigate. He was calling for the impossible. Leo stared at the men from work. They realized, whereas the others did not, that this word – *murder* – tarnished everyone in the room.

—Arkady was caught by a passing train. His death was an accident, a terrible accident.

—Then why was he naked? Why was his mouth stuffed with dirt?

Leo tried to fathom what had just been said. The boy was naked? That was the first he'd heard of it. He opened the report.

> *The boy was found clothed.*

Now that he read the line again it struck him as an odd stipulation. But there it was: the boy was clothed. He continued to scan the document:

> *Having been dragged along the ground his mouth contained dirt.*

He closed the report. The room was waiting.

—Your boy was found fully clothed. Yes, there was dirt in his mouth. But his body was dragged by the train; some dirt in his mouth is to be expected.

An elderly woman stood up. Although stooped by age, her eyes were sharp.

—*That is not what we were told.*

—*It's very unfortunate, but you've been misinformed.*

The woman pressed ahead. Evidently she was a significant power behind this speculation.

—*The man who found the body – Taras Kuprin – was scavenging. He lives two streets away. He told us Arkady was naked, you hear? Not wearing a single item of clothing. A collision with a train doesn't undress a boy.*

—*This man, Kuprin, did indeed find the body. His statement is in this report. He claims the body was found on the tracks, fully clothed. He's quite clear about that. His words are here in black and white.*

—*Why did he tell us differently?*

—*Maybe he was confused. I don't know. But I have this man's signature on his statement and his statement is in the report. I doubt he would say anything differently if I asked him now.*

—*Have you seen the boy's body?*

Her question took Leo by surprise.

—*I'm not investigating this incident: that is not my job. But even if it were, there's nothing to investigate. This is a terrible accident. I'm here to speak to you, to make things clear when they've been unnecessarily confused. I can read you the entire report aloud if you like.*

The elderly woman spoke again.

—*That report is a lie.*

Everyone tensed. Leo remained silent, struggling to stay calm. They had to realize that there was no compromise. They had to concede, they had to accept that their little boy died an unfortunate death. Leo was here for their benefit. He turned to Fyodor, waiting for him to correct this woman.

Fyodor stepped forward.

—*Leo, we have new evidence, evidence which has come to light today. A woman who lives in an apartment looking out over the tracks saw Arkady with a man. We don't know any more than that. This woman is not a friend of ours. We've never met her before. She heard about the murder—*

—*Fyodor . . .*

—*She heard about my son's death. And if what we've been told is true, she can describe this man. She'd be able to recognize him.*

—*Where is this woman?*

—*We're waiting for her now.*

—*She's coming here? I'd be interested in hearing what she has to say.*

Leo was offered a chair. He waved it away. He'd stand.

No one spoke, everyone waiting for the knock on the door. Leo regretted not taking that chair. Almost an hour passed, in silence, before a faint knock was heard. Fyodor opened the door, introducing himself and showing the woman in. She was perhaps thirty years old: a kind face, large, nervous eyes. Startled at all the people, Fyodor tried to comfort her.

—*These are my friends and family. There's no need to be alarmed.*

But she wasn't listening. She was staring at Leo.

—*My name is Leo Stepanovich. I'm an MGB officer. I'm in charge. What is your name?*

Leo took out his pad, finding a fresh page. The woman didn't reply. He glanced up. She still hadn't said anything. Leo was about to repeat the question when she finally spoke.

—*Galina Shaporina.*

Her voice was a whisper.

—*And what did you see?*

—*I saw . . .*

She looked about the room, then at the floor, then back at Leo, relapsing into silence. Fyodor prompted her, tension evident in his voice:

—You saw a man?

—Yes, a man.

Fyodor, standing right beside her, his eyes drilling into her, sighed with relief. She continued:

—A man, a worker perhaps, on the railway – I saw him through my window. It was very dark.

Leo tapped his pad with his pencil.

—You saw him with a young boy?

—No, there was no boy.

Fyodor's mouth dropped, his words rushed out.

—But we were told you saw a man holding my little boy's hand.

—No, no, no – there was no boy. He was holding a bag, I think – a bag full of tools. Yes, that was it. He was working on the tracks, repairing them perhaps. I didn't see very much, a glimpse, that's all. I shouldn't really be here. I'm very sorry your son died.

Leo shut his pad.

—Thank you.

—Will there be any further questions?

Before Leo could answer, Fyodor took the woman by the arm.

—You saw a man.

The woman pulled her arm free. She looked about the room, at all the eyes on her. She turned to Leo.

—Will you need to visit me at a later date?

—No. You can go.

Galina dropped her face to the floor, hurrying to the front door. But before she reached it the elderly woman called out:

—You lose your nerve so easily?

Fyodor approached the elderly woman.

—Please, sit down.

She nodded, neither disgusted nor approving.

—Arkady was your son.

—Yes.

Leo couldn't see Fyodor's eyes. He wondered what silent communication was passing between these two people. Whatever it was, she took her seat. During all of this Galina had slipped away.

Leo was pleased Fyodor had intervened. He hoped that they'd reached a turning point. Scratching together gossip and rumour served no one. Fyodor returned to Leo's side.

—Forgive my mother, she's very upset.

—This is why I'm here. So we can talk this through within the confines of this room. What cannot happen is that once I leave this room, the conversation continues. If anyone asks you about your son you cannot say he was murdered. Not because I order you to but because it is not true.

—We understand.

—Fyodor, I want you to take tomorrow off. This has been authorized. If there's anything more I can do for you . . .

—Thank you.

At the door to the apartment Fyodor shook Leo's hand.

—We're all very upset. Forgive us any outbursts.

—They'll pass unrecorded. But, as I said, this ends here.

Fyodor's face stiffened. He nodded. As though the words were bitter he forced them out:

—My son's death was a terrible accident.

Leo walked down the stairs, breathing deeply. The atmosphere in that room had been suffocating. He was glad to be done, glad the matter had been resolved. Fyodor was a good man. Once he came to terms with his son's death then the truth would be easier to accept.

He paused. There was the sound of someone behind him. He turned around. It was a boy, no more than seven or eight years old.

—*Sir, I am Jora. I'm Arkady's older brother. May I speak to you?*

—*Of course.*

—*It's my fault.*

—*What was your fault?*

—*My brother's death: I threw a snowball at him. I'd packed it with stones and dirt and grit. Arkady was hurt, it hit him in the head. He ran off. Maybe it made him dizzy, maybe that's why he couldn't see the train. The dirt they found in his mouth: that was my fault. I threw it at him.*

—*Your brother's death was an accident. There's no reason for you to feel any guilt. But you did well telling me the truth. Now go back to your parents.*

—*I haven't told them about the snowball with dirt and the mud and the stones.*

—*Perhaps they don't need to know.*

—*They'd be so angry. Because that was the last time I ever saw him. Sir, we played nicely most of the time. And we would've played nicely again, we would've made up, we would've been friends again, I'm sure of it. But now I can't make it up to him, I can't ever say sorry.*

Leo was hearing this boy's confession. The boy wanted forgiveness. He'd begun to cry. Embarrassed, Leo patted his head, muttering, as though they were the words of a lullaby:

—*It was no one's fault.*

The Village of Kimov
One Hundred and
Sixty Kilometres North of Moscow

Same Day

Anatoly Brodsky hadn't slept in three days. He was so tired that even the most basic tasks required concentration. The barn door in front of him was locked. He knew he'd have to force it open. Even so the idea seemed far-fetched. He simply didn't have the energy. Snow had begun to fall. He looked up at the night sky; his mind drifted and when he eventually remembered where he was and what he was supposed to be doing snow was settling on his face. He licked the flakes across his lips and realized that if he didn't get inside he was going to die. Concentrating, he kicked the door. The hinges shook, the door remained shut. He kicked again. Timbers splintered. Encouraged by the sound he summoned the last sparks of energy and aimed a third kick at the lock. The wood cracked, the door swung back. He stood at the entrance, adjusting to the gloom. On one side of the barn there were two cows in an enclosure. On the other side there were tools, straw. He spread some of the coarse sacks on the frozen ground, buttoned his coat and lay down, crossing his arms and closing his eyes.

*

From his bedroom window, Mikhail Zinoviev could see that the barn door was open. It was swaying backwards and forwards in the wind and snow was swirling into his barn. He turned around. His wife was in bed, asleep. Deciding not to disturb her, he quietly put on his coat, his felt boots and went outside.

The wind had picked up, whipping loose snow off the ground and flinging it into Mikhail's face. He raised his hand, sheltering his eyes. As he approached the barn, glancing through his fingers he could see the lock had been smashed, the door kicked open. He peered inside and after adjusting to the absence of moonlight he saw the outline of a man lying on the ground against the straw. Without any clear sense of what he was about to do, he entered the barn, took hold of a pitchfork, stepped up to the sleeping figure, raising the prongs above the man's stomach, ready to jab down.

Anatoly opened his eyes and saw snow-covered boots centimetres from his face. He rolled onto his back and looked up at the man looming over him. The prongs of a pitchfork were directly above his stomach, quivering. Neither man moved. Their breath formed a mist in front of their faces which appeared and disappeared. Anatoly didn't try to grab the pitchfork. He didn't try to move out of the way.

They remained like this, frozen mid-frame, until a feeling of shame overcame Mikhail. He gasped as though he'd been punched in the stomach by some invisible force, dropping the pitchfork harmlessly to the ground, sinking to his knees.

—*Please forgive me*.

Anatoly sat up. The adrenaline had jolted him awake but his body ached. How long had he been asleep? Not long, not long enough. His voice was hoarse, his throat dry.

—*I understand. I shouldn't have come here. I shouldn't have asked for your help. You have your family to think of. I've put you in danger. It is I who should be asking for your forgiveness.*

Mikhail shook his head.

—*I was afraid. I panicked. Forgive me.*

Anatoly glanced out at the snow and darkness. He couldn't leave now. He wouldn't survive. Of course he couldn't allow himself to sleep. But he did still need shelter. Mikhail was waiting for an answer, waiting for forgiveness.

—*There's nothing to forgive. You're not to blame. I might have done the same.*

—*But you're my friend.*

—*I'm still your friend and I'll always be your friend. Listen to me: I want you to forget that tonight ever happened. Forget that I ever came here. Forget that I ever asked for your help. Remember us as we were. Remember us as the best of friends. Do this for me and I shall do the same for you. By first light I'll be gone. I promise. You'll wake up and continue your life as normal. I assure you no one will ever know I was here.*

Mikhail's head dropped: he wept. Until tonight he'd believed he would've done anything for his friend. That was a lie. His loyalty, bravery and friendship had all been proved paper thin – they'd ripped at the first serious test.

When Anatoly had arrived unannounced that evening Mikhail had seemed understandably surprised. Anatoly had travelled to the village without warning. All the same he'd been welcomed warmly, offered food, drink, a bed. Only once his hosts had heard the news that he was making his way north to the Finnish border did they finally understand the reason for the sudden arrival. He'd never mentioned that he was wanted by the State Security Police, the MGB. He didn't need to. They understood. He was a fugitive. As that fact became clear the welcome had evaporated. The punishment for aiding and abetting a fugitive was execution. He knew this but had hoped his friend would be prepared to accept the risk. He'd even hoped his friend might travel north with him. The MGB weren't looking for two people and what's more Mikhail had acquaintances in towns all the way to Leningrad including Tver and Gorky. True, it was an enormous amount to ask, but Anatoly had once saved Mikhail's life and though he'd never considered it a debt that ever needed to be repaid, that was only because he'd never thought he'd need to call it in.

During their discussion it had become apparent that Mikhail wasn't prepared to take that kind of risk. In fact, he wasn't prepared to take any kind of risk. His wife had frequently interrupted their conversation asking to speak with her husband in private. At each interruption she'd glared at Anatoly with unmasked venom. Circumstances demanded prudence and caution as a part of everyday life. And there was no denying he'd brought danger to his friend's family, a family he loved. Lowering his expectations sharply he had told Mikhail that he wanted nothing more than a night's sleep in their barn. He'd be gone by tomorrow morning. He'd walk to the nearest railway station, the same way he'd arrived. In addition it'd been his idea to smash the lock to the barn. In the unlikely event that he was caught the family could claim ignorance and pretend there'd been an intruder. He'd believed that these precautions had reassured his hosts.

Unable to watch his friend cry, Anatoly leaned close.

—*There's nothing to feel guilty about. We're all just trying to survive.*

Mikhail stopped crying. He looked up, wiping his tears away. Realizing that this would be the last time they would ever see each other, the two friends hugged.

Mikhail pulled back.

—*You're a better man than me.*

He stood up, leaving the barn and taking care to shut the door, kicking up some snow to wedge it in position. He turned his back on the wind and trudged towards the house. Killing Anatoly and reporting him as an intruder would have guaranteed the safety of his family. Now he'd have to take his chances. He'd have to pray. He'd never thought of himself as a coward, and during the war, when it had been his own life at stake, he'd never behaved as one. Some men had even called him brave. But having a family had made him fearful. He was able to imagine far worse things than his own death.

Reaching the house he took off his boots and coat and went to the bedroom. Opening the door he was startled by a figure at the window. His wife was awake, staring out at the barn. Hearing him enter she turned around. Her small frame gave no indication of her capacity to lift and carry and cut, to work twelve-hour days, to hold her family together. She didn't care that Anatoly had once saved her husband's life. She didn't care about their history, their friendship. Loyalty and indebtedness were abstracts. Anatoly was a threat to their safety. That was real. She wanted him gone, as far away from her family as possible, and at this precise moment she hated him – this gentle decent friend whom she'd once loved and treasured as a guest – more than anyone else alive.

Mikhail kissed his wife. Her cheek was cold. He took her hand. She stared up at him, noticing that he'd been crying.

—*What were you doing outside?*

Mikhail understood her eagerness. She hoped that he'd done

what was necessary. She hoped he'd put his family first and killed that man. That would be the right thing to do.

—*He left the barn door open. Anyone could've seen it. I shut it.*

He could feel his wife's grip slacken, feeling her disappointment. She thought him weak. She was right. He had neither the strength to murder his friend nor the strength to help him. He tried to find some words of comfort.

—*There's nothing to worry about. No one knows he's here.*

Moscow

Same Day

The table had been smashed, the bed turned upside down, the mattress shredded, pillows torn apart and floorboards ripped up, yet so far the search of Anatoly Brodsky's apartment yielded no clue as to his whereabouts. Leo crouched down to examine the fireplace. Stacks of papers had been burnt. There were layers of fine ash where correspondence had been heaped and set alight. Using the muzzle of his gun he raked the remains hoping to find some fragment untouched by fire. The ashes fell apart – everything was burnt and black. The traitor had escaped. Leo was to blame. He'd given this man, a stranger, the benefit of the doubt. He'd presumed he was innocent; the kind of mistake a novice might make.

Better to let ten innocent men suffer than one spy escape.

He'd disregarded a fundamental principle of their work: the presumption of guilt.

Despite accepting responsibility, Leo couldn't help but wonder that if he hadn't been forced to waste the entire day dealing with the accidental death of that little boy, would Brodsky have escaped? Meeting relatives, stamping out hot-headed rumours — this wasn't the work of a senior MGB officer. Instead of personally running a surveillance operation he'd agreed to sideline himself, untangling what amounted to little more than a personal affair. He should never have said yes. He'd become complacent about the threat posed by this man Brodsky. His first serious misjudgement since joining State Security. He was aware that few officers ever got an opportunity to make a second mistake.

He hadn't thought much of the case: Brodsky was educated, with some competence in the English language, dealing with for-eigners on a regular basis. This was grounds for vigilance but, as Leo had pointed out, the man was a respected vet in a city with very few trained vets. Foreign diplomats had to take their cats and dogs to someone. Furthermore this was a man who'd served in the Red Army as a field doctor. His background was impeccable. According to his military records he'd volunteered and despite not being technically qualified as a doctor, despite his expertise being injured animals, he'd worked in several field hospitals and subse-quently received two commendations. The suspect must have saved hundreds of lives.

Major Kuzmin had quickly guessed the reason for his protégé's reservations. During Leo's own military career he'd been treated by field doctors for numerous injuries and clearly some kind of war camaraderie was holding him back. Kuzmin reminded Leo that sentimentality could blind a man to the truth. Those who appear the most trustworthy deserve the most suspicion. Leo rec-ognized it as a play on Stalin's well-known aphorism:

Trust but Check.

Stalin's words had been interpreted as:

Check on Those we Trust.

Since those who weren't trusted were scrutinized with the same vigour as those who were, it meant that there was at least a kind of equality.

The duty of an investigator was to scratch away at innocence until guilt was uncovered. If no guilt was uncovered then they hadn't scratched deep enough. In the case of Brodsky the question wasn't whether foreign diplomats met him because he was a vet but rather had this suspect become a vet in order that foreign diplomats could openly meet him. Why did he establish his practice within walking distance of the American Embassy? And why – shortly after he opened this practice – did several employees from the American Embassy obtain pets? Finally, why was it that the pets of foreign diplomats seemed to require more frequent attention than pets belonging to a typical citizen? Kuzmin had been the first to agree that there was a comical aspect to all of this and it was precisely this disarming quality which had made him uneasy. The innocence of the circumstances felt like a brilliant disguise. It felt like the MGB was being laughed at. There were few more serious crimes than that.

Having considered the case and noted his mentor's observations, Leo made the decision that instead of arresting the suspect outright they would have him followed, reasoning that if this citizen was working as a spy then it was an opportunity to discover who he was working with and arrest them all in one swoop. Though he never said as much, he was uncomfortable making an arrest without more evidence. Of course that was a qualm he'd lived with throughout his professional life. He'd made many arrests knowing only the citizen's name and address and the fact that someone mistrusted them. A suspect's guilt became real as soon as they became a suspect. As for evidence, that would be acquired during their interrogation. But Leo was no longer a lackey who merely followed orders, and he'd decided to make use of his authority and do things a little differently. He was an investigator. He'd wanted to investigate. He had little doubt that he'd eventually arrest Anatoly Brodsky, he just wanted proof; some sign of guilt other than mere conjecture. In short, he wanted to feel OK about arresting him.

As part of the surveillance operation, Leo had taken the day shift, following the suspect during the hours of eight in the morning through to eight in the evening. For three days he'd observed nothing out of the ordinary. The suspect worked, ate lunch out and went home. In short he seemed a good citizen. Perhaps it had been this innocuous appearance which had dulled Leo's senses. When, this morning, he'd been pulled aside by an irate Kuzmin, briefed on the Fyodor Andreev situation – the dead boy, the hysterical reaction – and ordered to fix it immediately, he didn't protest. Instead of putting his foot down and pointing out that he had far more important things to do he'd acquiesced. With hindsight how ridiculous it all seemed. How frustrating that he was conversing with relatives, coaxing children, whilst this suspect, this traitor, was making his escape, making a mockery of Leo. The agent delegated to maintain watch had idiotically thought nothing of the fact that there hadn't been a single customer at the veterinary practice all day. It wasn't until dusk that the agent had become suspicious and entered, intending to pose as a customer. He'd found the premises empty. A back window had been prised open. The suspect could've escaped at any time, most probably in the morning, soon after he'd arrived.

Brodsky is gone.

When Leo had heard those words he'd felt sick: he'd called an emergency meeting with Major Kuzmin at his home address. Leo now had the proof of guilt he'd been looking for but he no longer had the suspect. To his surprise his mentor had seemed gratified. The traitor's behaviour validated his theory: their business was mistrust. If an allegation contained only one per cent truth it was better to consider the entire allegation true than to dismiss it. Leo was instructed to catch this traitor at all costs. He was not to sleep, eat, rest, he was not to do anything until that man was in their custody, where – as Kuzmin had smugly pointed out – he should have been three days ago.

Leo rubbed his eyes. He could feel a knot in his stomach. At best he seemed naive, at worst incompetent. He'd underestimated an opponent and feeling a sudden, uncharacteristic burst of anger he considered kicking the upturned table. He decided against it. He had trained himself to keep his feelings locked out of view. A junior officer hurried into the room, probably keen to help, to prove his dedication. Leo waved him away, wanting to be alone. He took a moment to calm down, staring out of the window at the snow which had begun to fall over the city. He lit a cigarette, blowing smoke on a pane of glass. What had gone wrong? The suspect must have sighted the agents tailing him and planned his escape. If he was burning documents that meant he was keen to conceal material relating to his espionage or his current destination. Leo was sure that Brodsky had an escape plan, a way to get out of the country. He had to find some fragment of this plan.

The neighbours were a retired couple in their seventies who lived with their married son, his wife and their two children. A family of six in two rooms, not an unusual ratio. All six of them were sitting in their kitchen side by side with a junior officer standing behind them for the purpose of intimidation. Leo could see that they understood that they were all implicated in another man's guilt. He could see their fear. Dismissing this observation as irrelevant – he'd been guilty of sentimentality once already – he walked up to the table.

—Anatoly Brodsky is a traitor. If you help him in any way even by saying nothing you will be treated as an accomplice. The pressure is on you to prove your loyalty to the State. There is no pressure on us to prove your guilt. That, right now, is taken for granted.

The elderly man, the grandfather, no doubt a savvy survivor, was quick to offer every piece of information he had. Copying Leo's choice of words, he claimed the traitor had gone to work that morning a little earlier carrying the same case as usual, wearing the same coat and hat. Not wishing to seem uncooperative the grandfather offered opinions and suggestions as to where this traitor could be, all of which Leo sensed were nothing more than desperate guesswork. The grandfather concluded by saying how much everyone in their family disliked and mistrusted Brodsky as a neighbour and how the only person who liked him was Zina Morosovna, the lady living downstairs.

Zina Morosovna was aged somewhere in her fifties and trembling like a child, a fact she was trying unsuccessfully to hide by smoking. Leo found her standing beside a cheap reproduction of a famous Stalin portrait – smooth skin, wise eyes – hung prominently over her fireplace. Perhaps she thought it might protect her. Leo didn't bother to introduce himself, or show his identity card, cutting straight to the chase in an effort to disorient her.

—Why is it you're such good friends with Anatoly Brodsky when everyone else in this building disliked and mistrusted him?

Zina was caught off guard; her sense of discretion blunted by her indignation at this lie:

—*Everyone in this building liked Anatoly. He was a good man.*

—*Brodsky is a spy. Yet you call him good? Treachery is a virtue?*

Realizing her mistake too late, Zina began to qualify her comment.

—*All I meant was that he was very considerate with the noise. He was polite.*

These qualifications were stuttering and irrelevant. Leo ignored them. He took out a pad and wrote down her ill-chosen words in large visible letters.

HE WAS A GOOD MAN

He wrote clearly so that she could see exactly what he was writing: he was writing off the next fifteen years of her life. Those words were more than enough to convict her as a collaborator. She'd receive a lengthy sentence as a political prisoner. At her age she had little chance of surviving the Gulags. He didn't need to say any of these threats aloud. They were common currency.

Zina retreated to the corner of the room, stubbed out her cigarette and immediately regretted it, fumbling for another.

—*I don't know where Anatoly has gone but I do know that he has no family. His wife was killed in the war. His son died of tuberculosis. He rarely had any visitors. As far as I could tell he had few friends . . .*

She paused. Anatoly had been her friend. They'd spent many nights together, eating and drinking. There was a time when she'd even hoped that he might fall in love with her but he'd showed no

49

interest. He'd never got over the loss of his wife. Caught up in her recollections she glanced at Leo. He wasn't impressed.

—*I want to know where he is. I don't care about his dead wife or his dead son. His life story doesn't interest me unless it's relevant to where he is right now.*

Her life was in the balance – there was only one way to survive. But could she betray a man she loved? To her surprise the decision took less deliberation then she would've expected.

—*Anatoly kept himself to himself. However, he did receive and send letters. Occasionally he left them with me to post. The only regular correspondence was addressed to someone in the village of Kimov. It's somewhere north of here, I think. He mentioned that he had a friend there. I don't remember the name of the friend. That's the truth. That's all I know.*

Her voice was choked with guilt. While no outward display of emotion could ever be taken at face value Leo's instincts told him that she was betraying a confidence. He ripped out the incriminating page from his note-book and handed it to her. She accepted the sheet as payment for a betrayal. He saw contempt in her eyes. He didn't let it bother him.

The name of a rural village to the north of Moscow was a tenuous lead. If Brodsky was working as a spy it was much more likely he was being sheltered by the people he was working for. The MGB had long been convinced there was in existence a network of safe houses under foreign control. The idea of a foreign-funded traitor falling back on a personal connection – a collective farmer – ran contrary to the notion that he was a professional spy. And yet Leo felt sure this was a lead he should pursue. He brushed the discrepancies aside: his job was to catch this man. This was the only clue he had. Equivocation had already cost him.

He hurried to the truck parked outside and began rereading the case file, searching for something which might connect with the village of Kimov. He was interrupted by the return of his second in command, Vasili Ilyich Nikitin. Aged thirty-five, five years older than Leo, Vasili had once been one of the MGB's most promising officers. Ruthless, competitive, he harboured no loyalties to anyone except the MGB. Leo privately considered those loyalties to be less about patriotism and more about self-interest. In his early days as an investigator Vasili had signalled his dedication by denouncing his only brother for making anti-Stalinist remarks. Apparently the brother had made a joke at Stalin's expense. He'd been drunk at the time, celebrating his birthday. Vasili had written up the report and the brother had been given a twenty-year labour sentence. That arrest had worked in Vasili's favour until the brother escaped three years later, killing several guards and the camp doctor in the process. He was never caught, and the embarrassment of this incident hung around Vasili's neck. If he hadn't strenuously helped in the search for the fugitive his career might not have survived. Instead it survived in a much weakened state. With no more brothers left to denounce, Leo knew his deputy was on the lookout for some other way of getting back in favour.

Having just finished his search of the veterinary practice, Vasili was apparently pleased with himself. He handed Leo a crumpled letter which, he explained, he'd found caught behind the traitor's writing desk. All other correspondence had been burnt – as it had been in the apartment – yet in his hurry the suspect had missed this one. Leo read it. The letter was from a friend telling Anatoly he was welcome to stay with him at any time. The address was partially smudged but the name of the city was clear: Kiev. Leo folded the letter and handed it back to his deputy.

—This was written by Brodsky. Not a friend. He wanted us to find it. He's not heading to Kiev.

The letter had been hastily written. The handwriting was inconsistent, poorly disguised. The content was risible and seemed solely intended to convince the reader that the writer was a friend to whom Brodsky could turn in an hour of need. The address was deliberately smudged to prevent a quick identification of the genuine occupant and so proof of the letter's forgery. The location of the letter – dropped behind the desk – seemed staged.

Vasili protested the letter's authenticity.

—*It would be negligent not to fully investigate the Kiev lead.*

Though Leo had no doubts about the letter being a forgery he wondered if it wouldn't be shrewd to send Vasili to Kiev as a precautionary measure, to protect against any possible allegation that he'd ignored evidence. He dismissed the idea: it didn't matter how he conducted the investigation, if he failed to find the suspect his career was over.

He returned his attention to the file. According to the records, Brodsky was friends with a man called Mikhail Sviatoslavich Zinoviev, who had been discharged from the Red Army suffering chronic frostbite. Near death, several of his toes had been amputated: he'd been nursed back to health and given a discharge from military service. Brodsky had performed the operation. Leo's finger ran along the document, searching for a current address.

Kimov.

Leo turned to his men, catching Vasili's sour expression.
—*We're leaving.*

Thirty Kilometres North of Moscow

15 February

The roads out of Moscow were covered with icy mulch and despite the truck's tyres being fitted with snow chains their speed had rarely risen above twenty-five kilometres per hour. Wind and snow gusted around them with such ferocity it seemed as if they had some personal stake in Leo not reaching his destination. The windscreen wipers, attached to the roof of the front cabin struggled to keep even the smallest patch of window clear. With visibility less than ten metres the truck pushed forward. It was nothing less than desperation on Leo's part to attempt a journey in these conditions.

Hunched forward with maps spread across his lap, Leo was seated beside Vasili and their driver. All three of them were dressed as though they were outside – coats, gloves, hats. The steel cabin with its steel roof and steel floor was heated only by the residual warmth from the rattling engine. But at least the cabin offered some protection from the weather. In the back his nine heavily armed agents travelled in no such luxury. The ZiS-151 trucks had tarpaulin roofs which cold air and even snow whipped through. Since temperatures could fall to minus thirty, all rear compartments of the ZiS-151s were fitted with wood-burning stoves bolted to the floor. These pot-bellied contraptions were able to warm only those within touching distance of them, forcing the men to huddle and regularly rotate position. Leo had sat there many times himself: after every ten minutes the two nearest the stove reluctantly moved away from the heat, relegated to the coldest position at the furthest ends of the benches while the rest of the team shuffled up.

For the first time in his career Leo could sense dissent among his team. The reason wasn't the discomfort or the lack of sleep. His men were used to tough conditions. No, there was something else. Perhaps it was the fact that the mission could have been avoided. Perhaps they had no confidence in the Kimov lead. Yet he'd asked his men for their confidence before and he'd been given it. Tonight he felt hostility, resistance. Aside from Vasili he wasn't used to it. He pushed the thoughts aside. Right now his popularity was the least of his concerns.

If his theory proved correct, if the suspect was in Kimov, then Leo thought it likely that he'd be on the move at first light, whether on his own or aided by his friend. Leo was taking a chance betting that they'd get to the village in time. He'd decided against deploying the local militia stationed at Zagorsk, the nearest major town, since they were in his opinion amateurish, ill-disciplined and undertrained. Even the local MGB divisions weren't to be trusted with such an operation. Already alert to the fact he was a wanted man, Brodsky was unlikely to surrender. He might fight to the death. He needed to be taken alive. His confession was of paramount importance. Furthermore his escape had embarrassed Leo personally and he was determined to make amends, determined that he should be the one to make the arrest. This wasn't merely a matter of pride. Nor was it merely that his career depended upon success. The consequences ran deeper than that. Failure in such a high-profile espionage case might result in claims that Leo had deliberately sabotaged the investigation. Failure to recapture the suspect would further implicate him. His loyalty would be called into question.

Check on Those we Trust.

No one was exempt from that rule, not even those who enforced it.

If Brodsky wasn't in Kimov, if Leo was wrong, then Vasili would be the first in line with a testimonial detailing how his superior officer disregarded the promising Kiev lead. Sensing his weakness, others in the directorate, like animals circling a wounded prey, would almost certainly come forward to denounce him as a poor leader while Vasili positioned himself as Leo's logical successor. In the hierarchies of the State Security, fortunes could change overnight. For both men much depended upon the location of this traitor.

Leo glanced across at his deputy, a man both handsome and repulsive in equal measure — as if his good looks were plastered over a rotten centre, a hero's face with a henchman's heart. There were just the tiniest visible fractures in his attractive facade, appearing at the corners of his mouth, a slight sneer that, if you knew how to interpret it, hinted at the dark thoughts lying beneath his good looks. Perhaps sensing that he was the subject of attention, Vasili turned and smiled a thin, ambiguous smile. Something pleased him. Leo knew immediately that something must be wrong.

He checked the map. With a population of less than a thousand, Kimov was a speck of dust on the Soviet canvas. He'd warned the driver not to expect any road signs. Even at fifteen kilometres per hour this village would appear and disappear in the time it would take to change gear. Yet as Leo ran his finger over the road markings he began to suspect that they'd missed their turning. They were still travelling north when they should be travelling west. Since it was nearly impossible to take any kind of bearings based upon the surrounding landscape he calculated where they were in terms of kilometres. They were too far north. The driver had overshot the mark.

—*Turn around!*

Leo noticed that neither the driver nor Vasili seemed surprised by the request. The driver mumbled:

—*But we didn't see the exit.*

—*We've missed it. Stop the truck.*

The driver gently slowed, pumping the brake in short bursts in order to avoid sliding on the ice. The truck came to a gradual stop, Leo jumped out and in blizzard conditions began to direct the driver through an awkward U-turn, the ZiS-151 being almost as wide as the road. The turn was halfway complete, with the truck at right angles to the road, when the driver seemed to ignore Leo's instructions, reversing too far and too fast. Leo ran forward banging on the door but it was too late. One of the back tyres ran off the road. It was spinning uselessly in a snow drift. Leo's anger was tempered by his growing suspicions regarding this driver, who seemed to exhibit an improbable level of incompetence. Vasili had organized the truck, the driver. Leo opened the cabin door, shouting over the wind:

—*Get out!*

The driver stepped out. By now the officers in the back had also jumped out to survey the situation. They glared at Leo with disapproval. Was this annoyance at the delay, the mission itself, irritation with his leadership? He couldn't understand it. He ordered one of the other men to take the wheel whilst the entire team, including Vasili, pushed the truck out of the snow. The tyre spun, spraying dirty slush up their uniforms. Finally the snow chains caught the road and the truck lurched forward. Leo sent the disgraced driver to sit in the back. That kind of mistake was more than enough to warrant a written report and a Gulag sentence. Vasili must have guaranteed the driver immunity, a guarantee that would only hold up if Leo failed. Leo wondered how many other members of his team had more invested in his failure than his success. Feeling alone, isolated within his own unit, he took the wheel. He'd drive. He'd navigate. He'd get them there. He could trust no one. Vasili got in beside him, wisely opting to say nothing. Leo put the truck in gear.

By the time they were on the correct road, travelling west, on an approach to Kimov the storm had passed. A weak winter sun began to rise. Leo was exhausted. Driving through the snow had drained him. His arms and shoulders were stiff, his eyelids heavy. They were passing through the rural heartlands – fields, forests. Turning into a gentle valley he saw the village: a cluster of wooden farmhouses, some on the road, some set back, all with square bases and high triangular roofs, a vista that hadn't changed for a hundred years. This was old Russia: communities built around bucket wells and ancient myths, where the health of cattle was decided by the grace of the *Dvorovoi*, the yard spirit, where parents told their children that if they misbehaved spirits would steal them and turn them into bark. The parents had been told the stories as children and they'd never grown out of them, spending months stitching clothes only to give them away as offerings to forest nymphs, the *Rusalki*, who were believed to swing from the trees and could, if they so chose, tickle a man to death. Leo had grown up in the city and these rural superstitions meant nothing to him, baffled as to how their country's ideological revolution had done little to dislodge this primitive folklore.

Leo stopped the truck at the first farmhouse. From his jacket pocket he took out a glass vial filled with small, unevenly shaped dirty white crystals – pure methamphetamine – a narcotic much favoured by the Nazis. He'd been introduced to it while fighting on the Eastern Front as his country's army had pushed the invaders back, absorbing prisoners of war and also some of their habits. There had been operations where Leo couldn't afford to rest. This was one of them. Now prescribed to him by the MGB doctors, he'd used it repeatedly since the war, whenever a mission needed to run all night. Its usefulness couldn't be underestimated. But its price was a total crash about twenty-four hours later: complete exhaustion which could only be offset by taking more or sleeping for twelve hours. Side effects had begun to manifest themselves. He'd lost weight; the definition of his face had tightened. His powers of recall had faded, precise details and names eluded him, previous cases and arrests had become muddled in his memory and he now had to write notes to himself. It was impossible to judge whether or not he'd become more paranoid as a result of the drugs since paranoia was an essential asset, a virtue which should be trained and cultivated. If it had been amplified by the methamphetamines, that was all to the good.

He tapped a small amount onto his palm, then a little more, struggling to remember the correct dosage. Better too much than too little. Satisfied, he washed it down with the contents of a hip flask. The vodka stung his throat, failing to hide the acrid chemical taste, which made him want to gag. He waited for the sensation to pass, surveying his surroundings. Fresh snow covered everything. Leo was pleased. Outside Kimov itself there were few places to hide. A person would be visible for kilometres, their tracks through the snow easy to follow.

He had no idea which of these farms belonged to Mikhail Zinoviev. Since a military truck parked in the road took away any element of surprise Leo jumped out, drew his gun and moved towards the nearest house. Though the amphetamines hadn't yet taken hold he already felt more awake, sharpened as his brain prepared itself for the inevitable narcotic surge. He approached the porch, checking his weapon.

Before he'd even knocked on the door an elderly woman with leathery skin appeared. She was wearing a blue-patterned dress with white sleeves, and an embroidered shawl wrapped around her head. She didn't care for Leo, or his gun, his uniform, or his military truck. She was fearless and made no attempt to hide the lines of disdain carved into her brow.

—*I'm looking for Mikhail Sviatoslavich Zinoviev. Is this his farmhouse? Where is he?*

As though Leo were speaking a foreign language she cocked her head to one side and made no response. It was the second time in two days that an elderly woman had squared up to him, held him in open contempt. There was something about these women which made them untouchable; his authority meant nothing to them. Fortunately the stalemate was broken when the woman's son, a man with a strong build and nervous stammer, hurried out of the house.

—*Excuse her. She's old. What can I do for you?*

Once again sons made excuses for their mothers.

—*Mikhail Sviatoslavich. Where is he? Which is his farm?*

Realizing that Leo wasn't interested in arresting them, that he and his family were safe for another day, the son was greatly relieved. He gladly pointed out his friend's farm.

Leo returned to the truck. His men had assembled. He split the team into three groups. They'd advance on the house from different sides, one each from the front and back while the third team would approach and surround the barn. Each man was armed with a 9mm Stechkin APS automatic pistol devised specially for use by the MGB. In addition one man in each group carried an AK-47. They were ready for a pitched battle, if it came to that.

—We take the traitor alive. We need his confession. If you're in any doubt, any doubt at all, you don't fire.

Leo repeated this command with particular emphasis to the group headed by Vasili. Killing Anatoly Brodsky would be a punishable offence. Their own safety was secondary to the life of the suspect. In response Vasili took command of his group's AK-47.

—Just to be sure.

In an attempt to limit Vasili's potential to sabotage this operation Leo gave them the least important area to secure.

—Your group will search the barn.

Vasili moved off. Leo grabbed his arm.

—We take him alive.

Halfway towards the house the men divided into the three groups, breaking off in different directions. Neighbours stole glances from their windows then disappeared inside. Thirty paces from the door Leo paused, allowing the other two groups to get in position. Vasili's team encircled the barn while the third group arrived at the back of the house, all of them waiting for Leo's signal. There was no sign of life outside. A whisper of smoke rose from the chimney. Ragged cloth hung in front of the small windows. It was impossible to see into the rooms. Except for the click of AK-47 safety catches there was silence. Suddenly a young girl stepped out from a small rectangular building, the pit toilet – set back from the main house. She was humming; the sound carried across the snow. The three officers nearest Leo swung round, training their guns on her. The little girl froze, terrified. Leo raised his hands.

—*Don't shoot!*

He held his breath, hoping not to hear the report of machine-gun fire. No one moved. And then the girl broke into a run, sprinting towards the house as fast as she could, screaming for her mother.

Leo felt the first amphetamine kick – his fatigue evaporated. He leapt forward, his men followed, moving in on the house like a noose tightening around a neck. The little girl threw open the front door, scampered inside. Leo was only seconds behind, hitting the front door with his shoulder, raising his gun and barging into the house. He found himself inside a small, warm kitchen surrounded by the smell of breakfast. There were two young girls – the elder was maybe ten years old and the younger four years old – standing by a small fire. Their mother, a stout, tough looking woman who looked like she could swallow bullets and spit them back out, was in front of them, shielding them with one hand on each of their chests. A man in his forties entered from the back room. Leo turned to him.

—*Mikhail Sviatoslavich?*

—*Yes?*

—*My name is Leo Stepanovich Demidov, officer of the MGB. Anatoly Tarasovich Brodsky is a spy. He's wanted for questioning. Tell me where he is.*

—*Anatoly?*

—*Your friend. Where is he? And don't lie.*

—*Anatoly lives in Moscow. He works as a vet. I haven't seen him for years.*

—If you tell me where he is I will forget that he ever came here. You and your family will be safe.

Mikhail's wife directed her husband a glance: she was tempted by the offer. Leo felt an overwhelming sense of relief. He'd been right. The traitor was here. Without waiting for an answer, Leo gestured for his men to begin searching the house.

*

Vasili entered the barn, gun raised, finger against the trigger. He stepped towards the pile of straw, the only place to hide, high enough to conceal a man. He fired several short bursts. Wisps of straw flew up. Smoke rose from the barrel of his gun. The cows behind him snorted, shuffled away, kicking the ground. But no blood seeped out. There was no one here, they were wasting their time. He went outside, slung the machine gun over his shoulder and lit a cigarette.

Alarmed by the sound of gunfire, Leo ran out of the house. Vasili called to him:

—There's no one here.

Buzzing with narcotic energy Leo hurried towards the barn, his jaw clamped tight.

Annoyed at being ignored, Vasili tossed the cigarette into snow, watching as it melted down to the ground.

—Unless he can disguise himself as a cow he's not in there. Maybe you should shoot them just in case.

Vasili glanced around for laughter and the men obliged. He wasn't deluded: he recognized that none of them thought he was funny. Far better than that, their laughter was an indication that the balance of power had begun to shift. Their allegiance to Leo was weakening. Maybe it was the exhausting journey. Maybe it had been Leo's decision to let Brodsky remain free when he should've been arrested. But Vasili wondered if it had something to do with Fyodor and the death of his little boy. Leo had been sent to clear that matter up. Many of the men here were Fyodor's friends. If there was resentment it could be mined, manipulated.

Leo bent down, examining the tracks in the snow. There were fresh boot prints; some belonged to his officers but underneath those were a set leading out from the barn and heading to the fields. He stood up and entered the barn. Vasili called out after him:

—*I've searched there already!*

Ignoring him, Leo touched the smashed lock on the door: he saw the grain sacks spread on the ground and returned outside, staring in the direction of the fields.

—*I want three men to follow me, the fastest three. Vasili, you'll remain here. Continue searching the house.*

He took off his heavy winter jacket. Without meaning it as an intentional snub he gave it to his deputy. Unimpeded, able to run, he began following the tracks towards the fields.

The three agents who'd been ordered to follow didn't bother removing their coats. Their superior officer was asking them to run through the snow without their jackets when he couldn't even bother to examine the body of their colleague's dead son. A boy's death had been dismissed as though it were a trifle. The men certainly weren't going to catch pneumonia, not in blind obedience to a man whose authority might be coming to an end, a man who had no interest in looking after them. All the same, Leo was still their superior officer, for the moment at least, and after exchanging looks with Vasili the three men began sluggishly jogging in an imitation of obedience, following a man who was already several hundred metres ahead of them.

Leo was picking up speed. The amphetamines focused him:

nothing else existed except the tracks in the snow, the rhythm of his steps. He was incapable of stopping or slowing, incapable of failure, incapable of feeling the cold. Even though he guessed the suspect had at least an hour's head start, that fact didn't concern him. The man had no idea he was being followed, he'd almost certainly be walking.

Up ahead was the crest of a gentle hill and Leo hoped that from the top he'd be able to see the suspect. Reaching the top he paused, surveying the landscape around him. There were snow-covered fields in every direction. Some distance ahead there was the edge of a dense forest but before that, a kilometre away, downhill, there was a man shuffling through the snow. This was no farmer or labourer. It was the traitor. Leo was sure of it. He was making his way north on course towards the forest. If he managed to reach the trees he'd be able to hide. Leo had no dogs to track him. He checked over his shoulder – his three agents were lagging. Some tie between him and them had snapped. They couldn't be counted on. He'd have to catch the traitor himself.

As though some sixth sense had alerted him, Anatoly stopped walking and turned around. There, running down the small hill towards him, was a man. There could be no doubt that this was an officer of the State. Anatoly had been certain that all evidence connecting him to this remote village had been destroyed. For this reason he stood for a moment, doing nothing at all, mesmerized by the sight of his pursuer. He'd been found. He felt his stomach heave, his face flush red and then, realizing this man meant death, he spun around and began running towards the woods. His first few steps were clumsy and panicked, staggering sideways into the deeper snow drifts. He quickly understood that his coat was a hindrance. He pulled it off, dropping it on the ground, running for his life.

Anatoly no longer made the mistake of glancing behind him. He was concentrating on the woods ahead. At this rate he was going to reach them before his pursuer could catch up. The woods offered a chance to disappear, to hide. And if it came to a fight he'd have a better chance in there, where there were branches and stones, than unarmed and out in the open.

Leo increased his speed, pushing himself harder, sprinting as though on a running track. Some part of his mind remembered that the terrain was treacherous and running at this speed precarious. But the amphetamines made him believe anything was possible – he could leap this distance between them.

Suddenly Leo lost his footing, sliding to the side before tumbling face down into a snow drift. Dazed, buried in snow, he rolled onto his back, wondering if he was hurt whilst staring up at the pale-blue sky. He felt no pain. He got up, brushing the snow off his face and hands, regarding with cool detachment the cuts on his hands. He looked for the figure of Brodsky, expecting to see him disappearing into the edge of the forest. But to his surprise the suspect had also stopped running. He was standing still. Confused, Leo hurried forward. He didn't understand – just as escape seemed possible this man seemed to be doing nothing at all. He was staring at the ground in front of him. Barely a hundred metres now separated them. Leo drew his gun, slowing to a walk. He took aim, knowing full well he couldn't risk a shot from this range. His heart was pounding, two thumps for each footstep. Another surge of methamphetamine energy: the roof of his mouth went dry. His fingers trembled with an excess of energy, sweat seeped down his back. There were barely fifty paces between them. Brodsky turned around. He wasn't armed. He had nothing in his hands; it was as though he'd suddenly and inexplicably given up. Leo continued forward, closer and closer. Finally he could see what had stopped

Brodsky. There was an ice-covered river some twenty metres wide in between him and the woods. It hadn't been visible from the hill, hidden under a blanket of heavy snow which had settled across the frozen surface. Leo called out:

—*It's over!*

Anatoly considered this remark, turned back towards the forest and stepped out onto the ice. His footsteps were unsteady, sliding across the smooth surface. The ice sheet creaked under his weight, barely holding him. He didn't slow down. Step after step after step, the ice was beginning to crack – black, crooked lines formed on the surface, criss-crossing and fanning out from underneath his feet. The faster he moved, the faster the lines appeared, multiplying in all directions. Icy water seeped up through the joints. He pressed forward: he was at the middle of the river, another ten metres to go to the other side. He looked down at dark, freezing water flowing beneath him.

Leo reached the edge of the riverbank, holstered his gun, stretched out his hand.

—*The ice won't hold. You won't reach the woods.*

Brodsky stopped and turned.

—*I'm not trying to reach the woods.*

He raised his right leg and with a sudden movement brought his boot crashing down, splintering the surface and puncturing through to the river underneath. Water rushed up, the ice broke apart and he fell through.

Completely numb, in shock, he allowed himself to sink: looking up at the sunlight. Then, feeling the pull upwards, he kicked himself downstream away from the break in the ice. He had no intention of surfacing. He'd disappear into this dark water. His lungs were beginning to sting and already he could feel his body fighting his decision to die. He kicked himself further downstream swimming as far away from the light as possible, away from any chance of survival. Finally his natural buoyancy lifted him to the surface; instead of air his face rose up against a solid sheet of ice. The slow-moving current dragged him further downstream.

*

The traitor wasn't going to surface, no doubt he was swimming away from the air hole in an attempt to kill himself and protect his accomplices. Leo hurried down the riverbank, estimating where under the ice he might be. He unfastened his heavy leather belt and gun, dropped them on the ground and stepped out onto the frozen river, his boots slipping across the surface. Almost immediately the ice began to strain. He kept moving, trying to keep his footsteps light, but the ice was splintering and he could feel it sinking under his weight. Reaching the middle of the river, he crouched down, frantically brushing away the snow. But the suspect was nowhere to be seen – just dark water all around. Leo moved further downstream but fracture lines were chasing his every step, surrounding him from all sides. Water began to swell, the cracks came together. He looked up to the sky, filling his lungs, bracing himself as he heard a snap.

The ice collapsed.

Although he didn't feel the full extent of the cold, doped up on amphetamines, he knew he had to move fast. At this temperature he had a matter of seconds. He spun around. There were shafts of light where the ice had broken in two places but beyond that the water was dark, shielded from the sun by a dense canopy of snow. He pushed away from the bottom, heading downstream. Unable to see anything he swam further and further, blindly groping right and left. His body was screaming for air. In response he increased his speed, kicking harder, pulling himself faster through the water. Soon he'd have no choice but to turn back or die. Realizing he wouldn't get a second chance, that returning empty-handed might mean execution, he took another stroke downstream.

His hand brushed something: material, cloth, a trouser leg. It was Brodsky, lank against the ice. But as though his touch brought him back to life he started struggling. Leo swam underneath him, gripped him around the neck. The pain inside Leo's chest was sharp. He had to get back to the surface. With one arm around the suspect's neck he tried punching the ice above him but his blows glanced off the smooth hard surface.

Brodsky stopped moving. Concentrating, overriding every impulse in his body, he opened his mouth, filling his lungs with freezing water, welcoming death.

Leo focused on the shafts of sunlight upstream. He kicked hard, propelling them both towards the light. His prisoner was motionless, unconscious. Light-headed, Leo couldn't hold his breath any longer. He took another kick – felt sunlight across his face – pushed upwards. The two men broke the water's surface.

Leo gasped and gasped again. But Brodsky wasn't breathing. Leo pulled him towards the riverbank, smashing his way through the fractured chunks of ice. His feet touched the riverbed. He pulled himself up onto the bank, dragging his prisoner with him. Their skin was pale blue. Leo couldn't stop shaking. In contrast the suspect remained perfectly still. Leo opened the man's mouth, tipping the water out, blowing air into his lungs. He pushed down on his chest, blew air into his lungs, he pushed down on his chest, blew air into his lungs.

—*Come on!*

Brodsky spluttered back into consciousness, doubling over and vomiting up the icy water that filled his stomach. Leo didn't have time to feel relief. They had minutes before they'd die from hypothermia. He stood up. He could see his three officers in the near distance.

The men had spotted Leo disappearing into the river and realized that their superior officer had been right all along. In a split second the balance of power shifted away from Vasili and back to Leo. Their disgruntled feelings towards his handling of Fyodor now meant nothing. The only reason they'd felt safe enough to let their emotions poke through had been their expectation that this operation would fail and Leo would be relieved of his power. That was not the case: his position would be stronger than ever. They were running as fast as they could; their lives depended on it.

Leo dropped down to the prisoner's side. Brodsky's eyes were closing – he was drifting back into unconsciousness. Leo hit him across the face. It was essential he remain awake. He hit him again. The suspect opened his eyes but almost immediately began to close them again. Leo hit him again and again and again. They were running out of time. He stood up, calling to his men.

—*Hurry!*

His voice was becoming softer, his energy sapping as finally the cold caught up with him and his chemical invincibility began to melt away. The drugs had passed their peak. An extraordinary fatigue was repossessing his body. His officers arrived.

—*Take off your jackets. Get a fire started.*

All three took their jackets off, wrapping one around Leo and the other two around Brodsky. That wasn't going to be enough. They needed a fire. The three officers looked for wood. There was a picket fence some distance away and two of the agents ran towards it while the third agent began ripping the sleeve of his coarse cotton shirt into strips. Leo remained focused on his prisoner, hitting him to keep him awake. But Leo was also feeling sleepy. He wanted to rest. He wanted to close his eyes.

—*Hurry!*

Though he'd meant to shout, his voice was barely audible.

The two officers returned with planks ripped from the fence. They cleared an area of ground, kicking aside the snow and laying timbers across the frozen soil. Upon these timbers they positioned the strips of cotton. Building around these strips they balanced thin wooden shards, creating a pyramid formation. One of the officers took out his lighter, tipping the fluid over the cotton. The flint sparked, the cotton caught light, began to burn. The wood smouldered. But it was damp and refused to catch. Smoke spiralled upwards. Leo couldn't feel any heat. The wood was taking too long to dry out. He ripped the lining from the inside of the jacket, adding this to the fire. If it went out they'd both die.

Between them they only had one lighter remaining. The officer carefully pulled the components apart and tipped the last of the lighter fuel over the struggling fire. The flames grew, aided by a crumpled cigarette carton and shredded cigarette papers. All the officers were on their knees, stoking the fire. The timbers began to burn.

Anatoly opened his eyes, staring at the flames in front of him. The wood was crackling in the heat. Despite his desire to die the warmth felt wonderful on his skin. As the flames grew and the embers glowed red, he realized with muddled emotions that he was going to survive.

Leo sat, his gaze concentrated on the fire's centre. Steam rose from his clothes. Two of the officers, keen to recover his approval, carried on collecting firewood. The third officer stood guard. Once there was no danger of the fire burning out, Leo ordered one of the men to return to the house and make preparations for their return to Moscow. Addressing his prisoner, Leo asked:

—Are you well enough to walk?

—I used to go fishing with my son. At night we'd build fires just like this and sit around them. He didn't much like to fish but I think he enjoyed the fires. Had he not died he would've been roughly the same age as you are now.

Leo said nothing. The prisoner added:

—If it's all right with you, I'd like to stay a little longer.

Leo added some more wood to the fire. They could wait a little longer.

*

On the walk back none of the men spoke. The distance Leo had covered in less than thirty minutes took them almost two hours to retrace. Each footstep seemed heavier and heavier as the methamphetamines disappeared from his system. Only the fact of his success sustained him now. He'd return to Moscow having proved himself, having recovered his status. He'd stood on the brink of failure and stepped back from it.

Nearing the farmhouse Anatoly began to wonder how they'd found him. He realized that he must have mentioned his friendship with Mikhail to Zina. She'd betrayed him. But he felt no anger towards her. She was only trying to survive. No one could begrudge her that. Anyway, it was irrelevant. All that mattered now was convincing his captors that Mikhail was innocent of any collaboration. He turned to his captor.

—When I arrived last night the family told me to leave. They wanted nothing to do with me. They threatened to call the authorities. That's why I was forced to break into their barn. They thought I'd gone. The family has done nothing wrong. They're good people, hard-working people.

Leo tried to imagine what had really happened last night. The traitor had sought his friend's help but that help had not been forthcoming. It was not much of an escape plan. It was certainly not the escape plan of a competent spy.

—*I have no interest in your friends.*

They reached the perimeter of the farm. Just ahead of them, lined up on their knees outside the entrance to the barn, were Mikhail Zinoviev, his wife and their two young daughters. Their hands were tied behind their backs. They were shivering, freezing cold in the snow. It was obvious they'd been positioned like this for some time. Mikhail's face was battered. There was blood dripping from his smashed nose; his jaw hung at an awkward angle. It was broken. The officers were in a loose, uncertain ring around them. Vasili stood directly behind the family. Leo stopped walking, about to speak, when Vasili uncrossed his arms, revealing his gun. He lined up the muzzle and fired a shot into the back of Zinoviev's head. The sound rang out. The man's body fell forward into the snow. His wife and daughters remained motionless, staring at the body before them.

Only Brodsky reacted, making a noise, an inhuman noise – no words but grief and anger mixed together. Vasili took a step to the side and positioned his gun behind the wife's head. Leo raised his hand.

—*Lower your gun! That's an order.*

—*These people are traitors. We need to make an example.*

Vasili pulled the trigger, his hand recoiled, a second shot rang out and the woman's body slumped into the snow beside that of her husband. Brodsky tried to break free but the two officers escorting him kicked him to his knees. Vasili took another side-step, positioning the gun behind the head of the elder daughter. Her nose was red with the cold. Her body was shaking slightly. She was staring at her mother's body. She would die in the snow beside her parents. Leo drew his gun, pointing it at his deputy.

—*Lower your gun.*

Suddenly all his tiredness disappeared, not as the result of some narcotic. Outrage and adrenaline swept through him. His hand was steady. He closed one eye and took careful aim. At this range he wouldn't miss. If he fired now the girl would survive. Both girls would survive – no one would be murdered. Without thinking about it the word had sprung into his head:

Murdered.

He cocked his gun.

Vasili had been wrong about Kiev. He'd been duped by Brodsky's letter. He'd assured the other men they were wasting their time going to Kimov. He'd hinted that tonight's failure would result in him becoming the new boss. These embarrassing mistakes would all be in Leo's report. Right now Vasili could sense the other officers watching him. His status had been struck a humiliating blow. Part of him wanted to see if Leo had the nerve to kill him. The repercussions would be severe. Yet he was no fool. He knew in his heart that he was a coward just as surely as he knew that Leo was not. Vasili lowered his gun. Pretending to be satisfied, he gestured to the two children.

—*The girls have learned a valuable lesson. Maybe they'll grow up to be better citizens than their parents.*

Leo moved towards his deputy, passing the two dead bodies, leaving a boot print in the bloody snow. In a swift arc he swung his gun, cracking the edge of his weapon against the side of Vasili's head. Vasili fell back, clutching his temple. There was a trickle of blood where the skin had broken. But before he could stand up straight he felt the barrel of Leo's gun pressing against his temple. Except for the two girls, who were staring down, waiting to die, everyone watched.

Very slowly, Vasili tilted his head and looked up, his jaw quivering. He was afraid of death; this man to whom the death of others was so casual. Leo's finger touched the trigger. But he couldn't do it. Not in cold blood. He would not be this man's executioner. Let the State punish him. Trust in the State. He holstered his gun.

—You'll remain here and wait for the militia. You'll explain what has happened and assist them. You can make your own way back to Moscow.

Leo helped the two girls to their feet and walked them to the house.

Three agents were needed to carry Anatoly Brodsky to the back of the truck. His body was slack as though life had been sucked out of it. He was muttering incomprehensibly, insane with grief and oblivious as the other officers told him to shut up. They didn't want to listen to his crying.

*

Inside the house the two young girls said nothing, still unable to comprehend that the bodies lying outside in the snow were their parents. At any moment they expected their father to make them breakfast or their mother to return from the fields. Nothing felt real. Their parents were their entire world. How could the world exist without them?

Leo asked if they had any other family. Neither girl said a word. He told the elder girl to pack – they were coming to Moscow. Neither of them moved. He went to the bedroom and began to pack for them, looking for their things, their clothes. His hands began to shake. He stopped, sat on the bed and looked down at his boot. He clumped his heels together and stared at the thin, compact ridges of blood-soaked snow that fell to the floor.

*

Vasili watched from the roadside, smoking his last cigarette, as the truck pulled away. He glimpsed the two girls sitting in the front beside Leo where he should've been. The truck turned and disappeared down the road. He looked around. There were faces at the windows of nearby farms. This time they didn't shy away. He was glad he still had his machine gun. He walked back to the house glancing at the bodies lying in the snow. He entered the kitchen, warmed up some water and brewed some tea. It was strong and he sweetened it with sugar. The family had a small pot of sugar, probably meant to last a month. He poured almost all of it into his glass, creating a sickly treat. He sipped it and suddenly felt tired. He took off his boots and jacket, went to the bedroom, pulled back the covers and lay down. He wished it were possible to choose his dreams. He'd choose to dream of revenge.

Moscow

16 February

Even though it had been his place of work for the past five years, Leo had never felt comfortable in the Lubyanka, the head-quarters of the MGB. Casual conversations were rare. Reactions were guarded. All this was hardly surprising considering the nature of their occupation but to his mind there was something about the building itself which made people uneasy, as though fear had been factored into the design. He accepted his theory was nonsense in so far as he knew nothing of the architect's intention. The building predated the Revolution, existing as nothing more than an insurance office before being taken over by the Bolshevik secret security force. Yet he found it difficult to believe they'd by chance chosen a building whose proportions were so unsettling: neither tall nor squat, wide nor narrow, it was somewhere awkwardly in between. Its facade created the impression of watchfulness: rows and rows of windows crammed together, stacked up and up, rising to a clock at the top which stared out over the city as though it were a single beady eye. An invisible borderline existed around the building. Passers-by steered clear of this imaginary perimeter as if fearful they were going to be pulled in.

Crossing that line meant you were either staff or condemned. There was no chance you could be found innocent inside these walls. It was an assembly line of guilt. Perhaps the Lubyanka hadn't been constructed with fear in mind but fear had taken over all the same, fear had made this former insurance office its own, its home.

Leo handed over his identity card; a card which meant not only that he could enter the building but also that he could leave. The card-less men and women led through these doors were often never seen again. The system might carry them into the Gulags or to a building just behind this one, on Varsonofyevsky Lane, another State Security compound fitted with sloping floors, log-panelled walls to absorb bullets and hoses to wash away the rivulets of blood. Leo didn't know the precise execution capacity but the numbers were high, up to several hundred a day. At those levels practical considerations, such as how easily and quickly human remains could be cleaned away, became an issue.

Entering the main corridor, Leo wondered how it would feel to be led down to the basements with no leave to appeal and no one to call for help. The judicial system could be bypassed entirely. Leo had heard of prisoners who lay abandoned for weeks and doctors who served no other purpose than the study of pain. He taught himself to accept that these things existed not just for their own sake. They existed for a reason, a greater good. They existed to ter-rify. Terror was necessary. Terror protected the Revolution. Without it, Lenin would've fallen. Without it, Stalin would've fallen. Why else would rumours concerning this building be delib-erately spread by MGB operatives, muttered on the metro or on tramcars as strategically as if they were releasing a virus into the population? Fear was cultivated. Fear was part of his job. And for this level of fear to be sustained it needed a constant supply of people fed to it.

Of course the Lubyanka wasn't the only building to fear. There was Butyrka prison with its tall towers and squalid wings filled with cramped cells where inmates played with matchsticks whilst waiting for their deportation to the labour camps. Or there was Lefortovo, where criminals under active investigation were transported for interrogations and where screams could be heard from neighbouring streets. But Leo understood that the Lubyanka held a special place in the people's psyche, representing the place where those guilty of anti-Soviet agitation, counter-revolutionary activity and espionage were processed. Why did that category of prisoner strike particular dread into everyone's heart? While it was easy to comfort yourself that you would never steal or rape or murder, no one could ever be sure they weren't guilty of anti-Soviet agitation, counter-revolutionary activity and espionage since no one, including Leo, could ever be sure exactly what these crimes were. In the one hundred and forty articles of the criminal code Leo had just one article to guide him, a subsection defining the political prisoner as a person engaged in activity intended to:

Overthrow, subvert, or weaken the Soviet Power.

And that was more or less it: an elastic set of words stretching to accommodate anyone from top-ranking Party officials to ballet dancers to musicians to retired cobblers. Not even those who worked within the Lubyanka's walls, not even those who kept this machinery of fear ticking could be certain that the system they sustained would not one day swallow them too.

Despite the fact that Leo was indoors he was still wearing his outdoor attire, including leather gloves and a long woollen overcoat. He was shivering. When he stood still the floor seemed to rock from side to side. Dizzy spells came over him, lasting for several seconds. He felt as if he was going to collapse. He hadn't eaten in two days yet the thought of food made him sick. Even so he stubbornly refused to consider the possibility he was ill: he was a little cold certainly, tired perhaps, but that would pass. In the post-amphetamine crash, he just needed to sleep. There was no way he could take a day off. Not today, not when there was the matter of Anatoly Brodsky's interrogation.

Interrogations were technically not part of his duties. The MGB had specialists who did nothing but interview suspects, moving from cell to cell, extracting confessions with professional indifference and personal pride. They were motivated, like most employees, by simple things such as the prospect of a performance-related-pay bonus, rewarded if the suspect signed promptly and unconditionally without amendments. Leo knew a little of their methods. He knew none of them personally. Interrogators formed something of a clique, working as a team, often sharing the same suspects, combining their particular gifts to attack resilience from a variety of different angles. Brutal, articulate, disarming: all of these qualities had their place. Outside of work these men and women ate together, walked together, shared stories and compared methods. Though they looked more or less like anyone else it was for some reason relatively easy for Leo to point them out. Many of their more extreme operations were confined to the basement, where they were able to control environmental elements such as heat and light. In contrast, Leo's role as investigator meant he spent most of his time either upstairs or outside. The basement was a world he rarely descended to, a world he'd closed his eyes to, a world he preferred to keep under his feet.

After a short wait Leo was called in. Unsteady, he entered Major Kuzmin's office. Nothing in this room was accidental: everything had been meticulously planned and positioned. The walls were decorated with framed black-and-white photos, including one in which Stalin was shaking Kuzmin's hand, a photo taken at the Leader's seventieth birthday. Surrounding these were a selection of framed propaganda posters collected from different decades. Leo supposed the age range was intended to suggest that Kuzmin had always occupied this office even during the purges of the 1930s, which was not the case, he had been in army intelligence. There was a poster of a plump white rabbit in a cage. *EAT MORE RABBIT MEAT!* There were three powerful red figures smashing their red hammers against the heads of sulky-looking unshaven men. *FIGHT LAZY WORKERS!* There were three smiling women heading into a factory. *TRUST YOUR SAVINGS TO US!* The *US* in the last poster didn't refer to the three smiling women but rather to the national savings account. There was a poster of a bulbous man dressed in a suit and top hat carrying two bags brimming with money. *CAPITALIST CLOWNS!* There were blocky images of docks, ship-building, railways, smiling workers, angry workers and a fleet of locomotives all in honour of Lenin. *BUILD!* These posters were rotated regularly and Kuzmin was fastidious about showing off his extensive collection. Equal care was spent on his book collection. His shelves were stocked with all the appropriate titles whilst his copy of *The History of the All-Union Communist Party: Short Course,* the text ushered in by Stalin himself, rarely left his desk. Even the waste-paper basket contained only rigorously selected items. Everyone from the lowliest clerk to the highest-ranking officer understood that if you genuinely wanted to dispose of something you sneaked it out, discreetly getting rid of it on the way home.

Kuzmin stood by the window overlooking Lubyanka Square. He was squat and wearing, as he tended to do, a uniform one size too small for his frame. His glasses were thick and often slid down his nose. In short he was a ridiculous-looking man and not even the supreme power of life and death had bestowed upon him any gravitas. Although, as far as Leo was aware, Kuzmin no longer took part in interrogations it was rumoured that in his day he'd been something of an expert, preferring to use his small, fat hands. Looking at him now, it was hard to believe.

Leo sat down. Kuzmin remained standing by the window. He preferred to pose questions whilst looking outside. This was because he believed, and often reminded Leo, that outward displays of emotion should be treated with extreme scepticism unless the person was unaware that he or she was being observed. He'd become adept at appearing to gaze out at the view whilst actually watching people in the reflection. The usefulness of this trick was significantly reduced by the fact that almost everyone, including Leo, was aware they were being watched. And anyway very few people lowered their guard inside the Lubyanka.

—*Congratulations, Leo. I knew you'd get him. The experience was a valuable lesson for you.*

Leo nodded.

—*Are you ill?*

Leo paused. Evidently he looked worse than he imagined.

—*It's nothing. A cold perhaps but it will pass.*

—*My guess is that you're annoyed with me for having taken you off the Brodsky case to make you deal with Fyodor Andreev. Am I correct? You think Fyodor was an irrelevance and I should've left you to continue the operation against Brodsky.*

He was smiling, something amused him. Leo concentrated, sensing danger.

—*No, Major, I'm not annoyed. I should've arrested Brodsky immediately. It was my fault.*

—Yes, but you did not arrest him immediately. So, in those circumstances, was I wrong to take you off the case of the spy and make you speak to a grieving father? That is my question.

—I had only thought about my own failure to arrest Brodsky immediately.

—That's evasive of you. My point is simply this: Fyodor's family wasn't a trivial issue. It was a corruption within the very MGB itself. One of your men had become twisted by grief and unwittingly made himself and his family enemies of the State. While I'm pleased you caught Brodsky, I considered your work with Fyodor the more important.

—I understand.

—Then we come to the matter of Vasili Nikiyin.

It was inevitable that his actions would be reported. Vasili wouldn't hesitate to try and use them against him. Leo couldn't presume on Kuzmin's support or guess which aspect of the incident concerned him the most.

—You pointed a gun at him? And then you hit him? He says you were out of control. He says you were taking narcotics. They've made you irrational. He's pushing for your suspension. He's upset, you understand.

Leo understood perfectly: the executions were not the issue here.

—I was ranking officer and I gave an order. Vasili disobeyed. How can I maintain the line of command, how can any of us maintain command, if orders are ignored? The system collapses. Perhaps it's my military background. In military operations disobedience and insubordination are punishable by death.

Kuzmin nodded. Leo had chosen his defence wisely – the principles of military decorum.

—You're right, of course. Vasili is hot-headed. He admits as

much. He disobeyed an order. This is true. But he was enraged by the family's collaboration. I'm not condoning what he did, you understand. We have a system in place for such violations. They should've been brought here. And Vasili has been appropriately reprimanded. As for the drugs—

—I hadn't slept in twenty-four hours. And they are supplied to me by the doctors here.

—They don't concern me in the least. I told you to do whatever it takes, which I suppose extends to taking whatever it takes. But I wish to give you a word of warning. Hitting a fellow officer gets you noticed. People will quickly forget that your reasons were sound. As soon as Vasili lowered his gun that should've been the end of it. If you wished to punish him further you should have reported his insubordination to me. You took justice into your own hands. That is not acceptable. That is never acceptable.

—I apologize.

Kuzmin moved away from the window. Standing by Leo's side, he put a hand on his shoulder.

—Enough of all that. Consider the matter closed. I have a different challenge for you: Brodsky's interrogation. I want you to handle it personally. You may call on whoever you like to assist you – a specialist interrogator – but I want you to be present when he cracks. It's important that you see this man for who he really is, particularly since you were duped by his apparent innocence.

It was an unusual request. Kuzmin noted Leo's surprise.

—It will be good for you. We should measure a man by what they're prepared to do themselves. Not by what they're prepared to have others do for them. Do you have any objection?

—None.

Leo stood up, straightening his jacket.

—*I'll begin immediately.*

—*One last thing: I want you and Vasili to work together on this.*

*

There were three types of cell. There were the holding cells: square rooms, a floor covered with straw, with enough space for three adult men to lie side by side. There were always five men in any one cell, packed so tightly that one man couldn't scratch himself without the others also moving, a human jigsaw of limbs. Since there was no latrine, space also had to be made for the bucket which the men were obliged to use in each other's company. Once it was brimming prisoners were made to carry it to the nearest drain and told that if they spilled even the smallest drop they would be shot. Leo had listened to the guards discussing the prisoners' comical expressions of concentration as they stared at the quivering level of faeces and urine, a level which decided whether they lived or died. Barbarity, certainly, but barbarity for a reason, barbarity for the greater good.

Greater Good the Greater Good

It was necessary to repeat it, to carve it onto every thought, so that it ran like ticker tape across the bottom of your mind.

After the holding cells, there were punishment cells of various designs. Some were ankle deep in freezing water, the walls covered in mould and slime. A five-day stretch was sufficient to ensure the body never recovered, sickness permanently stitched into a prisoner's lungs. There were narrow closets, like wooden coffins, where bedbugs had been left to multiply and in which a prisoner would remain, naked, feasted upon, until ready to sign a confession. There were cork-lined rooms where prisoners were heated, cooked by the building's ventilation system, until blood seeped out of their pores. There were rooms with hooks and chains and electric wires. There were all kinds of punishments for all kinds of people. The imagination was the only barrier and not much of one at that. All these horrors seemed small when placed beside the size and magnitude of the greater good.

Greater Good the Greater Good the Greater Good

The justification of such methods was simple and persuasive and needed constant repeating: these people were enemies. Had Leo not seen equally extreme measures during war? Yes, and worse. Had that war not won them freedom? Was this not the same, a war against a different kind of enemy, an enemy within but an enemy all the same? Was it necessary? Yes, it was. The survival of their political system justified anything. The promise of a golden age where none of this brutality would exist, where everything would be in plenty and poverty would be a memory, justified anything. These methods were not desirable, they were not to be celebrated and the officers who took pleasure from their work were incomprehensible. Yet Leo was no fool. Within this polished and practised sequence of self-justification there was a small amount of denial, denial which sat dormant in the pit of his stomach like an undigested seed pod.

Finally, the last type of cells, were the interrogation cells. Leo had arrived at one such cell where they were holding the traitor: a plate-steel door with a viewing hole. He knocked, wondering what he would find inside. The door was unlocked by a boy barely seventeen years old. The cell itself was small and rectangular with stark concrete walls and stark concrete floors but so brightly lit that Leo squinted as he entered. Five powerful bulbs hung from the ceiling. Against the back wall, incongruous in the bleak setting, was a sofa. Anatoly Brodsky was sitting on it, his wrists and ankles tied with rope. The young officer proudly explained:

—*He keeps shutting his eyes, keeps trying to sleep. But me, I keep hitting him. He hasn't had a moment's rest, I promise you. That sofa's the best part. All he wants to do is sit back and doze off. It's comfortable, really soft. I've sat on it. But I won't let him sleep. It's like putting food just out of reach of a starving man.*

Leo nodded and could see the young officer was a little disappointed not to receive more gushing praise of his dedication. The officer took up position in the corner of the room, armed with his black wooden baton. Rigid, earnest, with red cheeks, he looked like a toy soldier.

Brodsky was sat on the edge of the sofa, hunched forward, his eyes half closed. There were no other chairs and Leo sat on the sofa beside him. It was a preposterous arrangement. The sofa was indeed very soft and Leo sank back, appreciating the peculiar torture of this room. But he didn't have time to waste, he had to work quickly. Vasili would be here any minute and Leo hoped that Anatoly could be persuaded to cooperate before he arrived.

Anatoly looked up, his eyes widening a fraction. It took him a moment before his sleep-deprived brain recognized the man seated beside him. This was the man who'd caught him. This was the man who'd saved his life. Drowsy, his words slurred, he said as though he'd been drugged.

—*The children? Mikhail's daughters? Where are they now?*

—*They've been placed in an orphanage. They're safe.*

An orphanage – was that meant as a joke, was that part of this punishment? No, this man wouldn't make a joke. He was a believer.

—*Have you ever been to an orphanage?*

—No.

—The girls would've had a better chance of surviving if you'd left them on their own.

—The State is looking after them now.

To Leo's surprise the prisoner reached up and, with his wrists still bound, felt his brow. The junior officer sprang forward, raising the wooden baton, ready to crack a blow across the prisoner's knees. Leo waved him away and the officer reluctantly stepped back.

—You have a fever. You should be at home. You men have a home? Where you sleep and eat and do all the things normal men do?

Leo wondered at this man. He was still a doctor, even now. He was still irreverent, even now. He was brave, rude and Leo couldn't help but like him.

Leo pulled back, wiping his clammy forehead with the sleeve of his jacket.

—You can save yourself unnecessary suffering by talking to me. There's not a person we've questioned who didn't wish they'd admitted everything straightaway. What will you gain by silence?

—I will gain nothing.

—Then will you tell me the truth?

—Yes.

—Who are you working for?

—Anna Vladislovovna. Her cat is going blind. Dora Andreyeva. Her dog refuses to eat. Arkadi Maslow. His dog has broken its front leg. Matthias Rakosi. He has a collection of rare birds.

—If you're innocent, why did you run?

—I ran because you were following me. There was no other reason.

—That doesn't make sense.

—I agree but it's true all the same. Once you're followed you're always arrested. Once you're arrested you're always guilty. No innocent people are ever brought here.

—Which officials from the American Embassy are you working with and what information have you been passing them?

At last Anatoly understood. Several weeks ago a junior clerk working for the American Embassy had brought his dog in for examination. The dog was suffering from an infected cut. It needed a course of antibiotics but since the antibiotics were unavailable he'd cleaned the animal carefully, sterilized the injury and kept it in under observation. Not long after that he'd spotted a man loitering outside his home. He hadn't slept that night, unable to figure out what he'd done wrong. The next morning he'd been followed into work and followed home again. This continued for three days. After the fourth sleepless night he'd decided to run. Now, finally, here were the details of his crime. He'd treated a foreigner's dog.

—I have no doubt that I will eventually say whatever it is you want me to say but right now I will say this: I – Anatoly Tarasovich Brodsky – am a vet. Soon your records will say that I was a spy. You will have my signature and my confession. You will force me to give you names. There will be more arrests, more signatures and more confessions. But whatever I eventually tell you will be a lie because I am a vet.

—You're not the first guilty man to claim that he's innocent.

—Do you really believe I'm a spy?

—From this conversation alone I have enough to convict you for subversion. You've already made it quite clear that you hate this country.

—I don't hate this country. You hate this country. You hate the people of this country. Why else would you arrest so many of them?

Leo grew impatient.

—*Are you aware of what will happen to you if you don't talk to me?*

—*Even children are aware of what goes on in here.*

—*But you still refuse to confess?*

—*I will not make this easy for you. If you want me to say I'm a spy you will have to torture me.*

—*I'd hoped this could be avoided.*

—*You think you can remain honourable down here? Go get your knives. Get your tool kit. When your hands are covered in my blood then let's hear you sound reasonable.*

—*All I need is a list of names.*

—*There's nothing more stubborn than a fact. That is why you hate them so much. They offend you. That is why I can upset you simply by saying that I – Anatoly Tarasovich Brodsky – am a vet. My innocence offends you because you wish me to be guilty. You wish me to be guilty because you've arrested me.*

There was a knock on the door. Vasili had arrived. Leo stood up, muttering:

—*You should have taken my offer.*

—*Perhaps one day you'll understand why I could not.*

The young officer unlocked the door. Vasili entered. He was wearing a sterilized dressing at the point where he'd been hit, which Leo suspected was of no practical value, intended only to trigger conversation and enable him to describe the incident to as many people as possible. Vasili was accompanied by a middle-aged man with thinning hair and dressed in a crumpled suit. Seeing Leo and Anatoly together, Vasili seemed concerned.

—*Has he confessed?*

—*No.*

Evidently relieved, Vasili signalled for the junior officer to get the prisoner to his feet whilst the middle-aged man in the brown suit stepped forward, smiling, offering Leo his hand.

—*Doctor Roman Hvostov. I'm a psychiatrist.*

—*Leo Demidov.*

—*Pleased to meet you.*

They shook hands. Hvostov gestured at the prisoner.

—*Don't worry about him.*

Hvostov led them to his surgery, the door to which he unlocked, gesturing for them to come in, as though they were children and this was his playroom. The surgery was small and clean. There was a red leather chair bolted to the white-tiled floor. By using a series of levers the chair could be lowered to become a bed and then raised upright again. On the walls were glass cabinets filled with bottles and powders and pills, labelled with neat white stickers and careful, tidy black handwriting. Hanging beneath the cabinet was an array of steel surgical instruments. There was a smell of disinfectant. Brodsky didn't struggle as he was strapped to the chair. His wrists, ankles and neck were fastened with black leather straps. Leo tied his feet whilst Vasili tied his arms. Once they were finished he was unable to move any part of his body. Leo stepped back. Hvostov scrubbed his hands at the sink.

—*For a time I worked in a Gulag, near the city of Molotov. The hospital was full of people pretending to be mentally ill. They would do anything to get out of work. They would run around like animals, screaming obscenities, tearing their clothes off, masturbating in full view, defecating on the floor, anything and everything to convince me they were deranged. You could trust none of it. My job was to identify who was lying and who was genuine. There were numerous academic tests but prisoners quickly caught on and this information was shared and soon everyone knew how to behave in order to cheat the system. For example a prisoner who thought he was Hitler or a horse or something equally and obviously out-landish was almost certainly pretending to be insane. And so prisoners stopped pretending to be Hitler and became much more subtle and sophisticated in their deceptions. In the end there was only one way of getting to the truth.*

He filled a syringe with thick yellow oil, then positioned it on a steel tray and carefully cut away part of the prisoner's shirt, tying a rubber tourniquet around the top of his arm in order to expose a wide blue vein which popped up. Hvostov addressed the prisoner:

—*I hear you have some medical knowledge. I'm about to inject camphor oil into your bloodstream. Do you understand what that will do to you?*

—*My medical experience is limited to helping people.*

—*This can help people too. It can help the deluded. It will induce a seizure. While you are in this seizure you will be unable to lie. In fact you will not have the ability to do very much at all. If you are able to speak you will only be able to speak the truth.*

—*Then go ahead. Inject your oil. Hear what I have to say.*

Hvostov addressed Leo.

—*We'll use a rubber gag. This is to stop him biting off his tongue during the most intense part of the seizure. However, once he calms down we can safely remove the gag and you may ask your questions.*

Vasili picked up a scalpel and began using the tip to clean his fingernails, wiping the line of dirt on the side of coat. Once he was done he put the scalpel down and reached into his pocket, pulling out a cigarette. The doctor shook his head.

—*Not in here, please.*

Vasili put the cigarette away. The doctor inspected the syringe – there was a yellow dewdrop of oil at the needle's tip. Satisfied, he sank the needle into Brodsky's vein.

—*We need to do this slowly. Too quick and he'll suffer an embolism.*

He pushed down on the plunger and the treacle-thick yellow oil moved from the syringe into the prisoner's arm.

The effects did not take long. Suddenly all intelligence left Anatoly Brodsky's eyes: they rolled back in his head and his body began to shake as if the chair he was strapped to was charged with a thousand volts. The needle was still in his arm and only a small fraction of the oil had been injected.

—*And now we inject a little more.*

Another five millilitres was injected and bubbles appeared at the corners of Brodsky's mouth, small white bubbles.

—*And now we wait, we wait, we wait, and now we inject the rest.*

Hvostov injected the remaining oil, pulling the needle out and pressing a cotton pad against the entry point on the arm. He stepped back.

Brodsky was less like a human and more like a machine gone wrong, an engine pushed past its limits. His body was pulling against the restraints in a way that suggested that there was some external force acting upon him. There was a crack. A bone in his wrist snapped as it jerked against the restraint. Hvostov peered at the injury, which was already swelling up:

—*That's not unusual.*

He said, glancing at his watch:

—*Wait a little longer.*

Two separate streams of foam dribbled down from either side of the prisoner's mouth, running underneath his chin and dripping onto his legs. The vibrations were slowing down.

—*OK. Ask your questions. See what he says.*

Vasili stepped forward and untied the rubber gag. Brodsky

vomited foam and saliva onto his lap. Vasili turned around with an incredulous look.

—*What the fuck is he going to tell us like this?*

—*Try.*

—*Who are you working with?*

In response the man's head slumped against the restraint. He gurgled. Blood ran out of his nose. Hvostov used a tissue to wipe away the blood.

—*Try again.*

—*Who are you working with?*

Brodsky's head rolled to the side, like a puppet, a doll: lifelike, capable of motion, but not actually alive. His mouth opened and shut, his tongue extended – the mechanical imitation of speech but there was no sound.

—*Try again.*

—*Who are you working with?*

—*Try again.*

Vasili shook his head, turning to Leo.

—*This is stupid. You try.*

Leo's back was pressed against the wall, as though trying to move as far away as possible. He stepped forward.

—*Who are you working with?*

A noise came from Brodsky's mouth. It was ridiculous, comical, like a baby's spluttering. Hvostov crossed his arms and peered into Brodsky's eyes.

—*Try again. Ask simple questions to start off with. Ask him his name.*

—*What is your name?*

—*Try again. Trust me. He's coming out of it. Try again. Please.*

Leo stepped closer. He was close enough to reach out and touch his brow.

—*What is your name?*

His lips moved.

—*Anatoly.*

—*Who are you working with?*

He was no longer shaking. His eyes rolled forward.

—*Who are you working with?*

There was silence for a moment. And then he spoke, faint, hurried – as a man might speak in his sleep.

—*Anna Vladislovovna. Dora Andreyeva. Arkadi Maslow. Matthias Rakosi.*

Vasili reached for his notepad, scribbling down the names, asking:

—*Recognize any of those names?*

Yes, Leo recognized those names: Anna Vladislovovna: her cat is going blind. Dora Andreyeva: her dog refuses to eat. Arkadi Maslow: his dog has broken its front leg. The seed of doubt, sitting dormant and undigested in the pit of Leo's stomach, cracked open.

Anatoly Tarasovich Brodsky was a vet.

Anatoly Tarasovich Brodsky was nothing more than a vet.

17 February

Dr Zarubin put on his mink-fur-lined hat, picked up his leather bag and nudged his way off the crowded tramcar, half-heartedly apologizing. The pavement was icy and, stepping down, he held on to the side of the tramcar for support. He felt old suddenly; unsteady on his feet, fearful of slipping over. The tramcar pulled away. He looked around, hoping this was the right stop – the eastern outskirts were a district he knew vaguely. But it proved a simple matter to get his bearings – his destination dominated the grey winter skyline. On the opposite side of the road stretching many hundreds of metres above him and above everything else was a set of four U-shaped apartment blocks arranged in pairs with each block positioned as if one were the reflection of the other. The doctor marvelled at this modern design, home to thousands of families. This wasn't just a housing project. It was a monument to a new era. No more privately owned one- or two-storey properties. Those were gone, flattened, smashed to brick dust, and in their place stood perfectly formed, government-designed and owned apartments, each painted grey and stacked up and up and side by side. Nowhere had he seen exactly the same shapes repeated so many times in so many directions, each apartment a perfect facsimile of the next. The thick layer of snow which capped the roof of each building was as though God had drawn a white line and said no further, the rest of the sky is mine. That, Zarubin thought, was their next challenge: the rest of the sky. It certainly didn't belong to God. Somewhere in one of these four buildings was apartment 124 – the home of MGB officer Leo Stepanovich Demidov.

Earlier this morning the doctor had been briefed by Major Kuzmin on the details of Leo's sudden departure. He'd left at the beginning of a crucial interrogation, claiming to feel feverish and unable to continue his duties. The major was concerned by the timing of the departure. Was Leo really sick? Or was there another reason for his absence? Why had he given assurances that he was well enough to work only to change his mind after being set the task of interrogating the suspect? And why had he attempted to interview the traitor alone? The doctor had been dispatched to investigate the authenticity of Leo's illness.

From a medical standpoint the doctor supposed, even before an examination, that Leo's poor health was due to his prolonged exposure to icy water, possibly pneumonia exacerbated by his use of narcotics. And if this was the case, if he was genuinely sick, then Zarubin was to behave as a doctor and facilitate his recovery. If, however, he was feigning sickness for whatever reason then Zarubin was to behave as an MGB officer and dope him with a powerful sedative, which he would administer by pretending it was a medicine or tonic. Leo would be bedridden for twenty-four hours preventing him from escape and giving the major time to decide how best to proceed.

According to the steel floor plan affixed to a concrete pillar at the base of the first building apartment number 124 was located in the third block on the fourteenth floor. The elevator, a metal box with space for two, or four if you didn't mind snuggling against each other, rattled its way up to the thirteenth floor where it paused briefly, as though taking a breath, before making up the final distance. Zarubin needed both hands to pull the stiff grate sideways. At this height the wind over the exposed concrete walkway brought tears to his eyes. He glanced out at the panorama over the tatty fringes of a snow-covered Moscow before turning left and arriving at apartment 124.

The door was opened by a young woman. The doctor had read Leo's file and knew that he was married to a woman called Raisa Gavrilovna Demidova: twenty-seven years old, a schoolteacher. The file hadn't mentioned that she was beautiful. She was, notably so, and it should've been in the file. These things mattered. He hadn't prepared himself for it. He had a weakness for beauty; not the ostentatious, self-regarding kind. His preference was for understated beauty. Here was such a woman: it wasn't that she'd made no effort over her appearance, on the contrary, she'd made every effort to appear unremarkable, to play down her beauty. Her hair, her clothes were styled in the most common of fashions, if they could be called fashions at all. Evidently she did not seek the attention of men, a fact which made her all the more attractive to the doctor. She would be a challenge. In his younger years the doctor had been a womanizer, legendary in fact among certain social circles. Inspired by the memories of his previous successes he smiled at her.

Raisa glimpsed a set of stained teeth, no doubt yellow from years of heavy smoking. She smiled in response. She'd expected the MGB to send someone even though they'd given no warning and she waited for this man to introduce himself.

—*I'm Doctor Zarubin. I've been sent to look in on Leo.*

—*I'm Raisa, Leo's wife. You have identification?*

The doctor took off his hat, found his card and presented it.

—*Please: call me Boris.*

There were candles burning in the apartment. Raisa explained that there was only intermittent power at the moment – there was a recurrent problem with the electricity on all floors above the tenth. They suffered periodic blackouts, sometimes lasting for a minute, sometimes for a day. She apologized, she didn't know when the power might be coming back on. Zarubin made what seemed to be a joke.

—*He'll survive. He's not a flower. As long as he's kept warm.*

She asked if the doctor wanted a drink: something hot perhaps since it was cold outside. He accepted her offer: touching the back of her hand as she took his coat.

In the kitchen, the doctor leant against the wall, his hands in his pockets, watching as she prepared tea.

—*I hope the water is still hot.*

She had a pleasant voice, soft and calm. She brewed loose leaves in a small pot before pouring it into a tall glass. The tea was strong, almost black, and once the glass was half full she turned to him.

—*How strong do you like it?*

—*As strong as you can make it.*

—*Like this, then?*

—*Perhaps just a little more water.*

As she topped it up with water from the samovar, Zarubin's eyes drifted down her body, roaming over the outline of her breasts, her waist. Her clothes were dowdy – a grey cotton dress, thick stockings, a knitted cardigan over a white shirt. He wondered why Leo hadn't used his position to dress her in foreign tailored luxuries. But even mass-produced garments and coarse material didn't make her any less desirable.

—*Tell me about your husband.*

—*He has a fever. He claims to feel cold when he's hot. He's shaking. He refuses to eat.*

—If he has a fever it's best that he doesn't eat for the time being. However, his lack of appetite might also be due to his use of amphetamines. Do you know anything about this?

—If it's to do with his work I know nothing.

—Have you noticed any changes in him?

—He skips meals, he's out all night. But then his work demands that. I've noticed that after working long stretches he tends to become a little absent-minded.

—He forgets things?

She handed the doctor his glass.

—Would you like sugar?

—Jam would be nice.

She reached for the top shelf. As she did the back of her shirt lifted up revealing a patch of pale, perfect skin. Zarubin felt his mouth go dry. She took down a jar of dark purple jam, unscrewing the lid and offering him a spoon. He scooped out a clump of jam and placed it on his tongue, sipping the hot tea, feeling the jam dissolve. With a deliberate intensity he stared into her eyes. Made aware of his desire, she blushed. He watched as the flush of red spread around her neck.

—Thank you.

—Perhaps you'd like to get on with the examination?

She screwed the lid back on the jar, leaving it on the side and stepping towards the bedroom. He didn't move.

—I'd like to finish my tea first. There's no rush.

She was forced to return. Zarubin pursed his lips and blew across the surface. The tea was hot and sweet. She was flustered. He was enjoying making her wait.

The windowless bedroom was hot, the air stale. Zarubin knew from the smell alone that the man lying in bed was ill. To his surprise he felt something like disappointment. Pondering what underlay this feeling he sat down on the bed, beside Leo. He took his temperature. It was high but not dangerously so. He listened to Leo's chest. He could hear nothing out of the ordinary. Leo wasn't suffering from tuberculosis. There were no indications that this was anything more than a cold. Raisa stood beside him, watching. The doctor could smell soap on her hands. He liked being this close to her. He took a brown glass bottle from his bag and measured out a spoonful of thick green liquid.

—*Please lift his head*.

She helped her husband into a sitting position. Zarubin tipped the liquid down his throat. Once he'd swallowed she lowered Leo's head onto the pillow.

—*What was that for?*

—*It's a tonic – to help him sleep*.

—*He needs no help with that*.

The doctor didn't reply. He couldn't be bothered to think up a lie. The drug administered in the guise of a medicine was in fact the doctor's own creation: a combination of a barbiturate, a hallucinogenic and, to disguise the taste, flavoured sugar syrup. Its purpose was to incapacitate the body and mind. Administered orally, in less than an hour the muscles went first – becoming slack, relaxed to the point where even the slightest movement felt like unimaginable hard work. The hallucinogenic kicked in shortly after.

An idea had taken hold of Zarubin: it had taken shape in the kitchen when Raisa had blushed and crystallized into a plan the moment he'd smelt soap on her hands. If he reported that Leo wasn't sick, that he was faking his leave of absence, then he would almost certainly be arrested and interrogated. With all the other doubts surrounding his behaviour there would be a heavy weight of suspicion. He'd most probably be imprisoned. His wife, his beautiful wife, would end up alone and vulnerable. She'd be in need of an ally. Zarubin's status within the State Security forces matched or even surpassed Leo's and he felt sure he could offer an acceptable, comfortable alternative. Zarubin was married but he could take her as a mistress. He was convinced that Raisa's survival instinct was highly tuned. Yet all things considered there might be a less complicated way of getting what he wanted. He stood up.

—*Can we speak in private?*

In the kitchen, Raisa crossed her arms. There was a furrow in her brow — a tiny crinkle in her otherwise perfect pale skin. Zarubin wanted to run his tongue along it.

—*Will my husband be OK?*

—*He's suffering from a fever. And I would be prepared to say that.*

—*You would be prepared to say what?*

—*I'd be prepared to say that he was genuinely sick.*

—*He is genuinely sick. You just said so yourself.*

—*Do you understand why I'm here?*

—*Because you're a doctor and my husband is ill.*

—*I've been sent to discover if your husband is genuinely ill or if he's merely trying to avoid work.*

—*But it's obvious that he's sick. Doctor or not, anyone could see that.*

—*Yes, but I'm the one who's here. I'm the one who decides. And they'll believe what I say.*

—*Doctor, you just said he was sick. You said he was suffering from a fever.*

—*And I would be prepared to say that, on the record, if you were prepared to sleep with me.*

Remarkably she didn't even blink. No visible reaction. Her coolness made Zarubin want her even more. He continued:

—It would only be once, of course, unless you took a fancy to me, in which case it could continue. We could come to some arrangement: you'd be rewarded with whatever you wanted, within reason. The point is that no one need ever know.

—And if I said no?

—I would say that your husband was a liar. I would say that he was desperate to avoid work for reasons unknown to me. I would recommend that he be investigated.

—They wouldn't believe you.

—Are you sure of that? The suspicion is already there. All it needs is a slight push from me.

Taking her silence as acceptance of his offer, Zarubin stepped towards her tentatively pressing a hand against her leg. She didn't move. They could have sex in the kitchen. No one would know. Her husband wouldn't wake. She could moan with pleasure, she could make as much noise as she liked.

Raisa glanced sideways, disgusted, unsure what to do. Zarubin's hand slid down her leg.

—Don't worry. Your husband is fast asleep. He won't disturb us. We won't disturb him.

His hand moved under her skirt.

—You might even enjoy it. Many other women have.

He was so close she could smell his breath. He leaned towards her, his lips parting, his yellow teeth nearing her as though she were an apple he was about to bite into. She pushed past him. He grabbed her wrist.

—Ten minutes is hardly a high price to pay for the life of your husband. Do it for him.

He pulled her closer, his grip tightening.

Suddenly he let go, raising both his hands in the air. Raisa had a knife against his throat.

—If you're unsure of my husband's condition, please inform Major Kuzmin – a good friend of ours – to send another doctor. A second opinion would be most welcome.

The two of them sidestepped around each other, the knife against his neck, until Zarubin backed out of the kitchen. Raisa remained at the entrance to the kitchen, holding the knife at waist height. The doctor took his coat, leisurely putting it on. He picked up his leather bag, opening the front door and squinting as he adjusted to the bright winter sunlight:

—Only children still believe in friends and only stupid children at that.

Raisa stepped forward, snatching his hat from the peg and tossing it at his feet. As he bent down to pick it up she slammed the front door shut.

Hearing him walk away, her hands were shaking. She was still holding the knife. Perhaps she'd given him some reason for thinking she'd sleep with him. She ran the events through her mind: opening the door, smiling at his ridiculous joke, taking his coat, making tea. Zarubin was deluded. There was nothing she could've done about that. But maybe she could've flirted with his proposition, pretended that she was tempted. Maybe the old fool only needed to think that she was flattered by his advances. She rubbed her brow. She'd handled that badly. They were in danger.

She entered the bedroom and sat down beside Leo. His lips were moving as though in silent prayer. She leaned closer, trying to make sense of his words. They were barely audible, fragments which didn't match up. He was delirious. He gripped her hand. His skin was clammy. She pulled her hand free and blew the candle out.

*

Leo was standing in snow, the river before him, Anatoly Brodsky on the opposite side. He'd made it across and was almost at the safety of the forests. Leo stepped after him only to see that under his feet, locked within the thick sheet of ice, were the men and women he'd arrested. He looked left and right – the entire river was filled with their frozen bodies. If he wanted to get to the forests, if he wanted to catch that man, he had to walk over them. With no choice – it was his duty – Leo quickened his pace. But his footsteps seemed to bring the bodies to life. The ice began to melt. The river came alive, writhing. Sinking into a slush Leo now felt faces under his boots. It didn't matter how fast he ran, they were everywhere, behind, in front. A hand caught his foot – he shook it free. Another hand grabbed his ankle, a second, a third, a fourth. He closed his eyes, not daring to look, waiting to be dragged down.

When Leo opened his eyes he was standing in a drab office. Raisa was beside him, wearing a pale red dress, the dress she'd borrowed from a friend on the day of their wedding, hastily adjusted so that it didn't look too big on her. In her hair she wore a single white flower picked from the park. He was wearing an ill-fitting grey suit. The suit wasn't his: he'd borrowed it from a colleague. They were in a rundown office in a rundown government building, standing side by side, in front of a table where a balding man was hunched over paperwork. Raisa presented their documentation and they waited whilst their identities were checked. There were no vows, no ceremony or bouquets of flowers. There were no guests, no tears or well-wishers – there was just the two of them, wearing the best clothes they could manage. No fuss: it was bourgeois to make a fuss. Their only witness, this balding civil servant, entered their details into a thick, well-thumbed ledger. Once the paperwork was completed they were handed a marriage certificate. They were man and wife.

Back at his parents' old apartment, the place where they'd celebrated their wedding, there were friends, neighbours, all keen to take advantage of the hospitality. Elderly men sang unfamiliar songs. Yet there was something wrong with this memory. There were faces that were cold and hard. Fyodor's family was here. Leo was still dancing but the wedding had become a funeral. Everyone was staring at him. There was a tap at the window. Leo turned to see the outline of a man, pressed up against the glass. Leo walked towards him, wiping away the condensation. It was Mikhail Sviatoslavich Zinoviev, a bullet through his head, his jaw smashed, his head battered. Leo stepped back, turned around. The room was now completely empty except for two young girls – Zinoviev's daughters, dressed in filthy rags. Orphans, their stomachs were swollen, their skin blistered. Lice crawled across their clothes, their eyebrows and in amongst their matted black hair. Leo closed his eyes and shook his head.

Shivering, freezing cold, he opened his eyes. He was underwater and sinking fast. The ice was above him. He tried to swim upwards but the current was pulling him down. There were people on the ice, looking down at him, watching him drown. An intense pain burned in his lungs. Unable to hold his breath, he opened his mouth.

*

Leo gasped, opening his eyes. Raisa was seated beside him, trying to calm him. He looked around, confused: his mind half in the dream world, half in this one. This was real: he was back in his apartment, back in the present. Relieved, he took hold of Raisa's hand, whispering in a hurried unbroken stream.

—Do you remember the first time we saw each other? You thought I was rude, staring at you. I got off at the wrong metro stop

just to ask your name. And you refused to tell me. But I wouldn't leave until you did. So you lied and told me your name was Lena. For an entire week all I could talk about was this beautiful woman called Lena. I'd tell everyone, Lena's so beautiful. When I finally saw you again and convinced you to walk with me I called you Lena the entire time. At the end of the walk I was ready to kiss you and you were only ready to tell me your real name. The next day I told everyone how wonderful this woman Raisa was and everyone laughed at me saying last week it was Lena this week it's Raisa and next week it'll be someone else. But it never was. It was always you.

Raisa listened to her husband and wondered at this sudden sentimentality. Where had it come from? Maybe everyone got sentimental when they were sick. She made him lie back and before long he was asleep again. It had been almost twelve hours since Dr Zarubin had left. A slighted, vain old man was a dangerous enemy. To take her mind off her anxieties she made soup – a thick chicken broth with strips of meat, not just boiled vegetables and chicken bones. It bubbled on a slow heat, ready for Leo when he was able to eat again. She stirred the soup, filling a bowl for herself. No sooner had she done so than there was a knock on the door. It was late. She wasn't expecting visitors. She picked up the knife, the same knife, placing it behind her back before moving closer to the door.

—Who is it?

—It's Major Kuzmin.

Her hands shaking, she opened the door.

Major Kuzmin was standing outside with his escort, two young, tough-looking soldiers.

—Dr Zarubin has spoken to me.

Raisa blurted out:

—Please, take a look at Leo for yourself—

Kuzmin seemed surprised.

—*No, that isn't necessary. I don't need to disturb him. I trust the doctor on medical matters. Plus, and don't think me a coward, I'm fearful of catching his cold.*

She couldn't understand what had happened. The doctor had told the truth. She bit her lip, trying not to let her relief show. The major continued:

—*I've spoken to your school. I've explained that you'll be taking leave in order to help Leo recover. We need him fit. He's one of our finest officers.*

—*He's lucky to have such concerned colleagues.*

Kuzmin waved this comment aside. He gestured at the officer standing beside him. The man was holding a paper bag. He stepped forward, offering it to her.

—*This is a gift from Dr Zarubin. So there's no need to thank me.*

Raisa was still holding the knife behind her back. In order to accept the bag she'd need both hands. She slipped the blade down the back of her skirt. Once it was in place she reached forward, accepting the bag, which was heavier than she expected.

—*Will you come in?*

—*Thank you, but it's late and I'm tired.*

Kuzmin bade Raisa goodnight.

She shut the door and walked to the kitchen, putting the bag on the table and taking the knife from the back of her skirt. She opened the bag. It was filled with oranges and lemons, a luxury in a city of food shortages. She shut her eyes, imagining the satisfaction Zarubin was enjoying from her feelings of gratitude, not for the fruit, but for the fact that he'd merely done his job, for the fact that he'd reported that Leo was genuinely sick. The oranges and lemons were his way of saying she should feel indebted to him.

Had another whim taken him, he might have had them both arrested. She emptied the bag into the bin. She stared at the bright colours before picking out every piece of fruit. She'd eat his gift. But she refused to cry.

19 February

This was the first time in four years that Leo had taken an unscheduled leave of absence. There was an entire category of Gulag prisoner convicted under violations of work ethic; people who'd left their station for an undue amount of time or who'd turned up for their shift half an hour late. It was far safer to go to work and collapse on the factory floor than to pre-emptively stay at home. The decision whether or not to work never resided with the worker. Leo was unlikely to be in any danger, however. According to Raisa he'd been checked on by a doctor and Major Kuzmin had paid him a visit, giving the OK to take time off. This meant that the anxiety he was feeling had to be about something else. The more he thought about it the more obvious it became. He didn't want to go back to work.

For the past three days he hadn't left his apartment. Shut off from the world, he'd stayed in bed, sipping hot lemon and sugar water, eating borscht and playing cards with his wife, who'd made no allowance for him being ill, winning almost every hand. For the most part he'd slept and after that first day he'd suffered no more nightmares. But in their place he'd felt a dullness. He'd expected the feeling to fade, convinced that his melancholy was a side effect of the methamphetamine slump. The feeling had got worse. He'd taken his supply of the drug – several glass phials of dirty white crystals – and tipped it down the sink. No more narcotic fuelled arrests. Was it the drugs? Or was it the arrests? As he'd grown stronger he found it easier to rationalize the events of the past few days. They'd made a mistake: Anatoly Tarasovich Brodsky had been a mistake. He was an innocent man caught up and crushed in the cogs of a vital and important but not infallible State machine. It was as simple and as unfortunate as that. A single man didn't dent the meaningfulness of their operations. How could he? The principles of their work remained sound. The protection of a nation was bigger than one person, bigger than a thousand people. How much did all of the Soviet Union's factories and machines and armies weigh? Compared to this the mass of an individual was nothing. It was essential that Leo keep matters in proportion. The only way to carry on was to keep things in proportion. The reasoning was sound and he believed none of it.

In front of him stood the statue of Feliks Dzerzhinsky, in the centre of Lubyanka Square, framed by a patch of grass and circled by traffic. Leo knew Dzerzhinsky's story by heart. Every agent knew his story by heart. As the first leader of the Cheka, the name of the political police created by Lenin after the overthrow of the Tsarist regime, Dzerzhinsky was the forefather of the NKVD. He was a role model. Training manuals were littered with quotes attributed to him. Perhaps his most famous and often referenced speech described how.

An officer must train his heart to be Cruel.

Cruelty was enshrined in their working code. Cruelty was a virtue. Cruelty was necessary. Aspire to Cruelty! Cruelty held the keys that would unlock the gates to the perfect State. If being a Chekist was akin to following a religious doctrine then cruelty was one of their central commandments.

Leo's education had been centred on his athleticism, his physical prowess – a fact that had so far helped rather than hindered his career, giving him the guise of a man who could be trusted in the way that a scholar was to be suspected. But it did mean that he was forced to devote at least one night a week writing out in laborious longhand all the quotes that an agent should know by heart. Burdened with a poor memory, a condition exacerbated by his drug use, he was not a bookish man. However, an ability to recall key political speeches was essential. Any slips showed a lack of faith and dedication. And now, after three days away, as he approached the doors to the Lubyanka and looked back at Dzerzhinsky's statue, he realized that his mind was patchy – phrases came back to him but not in their entirety and not in their correct order. All he could remember exactly, out of the thousands and thousands of words, out of the entire Chekist bible of axioms and principles, was the importance of cruelty.

Leo was shown into Kuzmin's office. The major was seated. He indicated that Leo should take the chair opposite.

—*You're feeling better?*

—*Yes, thank you. My wife told me that you visited.*

—*We were concerned about you. It's the first time you've been ill. I checked your records.*

—*I apologize.*

—*It wasn't your fault. You were brave, swimming in that river. And we're glad you saved him. He's provided some critical information.*

Kuzmin tapped a thin black file at the centre of his desk.

—*In your absence Brodsky confessed. It took two days, two camphor shock treatments. He was remarkably stubborn. But in the end he broke. He gave us the name of seven Anglo-American sympathizers.*

—*Where is he now?*

—*Brodsky? He was executed last night.*

What had Leo expected? He concentrated on keeping his expression still, as though he'd just been told it was cold outside. Kuzmin picked up the black file, handing it to Leo.

—*Inside you have the full transcript of his confession.*

Leo opened the file. His eyes caught the first line.

I – Anatoly Tarasovich Brodsky – am a spy.

Leo flicked through the typed pages. He recognized the pattern, opening with an apology, expressing regret before describing the nature of his crime. He'd seen this template a thousand times. They varied only in the details: the names, the places.

—*Would you like me to read it now?*

Kuzmin shook his head, handing him a sealed envelope.

—*He named six Soviet citizens and one Hungarian man. They're collaborators working with foreign governments. I've given six of the names to other agents. The seventh name is yours to investigate. Considering you're one of my best officers I've given you the hardest. Inside that envelope you have our preliminary work, some photographs and all the information we currently hold on the individual, which, as you will see, is not very much. Your orders are to collect further information and if Anatoly was right, if this person is a traitor, you're to arrest them and bring them here, the usual process.*

Leo ripped open the envelope, pulling out several large black-and-white photographs. They were surveillance photographs taken at some distance from across a street.

They were photographs of Leo's wife.

Same Day

Raisa was relieved to be nearing the end of the day. She'd spent the past eight hours teaching exactly the same lesson to all her year groups. Normally she taught compulsory political studies but this morning she'd received instructions posted to the school from the Ministry of Education ordering her to follow the enclosed lesson plan. It seemed these instructions had been sent to every school in Moscow and were to be implemented with immediate effect, ordinary lessons could resume tomorrow. The instructions stipulated that she spend the day discussing with each class how much Stalin loved his country's children. Love itself was a political lesson. There was no more important love than the Leader's Love, and consequently, one's Love for the Leader. As part of that Love, Stalin wanted all of his children, no matter how old they were, to be reminded of certain basic precautions which they should make part of their daily life. They were not to cross roads without looking twice, they were to be careful when travelling on the metro and finally, and this was to be emphasized particularly, they were not to play on the railway tracks. Over the past year there had been several tragic accidents on the railways. The safety of the State's children was paramount. They were the future. Various faintly ridiculous demonstrations had been given. Each class had concluded with a short quiz to make sure all the information had been absorbed.

> *Who loves you most? Correct answer: Stalin.*
> *Who do you love most? Correct answer: see above*
> *(wrong answers to be logged).*
> *What should you never do? Correct answer:*
> *play on the railway tracks.*

Raisa could only presume that the reason behind this latest edict was that the Party was worried about population levels.

As a rule her classes were tiring, perhaps more so than other subjects. Whereas there was no expectation that students should clap the completion of every mathematical equation there was an expectation that every pronouncement she made regarding Generalissimo Stalin, the state of the Soviet Union or the prospects for worldwide revolution be met with applause. Students were competitive with each other, none of them wanting to seem less dedicated than their neighbour. Every five minutes the class would come to a halt as the children rose to their feet, stamping their shoes on the floor or banging their desks with their fists, and Raisa was duty bound to stand and join in. In order to stop her hands chafing, she clapped in a fashion whereby her palms would barely touch, gliding over each other in the imitation of enthusiasm. Initially she'd suspected that the children enjoyed this raucous behaviour and exploited any opportunity to interrupt a class. She'd come to realize this was not the case. They were afraid. Consequently discipline was never a problem. She rarely needed to raise her voice and never made threats of any kind. Even from the age of six the children understood that to disrespect authority, to speak out of turn, was to take your life into your own hands. Youth provided no protection. The age at which a child could be shot for their crimes, or their father's crimes, was twelve. That was a lesson Raisa wasn't allowed to teach.

Despite the large class sizes, which would have been larger still had it not been for the war playing havoc with demographics, she'd originally set out with the objective of remembering every student's name. Her intention had been to show that she cared about each student individually. Yet very quickly she'd noticed her ability to recall names struck a peculiar note of unease. It was as though there were some implied menace.

If I can remember your name I can denounce you.

These children had already grasped the value of anonymity and Raisa had realized they'd prefer it if she paid them as little individual attention as possible. After less than two months she'd stopped calling them by their names and reverted to pointing.

Yet, comparatively, she had little reason to complain. The school she taught in, Secondary School 7 — a rectangular building raised on stubby concrete legs — happened to be one of the gems of the State education policy. Much photographed and publicized, it was opened by none other than Nikita Khrushchev, who'd made a speech in the new gymnasium, the floor of which had been waxed to such an extent that his bodyguards struggled not to slip. He'd claimed that education must be tailored to the country's needs. And what the country needed were highly productive, healthy young scientists, engineers and Olympic gold-medal-winning athletes. The cathedral-sized gymnasium, adjacent to the main building, was wider and deeper then the school itself, equipped with an indoor running track, an array of mats, hoops, rope ladders and springboards, all of which were put to good use by an extra-curricular timetable that included an hour of training every day for every student regardless of age or ability. The implication of both his speech and the design of the school itself had been always very clear to Raisa: the country didn't need poets, philosophers and priests. It needed productivity that could be measured and quantified, success that could be timed with a stopwatch.

Raisa counted only one friend amongst her colleagues – Ivan Kuzmitch Zhukov, a language and literature teacher. She didn't know his exact age, he wouldn't say, but he was around about forty. Their friendship had occurred by chance. He'd casually lamented the size of the school library – a cupboardlike room in the basement next to the boiler stocked with pamphlets, back issues of *Pravda*, approved texts and not a single foreign author. Hearing him, Raisa had whispered that he should be more careful. That whisper had been the beginning of an unlikely friendship which, from her point of view, might have been strategically unwise considering Ivan's tendency to speak his mind. He was in many people's eyes already a marked man. Other teachers were convinced that he hoarded forbidden texts under his floorboards or, far worse, he was writing a book of his own and smuggling the no doubt subversive pages out to the West. It was true that he'd loaned her an illegal translation of *For Whom the Bell Tolls*, which she'd been forced to read in parks over the summer and which she'd never dared take back to her apartment. Raisa could afford the association only because her own loyalty had never been too closely scrutinized. She was, after all, the wife of a State Security officer, a fact known by almost everyone, including some of the students. Logically, Ivan should have kept his distance. No doubt he reassured himself with the deduction that if Raisa had wanted to denounce him she would have done so already, considering how many imprudent things she'd heard him say and how easy it would for her to whisper his name across the pillow into the ear of her husband. So it came to be that the only person she trusted amongst the staff was the man most mistrusted and the only person he trusted was the woman he should trust least of all. He was married, with three children. All the same she suspected he was in love with her. It was not something she dwelt on and she hoped for both their sakes that it was not something he dwelt on either.

*

Outside the main entrance to the school, across the road, in the foyer of a low-rise apartment block, stood Leo. He'd changed out of his uniform and was wearing civilian clothing, clothing he'd borrowed from work. In the Lubyanka there were cupboards full of odds and ends: coats, jackets, trousers – all of various sizes and differing in quality, kept for exactly this purpose. Leo hadn't thought about where these clothes had come from until he'd found a spot of blood on the cuff of a cotton shirt. They were the clothes of those executed in the building on Varsonofyevsky Lane. They'd been washed, of course, but some stains were stubborn. Dressed in an ankle-length grey woollen coat and a thick fur hat pulled down over his forehead, Leo was convinced his wife wouldn't recognize him if by chance she glanced in his direction. He stamped his feet to keep warm, checking his watch, a stainless-steel Poljot Aviator – a birthday present from his wife. There wasn't long until her classes were finished for the day. He glanced at the light above him. Using an abandoned mop he reached up and smashed the bulb, plunging the foyer into shadow.

This wasn't the first time his wife had been followed. Three years ago Leo had arranged surveillance for reasons that had nothing to do with whether or not she was a security risk. They'd been married less than a year. She'd become increasingly distant. They were living together yet living apart, working long hours, glimpsing each other briefly in the morning and evening with as little interaction as two fishing boats which set sail each day from the same port. He didn't believe that he'd changed as a husband and so couldn't understand why she'd changed as a wife. Whenever he broached the subject she'd claimed she felt unwell yet she refused to see a doctor and anyway who was unwell month after month after month? The only explanation he could come up with was that she was in love with another man.

Duly suspicious he'd dispatched a newly recruited, promising young agent to follow his wife. This agent had done so every day for a week. Leo had justified this course of action because although unpleasant it was motivated by love. However, it had been a risk, not merely in the sense that Raisa might find out. If his colleagues had found out they might have interpreted this matter differently. If Leo couldn't trust his wife sexually how could they trust her politically? Unfaithful or not, subversive or not, it would be better for everyone if she was sent to the Gulags. Just to be sure. But Raisa hadn't been having an affair and no one ever found out about the surveillance. Relieved, he had accepted that he simply needed to be patient, attentive and help her with whatever difficulty she was going through. Over the months their relationship had gradually improved. Leo had transferred the young agent to a post in Leningrad, a move which he'd packaged as a promotion.

This mission, however, was something entirely different. The order to investigate had come from above. This was official State business; a matter of national security. At stake was not their marriage but their lives. There was no doubt in Leo's mind that Raisa's name had been inserted into Anatoly Brodsky's confession by Vasili. The fact that another agent corroborated the details of the confession meant nothing: either it was a conspiracy, a bare-faced lie, or Vasili had planted the name in Brodsky's head at some point during his interrogation, an easy enough thing to do. Leo blamed himself. Taking time off work had given Vasili an opportunity which he'd exploited with perfect ruthlessness. Leo was trapped. He couldn't claim the confession itself was a lie – it was an official document as valid and true as every other confession. The only course of action had been to register his profound disbelief, suggesting that the traitor Brodsky was trying to incriminate Raisa as an act of revenge. Upon hearing this explanation Kuzmin had asked how the traitor knew that he was married. Desperate, Leo had been forced to lie, claiming that he'd mentioned his wife's name in the course of their conversations. Leo was not a skilful liar. By defending his wife he was incriminating himself. To stand up for someone was to stitch your fate into the lining of theirs. Kuzmin had concluded that such a potential breach of security would have to be thoroughly investigated. Either Leo could do it himself or allow another operative to take over. Hearing this ultimatum, he'd accepted the case on the basis that he was simply trying to clear his wife's name. In much the same way that three years ago he'd put to bed his doubts about her faithfulness, now he had to put to bed doubts about her faithfulness to the State.

Across the road children poured out of the school, breaking off in all directions. One young girl ran across the road, heading straight towards Leo and entering the apartment block where he was hiding. As she passed by in the gloom, her feet crunching on the shards of bulb glass, she paused, weighing up whether or not to speak. Leo turned to look at her. The girl had long black hair tied with a red band. She was perhaps seven years old. Her cheeks were pink with the cold. Quite suddenly she broke into a run, her little shoes tapping up the flight of stairs, away from this stranger and back home where she was still young enough to believe she was safe.

Leo moved to the glass door, watching as the last of the students filed out of the building. He knew Raisa wasn't timetabled for any extracurricular activities – she'd be leaving soon. There she was, at the entrance, standing with a male colleague. He had a trim grey beard, round glasses. Leo noted that he was not an unattractive man. He looked educated, cultivated, refined, with busy eyes and a satchel brimming with books. This must be Ivan: Raisa had mentioned him, the language teacher. At a guess Leo reckoned this man was older than him by at least ten years.

Leo willed them to separate at the gates but instead they set off together, walking side by side in casual conversation. He waited, allowing them to get ahead. They were familiar with each other, Raisa laughed at a joke and Ivan seemed pleased. Did Leo make her laugh? Not really, not often. He certainly didn't object to being laughed at when he was foolish or clumsy. He had a sense of humour in that regard but no, he didn't tell jokes. Raisa did. She was playful, verbally, intellectually. Ever since they'd first met, ever since she'd tricked him into believing she was called Lena, he'd never been in any doubt that she was smarter than him. Considering the risks associated with intellectual agility, he'd never been jealous – until now, watching her with this man.

Leo's feet were numb. He was glad to be on the move, trailing his wife at a distance of about fifty metres. In the weak orange glow of the street lights it wasn't difficult to follow her – there were hardly any other people on the street. That changed when they turned on Avtozavodskaya, the main road, which was also the name of the metro station to which they were almost certainly heading. There were queues of people lined up outside grocery stores, clogging the pavements. Leo found it hard to keep track of his wife, made harder by her nondescript clothes. He had no choice but to shorten the distance between them, quickening his pace. He was less than twenty metres behind her. At this distance there was a danger she'd see him. Raisa and Ivan turned into

Avtozavodskaya station, disappearing from view. Leo hurried forward, weaving in and out of the pedestrians. In the commuter crowds she might easily disappear. This was, as *Pravda* frequently boasted, the busiest and best metro system in the world.

Reaching the entrance to the station he descended the stone steps to the lower hall – an opulent chamber, an ambassador's reception, with cream marble pillars, polished mahogany banisters illuminated by domes of frosted glass. Rush hour and not a centimetre of floor could be seen. Thousands of people wrapped up in long coats and scarves hustled in line at the ticket barriers. Going against the flow, Leo backtracked up the steps, using this slight elevation to survey the heads of the crowd. Raisa and Ivan had passed through the steel ticket barrier and were waiting for a place on the escalator. Leo rejoined the throng, sliding into gaps, edging forward. But stuck behind a mass of bodies he had no option but to resort to less polite methods, using his hands to steer people aside. No one dared do anything more than look annoyed, no one knew who Leo might be.

Reaching the ticket barrier, he was in time to see his wife move out of sight. He passed through, queuing and taking the first available position on the escalator. Stretching down the flight of mechanical wooden steps in a diagonal line to the bottom were the tops of a hundred winter hats. Unable to distinguish one from the other he leaned to the right. Raisa was maybe fifteen steps below him. In order to talk to Ivan, who was standing on the step behind and above her, she'd turned round and was facing upwards. Leo was in her line of view. He pulled back behind the man in front of him and, not wanting to risk another glance, waited until he was almost at the lower level before looking again. The passageway divided into two tunnels, for trains travelling north and south, each filled with passengers, shuffling forward, trying to make their way onto the platforms, vying for a position on the next train. Leo couldn't see his wife anywhere.

If Raisa was en route home she'd be heading three stops north on the Zamoskvoretskaya line to Teatral'naya, where she'd change. With no choice other than to suppose this was what she was doing, he moved down the platform, looking right and left, studying the faces lined up, crammed together, staring out in the same direction, waiting for the train. He was halfway down the platform. Raisa wasn't here. Could she have taken a train in the other direction? Why would she go south? Suddenly a man moved and Leo caught a glimpse of a satchel. There was Ivan. Raisa was by his side, both of them standing by the platform's edge. Leo was so close he could almost reach out and touch her cheek. If she turned her head even a fraction they'd be eye to eye. He was almost certainly in her peripheral vision; if she hadn't seen him it was only because she wasn't expecting to see him. There was nothing he could do, nowhere to hide. He continued down the platform, waiting for her to call his name. He wouldn't be able to explain this as a coincidence. She'd see through his lie, she'd know he was following her. He counted twenty steps then came to a stop by the edge of the platform, staring at the mosaic in front of him. Three separate lines of sweat ran down the side of his face. He didn't dare wipe them away or turn to check in case she was looking in his direction. He tried to concentrate on the mosaic, a celebration of Soviet military strength – a tank with its barrel pointing straight out, flanked by heavy artillery and mounted by Russian soldiers in long sweeping coats brandishing guns. Very slowly he turned his head. Raisa was talking to Ivan. She hadn't seen him. A gust of warm air blew down the crowded platform. The train was approaching.

As everyone turned to watch, Leo caught sight of a man looking in the opposite direction, away from the oncoming train, looking directly at him. It was the briefest of glances, eye contact for a fraction of a second. The man was maybe thirty years old. Leo had never seen him before. Yet he knew immediately this man was a fellow Chekist, a State Security operative. There was a second agent on the platform.

The crowd surged forward towards the train doors. The agent was gone, out of sight. The doors opened. Leo hadn't moved; his body was turned away from the train, still staring at the exact point where he'd seen those cool, professional eyes. Brushed aside by passengers disembarking he recovered from his surprise and boarded the train, one carriage down from Raisa. Who was that agent? Why did they need a second agent following his wife? Didn't they trust him? Of course they didn't. But he hadn't expected them to take such extreme supplementary measures. He pushed his way down towards the window through which he'd be able to see into the adjoining carriage. He could see Raisa's hand, holding the side bar. But there was no sign of this second agent. The doors were about to shut.

The second agent boarded the same carriage as Leo, slipping past him with apparent indifference and taking up position several metres away. He was well trained, calm, and had it not been for that brief glance Leo might not have spotted him. This agent wasn't following Raisa. He was following Leo.

He should've guessed that this operation wouldn't have been left entirely in his hands. There was the possibility he was compromised. They might even suspect he was working with Raisa if she was a spy. His superiors had an obligation to make sure he did his job properly. Anything he reported back would be cross-checked with the other agent. For this reason it was essential that

Raisa go straight home: if she went anywhere else, the wrong restaurant or bookshop, the wrong home where the wrong people lived, she'd be putting herself at risk. Her only chance of escape, and it was a slim chance, was by saying nothing, doing nothing, meeting nobody. She could work, shop and sleep. Any other activities were liable to be misconstrued.

If Raisa was travelling home she'd remain on this train for the next three stops, reaching Teatral'naya station, where she'd change to the Arbatsko–Pokrovskaya line and travel eastwards. Leo checked on the officer following him. Someone had stood to disembark and the agent slipped into a vacant seat. He was now casually staring out of the window, no doubt studiously watching Leo out of the corner of his eye. The agent knew he'd been sighted. Perhaps that had even been his intention. None of it mattered as long as Raisa went straight home.

The train pulled into the second station – Novokuznetskaya. One more stop till they changed. The doors opened. Leo watched as Ivan disembarked. He thought:

Please stay on the train.

Raisa got off the train, stepping down onto the platform and making her way towards the exit. She wasn't going home. Leo didn't know where she was going. To follow her would expose her to the scrutiny of the second agent. Not to follow her would put his life in jeopardy. He had to choose. Leo turned his head. The agent hadn't moved. From that position he couldn't have seen Raisa get off the train. He was taking his cue from Leo not Raisa, presuming that the movements of the two were synchronized. The doors were about to shut. Leo stayed where he was.

Leo glanced to the side, through the window, as though Raisa was still in the adjoining carriage, as though he was still checking on her. What was he doing? It had been an impulsive, reckless decision. His plan depended on the agent believing that his wife was on the train; a rickety plan at best. Leo hadn't counted on the crowds. Raisa and Ivan were still on the platform, moving towards the exit with excruciating slowness. Since the agent was staring out the window he'd see them as soon as the train began to move. Raisa edged closer to the exit, queuing patiently. She was in no hurry, she had no reason to be, unaware that both her life and Leo's were in danger unless she moved out of sight. The train began to roll forward. Their carriage was almost in line with the exit. The agent would see Raisa for sure – he'd know that Leo had deliberately failed.

The train picked up speed – it was parallel to the exit. Raisa was standing in plain view. Leo felt the blood rush from his stomach. He slowly turned his head to see the agent's reaction. A sturdy middle-aged man and his sturdy middle-aged wife were standing in the aisle, blocking any view the agent might have of the plat-form. The train rattled into the tunnel. He hadn't seen Raisa at the exit. He didn't know Raisa was no longer on the train. Barely able to conceal his relief, Leo resumed his pantomime of staring into the adjoining carriage.

At Teatral'naya station, Leo waited for as long as possible before getting off the train, acting as though he was still following his wife, as though she was heading home. He moved towards the exit. Glancing back he saw that the agent had also disembarked and was trying to catch up some of the ground between them. Leo pressed forward.

The passage funnelled out into a thoroughfare with access either to the different lines or to the street-level exit. He had to lose this tail without appearing to do so. The tunnel to the right

would take him to trains travelling east on the Arbatsko–
Pokrovskaya line, the route home. Leo turned right. Much
depended upon the arrival of the next train. If he could get far
enough ahead then he might be able to board the train before the
agent caught up and realized Raisa wasn't on the platform.

Now in the tunnel which led to the platform he was faced with
crowds of people in front of him. Suddenly he heard the sound of
an approaching train, pulling into the platform. There was no way
he could reach it in time, not with all these people in front of him.
He reached into his jacket pocket, taking out his State Security
identity card and tapping it on the shoulder of the man in front of
him. As though scalded, the man stepped aside, the woman
stepped aside, the crowd parted. With a clear path he was able to
hurry forward. The train was there, its doors open, ready to go. He
put his card away and boarded. He turned to see how close his tail
was. If the man managed to catch up and board this train, the
game was up.

The people who'd moved out of the way had closed ranks. The
agent was stuck behind them, resorting to less subtle methods,
pushing and shoving people out the way. He was catching up.
Why weren't the doors closing? The agent was now at the platform, only metres away. The doors began to close. His hand darted
out, grabbing the side of the door. But the mechanism wouldn't
be pulled back and the man – who Leo saw closely for the first
time – had no choice but to let go. Maintaining an air of casual
indifference Leo tried not to react, watching out of the corner of
his eyes as the agent was left behind. In the darkness of the tunnel
Leo took off his sweat-sodden hat.

Same Day

The elevator came to a stop on the fifth floor, the top floor, the doors opened and Leo stepped out into the narrow corridor. The hallway smelt of cooking. It was seven in the evening, the time at which many families ate *uzhin,* the last meal of the day. As he walked past the apartments he could hear the sound of dinner preparations through the thin plywood front doors. The closer he got to his parents' apartment the more tired he felt. He'd spent several hours criss-crossing the city. After losing the agent following him at Teatral'naya station he'd returned home, to apartment 124, turning on the lights and radio, drawing the curtains – a necessary precaution even though they were on the fourteenth floor. He'd left again, taking a deliberately circuitous route to the metro and travelling back into the city. He hadn't changed his clothes and he regretted not doing so. They'd become unpleasant; his shirt, drenched with sweat, had dried and stuck to his back. He was sure it stank although he couldn't smell it himself. He brushed these concerns aside. His parents wouldn't care. They'd be too distracted by the fact he was asking their advice; something he hadn't done in a long time.

The balance of their relationship had shifted – he now helped them far more than they helped him. Leo liked it that way. He enjoyed the feeling of being able to secure them easier jobs at their places of work. With nothing more than a polite enquiry his father had become a foreman at the munitions factory, taken off the assembly line, while his mother, who spent her days stitching parachutes, had been given a similar rise in status. He'd improved their access to food – no longer did they have to queue for several hours for basics such as bread and buckwheat; instead they were given access to the *spetztorgi*, the special shops not intended for the general public. In these restricted shops there were exotic delights such as fresh fish, saffron and even slabs of real dark chocolate, instead of the synthetic kind which substituted cocoa with a blend of rye, barley, wheat and peas. If his parents had trouble with a quarrelsome neighbour, that neighbour never remained quarrelsome for long. There was no violence involved, no crude threats, just a hint that they were dealing with a family better connected than their own.

This apartment, the apartment he'd managed to have them allocated, was in a pleasant residential area in the north of the city – a low-rise block where each apartment could boast of private washroom facilities and its own small balcony overlooking a small stretch of grass and a quiet road. They shared it with no one: extraordinary in this city. After fifty years of hardship they finally enjoyed a privileged life, a fact his parents keenly appreciated. They'd become addicted to comfort. And it all hung by the thread of Leo's career.

Leo knocked on the door. When his mother, Anna, opened the door she seemed surprised. That surprise, which rendered her briefly speechless, melted away. She stepped forward, hugging her son, speaking excitedly.

—*Why didn't you tell us you were coming? We heard you were ill. We came over to see you but you were asleep. Raisa let us in. We looked in on you, I even held your hand but what could we do? You needed your rest. You were sleeping like a child.*

—Raisa told me you came round. Thank you for the fruit – the oranges and the lemons.

—We didn't bring any fruit. At least I don't think we did. I'm getting old. Maybe we did!

Having heard the conversation his father, Stepan, appeared from the kitchen, gently nudging past his wife. She'd gained a little weight recently. They'd both gained a little weight. They looked well.

Stepan embraced his son.

—Are you better?

—Yes, much.

—That's good. We were worried about you.

—How's your back?

—It hasn't hurt for a while now. One of the benefits of an administrative job, all I do is oversee other people's hard work. I walk around with a pen and a clipboard.

—Enough with the guilt. You've done your time.

—Perhaps, but people look at you differently when you're no longer one of them. My friends are not quite so friendly any more. If someone is late, I'm the one who has to report them. Thankfully no one has been late so far.

Leo rolled these words around his head.

—What would you do if they were late? Would you report them?

—I just keep telling them every evening, don't be late.

No, in other words, his father would not report them. He'd probably already overlooked a couple of cases. Right now wasn't the time to warn him, but that kind of generosity was liable to be found out.

In the kitchen a head of cabbage was bubbling in a copper pot of water. His parents were in the middle of preparing *golubsty* and Leo told them to carry on, they could talk in the kitchen. He stood back and watched as his father mixed together mince (fresh meat, not dried, possible only because of Leo's job), fresh grated carrots (once again possible only because of him) and cooked rice. His mother set about peeling the colour-drained leaves from the cooked cabbage head. His parents knew something was wrong and waited, without prompting, for Leo to begin. He was glad they were busy with the food.

—*We've never spoken much about my work. That's for the best. There have been times when I've found my job difficult. I've done things of which I'm not proud but which were always necessary.*

Leo paused, trying to work out how best to proceed. He asked:

—*Have any of your acquaintances been arrested?*

The question was awkward, Leo appreciated that. Stepan and Anna glanced at each other before carrying on with the food, no doubt glad to have something to do. Anna shrugged.

—*Everyone knows someone who's been arrested. But we don't question it. I say to myself: you officers are the ones with the evidence. I know only what I see of people and it is very easy to appear to be nice and normal and loyal. It is your job to see past that. You know what's best for this country. It is not for people like us to judge.*

Leo nodded, adding.

—*This country has many enemies. Our Revolution is hated around the world. We must protect it. Unfortunately even from ourselves.*

He paused. He hadn't come here to repeat State rhetoric. His parents stopped working, turning to face their son, their fingers sticky with oils from the mince.

—*Yesterday I was asked to denounce Raisa. My superior officers believe she's a traitor. They believe she's a spy working for a foreign agency. I've been ordered to investigate.*

A single drop of oil dripped from Stepan's finger onto the floor. He stared at the drop of grease and then asked:

—*Is she a traitor?*

—*Father, she's a schoolteacher. She works. She comes home. She works. She comes home.*

—*Then tell them that. Is there any evidence? Why do they even think such a thing?*

—*There's the confession of an executed spy. He named her. He claimed he'd worked with her. But I know that confession is a lie. I know that the spy was in reality nothing more than a vet. We made a mistake in arresting him. I believe his confession to be the fabrication of another officer trying to implicate me. I know my wife is innocent. The whole thing is an act of revenge.*

Stepan wiped his hands clean on Anna's apron.

—*Tell them the truth. Make them listen. Expose this officer. You are in a position of authority.*

—*This confession, whether fabricated or not, has been accepted as the truth. It's an official document and her name is on it. If I defend Raisa I'm contesting the validity of a State document. If they admit one is flawed then they admit all of them are. They cannot go back. The repercussions would be enormous. It would mean all confessions were up for question.*

—*Can you not say that this spy – this vet – was mistaken?*

—*Yes. That is what I intend to do. But if I make a case and they don't believe me then not only will they arrest her they will arrest me too. If she is guilty and I've claimed she's innocent then I am guilty too. That isn't all. I know how these matters play out. There's a very strong chance that they will arrest both of you. Part of the judicial code targets any family members of a convicted criminal. We're guilty by association.*

—*And if you denounce her?*

—*I don't know.*

—*Yes you do.*

—*We'll survive. She won't.*

The water was still bubbling on the stove. At last Stepan spoke.

—*You're here because you're unsure what to do. You're here because you're a good man and you want us to tell you to do the right thing, the decent thing. You want us to give you the right advice. Which would be to tell them that they're wrong, to tell them that Raisa is innocent. And to brave the consequences that come from that.*

—*Yes.*

Stepan nodded, looking at Anna. After a moment he added:

—*But I can't give you that advice. And I'm not sure you believed I would give you that advice. How can I? The truth is I want my wife to live. I want my son to live. And I want to live. I would do whatever it takes to ensure that. As I understand the situation, it is one life for three. I'm sorry. I know that you expected more of me. But we're old, Leo. We wouldn't survive the Gulags. We'd be separated. We'd die alone.*

—*And if you were young what your advice be then?*

Stepan nodded.

—*You're right. My advice would be the same. But don't be angry with me. What did you expect when you came here? Did you expect us to say, fine, we don't mind dying? And what purpose would our deaths serve? Would your wife be saved? Would you live happily together? If that had been the case I would gladly have given up my life for the two of you. But that isn't what would happen. All that would happen is that we'd die – all of us, all four of us – but you'd die knowing that you'd done the right thing.*

Leo looked at his mother. Her face was as pale as the lank cabbage leaves she held in her hand. She was quite calm. She didn't contradict Stepan, asking instead:

—When do you have to decide?

—I have two days to gather evidence. Then I must report back.

His parents continued with the preparation of dinner, wrapping mince in the cabbage leaves, laying them side by side in a baking tray like a row of thick, dismembered thumbs. No one spoke until the tray was full. Stepan asked:

—You'll eat with us?

Following his mother into the living room, Leo saw that there were already three place settings.

—You're expecting a guest?

—We're expecting Raisa.

—My wife?

—She's coming for dinner. When you knocked on the door we thought you were her.

Anna laid a fourth plate on the table, explaining.

—She comes almost every week. She didn't want you to know how lonely she finds it, eating with only the radio for company. We've become very fond of her.

It was true that Leo was never home from work at seven. A culture of long working days had been fostered by Stalin, an insomniac, who would take no more than four hours of sleep a night. Leo had heard that no one in the Politburo was permitted to leave until the lights of Stalin's study were turned off, normally some time past midnight. Though this rule didn't apply exactly to the Lubyanka, similar levels of dedication were expected. Few officers worked anything less than ten-hour days, even if several of those hours were spent doing nothing at all.

There was a knock. Stepan opened the door, allowing Raisa into the hallway. She was as surprised as his parents to see Leo. Stepan explained:

—He was working nearby. For once we can eat together as a family.

She undid her jacket, which Stepan took from her. She stepped forward, close to Leo, looking him up and down.

—Whose clothes are these?

Leo glanced at the trousers, the shirt — these dead men's clothes.

—I borrowed them – from work.

Raisa leaned closer, whispering in Leo's ear.

—The shirt smells.

Leo moved towards the bathroom. At the door, he glanced back, watching as Raisa helped his parents with the table.

Leo had grown up without running hot water. His parents had shared their old apartment with his father's uncle and his family. There had been only two bedrooms, one bedroom for each family. The apartment had no inside toilet or bathroom, the occupants of the building had to use outdoor facilities which were without hot water. In the morning the queues were long and in the winter, snow would fall on them while they waited. A private sink full of hot water would've been an impossible luxury, a dream. Leo stripped off the shirt, washing himself. Finished, he opened the door, asking his father if he could borrow a shirt. Though his father's body was work-worn — stooped and shaped by the assembly line as surely as the tank shells that had been shaped by him — he was of a roughly similar frame to his son, a strong build with broad, muscular shoulders. The shirt was a close enough fit.

Changed, Leo sat down to eat. While the *golubsty* finished baking in the oven, they had *zakuski*, plates of pickles, mushroom salad and for each of them, a thin slice of veal tongue cooked with marjoram, left to cool in gelatine and served with horseradish. It was an exceptionally generous spread. Leo couldn't help but stare at it, calculating the cost of each dish. Whose death had paid for that marjoram? Had that slice of tongue been bought with Anatoly Brodsky's life? Feeling sick, he remarked:

—*I can see why you come here every week.*

Raisa smiled.

—*Yes. They spoil me. I tell them* kasha *would be fine but—*

Stepan interjected:

—*It's an excuse to spoil ourselves.*

Trying to sound casual, Leo asked his wife:

—*You come here straight after work?*

—*That's right.*

That was a lie. She'd gone somewhere with Ivan first. But before Leo could consider it further, Raisa corrected herself.

—*That's not true. Normally I come here straight after work. But tonight I had an appointment, which is why I'm a little late.*

—*An appointment?*

—*With the doctor.*

Raisa began to smile.

—*I'd meant to tell you when we were on our own but since it has come up . . .*

—*Tell me what?*

Anna stood up.

—*Would you like us to leave?*

Leo gestured for his mother to be seated.

—*Please. We're family. No secrets.*

—*I'm pregnant.*

20 February

Leo couldn't sleep. He lay awake, staring at the ceiling, listening to the slow breathing of his wife, her back pressed against his side not out of any deliberate expression of intimacy but through chance movements. She was an unsettled sleeper. Was that enough reason to denounce her? He knew it was. He knew how it could be written up:

Unable to rest easy, troubled by her dreams: my wife is clearly tormented by some secret.

He could pass responsibility for the investigation to another person. He could kid himself that he was deferring judgement. He was too close, too involved. But any such investigation would only come to one conclusion. The case had been opened. No one else would position against a presumption of guilt.

Leo got out of bed and stood by the living-room window, which had a view not of the city but of the apartment block opposite. A wall of windows with only three lights on, three out of a thousand or so, and he wondered what worries were troubling the occupants, what was keeping them from sleeping. He felt an odd kind of companionship with those three squares of pale yellow light. It was four in the morning, arresting hour – the best time to seize a person, to

136

grab them from their sleep. They were vulnerable, disorientated. Unguarded comments made as officers swarmed into their homes were often used against suspects in their interrogations. It was not easy to be prudent when your wife was being dragged across the floor by her hair. How many times had Leo smashed a door open with the sole of his boot? How many times had he watched as a married couple were pulled from their bed, flashlights shone in their eyes and up their nightclothes? How many times had he heard the sound of an officer laughing at the sight of someone's genitals? How many people had he pulled from their beds? How many apartments had he torn apart? And what of the children he'd held back as the parents were taken away? He couldn't remember. He'd blocked it out: the names, the faces. An indistinct memory served him well. Had he cultivated it? Had he taken amphetamines not to work longer hours but to erode the memories of that work?

There was a joke, popular among officers, who could tell it with impunity. A man and his wife were asleep in bed when they were woken by a sharp knock on the door. Fearing the worst they got up, kissed each other goodbye.

I love you, wife.
I love you, husband.

Having said their goodbyes they opened the front door. Standing before them was a frantic neighbour, a corridor full of smoke and flames as high as the ceiling. The man and his wife smiled with relief and thanked God: it was just the building on fire. Leo had heard variations on this joke. Instead of a fire there were armed bandits, instead of armed bandits there was a doctor with terrible news. In the past he'd laughed, confident that it would never happen to him.

His wife was pregnant. Did that fact change anything? It might change the attitude of his superiors to Raisa. They'd never liked her. She'd never given Leo any children. In these times it was expected, demanded that couples have children. After the millions who'd died fighting children were a social obligation. Why had Raisa not become pregnant? The question had dogged their marriage. The only conclusion was that there was something wrong with her. The pressure had been cranked up recently: questions asked with greater frequency. Raisa was seeing a doctor regularly in order to address the issue. Their sexual relations were pragmatic, motivated by external pressures. The irony didn't escape Leo that just as his superiors got what they wanted – Raisa pregnant – they wanted her dead. Perhaps he could mention that she was pregnant? He dismissed the idea. A traitor was traitor, there were no exonerating circumstances.

Leo showered. The water was cold. He got changed and made a breakfast of oatmeal. He had no desire to eat and watched it harden in the bowl. Raisa entered the kitchen, sat down, rubbing the sleep out of her eyes. He got up. Neither of them spoke as he waited for the oatmeal to warm up. He put a bowl before her. She said nothing. He made a glass of weak tea, placed it on the table alongside the jar of jam.

—*I'll try to be home a little earlier.*

—*You don't have to change your routine for me.*

—*I'll try anyway.*

—*Leo, you don't have to change your routine for me.*

Leo shut the front door. It was dawn. From the edge of the walkway he could see people waiting for the tramcar hundreds of metres down below. He made his way to the elevator. Once it had arrived he pressed the button for the top floor. On the thirtieth floor, the top floor, he stepped out and walked down the passage way to the service door at the end marked NO ENTRY. The lock had been smashed a long time ago. It led to a flight of stairs that in turn led to the roof. He'd been here before, when they'd first moved in. Facing west you could see the city. Facing east you could see the edge of the countryside where Moscow broke apart and gave way to snow-covered fields. Four years ago, admiring this view, he'd thought himself one of the luckiest men alive. He was a hero – he had the newspaper clipping to prove it. He had a powerful job, a beautiful wife. His faith in the State had been unquestioning. Did he miss that feeling – complete, unswerving confidence? Yes, he did.

He took the elevator down to the fourteenth floor, returning to his apartment. Raisa had gone to work. Her breakfast bowl sat unwashed in the kitchen. He took off his jacket and boots, warmed his hands, ready to begin his search.

Leo had organized and overseen the searches of many houses, apartments and offices. They were treated competitively by those who worked in the MGB. Stories were swapped about the extraordinary thoroughness which officers demonstrated in order to prove their dedication. Precious objects were smashed, portraits and works of art cut from the frames, books ripped apart, entire walls knocked down. Even though this was his home and these were his things Leo proposed to treat the search no differently. He ripped off the bed linen, pillowcases and sheets, turning the mattress upside down and feeling it carefully, every square inch, like a blind man reading Braille. Paper documents could be stitched into a mattress becoming invisible to the eye. The only way to locate these secret stashes was by touch. Finding nothing, he moved to the shelves. He went through every book checking if anything had been placed inside them. He found one hundred roubles, just under a week's wages. He looked at the money wondering what it could mean until remembering that the book belonged to him and this money was his own, a secret stash. Another agent might have declared it proof that the owner was a speculator. Leo put the money back. He opened the drawers, looking down at Raisa's neatly folded clothes. He picked up each garment, feeling and shaking it before dropping it in a heap on the floor. When all the drawers were emptied he checked the backs and sides. Finding nothing, he turned, studying the room. He pressed himself against the walls, running his fingers along them to see if there was the outline of a safe or a hollow. He took down the framed newspaper clipping, the photo of himself beside the burning panzer tank. It was peculiar to think of that moment, surrounded by death, as happier times. He took the frame apart. The slip of newspaper floated to the floor. Putting the clipping and the frame back together, he turned the bed on its side, leaning it against the wall. He got onto his knees. The floorboards were securely screwed down. He retrieved a screwdriver from the kitchen and took up every floorboard. Underneath there was nothing but dust and pipes.

He went into the kitchen, washed the dirt off his hands. There was, at last, warm water. He spent a leisurely amount of time lathering the small bar of soap: scrubbing his skin even after all the dirt had gone. What was he trying to wash off his hands? The betrayal, no – he had no interest in metaphors. He was washing his hands because they were dirty. He was searching his apartment because it had to be done. He mustn't over-think.

There was a knock on the front door. He rinsed his hands, which were covered from wrist to elbow in cream-coloured soap-spuds. There was a second knock. With water dripping from his arms he moved into the hallway, calling out:

—*Who is it?*

—It's Vasili.

Leo closed his eyes, feeling his heart rate quicken and trying to control the surge of anger. Vasili knocked again. Leo stepped forward, opened the door. Vasili was accompanied by two men. The first was a young officer Leo didn't recognize. He had soft features and paper-pale skin. He stared at Leo with expressionless eyes, like two glass marbles pushed into a ball of dough. The second officer was Fyodor Andreev. Vasili had selected these men carefully. The man with the pale skin was his protection, no doubt strong, a good shot or quick with a knife. He'd brought Fyodor along for spite.

—What is it?

—We're here to help. Major Kuzmin sent us.

—Thank you, but I have the investigation under control.

—I'm sure you do. We're here to assist.

—Thank you, but that's not necessary.

—Come on, Leo. We've travelled a long way. And it's cold out here.

Leo stepped aside, letting them in.

None of the three men took off their boots, which were encrusted with ice, chunks of which dropped from their soles, melting into the carpet. Leo shut the door, aware that Vasili was here to bait him. He wanted Leo to lose his temper. He wanted an argument, an ill-considered comment, anything to strengthen his case.

Leo offered his guests tea or vodka if they preferred. Vasili's love drink was well known, but it was considered the most minor of vices if a vice at all. He dismissed Leo's offer with a shake of his head and glanced into the bedroom.

—What have you found?

Without waiting for a reply Vasili entered the room, staring at the upturned mattress.

—You've not even cut it open.

He leant down, drawing his knife, ready to slice open the mattress. Leo caught hold of his hand.

—There's a way to feel for items stitched into the material. You don't have to cut it.

—So you're going to put the place back together again?

—That's right.

—You still think your wife is innocent?

—I've found nothing to suggest otherwise.

—May I give you some advice? Find another wife. Raisa is beautiful. But there are many beautiful women. Maybe you'd be better off with one who wasn't quite so beautiful.

Vasili reached into his pocket, pulling out a set of folded photographs. He offered them to Leo. They were photographs taken of Raisa outside the school with Ivan, the literature teacher.

—She's fucking him, Leo. She's a traitor to you and the State.

—These were taken at the school. They're both teachers. Of course it's possible to take photographs of them together. It proves nothing.

—Do you know his name?

—Ivan, I think.

—We've had an eye on him for some time.

—We have our eye on lots of people.

—Perhaps you're a friend of his also?

—I've never met him. I've never spoken to him.

Seeing the heap of clothes on the floor, Vasili bent down and picked up a pair of Raisa's underpants. He rubbed them between his fingers, crumpling them into a ball, placing them under his nose and never taking his eyes off Leo. Instead of feeling anger at this provocation Leo contemplated his deputy in a way that he'd never bothered to before. Who exactly was this man who hated him so much? Was he motivated by professional jealousy or by raw ambition? Watching him now, sniffing Raisa's clothes, Leo realized there was something personal about this hatred.

—*May I take a look around the rest of your apartment?*

Fearing a trap of some kind, Leo replied:

—*I'll come with you.*

—*No, I'd prefer to do it by myself.*

Leo nodded. Vasili moved off.

Hardly able to breathe, his throat constricted with anger, Leo stared at the upturned bed. He was surprised by a soft voice beside him. It was Fyodor.

—*You'd do all this. Search through your wife's clothes, turn your bed upside down, rip up your own floorboards – pull your own life apart.*

—*We should all be prepared to submit to such searches. Generalissimo Stalin—*

—*I've heard this too. Our Leader said even his apartment could be searched if need be.*

—*Not only can we all be investigated, we must all be investigated.*

—*And yet you would not investigate the death of my son? You would investigate your wife, yourself, your friends, your neighbours but you would not take a look at his body? You would not spare an hour to see how his stomach was cut open, and how he died with dirt shoved in his mouth?*

Fyodor was calm: his voice soft – his anger was no longer raw. It had turned to ice. He could speak in this fashion to Leo – openly, frankly – because he knew Leo was no longer a threat.

—*Fyodor, you didn't see his body either.*

—*I spoke to the old man who found his body. He told me what he saw. I saw in the old man's eyes his shock. I spoke to the eyewitness, the woman you scared away. A man was holding my son's hand, leading him along the tracks. She saw that man's face. She could describe him. But no one wants her to speak. And now she's too afraid to. My boy was murdered, Leo. The militia made all the witnesses change their statements. This I expected. But you were my friend. And you came to my home and instructed my family to keep our mouths shut. You threatened a grieving family. You read us a fiction and told us to commit those lies to our hearts. Instead of looking for the person who killed my son, you placed the funeral under scrutiny instead.*

—Fyodor, I was trying to help you.

—I believe you. You were telling us the way to survive.

—Yes.

—And in some ways I'm grateful. Otherwise, the man who murdered my son would also have murdered me and my family. You saved us. That is why I'm here, not to gloat, but to return the favour. Vasili is right. You must sacrifice your wife. Don't bother looking for any evidence. Denounce her and you'll survive. Raisa is a spy, it's been decided. I've read Anatoly Brodsky's confession. It's written in the same black ink as my son's incident report.

No, Fyodor was wrong. He was angry. Leo reminded himself that he had a simple objective – to investigate his wife and report his findings. His wife was innocent.

—I'm convinced the traitor's remarks concerning my wife were motivated by revenge and nothing more. So far my investigation supports that.

Vasili had re-entered the room. It was impossible to tell how much of their conversation he'd heard. He answered:

—Except that the other six names he listed have all been arrested. And all six have already confessed. Anatoly Brodsky's information has proved invaluable.

—*Then I'm pleased I was the one who apprehended him.*

—*Your wife was named by a convicted spy.*

—*I've read his confession and Raisa's name is the last on the list.*

—*The names weren't given in order of importance.*

—*I believe he added it out of spite. I believe he wanted to hurt me personally. It is unlikely to fool any one, an obvious, desperate trick. You're welcome to help with my search – if that is why you've come round. As you can see . . .*

Leo gestured at the ripped-up floorboards.

—*I've been thorough.*

—*Give her up, Leo. You need to be realistic. On the one hand you have your career, your parents – on the other hand you have a traitor and a slut.*

Leo glanced at Fyodor. His face showed no sign of pleasure, no malicious relish. Vasili continued:

—*You know she's a slut. That is why you had her followed before.*

Leo's anger was displaced by shock. They'd known. They'd known all along.

—*Did you think that was a secret? We all know. Denounce her, Leo. End this. End the doubt; end the niggling questions at the back of your mind. Give her up. We'll go drinking together afterwards. By the end of the night you'll have another woman.*

—*I'll report my findings tomorrow. If Raisa is a traitor, I'll say so. If she's not, I'll say so.*

—*Then I wish you luck, comrade. If you survive this scandal you'll one day be running the MGB. I'm sure of it. And it would be an honour to work under you.*

At the front door, Vasili turned:

—*Remember what I said. Your life and the lives of your parents are being weighed against hers. It's not a difficult decision.*

Leo shut the door.

Listening to them walk away, he noticed his hands were shaking. He returned to the bedroom, surveying the mess. He replaced all the floorboards, screwing them back down. He made the bed, carefully straightening all the sheets and then crumpling them slightly, in imitation of how he'd found them. He replaced all Raisa's clothes, folding and stacking them, conscious that he couldn't remember the exact order in which he'd pulled them out. An approximation would have to do.

As he lifted a cotton shirt a small object fell out, hitting his foot and rolling onto the floor. Leo bent down and picked it up. It was a copper rouble coin. He tossed it onto the top of his bedside cabinet. On impact the coin split in two, the separate halves rolling off opposite sides of the cabinet. Perplexed, he approached the cabinet. He knelt down and retrieved the two halves. The inside of one had been hollowed out. When slotted together it looked like an ordinary coin. Leo had seen one of these before. It was a device for smuggling microfilm.

21 February

Present at Leo's deposition were Major Kuzmin, Vasili Nikitin and Timur Raphaelovich – the officer who'd taken Leo's place during Anatoly Brodsky's interrogation. Leo knew him only in passing: an ambitious man of few words and much credibility. The discovery that Raphaelovich was prepared to vouch for everything in the confession including the reference to Raisa was devastating. This man was no lackey of Vasili. Raphaelovich didn't respect or fear him. Leo wondered whether Vasili could've inserted Raisa's name into the confession. He had no sway over Raphaelovich, no leverage, and according to their rank he would've been the subordinate officer during the interrogation. For the past two days Leo had been working under the assumption this had been an act of revenge by Vasili. He'd been mistaken. Vasili wasn't behind this. The only person who could've organized the fabrication of such a confession backed up with such a high-ranking witness was Major Kuzmin.

It was a set-up, orchestrated by none other than his mentor, the man who'd taken Leo under his wing. Leo had ignored his advice regarding Anatoly Brodsky and now he was being taught a lesson. What had Kuzmin told him?

Sentimentality can blind a man.

This was a test, an exercise. The issue under scrutiny here was Leo's suitability as an officer: it had nothing to do with Raisa, nothing at all. Why appoint the husband of a suspect to investigate his wife unless the primary concern was how the husband would conduct himself during that investigation? Hadn't Leo been the one who'd been followed? Hadn't Vasili come to check whether he was searching the apartment properly? He wasn't interested in the contents of the apartment: he was interested in Leo's approach. It all made sense. Vasili had goaded him yesterday, told him to denounce his wife, precisely because he hoped that Leo would do exactly the opposite and stand up for her. He didn't want Leo to denounce Raisa. He didn't want him to pass this test – he wanted him to put his private life above the Party. It was a trick. All he had to do was show Major Kuzmin that he was willing to denounce his wife, prove that his loyalties were absolutely with the MGB, prove his faith was unquestioning, prove that his heart could be cruel – if he did this then they'd all be safe: Raisa, his unborn child, his parents. His future with the MGB would be assured and Vasili would be an irrelevance.

Yet wasn't this a presumption? What if the traitor was, as he'd confessed to being, a traitor? What if he'd somehow been working with Raisa? Perhaps he'd spoken the truth. Why was Leo so sure that this man was innocent? Why was he so sure his wife was innocent? After all, why did she befriend a dissident literature teacher? What was that coin doing in their apartment? Hadn't the six other names listed in the confession been arrested and all been successfully interrogated? The list was proven and Raisa was on the list. Yes, she was a spy and here in his pocket was the copper coin, the evidence to prove it. He could place the coin on the desk and recommend that both she and Ivan Zhukov be taken in for questioning. He'd been played a fool. Vasili was right: she was a traitor. She was pregnant with another man's child. Hadn't he always known that she'd been unfaithful to him? She didn't love him. He was sure of that. Why risk everything for her — a woman who was cold to him, a woman who at best tolerated him? She was a threat to everything he'd worked for, everything he'd won for his parents and for himself. She was a threat to the country, a country Leo had fought to defend.

It was quite clear: if Leo said she was guilty then this would end well for both him and his parents. That was guaranteed. It was the only safe thing to do. If this was a test of Leo's character then Raisa would also be spared. And she would never need to know. If she was a spy then these men already had the evidence and were waiting to see if Leo was working with her. If she was a spy then he should denounce her, she deserved to die. The only course of action was to denounce his wife.

Major Kuzmin began the proceedings.

—*Leo Stepanovich, we have reason to believe your wife is working for foreign agencies. You personally are not suspected of any crimes. This is the reason we've asked you to investigate the allegations. Please tell us what you have found.*

Leo had the confirmation he was looking for. Major Kuzmin's offer was clear. If he denounced his wife he'd have their continued confidence. What had Vasili said?

If you survive this scandal you'll one day be running the MGB. I'm sure of it.

Promotion was a sentence away.

The room was silent. Major Kuzmin leaned forward.

—*Leo?*

Leo stood up, straightened the jacket of his uniform.

—*My wife is innocent.*

THREE WEEKS LATER

West of the Ural Mountains
the Town of Voualsk

13 March

The car-assembly line switched over to the late shift. Ilinaya stopped work and began scrubbing her hands using a bar of black rancid-smelling soap, the only kind available if any was available at all. The water was cold, the soap wouldn't lather – it simply disintegrated into greasy shards – but all she could think about were the hours between now and the beginning of her next shift. She had her night planned out. First, she'd finish scraping the oil and metal filings from under her fingernails. Then she was going home, changing her clothes, daubing some colour on her cheeks before heading to Basarov's, a restaurant near the railway station.

Basarov's was popular with people visiting on business, officials stopping over before they continued their journey on the Trans-Siberian railway east or west. The restaurant served food – millet soup, barley *kasha* and salted herring – all of which Ilinaya thought was terrible. More importantly it served alcohol. Since it was illegal to sell alcohol in public without selling food, meals were a means to an end, a plate of food was a permit to drink. In reality the restaurant was little more than a pick-up joint. The law that no individual was to be sold more than one hundred grams of vodka was ignored. Basarov, the manager and namesake of the restaurant, was always drunk and often violent and if Ilinaya wanted to ply her trade on his premises he wanted a cut. There was no way she could pretend she was drinking there for the fun of it whilst sneaking off with the occasional paying customer. No one drank there for the fun of it; it was a transient crowd, no locals. But that was an advantage. She couldn't get work off the locals any more. She'd been sick recently – sores, redness, rashes, that kind of thing. A couple of regulars had come down with more or less the same symptoms and bad-mouthed her around town. Now she was reduced to dealing with people who didn't know her, people who weren't staying in town for long and who wouldn't find out they were pissing pus until they reached Vladivostok or Moscow, depending on which way they were travelling. She didn't take any pleasure from the idea of passing on some kind of bug even if they weren't exactly nice people. But in this town seeing a doctor about a sexually transmitted infection was more dangerous than the infection itself. For an unmarried woman it was like handing in a confession, signed with a smear. She'd have to go to the black market for treatment. That required money, maybe a lot of money, and right now she was saving for something else, something far more important – her escape from this town.

By the time she'd arrived the restaurant was crowded and the windows steamed up. The air stank of *makhorka*, cheap tobacco. She'd heard drunken laughter fifty paces before stepping through the door. She'd guessed soldiers. She'd guessed right. There were often some kind of military exercises taking place in the mountains and off-duty personnel were normally directed here. Basarov catered specifically for this sort of clientele. He served watered-down vodka, claiming, if anyone complained and they often did, that it was a high-minded attempt to limit drunkenness. There were frequent fights. Even so, she knew that for all his talk about how hard his life was and how terrible his customers were, he made a tidy profit, selling the undiluted vodka he skimmed off. He was a speculator. He was scum. Just a couple of months ago she'd gone upstairs to pay him his weekly cut and, through a crack in his bedroom door, caught sight of him counting out rouble note after note after note, which he stored in a tin box tied shut with string. She'd watched, hardly daring to breathe, as he'd wrapped his box in a cloth before hiding it in his chimney. Ever since then she'd dreamed of stealing that money and making a break for it. Of course Basarov would snap her neck for sure if he caught up with her, but she figured that if he ever discovered his tin box was empty his heart would give out right there, by his chimney place. She was pretty sure his heart and that box were one and the same thing.

By her reckoning the soldiers were going to be drinking for another couple of hours. At the moment all they were doing was groping her, a privilege they weren't paying for unless you counted free vodka as payment, which she did not. She surveyed the other customers, convinced she could earn a little extra money before the soldiers started clocking on. The military contingent took up the front tables, relegating the remaining customers to the back. These customers were sitting on their own – just them and their drinks and their plates of untouched food. No doubt about it: they were looking for sex. There was no other reason to hang around.

Ilinaya straightened her dress, ditched her glass and made her way through the soldiers, ignoring the pinches and remarks until she found herself at one of the back tables. The man sitting there was maybe forty, maybe a little younger. It was hard to tell. He wasn't handsome, but she reckoned he'd probably pay a little more because of that. The better-looking ones sometimes got it into their heads money wasn't necessary, like the arrangement might be mutually pleasurable. She sat down, sliding her leg up against his thigh and smiling:

—*My name is Tanya*.

It helped, at times like these, to think of herself as someone else.

The man lit a cigarette and put his hand on Ilinaya's knee. Not bothering to buy her a drink he tipped half his remaining vodka into one of the many dirty glasses surrounding him and pushed it towards her. She toyed with the glass, waiting for him to say something. He finished his drink, showing no sign of wanting to talk. Trying not to roll her eyes, she pushed for a little conversation.

—*What's your name?*

He didn't reply, reaching into his jacket pocket, rummaging around. He pulled out his hand, his fist clenched shut. She understood this was a game of sorts and that she was expected to play along. She tapped his knuckles. He turned his fist upside down, slowly extending his fingers, one by one . . .

In the middle of his palm was a small nugget of gold. She leaned forward. Before she could get a good look he closed his hand and slipped it back into his pocket. He still hadn't said a word. She studied his face. He had bloodshot, boozy eyes and she didn't like him at all. But then she didn't like many people and certainly none of the men she slept with. If she wanted to get fussy she might as well call it quits, marry one of these locals and resign herself to staying in this town forever. The only way she was going to return to Leningrad, where her family lived, where she'd lived all her life until being ordered to move here, to a town she'd never even heard of, was if she could save up enough money to bribe the officials. Without any high-ranking, powerful friends to authorize the transfer, she needed that gold.

He tapped her glass, uttering his first word.

—*Drink.*

—*First you pay me. Then you can tell me what to do. That's the rule, that's the only rule.*

The man's face fluttered as if she'd tossed a stone onto the surface of his expression. For a moment she saw something beneath his bland, plump appearance, something unpleasant, something which made her want to look away. But the gold kept her looking at him, kept her in her seat. He took the nugget from his pocket, offering it. As she reached out and picked it from his sweaty palm he closed his hand, trapping her fingers. It didn't hurt but her fingers were trapped all the same. She could either surrender to his grip or pull her hand out without the gold. Guessing what was expected she smiled and laughed like a helpless girl, letting her arm go slack. He released his grip. She took the nugget and stared at it. It was the shape of a tooth. She stared at the man.

—*Where did you get it?*

—*When times are tough, people sell whatever they've got.*

He smiled. She felt sick. What kind of currency was this? He tapped the glass of vodka. That tooth was her ticket out of here. She finished her drink.

*

Ilinaya stopped walking.

—*You work in the mills?*

She knew he didn't but there weren't any houses around here except mill-worker houses. He didn't even bother to reply.

—*Hey, where are we going?*

157

—We're almost there.

He'd led her to the railway station on the edge of town. Though the station itself was new it was set in amongst one of the oldest districts, made up of ramshackle one-room huts with tin roofs and thin wood walls, huts lined up side by side along sewage-stinking streets. These huts belonged to the workers at the lumber mill, who lived five or six or seven to a room, no good for what they had in mind.

It was freezing cold. Ilinaya was sobering up. Her legs were getting tired.

—This is your time. The gold buys you one hour. That's what we agreed. If you take away the time I need to get back to the restaurant that leaves you twenty minutes from now.

—It's around the back of the station.

—There's just forest back there.

—You'll see.

He pressed forward, reaching the side of the station and pointing into the darkness. She pushed her hands into her jacket pockets, caught up with him, squinting in the direction he was pointing. She could see train tracks disappearing into the forest and nothing else.

—What am I looking at?

—There.

He was pointing at a small wood cabin to one side of the railway track not far from the edge of the forest.

—I'm an engineer. I work on the railways. That's a maintenance cabin. It's very private.

—A room is very private.

—I can't take you back where I'm staying.

—I know some places we could've gone.

—It's better like this.

—Not for me it isn't.

—There was one rule. I pay you, you obey. Either give me back my gold, or do as I say.

Nothing about this was good except for the gold. He stretched out his hand, waiting for the gold to be returned. He didn't seem angry or disappointed or impatient. Ilinaya found this indifference comforting. She began walking towards the cabin.

—Inside you get ten minutes, agreed?

No reply – she'd take that as a yes.

The cabin was locked but he had a set of keys and after fumbling for the right one struggled with the lock.

—It's frozen.

She didn't respond, turning her head to the side and sighing to indicate her disapproval. Secrecy was one thing and she'd already presumed he was married. But since he didn't live in this town she couldn't understand what his problem was. Perhaps he was staying with family or friends; perhaps he was a high-ranking Party member. She didn't care. She just wanted the next ten minutes over.

He crouched down, cupped his hands around the padlock and breathed on it. The key slipped in, the lock clicked open. She remained outside. If there wasn't going to be any light the deal was off and she'd keep the gold to boot. She'd already given this guy more than enough time. If he wanted to waste it on an expedition to nowhere that was up to him.

He stepped into the cabin, disappearing into the darkness. She heard the sound of a match being struck. Light flickered from the heart of a hurricane lamp. The man cranked up the lamp and hung it from a crooked hook sticking out from the roof. She peered inside. The cabin was filled with spare track, screws, bolts, tools and timber. There was a smell of tar. He began clearing one of the work stations. She laughed.

—*I'll get splinters in my bum*.

To her surprise he blushed. Improvising, he spread his coat across the work surface. She stepped inside.

—*A perfect gentleman* . . .

Normally she'd take off her coat, maybe sit on the bed and roll down a stocking, make a performance of it. But with no bed and no heating all she planned on allowing him to do was to lift up her dress. She'd keep the rest of her clothes on.

—*Hope you don't mind if my jacket stays on?*

She shut the door, not expecting it would make much difference to the temperature, which was almost as cold inside as it was out. She turned around.

The man was much closer than she remembered. She caught sight of something metallic coming towards her — she didn't have time to work out what it was. The object connected with the side of her face. Pain shot through her body from the point of impact travelling down her spine to her legs. Her muscles went slack; her legs slumped as though her tendons had been snipped. She fell back against the cabin door. Her eyesight blurred, her face felt hot, there was blood in her mouth. She was going to pass out, lose consciousness but she fought against it, forcing herself to stay awake, focusing on his voice.

—*You do exactly as I say*.

Would submission satisfy this man? Shards of broken tooth dug into her gum and convinced her otherwise. She didn't feel like believing in his mercy. If she was going to die in a town she hated, a town she'd been transferred to by compulsory State writ, one thousand seven hundred kilometres from her family, then she'd die scratching this bastard's eyes out.

He grabbed her arms, no doubt expecting any resistance to have evaporated. She spat a mouth full of blood and phlegm in his eyes.

He must have been surprised because he let go. She felt the door behind her and pushed against it – the door swung open and she fell into the snow outside, onto her back, staring up at the sky. He grabbed at her feet. She kicked frantically, trying to get out of reach. He grabbed hold of one foot, pulling her back into the cabin. She concentrated, taking aim: her heel caught his jaw. The contact was good, his head flicked round. She heard him cry out. He lost his grip. She rolled onto her stomach, got up and ran.

Staggering blindly, it took her a couple of seconds to realize she'd run straight out from the cabin, away from town, away from the station and down the railway tracks. Her instincts had been to get away from him. Her instincts had let her down. She was running away from safety. She checked behind. He was chasing her. Either she continued in this direction or she turned back towards him. There was no way she could get around him. She tried to scream but her mouth was full of blood. She choked, spluttered, breaking her rhythm and losing some of the distance between them. He was catching up.

Suddenly the ground began to vibrate. She looked up. A freight train was approaching, hurtling towards them, plumes of smoke rushing out of the high iron front. She raised her arms, waving. But even if the driver saw her there was no stopping in time with barely five hundred metres between them. There were only seconds before a collision. But she didn't step off the tracks, continuing towards the train, running faster – intent on throwing herself under it. The train gave no sign of slowing. There was no screech of metal brakes, no whistle. She was so close the vibrations almost shook her to her feet.

The train was about to smash into her. She flung herself to the side, off the tracks into the thick snow. The engine and wagons roared past, rocking the snow off the tips of the nearby trees.

Breathless, she peered behind her, hoping her pursuer had been cut down, crushed under the train or trapped on the other side of the tracks. But he'd held his nerve. He'd jumped to her side and was lying on the snow. He stood up, staggering towards her.

She spat the blood from her mouth and cried out: calling for help, desperate. This was a freight train, there was no one to hear or see her. She got up and ran, reaching the edge of the woods, not slowing down, smashing through the branches that jutted out. Her plan was to loop around and double back onto the tracks towards town. She couldn't hide here: he was too close, there was too much moonlight. Even though she knew it would be better to remain focused on running she gave in to temptation. She had to look. She had to know where he was. She turned around.

He was gone. She couldn't see him. The train was still thundering past. She must have lost him when she entered the forest. She changed direction, running back towards the town, towards safety.

The man stepped out from behind a tree, catching hold of her waist. They crashed down into the snow. He was on top of her, ripping at her jacket and shouting. She couldn't hear him over the sound of the train. All she could see were his teeth and tongue. Then she remembered: she'd prepared for this moment. She reached into her coat pocket, feeling for a chisel, stolen from work. She'd used it before but only as a threat, only to show she could fight if fighting was required. She clutched the wooden handle. She'd get one chance at this. As he put his hand up her dress she brought the metal tip into the side of his head. He sat upright, clutching his ear. She sliced at him again, cutting the hand that clutched his ear. She should have struck again and again, she should have killed him, but her desire to get away was too strong. She scrambled backwards on all fours like an insect, still holding the bloody chisel.

The man dropped onto his hands and knees, crawling after her. Part of his earlobe hung loose, dangling from a flap of skin. His expression twisted with anger. He lunged for her ankles. She managed to keep out of reach, barely, outpacing him until she backed into a tree trunk. With her brought to a sudden stop, he caught up, took hold of her ankle. She slashed at his hand, jabbing and cutting. He grabbed her wrist, pulling her towards him. Face to face, she leaned forward, trying to bite his nose. With his free hand he clasped her neck, squeezing, keeping out of her reach. She gasped, trying to break free, but his grip was too strong. She was suffocating. She threw her weight sideways. The two of them tumbled – rolling in the snow, over and over each other.

Inexplicably he let go, releasing her neck. She coughed, catching her breath. The man was still on top, pinning her down, but no longer looking in her direction. His attention was on something else, something to the side of them. She turned her head.

Sunken into the snow beside her was the naked body of a young girl. Her skin was pale, almost translucent. Her hair was blonde, almost white. Her mouth was wide open and had been stuffed with dirt. It formed a mound, rising above her thin blue lips. The girl's arms and legs and face appeared to be uninjured, covered in a light layer of snow which had been disturbed when they'd rolled into it. Her torso had been savaged. The organs were exposed, ripped, torn. Much of the skin was missing, cut away or peeled back, as though her body had been attacked by a pack of wolves.

Ilinaya looked up at her pursuer. He seemed to have forgotten about her. He was staring at the girl's body. He began to retch, doubled over and was sick. Without thinking she put a consoling hand on his back. Remembering herself, remembering who this man was and what he'd done to her, she pulled her hand away, got up and ran. This time her instincts didn't let her down. She broke through the edge of the forest, running towards the station. She had no idea if the man was chasing her or not. This time she didn't scream, didn't slow down and didn't look back.

Moscow

14 March

Leo opened his eyes. A flashlight blinded him. He didn't need to check his watch to know the time. Arresting hour – four in the morning. He got out of bed, heart pounding. In the dark he staggered, disorientated, bumping into one man, pushed to the side. He stumbled, regained his balance. The lights came on. Adjusting to the brightness he saw three officers: young men, not much older than eighteen. They were armed. Leo didn't recognize them but he knew the kind of officers they were: low ranking, unthinkingly obedient: they'd follow whatever orders they'd been given. They'd be violent without hesitation: any slight resistance would be answered with extreme force. They gave off a smell of cigarette smoke and alcohol. Leo supposed these men hadn't been to bed yet: drinking all night, staying up for this assignment. Alcohol would make them unpredictable, volatile. To survive these next few minutes Leo would have to be cautious, submissive. He hoped Raisa understood that as well.

Raisa was standing in her nightclothes, shivering but not from cold. She wasn't sure whether it was shock or fear or anger. She couldn't stop shaking. But she wouldn't look away. She wasn't embarrassed; let them be embarrassed at their violation, let them see her crumpled nightdress, her untidy hair. No, they were indifferent: it was all the same to them, part of their job. She saw no sensitivity in these boys' eyes. They were dull: flicking from side to side like a lizard – reptilian eyes. Where did the MGB find these boys with souls of lead? They made them that way, she was sure of it. She glanced at Leo. He was standing with his hands in front, his head dropped in order to avoid eye contact. Humility, meekness: maybe that was the smart way to behave. But she didn't feel smart right now. There were three thugs in their bedroom. She wanted him defiant, angry. Surely that was the natural reaction? Any ordinary man would feel outrage. Leo was political even now.

One of the men left the room, to return almost immediately holding two small cases.

—*This is all you can take. You can carry nothing on your person except your clothes and your papers. In one hour we leave whether you're ready or not.*

Leo stared at the cases, canvas stretched tight over a timber frame. They offered a modest space, enough for a day trip. He turned to his wife.

—*Wear as much as you can.*

He glanced behind him. One of the officers was watching, smoking.

—*Can you wait outside?*

—*Don't waste time making requests. The answer to everything is no.*

Raisa got changed, sensing this guard's reptile eyes roaming over her body. She wore as many clothes as she could reasonably manage: layers on top of layers. Leo did the same. It might have been comical, in other circumstances, their limbs swollen by cotton and wool. Dressed, she grappled with the question of what, of all their belongings, they should bring and what they were forced to leave behind. She examined the case. It was no more than ninety centimetres wide, maybe sixty centimetres high and twenty centimetres deep. Their lives had to reduce to fit this space.

Leo knew there was a chance they'd been told to pack merely as a way of being moved without any of the emotional fuss, the struggle which came with the realization that they were being sent to their deaths. It was always easier to move people around if they clung to the notion, no matter how small, that they were going to survive. However, what could he do? Give up? Fight? He made several quick calculations. Precious space had to be wasted with the inclusion of *The Book of Propagandists* and *The Short Course of the Bolshevik Party*, neither of which could be abandoned without it being construed as a subversive political gesture. In their current predicament such recklessness was nothing less than suicidal. He grabbed the books, putting them in the case, the first objects either of them had packed. Their young guard was watching everything, seeing what went in, what choices they made. Leo touched Raisa's arm.

—*Take our shoes. Pick the best, one pair each.*

Good shoes were rare, tradable, a valuable commodity.

Leo gathered up clothes, items of value, their collection of photos: photos of their wedding, his parents, Stepan and Anna, but none of Raisa's family. Her parents been killed in the Great Patriotic War, her village wiped out. She'd lost everything except the clothes she'd been wearing. With his case full Leo's eyes came to rest on the framed newspaper clipping hanging on the wall: the photo of himself, the war hero, the tank destroyer, the liberator of occupied soil. His past made no difference to these guards: with the signing of an arrest warrant every act of heroism and personal sacrifice had been made irrelevant. Leo took the clipping out of the frame. After years of carefully preserving it, revering it on the wall as though it were a holy icon, he folded it down the middle and tossed it in the case.

Their time was up. Leo shut his case. Raisa shut hers. He wondered if they'd ever see this apartment again. It was unlikely.

Escorted downstairs, all five of them crammed into the elevator, pressed together. There was a car waiting. Two of the officers sat in the front. One sat in the back, his breath stinking, sandwiched in between Leo and Raisa.

—*I'd like to see my parents. I'd like to say goodbye.*

—*No fucking requests.*

*

Five in the morning and the departure hall was already busy. There were soldiers, civilian passengers, station workers all orbiting the Trans-Siberian express train. The engine, still clad in armour plating from the war, was embossed on the side with the words HAIL TO COMMUNISM. While passengers boarded the train, Leo and Raisa waited at the end of the platform, holding their cases and flanked by their armed escort. As though they were infected with a contagious virus, no one approached them, an isolated bubble in a crowded station. They'd been given no explanation, nor did Leo bother asking for one. He had no idea where they were going or who they were waiting for. There was still a chance they'd be sent to different Gulags, never to see each other again. However, this was unmistakably a passenger train, not the *zak* cars, the red cattle trucks used to transport prisoners. Was it possible they were going to escape with their lives? There was no doubt that they'd been lucky so far. They were still alive, still together, more than Leo had dared to hope for.

After Leo's testimony he'd been sent home, placed under house arrest until a decision could be made. He'd expected it to take no more than a day. On the way to his apartment, on the fourteenth-floor landing, aware that he still had the incriminating hollow coin in his pocket, Leo had tossed it over the side. Maybe Vasili had planted it, maybe not, it no longer mattered. When Raisa had arrived back from school she'd found two armed officers outside their door; she'd been searched and ordered to remain inside. Leo had explained their predicament: the allegations against her, his own investigation and his denial of the charges. He hadn't needed to explain that their chances of survival were slim. As he'd talked she'd listened without comment or question, expression-less. When he'd finished her response had taken him by surprise.

—*It was naive to think this wouldn't happen to us too.*

They'd sat in their apartment, expecting the MGB to come at any minute. Neither of them had bothered to cook; neither of them had been hungry even though the sensible thing to do would've been to eat as much as possible in preparation for what might lay ahead. They hadn't got undressed for bed, they hadn't moved from the kitchen table. They'd sat in silence – waiting. Considering they might never see each other again Leo had felt an urge to talk to his wife: to say things that needed to be said. But he'd been unable to formulate what they might be. As the hours passed he'd realized this was the most time they'd spent together, face to face, uninterrupted, for as long as he could remember. Neither of them had known what to do with it.

The knock on the door hadn't come that night. Four in the morning had passed, there'd been no arrest. As it had approached midday the following day, Leo made breakfast, wondering why they were taking so long. When the first knock on the door finally came, he and Raisa had stood up, breathing fast, expecting this to be the end, the arrival of officers collecting them, splitting them apart and taking them to their separate interrogations. Instead it was some trivial matter: a changing of the guards, an officer using their bathroom, questions about buying food. Perhaps they couldn't find any evidence, perhaps they'd be cleared and the case against them would collapse. Leo had only flirted with these thoughts briefly: accusations never collapsed through lack of proof. All the same, a day became two days, two days became four days.

A week into their confinement, a guard had entered the apartment, ashen-faced. Seeing him, Leo had been certain their time had finally come, only to listen as the guard announced, in a voice trembling with emotion, that their Leader, Stalin, was dead. Only at this moment did Leo allow himself to contemplate whether or not they might just have a chance of surviving.

Able to gather the vaguest details of their Leader's demise — the newspapers had been hysterical, the guards hysterical — all Leo could piece together was that Stalin had died peacefully in his bed. His last words had purportedly been about their great country and their great country's future. Leo didn't believe it for a second, too schooled in paranoia and plot not to see the cracks in the story. He knew from his work that Stalin had recently arrested the country's foremost doctors, doctors who had spent their entire working lives keeping him well, as part of a purge of prominent Jewish figures. It struck him as no coincidence that Stalin had died of apparently natural causes at a time when there were no expert medical professionals to identify the source of his sudden illness. Morality aside, the great Leader's purge had been a tactical error. It had left him exposed. Leo had no idea whether Stalin had been murdered or not. With the doctors locked up that certainly gave any would-be assassins a free hand to do as they pleased, which was to sit back and watch him die, safe in the knowledge that the very men and women who could stop them were behind bars. Having said that, it was just as possible that Stalin had fallen ill and no one dared contradict his orders and release the doctors. If Stalin had recovered they might have been executed for disobedience.

This skulduggery was of little importance to Leo. What was important was that the man was dead. Everyone's sense of order and certainty had dissolved. Who would take over? How would they run the country? What decisions would they make? Which officers would be in favour and which would be out of favour? What was acceptable under Stalin might be unacceptable under new rule. The absence of a leader would mean temporary paralysis. No one wanted to make a decision unless they knew their decision would be approved. For decades no one had taken action according to what they believed was right or wrong but by what they thought would please their leader. People had lived or died depending on his annotations on a list: a line against a name saved a person, no mark meant they were left to die. That was the judicial system – line or no line. Closing his eyes, Leo had been able to imagine the muted panic within the corridors of the Lubyanka. Their moral compass had been neglected for so long it spun out of control: north was south and east was west. As for questions of what was right and wrong – they had no idea. They'd forgotten how to decide. In times like these the safest course of action was to do as little as possible.

In these circumstances the case of Leo Demidov and his wife, Raisa Demidova, which had no doubt proved divisive, inflammatory and problematic, was best shunted to the margins. That's why there'd been the delay. No one had wanted to touch it: everyone was too busy repositioning with the new power groups in the Kremlin. To complicate matters further, Lavrenti Beria, Stalin's closest aide – and if anyone had poisoned Stalin, Leo suspected it was him – had already assumed the mantle of Leader and dismissed the notion that there was a plot, ordering the doctors to be released. Suspects released because they were innocent – who'd heard of such a thing? Certainly Leo couldn't remember any precedent. In these circumstances, prosecuting a decorated war hero, a man who'd made the front page of *Pravda*, without any evidence might be deemed risky. So, on the sixth of March, instead of a knock on the door bringing news of their fate, Leo and Raisa had been granted permission to attend the State funeral of their great Leader.

Still technically under house arrest, Leo and Raisa and their two guards had dutifully joined the crowds, all of them making their way towards Red Square. Many had been crying, some uncontrollably – men and women and children – and Leo had wondered if there was a person in sight, out of all the hundreds of thousands gathered in their collective grief, who hadn't lost some family or friend to the man they were apparently mourning. The atmosphere, fraught, charged with an overwhelming sense of sadness, perhaps had something to do with an idolization of this dead man. Leo had heard many people, even in the most brutal of interrogations, cry out that if only Stalin knew about the *excesses* of the MGB he would intervene. Whatever the real reason behind the sadness, the funeral had offered a legitimate outlet for years of pent-up misery, an opportunity to cry, to hug your neighbour, to express a sadness that had never previously been allowed to show itself because it implied some criticism of the State.

The main streets around the State Duma had been packed so tight with people it was hard to breathe, moving forward with as little control as a rock caught in a rockslide. Leo had never let go of Raisa's hand and although shoulders pressed into him from all sides he'd made sure they weren't pulled apart. They'd quickly been separated from their guards. As they'd neared the Square the crowd contracted further. Feeling the squeeze, the mounting hysteria, Leo had decided enough. By chance, they'd been pushed to the edge of the crowd and he'd stepped into a doorway, helping Raisa out of the crowd. They'd sheltered there, watching as the streams of people continued past. It had been the right decision. Up ahead, people had been crushed to death.

In the chaos they could've attempted escape. They'd considered it, debated it, whispering to each other in that doorway. The guards accompanying them had been lost. Raisa had wanted to run. But running would've given the MGB all the reason they needed to execute them. And from a practical point of view they had no money, no friends and no place to hide. If they'd decided to run Leo's parents would've been executed. They'd been lucky so far. Leo had staked their lives on braving it out.

*

The last of the passengers had finished boarding. The station master, seeing the uniforms clustered on the platform by the engine, was holding the departure for them. The train driver leant out of his cabin, trying to figure out what the problem was. Curious passengers were stealing glances out of windows at this young couple in some sort of trouble.

Leo could see a uniformed officer walking towards them. It was Vasili. Leo had been expecting him. He'd hardly miss the opportunity to gloat. Leo felt a flicker of anger but it was imperative he kept his emotions under control. There was, perhaps, a trap still to be set.

Raisa had never seen Vasili before but she'd heard Leo's description of him.

A hero's face, a henchman's heart.

Even at a glance she could tell there was something not quite right about him. He was handsome, certainly, but he was smiling as though a smile had been invented to express nothing other than ill will. When he finally reached them she noticed his pleasure at Leo's humiliation and his disappointment that it wasn't greater.

Vasili widened his smile.

—I insisted that they wait, so I could say goodbye. And explain what has been decided for you. I wanted to do it personally, you understand?

He was enjoying himself. As much as this man appalled Leo it was stupid to risk angering him when they'd survived so much. In a voice barely audible he muttered:

—I appreciate that.

—You've been reassigned. It was impossible to keep you in the MGB with so many unanswered questions over your head. You're going to join the militia. Not as a syshchik, *not as a detective, but as the lowest entry position, an* uchastkovyy. *You'll be the man who cleans the holding cells, the man who takes notes – the man who does as he's told. You need to get used to taking orders if you're to survive.*

Leo understood Vasili's disappointment. This punishment – employed exile in the local police force – was light. Considering the severity of the allegations they could've faced twenty-five-year terms mining gold in Kolyma, where temperatures were fifty below freezing and prisoners' hands were deformed by frostbite and where the life expectancy was three months. They'd escaped not only with their lives but with their freedom. Leo didn't imagine that Major Kuzmin had done it out of sentimentality. The truth was that he would've embarrassed himself by prosecuting his protégé. In a time of political instability it was far better, far shrewder to simply send him away under the guise of a relocation. Kuzmin didn't want his judgement scrutinized; after all if Leo was a spy why had Kuzmin favoured him with promotions? No, those questions were awkward. It was easier and safer just to brush him under the corner of some rug. Understanding that any sign of relief would aggravate Vasili, Leo did his best to look crestfallen.

—*I'll do my duty wherever I'm needed.*

Vasili stepped forward, pressing the tickets and paperwork into Leo's hands. Leo took the documents and moved towards the train.

Raisa stepped up onto the carriage. As she did, Vasili called out.

—*It must have been difficult to hear that your husband had followed you. And not just once, I'm sure he'd told you about that. He followed you twice. On the other occasion it wasn't State business. He didn't think you were a spy. He thought you were a slut. You must forgive him that. Everyone has their doubts. And you are pretty. Personally, I don't think you're worth giving up everything for. I suspect when your husband comes to realize what a shithole we've sent him to he'll grow to hate you. Me, I would've kept the apartment and had you shot as a traitor. All I can suppose is that you must be some great fuck.*

Raisa wondered at this man's obsession with her husband. But she remained silent: a retort might cost them their lives. She took her suitcase and opened the carriage door.

Leo followed her, carefully not to turn around. There was a chance, if he saw Vasili's smirk, that he might not be able to control himself.

*

Raisa stared out of the window. The train departed the station. There were no seats available and they were forced to stand, cramped together. Neither of them spoke for some time, watching the city roll past. Finally, Leo said:

—*I'm sorry.*

—*I'm sure he was lying. He would've said anything to get under your skin.*

—*He was telling the truth. I had you followed. And it had nothing to do with my work. I thought . . .*

—*That I was sleeping with someone else?*

—*There was a time when you wouldn't talk to me. You wouldn't touch me. You wouldn't sleep with me. We were strangers. And I couldn't understand why.*

—*You can't marry an MGB officer and not expect to be followed. But tell me, Leo, how could I be unfaithful? I'd be risking my life. We wouldn't have argued about it. You'd just have me arrested.*

—*Is that what you think would happen?*

—*You remember my friend Zoya, you met her once, I think?*

—*Perhaps, I don't know.*

—*Yes, that's right – you never remember anyone's name, do you? I wonder why? Is that how you're able to sleep at night, by blanking events from your mind?*

Raisa spoke quickly, calmly and with an intensity Leo hadn't heard before. She continued:

—*You did meet Zoya. Perhaps she didn't register, but then she wasn't very important in Party terms. She was given a twenty-year sentence. They arrested her as she stepped out of a church, accusing her of anti-Stalinist prayers. Prayers, Leo – they convicted her on the basis of prayers they hadn't even heard. They arrested her on the basis of the thoughts in her head.*

—*Why didn't you tell me? I might've helped.*

Raisa shook her head. Leo asked:

—You think I denounced her?

—Would you even know? You can't even remember who she is.

Leo was taken aback: he and his wife had never spoken like this before, never spoken about anything other than the household chores, polite conversation – they'd never raised their voices, never had an argument.

—Even if you didn't denounce her, Leo, how could you have helped? When the men who arrested her were men like you – dedicated, devoted servants of the State? That night you didn't come home. And I realized you were probably arresting someone else's best friend, someone else's parents, someone else's children. Tell me, exactly how many people have you arrested? Do you have any idea? Say a number – fifty, two hundred, a thousand?

—I refuse to give them to you.

—They weren't after me. They were after you. Arresting strangers, you were able to fool yourself that they might just be guilty. You could believe that what you were doing served some purpose. But that wasn't enough for them. They wanted you to prove that you'd do whatever they asked even if you knew it in your heart to be wrong, even if you knew it to be meaningless. They wanted you to prove your blind obedience. I imagine wives are a useful test for that.

—Maybe you're right, but we're free of that now. Do you understand how lucky we are to even get this second chance? I want us to start a new life, as a family.

—Leo, it's not as simple as that.

Raisa paused, studying her husband carefully, as though they were meeting for the first time.

—The night we ate dinner at your parents' apartment I heard you talking through the front door. I was in the hallway. I heard the discussion about whether or not you should denounce me as a spy. I

*didn't know what to do. I didn't want to die. So I went back down
to the street and walked for a while, trying to collect my thoughts.
I wondered – will he do it? Will he give me up? Your father made
a convincing case.*

—*My father was scared.*

—*Three lives weighed against one? It's hard to argue with those
numbers. But what about three lives against two?*

—*You're not pregnant?*

—*Would you have vouched for me if I wasn't?*

—*And you waited until now before telling me?*

—*I was afraid you might change your mind.*

This was their relationship: stripped bare. Leo felt unsteady.
The train he was standing on, the people near him, the cases,
his clothes, the city outside – none of it felt right now. He could
trust none of it, not even the things he could see and touch and
feel. Everything he'd believed in was a lie.

—*Raisa, have you ever loved me?*

A moment passed in silence, the question lingering like a bad
smell, the two of them rocking with the motion of the train.
Finally, instead of answering, Raisa knelt down and tied her
shoelace.

Voualsk

15 March

Varlam Babinich was sitting cross-legged on a filthy concrete floor in the corner of an overcrowded dormitory, his back to the door, using his body to shield from view the objects arranged in front of him. He didn't want the other boys to interfere as they had a tendency to if something caught their interest. He glanced around. The thirty or so boys in the room weren't paying him any attention; most of them lay side by side on the eight piss-sodden beds they were forced to share. He watched two of them scratching the bug bites swelling up across each other's backs. Satisfied that he wasn't going to be pestered, he returned to the objects arranged in front of him, objects he'd collected over the years, all of them precious to him, including his most recent addition, stolen this morning – a four-month-old baby.

Varlam was dimly aware that by taking the baby he'd done something wrong and that if he was caught he'd be in trouble, more trouble than he'd ever been in before. He was also aware that the baby wasn't happy. It was crying. He wasn't particularly worried about the noise since no one was going to notice another screaming child. As it happened he was less interested in the baby itself than in the yellow blanket it was wrapped in. Proud of his new possession, he positioned the baby at the centrepiece of his collection, among a yellow tin, an old yellow shirt, a yellow-painted brick, a ripped portion of a poster with a yellow background, a yellow pencil and a book with a soft yellow paper cover. In the summer he added to this collection wild yellow flowers, which he picked from the forest. The flowers never lasted long and nothing made him sadder than watching their shades of yellow fade, the petals becoming lank and brown. He used to wonder:

Where does the yellow go?

He had no idea. But he hoped he'd go there too some day, maybe when he died. The colour yellow was more important to him than anything or anybody. Yellow was the reason he'd ended up here, in Voualsk's *internat*, a State-run facility for children with mental deficiencies.

As a small boy he'd chased after the sun, certain that if he ran far enough he'd eventually catch up with it, snatch it from the sky and carry it home. He'd run for almost five hours before being caught and brought back, screaming in anger at his quest being cut short. His parents, who'd beaten him in the hope that it would straighten out his peculiarities, finally accepted that their methods weren't working and handed him over to the State, which had adopted more or less the same methods. For his first two years in the *internat* he'd been chained to a bed frame, like a farm dog chained to a tree. However, he was a strong child, with broad shoulders and a stubborn determination. Over several months he'd managed to break the bed frame, pulling the chain loose and escaping. He'd ended up on the edge of town, chasing a yellow carriage of a moving train. Eventually he'd been returned to the *internat* suffering from exhaustion and dehydration. This time he'd been locked in a cupboard. But all that was a long time ago – the staff trusted him now he was seventeen years old and smart enough to understand that he couldn't run far enough to reach the sun or indeed climb high enough to pick it out of the sky. Instead, he concentrated on finding yellow closer to home, such as this baby, which he'd stolen by reaching in through an open window. If he hadn't been in such a hurry he might have tried to unwrap the blanket and leave the baby behind. But he'd panicked, afraid that he was going to get caught, and so he'd taken them both. Now, staring down at the screaming infant he noticed that the blanket made the baby's skin appear faintly yellow. And he was glad that he'd stolen them both after all.

*

Outside two cars pulled up and six armed members of the Voualsk militia stepped out, led by General Nesterov, a middle-aged man with the broad, stocky build of a *kolkhoz* labourer. He gestured for his team to surround the premises while he and his deputy, a lieutenant, approached the entrance. Although the militia were not normally armed, today Nesterov had instructed his men to carry guns. They were to shoot to kill.

The administrative office was open: a radio playing on a low volume, a game of cards abandoned on the table, a reek of alcohol hanging in the air. There were no members of staff to be seen. Nesterov and his lieutenant moved forward, entering a corridor. The smell of alcohol gave way to the smell of faeces and sulphur. Sulphur was used to keep away bed bugs. The smell of faeces needed no explanation. There was shit on the floor and on the walls. The dormitories they passed were overrun with young children, maybe forty to a room, wearing nothing more than a dirty shirt or a pair of dirty shorts but never, it seemed, both. They were sprawled on their beds, three or four layered across a thin, filthy mattress. Many weren't moving – staring up at the ceiling. Nesterov wondered if some of them were dead. It was difficult to tell. The children on their feet ran forward, trying to grab the guns, touching their uniforms, starved of adult interaction. The men were quickly encircled by clambering hands. Even though Nesterov had braced himself for terrible conditions he found it difficult to comprehend how things could have got this bad. He intended to bring it up with the director of the establishment. However, that was for another time.

Having searched the ground floor, Nesterov made his way upstairs while his lieutenant tried to keep the pack of children from following, communicating with stern looks and gestures which only caused them to laugh as though this were a game. When he gently pushed the children back they immediately rushed forward, wanting to be pushed back again. Impatient, Nesterov remarked:

—*Leave them, let them be.*

They had no choice but to allow them to trail behind.

The children in the rooms upstairs were older. Nesterov guessed that the dormitories were loosely arranged according to age. Their suspect was seventeen years old – the age limit at this institution, after which they were sent out into the most back-breaking, unappealing jobs available, jobs no sane man or woman would want, jobs where the life expectancy was thirty years. They were coming to the end of the corridor. There was only one dormitory left to search.

With his back to the door, Varlam was preoccupied with stroking the baby's blanket, wondering why the child wasn't crying any more. He prodded it with a dirty finger. Suddenly a voice cut across the room, causing his back to stiffen.

—*Varlam: stand up and turn around, very slowly.*

Varlam held his breath and closed his eyes as though this might make the voice disappear. It didn't work.

—*I'm not going to tell you again. Stand up and turn around.*

Nesterov stepped forward, approaching Varlam's position. He couldn't see what the boy was sheltering. He couldn't hear the sound of a baby crying. All the other boys in the dormitory were sitting upright, staring, fascinated. Without warning Varlam sprang to life, scooping something up in his arms, standing and turning round. He was holding the baby. It started crying. Nesterov was relieved: the child was alive at least. But not out of danger. Varlam was holding it tight against his chest, his arms wrapped around the baby's fragile neck.

Nesterov checked behind him. His deputy had remained by the door with the other curious children clustered around. He took aim at Varlam's head, cocking his gun, ready to kill, waiting for the order. He had a clear line. But at best he was an average shot. At the sight of his gun some of the children began screaming, others laughing and banging the mattresses. The situation was getting out of control. Varlam was beginning to panic. Nesterov holstered his weapon, raising his hands in an attempt to pacify Varlam, speaking over the din.

—*Give me the child.*

—*I'm in so much trouble.*

—*No, you're not. I can see the baby's OK. I'm pleased with you. You've done a good job. You've looked after him. I'm here to congratulate you.*

—*I did a good job?*

—*Yes, you did.*

—Can I keep it?

—I need to check that the baby's OK, just to be sure. Then we'll talk. Can I check on the child?

Varlam knew they were angry and they were going to take the baby from him and lock him in a yellow-less room. He pulled the baby closer, tighter, squeezing it so that the yellow blanket pressed up against his mouth. He stepped back towards the window, looking out at the militia cars parked in the street and the armed men surrounding the building.

—I'm in so much trouble.

Nesterov edged forward. There was no way he could extricate the baby from Varlam's grip by force – it could be crushed in the struggle. He glanced at his lieutenant who nodded, indicating that he'd lined up a shot: he was ready. Nesterov shook his head. The baby was too close to Varlam's face. The risk of an accident was too great. There had to be another way.

—Varlam, no one is going to hit you or hurt you. Give me the child and we'll talk. No one will be angry. You have my word. I promise.

Nesterov took another step closer, blocking his lieutenant's shot. Nesterov glanced down at the collection of yellow items on the floor. He'd encountered Varlam in a previous incident, when a yellow dress had been stolen from a clothes line. It had not slipped his attention that the baby was wrapped in a yellow blanket.

—If you give me the child, I'll ask the mother if you can have the yellow blanket. I'm sure she'll say yes. All I want is the baby.

Hearing what seemed like a fair deal, Varlam relaxed. He stretched out his arms, offering the child. Nesterov sprang forward, snatching the child from his hands. He checked that the child seemed to be unharmed before passing it to his deputy.

—Take it to the hospital.

The lieutenant hurried out.

As though nothing had happened, Varlam sat down with his back to the door, rearranging the items in his collection to fill the space created by the absent baby. The other children in the dormitory were quiet again. Nesterov knelt down beside him. Varlam asked:

—*When can I have the blanket?*

—*You have to come with me first.*

Varlam continued rearranging his collection. Nesterov glanced at the yellow book. It was a military manual, a confidential document.

—*How did you get that?*

—*I found it.*

—*I'm going to have a look. Will you stay calm if I have a look?*

—*Are your fingers clean?*

Nesterov noticed that Varlam's fingers were filthy.

—*My fingers are clean.*

Nesterov picked it up, casually flicking through. There was something in the middle, pressed between the pages. He turned the book upside down and shook it. A thick lock of blonde hair fell to the floor. He picked it up, rubbing it between his fingers. Varlam blushed.

—*I'm in so much trouble.*

Eight Hundred Kilometres East of Moscow

16 March

Asked whether or not she loved him, Raisa had refused to answer. She'd just admitted to lying about being pregnant so even if she'd said — *Yes, I love you, I've always loved you* — Leo wouldn't have believed her. She certainly wasn't about to stare into his eyes and spell out some fanciful description. What was the point of the question anyway? It was as though he'd had some kind of epiphany, a revelation that their marriage wasn't built on love and affection. If she'd answered truthfully — *No, I've never loved you* — all of a sudden he would've been the victim, the implication being that their marriage had been a trick played on him by her. She was the con-artist who'd toyed with his gullible heart. Out of nowhere, he was a romantic. Perhaps it was the shock of losing his job. But since when had love been part of the arrangement? He'd never asked her about it before. He'd never said:

I love you.

She hadn't expected him to. He'd asked her to marry him, true.

She'd said yes. He'd wanted a marriage, he'd wanted a wife, he'd wanted her and he'd got what he wanted. Now that wasn't enough. Having lost his authority, having lost the power to arrest whoever he wanted, he was choked with sentimentalism. And why was it her pragmatic deceit, rather than his profound mistrust, that had brought this illusion of marital contentment crashing down around them? Why couldn't she demand that he had to convince her of his love? After all, he'd presumed incorrectly that she'd been unfaithful, he'd set up an entire surveillance team, a process which could easily have resulted in her arrest. He'd broken trust between them long before she'd been forced to. Her motivation for doing so had been survival. His had been a pathetic male anxiety.

Ever since they'd entered their names as man and wife into the ledger, even before that, ever since they started seeing each other, she'd been conscious that if she displeased him he could have her killed. It had become a blunt reality of her life. She had to keep him happy. When Zoya had been arrested, the very sight of him – his uniform, his talk about the State – made her so angry she found it impossible to utter more than a couple of words to him. In the end the question was very simple. Did she want to live? She was a survivor and the fact of her survival, the fact that she was the only remaining member of her family, defined her. Indignation at Zoya's arrest was a luxury. It achieved nothing. And so she'd got into his bed and slept beside him, slept with him. She'd cooked him dinner – hating the sound of him eating. She'd washed his clothes – hating his smell.

For the past few weeks she'd sat idle in their apartment, knowing full well he'd been weighing up whether he'd made the right decision. Should he have spared her life? Was she worth the risk? Was she pretty enough, nice enough, good enough? Unless every gesture and glance pleased him she'd be in mortal danger. Well, that time was over. She was sick of the powerlessness, the dependency upon his good will. Yet now he seemed to be under the impression that she was in his debt. He'd stated the obvious: she wasn't an international spy, she was a secondary-school teacher. In repayment he wanted a declaration of her love. It was insulting. He was no longer in a position to demand anything. He had no leverage over her just as she had none over him. They were both in the same dire straits: their life's possessions reduced to one suitcase each, exiled to some far-flung town. They were equals as they had never been equal before. If he wanted to hear about love, the first verse was his to sing.

Leo brooded over Raisa's remarks. It seemed that she'd granted herself the right to judge him, to hold him in contempt while pretending that her hands were clean. But she'd married him knowing what he did for a living, she'd enjoyed the perks of his position, she'd eaten the rare foods he'd been able to bring home, she'd bought clothes from the well-stocked *spetztorgi*, stores restricted to state officials. If she was so appalled by his work, why hadn't she rejected his advances? Everyone understood that it was necessary, in order to survive, to compromise. He'd done things that were distasteful – morally objectionable. A clear conscience was, for most people, an impossible luxury and one Raisa could hardly lay claim to. Had she taught her classes according to her genuine beliefs? Evidently not, considering her indignation at the State Security apparatus – but at school she must have expressed her support for it, explained to her students how their State operated, applauded it, indoctrinated them to agree with it and even encouraged them to denounce one another. If she hadn't she would've almost certainly been denounced by one of her own students. Her job was not only to toe the line but to shut down her pupils' questioning faculties. And it would be her job to do it again in their new town. As far Leo was concerned, he and his wife were spokes in the same wheel.

The train stopped at Mutava for an hour. Raisa broke the day-long silence between them.

—*We should eat something.*

By which she meant that they should stick to practical arrange-ments: it had been the foundation for their relationship this far. Surviving whatever challenges they had coming, that was the glue between them, not love. They got out of the carriage. A woman was pacing the platform with a wicker basket. They bought hard-boiled eggs, a paper pouch of salt, chunks of tough rye bread. Sitting side by side on a bench they peeled their eggs, collecting the shell in their laps, sharing the salt and saying nothing at all to each other.

*

The train's speed dropped as it climbed towards the mountains, passing through black pine forests. In the distance, over the tree tops, the mountains could be seen jutting upwards like the uneven teeth in a bottom jaw.

The tracks opened out into a clearing – sprawled before them was a vast assembly plant, tall chimneys, interconnected ware-house-like buildings suddenly appearing in the middle of a wilderness. It was as though God had sat on the Ural Mountains, smashed his fist down on the landscape before him, sending trees flying, and demanded that this newly created space be filled with chimneys and steel presses. This was the first glimpse of their new home.

Leo's knowledge of this town came from propaganda and paperwork. Previously little more than timber mills and a collection of timber huts for the people who worked in them, the once modest settlement of twenty thousand inhabitants had caught Stalin's eye. Upon closer examination of its natural and man-made resources he'd declared it insufficiently productive. The river Ufa ran nearby, there were the steel- and iron-processing plants in Sverdlovsk only a hundred and sixty kilometres east and ore mines in the mountains, and it had the benefit of the Trans-Siberian railway – vast locomotives passed through this town each day and nothing more was added to them than planks of wood. He'd decided that this would be the ideal location to assemble an automobile, the GAZ-20, a car intended to rival the vehicles produced in the West, built according to the highest specifications. Its successor, currently under design – the Volga GAZ-21 – was being upheld as the pinnacle of Soviet engineering, designed to survive the harsh climate with high ground clearance, enviable suspension, a bullet-proof engine and rust-proofing on a scale unheard of in the United States of America. Whether that was true or not, Leo had no way of knowing. He knew it was a car only a tiny per cent of Soviet citizens could afford, far beyond the financial reach of the men and women employed in its assembly.

Construction on the factory began some time after the war and eighteen months later the Volga assembly plant stood in the middle of the pine forests. He couldn't remember the number of prisoners reported to have died in its construction. Not that the numbers were reliable anyway. Leo had only become actively involved after the factory had been completed. Thousands of *free* workers had been vetted and transferred by compulsory writ from cities across the country to fill the newly created labour gap: the population rising fivefold over the space of five years. Leo had done background checks on some of the Moscow workers transferred here. If they'd passed the checks, they were packed up and moved out within the week. If they failed, they were arrested. He'd been one of the gatekeepers to this town. He was sure that this was one of the reasons that Vasili had picked this place. The irony must have amused him.

Raisa missed this first glimpse of their new home. She was asleep, wrapped up in her coat, her head resting against the window, rocking slightly with the motion of the train. Moving to the seat beside his wife and facing in the direction they were travelling, he could see how the main town was latched onto the side of the vast assembly plant as though it was a tic sucking on the neck of a dog. First and foremost this was a place of industrial production, a distant second, a place to live. The lights of apartment blocks glowed dim orange against a grey sky. Leo nudged Raisa. She woke, looking at Leo, then out of the window.

—*We're here.*

The train pulled into the station. They collected their cases, stepping down onto the platform. It was colder than Moscow — the temperature had dropped by at least a couple of degrees. They stood like two evacuee children arriving in the country for the first time, staring at their unfamiliar surroundings. They'd been given no instructions. They knew no one. They didn't even have a number to call. No one was waiting for them.

The station building was empty except for a man seated at the ticket booth. He was young, not much more than twenty. He watched them intently as they entered the building. Raisa approached him.

—*Good evening. We need to get to the headquarters of the militia.*

—*You're from Moscow?*

—*That's right.*

The man opened the door of his ticket booth, stepping out onto the concourse. He pointed out of the glass doors towards the street outside.

—*They're waiting for you.*

One hundred paces from the station entrance was a militia car.

Passing a snow-capped stone carving of Stalin's profile, chiselled into a slab of rock like a fossilized impression, Raisa and Leo moved towards the car, a GAZ-20, no doubt one of the cars produced by this town. As they got closer they could see two men sitting in the front. The door opened, one of the men stepped out, a middle-aged man with broad shoulders.

—*Leo Demidov?*

—*Yes.*

—*I'm General Nesterov, head of Voualsk's militia.*

Leo wondered why he'd bothered to meet them. Surely Vasili had given instructions to make the experience as unpleasant as possible? But it didn't matter what Vasili had said – the arrival of a former MGB agent from Moscow was going to put the militia on their guard. They wouldn't believe that he was merely here to join their ranks. They almost certainly suspected an ulterior agenda and presumed that, for whatever reason, he'd be reporting back to Moscow. The more Vasili had tried to convince them otherwise, the more suspicious they would've become. Why would an agent travel hundreds of kilometres to join a small-scale militia operation? It didn't make sense – in a classless society the militia were near the bottom of the heap.

Every schoolchild was taught that murder, theft and rape were symptoms of a capitalist society, and the role of the militia had been ranked accordingly. There was no need to steal and no violence between citizens because there was equality. There was no need for a police force in a Communist state. It was for this reason that the militia were nothing more than a lowly subsection of the

Ministry of the Interior: poorly paid, poorly respected – a force comprised of secondary-school dropouts, farm workers kicked off the *kolkhoz*, discharged army personnel and men whose judgement could be bought with a half bottle of vodka. Officially the USSR's crime rates were close to zero. The newspapers frequently pointed out the vast sums of money the United States of America was forced to waste on crime prevention with its need for gleaming police cars and police officers in crisp, clean uniforms visible on every street corner, without which its society would crumble. The West employed many of their bravest men and women fighting crime, citizens who could've better spent their time building something. None of that manpower was squandered here: all that was needed was a ragtag group of strong but otherwise useless men who were good for nothing more than breaking up drunken brawls. That was the theory. Leo had no idea what the real crime statistics were. He had no desire to find out since those who knew were probably liquidated on a regular basis. Factory production figures filled *Pravda*'s front page, the middle pages and the back pages too. Good news was the only news worth printing – high birth rates, mountain-top train lines and new canals.

Taking this into account, Leo's arrival was a striking anomaly. A post in the MGB held more *blat*, respect, more influence, more material benefit than almost any other job. An officer wouldn't voluntarily step down. And if he was disgraced, why hadn't he simply been arrested? Even disavowed from the MGB, he still carried its shadow – potentially a valuable asset.

Nesterov carried their cases to the car as effortlessly as if they'd been empty. He loaded them into the boot, before opening the back door for them. Inside, Leo watched his new superior officer as he climbed into the front passenger seat. He was too large, even for this impressive vehicle. His knees came up near his chin. There was a young officer seated behind the wheel. Nesterov didn't bother to introduce him. In similar fashion to the MGB there were drivers responsible for each vehicle. Officers weren't given their own car and didn't drive themselves. The driver put the car into gear, pulling out into an empty road. There wasn't another car in sight.

Nesterov waited a while, no doubt not wanting to seem like he was interrogating his new recruit, before glancing at Leo in the rear-view mirror and asking:

—*We were told three days ago that you were coming here. It's an unusual transfer.*

—*We must go where we're needed.*

—*No one has been transferred here for some time. I certainly made no request for any additional men.*

—*The output of the factory is considered a high priority. You can never have too many men working to ensure the security of this town.*

Raisa turned towards her husband, guessing that his enigmatic answers were deliberate. Even demoted, even tossed out of the MGB, he was still making use of the fear it instilled. In their precarious circumstances it seemed a sensible thing to do. Nesterov asked:

—*Tell me: are you to be a* syshchik, *a detective? We were confused about the orders. They said no. They said you were to be an* uchastkovyy, *which is a significant demotion in responsibility for a man of your status.*

—*My orders are to report to you. I leave my rank in your hands.*

There was silence. Raisa supposed the general didn't like having the question pushed back at him. Uncomfortable with the situation he gruffly added:

—*For the moment you'll stay in guest accommodation. Once an apartment has been found it will be assigned to you. I should warn you that there's a very long waiting list. And there's nothing I can do about that. There are no advantages to being a* militsioner.

The car stopped outside what appeared to be a restaurant. Nesterov opened the boot, picking up the cases and depositing them on the pavement. Leo and Raisa stood, awaiting instructions. Addressing Leo, Nesterov said:

—*Once you've taken your cases to your room please come back to the car. Your wife doesn't need to come.*

Raisa suppressed her irritation at being spoken about as if she wasn't present. She watched as Leo, mimicking Nesterov, picked up both their cases. She marvelled at this bravado but decided against embarrassing him. He could struggle with her case if he wanted to. Walking just in front she pushed open the door, entering the restaurant.

Inside it was dark, the shutters were closed and the air stank of stale smoke. Last night's dirty glasses cluttered the table. Leo put the cases down and knocked on one of the greasy tabletops. The silhouette of a man appeared at the door.

—*We're not open.*

—*My name is Leo Demidov. This is my wife, Raisa. We've just arrived from Moscow.*

—*Danil Basarov.*

—*I've been told by General Nesterov you have accommodation for us.*

—*You mean the room upstairs?*

—*I don't know, yes, I suppose.*

Basarov scratched the rolls of his stomach.

—*Let me show you to your room.*

The room was small. Two single beds had been pushed together. There was a gap down the middle. Both mattresses dipped. The wallpaper was bubbled like adolescent skin, lined with some kind of grease, sticky to touch. Leo figured it must be cooking oil, since the bedroom was directly over the kitchen, which could be seen through cracks in the floorboards, cracks which ventilated the room with the smell of whatever had been or was cooking below – boiled offal, gristle and animal fat.

Basarov was put out by Nesterov's request. These beds, and this room, had been used by his *staff*, which is to say the women who worked his customers. However, he'd been unable to decline the request. He didn't own the building. And he required the goodwill of the militia in order to function as a business. They knew he was making a profit and they were fine with it as long as they got a share. It was undeclared, unofficial – a closed system. If the truth was told he was a little nervous of his guests, having heard they were MGB. It stopped him being as rude as he would naturally have been. He pointed down the hall towards a door which was partly ajar.

—*There's the bathroom. We've got one indoors.*

Raisa tried to open the window. It had been nailed shut. She stared at the view. Ramshackle housing, dirty snow: this was home.

Leo felt tired. He'd been able to handle his humiliation while it had remained a concept but now that it had a physical form – this room – he just wanted to sleep, to close his eyes and shut out the world. Obliged to go back outside, he put his case on the bed, unable to look at Raisa, not out of anger, but out of shame. He walked out without saying a word.

*

Driven to the town's telephone exchange, Leo was led inside. There was a queue of several hundred people waiting for their allotted time, a couple of minutes. Since most of them had been forced to leave behind their families in order to work here, Leo could appreciate that these minutes were extremely precious. Nesterov had no need to queue, heading into a cubicle.

Once he'd set up the call, which involved a conversation Leo couldn't hear, he handed the receiver to him. Leo put the receiver to his ear. He waited.

—*How's the accommodation?*

It was Vasili. He continued:

—*You want to hang up, don't you? But you can't. You can't even do that.*

—*What is it you want?*

—*To stay in touch so you can tell me about life over there and I can tell you about life here. Before I forget, the pleasant apartment you'd arranged for your parents, it's been taken back. We've found them somewhere more suitable to their status. It's a little cold and crowded, perhaps. Dirty, certainly. They're sharing with a family of seven, I think, including five young children. By the way, I didn't know your father suffered from terrible back pain. Shame that he has to return to the assembly line floor only a year from retirement: one year can be made to feel like ten when you're not enjoying your job. But you'll soon know all about that.*

—*My parents are good people. They've worked hard. They've done you no harm.*

—*But I'm going to hurt them all the same.*

—*What do you want from me?*

—*An apology.*

—*Vasili, I'm sorry.*

—*You don't even know what you're sorry for.*

—*I treated you badly. And I'm sorry.*

—What are you sorry for? Be specific. Your parents are depending on you.

—I shouldn't have hit you.

—You're not trying hard enough. Convince me.

Desperate, Leo's voice was trembling.

—I don't understand what you want. You have everything. I have nothing.

—It's simple. I want to hear you beg.

—I'm begging you, Vasili, listen to my voice. I am begging you. Leave my parents alone. Please . . .

Vasili had hung up.

Voualsk

17 March

Having walked all night – his feet blistered, his socks sodden with blood – Leo sat down on a park bench, put his head in his hands and wept.

He hadn't slept, he hadn't eaten. Last night, when Raisa had tried to talk to him, he'd ignored her. When she'd brought him food from the restaurant he'd ignored that too. Unable to stay in their tiny stinking room any longer he'd gone downstairs, elbowed his way through the crowd, making his way outside. He'd walked without any sense of direction, too frustrated, too angry to sit still and do nothing although he realized that was exactly the nature of his predicament – he could do nothing. Once again he was faced with an injustice, but this time he was no longer able to intervene. His parents wouldn't be shot in the back in the head – that would be too swift, too much an approximation of mercy. Instead they'd be persecuted drip by drip. He could imagine the variety of options open to a methodical, sadistic and petty mind. In their respective factories they'd be demoted, given the hardest, dirtiest jobs – jobs a young man or woman would struggle with. They'd be goaded with stories of Leo's pitiful exile, his disgrace and humiliation. Perhaps they'd even be told that he was in a Gulag, sentenced to twenty years of *katorga*, hard labour. As for the family that his parents were forced to share an apartment with, there was no doubt that they'd be as disruptive and unpleasant as possible. The children would be promised chocolate if they made a lot of noise, the adults promised their own apartment if they stole food, argued and, through whatever means available, made home life intolerable. He didn't need to guess the details. Vasili would enjoy reporting them, knowing that Leo wouldn't dare hang up the phone since he was afraid that whatever hardships his parents were experiencing would double as a result. Vasili would break him from afar, systematically applying pressure where he was vulnerable – his family. There was no defence. With a little work Leo could discover his parents' address but all he could do, if his letters weren't intercepted and burnt, would be to reassure them he was safe. He'd built them a comfortable life only to have it ripped from under their feet at a time when they could least handle the change.

He stood up, shivering with cold. With some difficulty, and no idea what he was going to do next, he began to retrace his steps, back to his new home.

*

Raisa was downstairs sitting at a table. She'd been waiting for him all night. She knew, just as Vasili had predicted, that Leo now regretted his decision not to denounce her. The price was too high. But what was she supposed to do? Pretend that he'd risked everything for a perfect love? It wasn't something she could just conjure on demand. Even if she'd wanted to pretend she didn't know how: she didn't know what to say, what motions to go through. She could've been easier on him. In truth, some part of her must have relished his demotion. Not out of spite or vindictiveness but because she wanted him to know:

This is how I feel every day.

Powerless, scared — she'd wanted him to feel it too. She'd wanted him to understand, to experience it for himself.

Exhausted, her eyes heavy with sleep, she looked up as Leo entered the restaurant. She stood, approaching her husband, noticing his bloodshot eyes. She'd never seen him cry before. He turned away and poured himself a drink from the nearest bottle. She put a hand on his shoulder. It happened in a fraction of second: Leo spun around, grabbing her by the neck and squeezing.

—*You did this.*

Her veins constricted, her face flushed red — she couldn't breathe, she was choking. Leo lifted her up: she was on the tips of her toes. Her hands fumbled at his grip. But he wouldn't let go and she couldn't break his hold.

She reached towards a tabletop, her fingers straining for a glass, her eyesight blurring. She managed to touch a glass, tipping it over. It fell within reach: she grabbed it, swinging and smashing it against the side of Leo's face. The glass cracked in her hand, cutting her palms. As if a spell had been broken he released her. She fell back, coughing, holding her neck. They stared at each other, strangers, as though their entire history had been washed away in that fraction of a second. A shard of glass was embedded in Leo's cheek. He touched it and pulled the splinter out, surveying it in the palm of his hand. Without turning her back, she edged to the stairs, hurrying up, leaving him.

Instead of following his wife, Leo downed the drink he'd already poured and then poured another and then another and by the time he heard Nesterov's car outside he'd finished most of the bottle. Unsteady on his feet, unwashed and unshaven, drunk, brutish and senselessly violent – it had taken him less than a day to sink to the level expected of the militia.

During their car journey, Nesterov didn't mention the gash down Leo's face. He spoke in short bursts about the town. Leo wasn't listening, barely conscious of his surroundings, preoccupied with the question of what he'd just done. Had he tried to strangle his wife or was that some trick of his sleep-deprived brain? He touched the cut on his cheek, saw blood on his fingertip – it was true, he'd done it and he'd been capable of more. Another couple of seconds, a slight tightening of his grip, and she would've died. His provocation was that he'd given up everything – his parents, his career – all on a false pretext, the promise of a family, the notion that there was some tie between them. She'd tricked him, fixed the odds, skewering his decision. Only once she was safe and his parents were suffering did she admit the pregnancy was a lie. Then she went further, openly describing how she'd held him in contempt. She'd manipulated his sentimentality and then spat in his face. In exchange for his sacrifice, in exchange for overlooking incriminating evidence of her guilt, he'd gotten nothing.

But Leo didn't believe it for a second. The time of self-justification had ended. What he had done was unforgivable. And she was right to hold him in contempt. How many brothers and sisters, mothers and fathers had he arrested? How different was he from the man he considered his moral opposite, Vasili Nikitin? Was the difference merely that Vasili was senselessly cruel while he'd been idealistically cruel? One was an empty, indifferent cruelty while the other was a principled, pretentious cruelty which thought of itself as reasonable and necessary. But in real terms, in destructive terms, there was little to separate the two men. Had

Leo lacked the imagination to realize what he was involved in? Or was it worse than that – had he chosen not to imagine it? He'd shut down those thoughts, brushed them aside.

Out of the rubble of his moral certainties one fact remained. He'd laid down his life for Raisa only to try and kill her. That was insanity. At this rate he'd have nothing, not even the woman he'd married. He wanted to say, the woman he loved. Did he love her? He'd married her, wasn't that the same? No, not really – he'd married her because she was beautiful, intelligent and he was proud to have her by his side, proud to make her his. It was another step towards the perfect Soviet life – work, family and children. In many ways she was a cipher, a cog in the wheels of his ambitions, the necessary domestic background to his successful career, his status as a Model Citizen. Was Vasili right when he'd said she could be substituted for another? On the train he'd asked her to declare her love for him, to soothe him, to reward him with a romantic fantasy in which he was the hero. It was pathetic. Leo let out an audible sigh, rubbing his forehead. He was being outplayed – and that's exactly what this was to Vasili, a game, with the playing chips being denominations of misery. Instead of Vasili striking his wife, hurting her, Leo had done it for him, acting out every part of his plan.

They'd arrived. The car had stopped. Nesterov was already out of the car and waiting for him. With no idea how long he'd been sitting there, Leo opened the car door, stepping out and following his superior officer into the militia headquarters to begin his first morning at work. Introduced to staff, shaking hands, nodding, agreeing but unable to take anything in; names, details – they washed over him – and it wasn't until he was alone in the locker room with a uniform hanging before him that he began to refocus on the present. He took off his shoes, slowly peeling back the socks from his bloody toes and running his feet under cold water, watching as the water turned red. Since he had no new socks and couldn't bring himself to ask for a new pair, he was forced to put the old socks back on, wincing in pain as he slid the material over his raw blisters. He stripped, leaving his civilian clothing in a heap at the bottom of a locker and buttoning up his new uniform, coarse trousers with red piping and a heavy military jacket. He looked at himself in the mirror. There were black marks under his eyes, a weeping cut down his left cheek. He glanced at the insignia on his jacket. He was an *uchastkovyy*, he was nothing.

The walls of Nesterov's office were decorated with framed certificates. Reading them, Leo discovered that his boss had won amateur wrestling competitions and rifle-shooting tournaments, and had received commendations as Officer of the Month on numerous occasions both here and at his former place of residence, Rostov. It was an ostentatious display, understandable considering that his position was held in such low esteem.

Nesterov studied his new recruit, unable to work him out. Why was this man, a former high-ranking MGB officer with a decorated war record, in such a bedraggled state – his fingernails filthy, his face bleeding, his hair unwashed, stinking of alcohol and apparently indifferent to his demotion? Perhaps he was exactly as he'd been described: grossly incompetent and unworthy of responsibility. His appearance certainly fitted the bill. But Nesterov wasn't convinced: maybe this dishevelled appearance was a trick. He'd been uneasy from the moment he'd heard about the transfer. This man had the potential to do untold damage to him and his men. One damning report, that was all it would take. Nesterov had decided the best course of action would be to observe this man, test him and keep him close. Leo would eventually reveal his hand.

Nesterov presented Leo with a file. Leo stared at it for a moment, trying to work out what was expected of him. Why was he being given this? Whatever it was, he didn't care. He sighed, forcing himself to study the file. Inside there were black-and-white photographs of a young girl. She was lying on her back, surrounded by black snow. Black snow . . . black because it was soaked in blood. It seemed as though the girl was screaming. On closer inspection there was something inside her mouth. Nesterov explained:

—*Her mouth was stuffed with soil. So she couldn't scream for help.*

Leo's fingers tightened on the photo, all his thoughts about Raisa, his parents, about himself — evaporated as his eyes focused on this girl's mouth. It was wide open, stuffed with dirt. He glanced at the next photo. The girl was naked: her skin, where it was undamaged, was as white as the snow. Her midriff had been savaged, torn open. He flicked to the next photo and the next and the next, not seeing a girl but instead Fyodor's little boy, a boy who hadn't been stripped naked, or had his stomach cut open, a boy whose mouth hadn't been stuffed with dirt — a boy who hadn't been murdered. Leo put the photos down on the table. He said nothing, staring at the certificates hanging on the wall.

Same Day

The two incidents had nothing to do with each other, the death of Fyodor's young boy and the murder of this young girl — it was impossible. They'd taken place hundreds of kilometres apart. This was a vicious irony, nothing more. But Leo had been wrong to dismiss Fyodor's allegations. Here was a child murdered as Fyodor had described. Such a thing was possible. There was now no way of knowing what had really happened to Fyodor's son, Arkady, because Leo had never bothered to examine the boy's body for himself. Perhaps that death had been an accident. Or perhaps the matter had been hushed up. If the latter was true then Leo had been instrumental in orchestrating a cover-up. He'd done so unquestioningly — ridiculing, bullying and finally threatening a grieving family.

General Nesterov was frank about the details of this murder, calling it by no other name — *murder* — and giving no indication of wanting to portray it as anything other than a brutal and horrific crime. His frankness worried Leo. How could he be so cool? The yearly statistics for his department were supposed to conform to predetermined patterns: decreasing crime rates, increasing social harmony. Although the town had undergone a vast increase in population, an influx of eighty thousand uprooted workers, crime should have declined since the theory dictated that there was more work, more fairness, less exploitation.

The victim's name was Larisa Petrova; she'd been found four days ago, in the forest, not far from the train station. The details regarding the discovery of the body were vague and when Leo had pressed the issue Nesterov had seemed eager to brush the point aside. All Leo could gather was that the body had been discovered by a couple who'd drunk too much and had retreated into the forest to fornicate. They'd stumbled across the little girl, who'd been lying in the snow for several months, her body perfectly preserved in the freezing cold. She was a schoolchild, fourteen years old. The militia knew her. She had a reputation for having a disorderly sex life not just with boys of her own age but with older men; she could be bought for a litre bottle of vodka. Larisa had argued with her mother on the day she went missing. Larisa's absence had been dismissed; she'd threatened to run away and it seemed she'd followed through on her word. No one had looked for her. According to Nesterov her parents were respected members of the community. Her father was an accountant at the assembly plant. They were ashamed of their daughter and wanted nothing to do with the investigation, which was to be kept secret; not covered up, but not publicized either. The parents agreed not to have a funeral for their child and were prepared to pretend that she was merely missing. There was no need for the community at large to know. Only a handful of people outside the militia were aware of the murder. Those people, including the couple who'd found the body, had been made clear of the consequences of talking. The matter would be concluded swiftly because they already had a man in custody.

Leo was aware that the militia could only investigate after a criminal case had been opened and that a criminal case was only opened if it was certain it would be concluded successfully. Failure to convict a suspect was unacceptable and the consequences severe. Bringing a case to court was supposed to mean one thing: that the suspect was guilty. If a case was difficult, complex, ambiguous, it simply wouldn't be opened. For Nesterov and his subordinates to be this calm could only mean that they were convinced they had their man. Their job was done. The brainwork of investigations, the presentation of evidence, interrogations and ultimately the prosecution itself were the duties of the State's investigative team, the procurator's office and their team of *sledovatyel*, lawyers. Leo wasn't being asked to assist: he was being given a tour, expected to marvel at their efficiency.

The cell was small with none of the ingenious modifications typical of those in the Lubyanka. There were concrete walls, a concrete floor. The suspect was seated, his hands cuffed behind his back. He was young, perhaps no more than sixteen or seventeen, with an adult's muscular frame but a child's face. His eyes seemed to roam with no particular sense of purpose. He didn't seem afraid. He was calm although not in an intelligent way and showed no signs of physical abuse. Of course there were ways of inflicting injuries so the marks didn't show but Leo's gut reaction was that the boy hadn't been harmed. Nesterov pointed at the suspect.

—*This is Varlam Babinich*.

At the sound of his name, the young man stared at Nesterov as a dog might stare at its owner. Nesterov continued:

—*We found him in possession of a lock of Larisa's hair. He has a history of stalking Larisa – lingering outside her house, propositioning her in the street. Larisa's mother remembers seeing him on numerous occasions. She remembers her daughter complaining about him. He used to try and touch her hair.*

Nesterov turned to the suspect, speaking slowly.

—*Varlam, tell us what happened, tell us how you had a lock of her hair in your possession.*

—I cut her. It was my fault.

—Tell this officer why you killed her.

—I liked her hair. I wanted it. I have a yellow book, a yellow shirt, a yellow tin and some yellow hair. This is why I cut her. I'm sorry. I shouldn't have done that. When can I have the blanket?

—Let's talk about that later.

Leo interrupted:

—What blanket?

—Two days ago he kidnapped a baby. It was wrapped in a yellow blanket. He has an obsession with the colour yellow. Fortunately the baby was unhurt. However, he has no sense of right or wrong. He does whatever he feels like without regard for consequence.

Nesterov moved closer to the suspect.

—When I found Larisa's hair in your book, why did you think you'd be in trouble? Tell this man what you told me.

—She never liked me, she kept telling me to go away but I wanted her hair. I wanted it so bad. And when I cut her hair she didn't say anything at all.

Nesterov turned to Leo, offering the questioning to him.

—Do you have any questions?

What was expected of him? Leo thought for a moment before asking:

—Why did you stuff her mouth with soil?

Varlam didn't answer immediately. He seemed confused.

—Yes, there was something in her mouth. I remember that now. Don't hit me.

Nesterov answered:

—No one is going to hit you, answer the question.

—I don't know. I forget things. There was dirt in her mouth, yes.

Leo continued:

—Explain what happened when you killed her.

—I cut her.

—You cut her or you cut her hair?

—I'm sorry, I cut her.

—Listen to me carefully. Did you cut her body or did you cut her hair?

—I found her and I cut her. I should have said to somebody but I was worried. I didn't want to get in trouble.

Varlam began to cry.

—I'm in so much trouble. I'm sorry. I just wanted her hair.

Nesterov stepped forward.

—That's enough for the moment.

With those words of reassurance, Varlam stopped crying. He was calm again. It was impossible to tell from his face that this was a man in the frame for murder.

Leo and Nesterov stepped outside. Nesterov shut the door to the cell:

—We have evidence that he was at the crime scene. Snow prints match his boots exactly. You understand that he's from the inter-nat? He's a simpleton.

Leo now understood Nesterov's bravery in addressing this murder head on. They had a suspect who suffered from a mental disorder. Varlam was outside Soviet society, outside Communism, politics – he was explainable. His actions didn't reflect on the Party, they didn't alter the truism about crime because the suspect was not a real Soviet. He was an anomaly. Nesterov added:

—That shouldn't lull you into thinking he's incapable of vio-lence. He's admitted killing her. He has a motive, an irrational one, but a motive. He wanted something he couldn't have – her blonde hair. He has a history of committing crimes when he can't get what he wants: theft, kidnapping. Now he's turned to murder. To him,

killing Larisa was no different from stealing a baby. His morality is undeveloped. It's sad. He should have been locked up a long time ago. This is a matter for the sledovatyel *now.*

Leo understood. The investigation was over. This young man was going to die.

Same Day

The bedroom was empty. Leo dropped to his knees, putting his head to the floorboards. Her case was missing. He stood up, ran out of the room, down the stairs and into the restaurant kitchen. Basarov was cutting fatty strips off an unidentifiable joint of yellow meat.

—*Where's my wife?*

—*Pay for the bottle and I'll tell you.*

He pointed to an empty bottle, the bottle of cheap vodka Leo had finished in the early hours of the morning, adding:

—*I don't care if it was you or your wife who drank it.*

—*Please, just tell me where she is.*

—*Pay for the bottle.*

Leo didn't have any money. He was still wearing his militia uniform. He'd left everything in the locker room.

—*I'll pay you later. However much you want.*

—*Later, sure, later you'll pay me a million roubles.*

Basarov continued cutting the meat, signalling his refusal to budge.

Leo ran back upstairs, rifling through his case, throwing everything out. In the back of the *Book of Propagandists* he had twenty-five-rouble notes, four of them, an emergency stash. He got to his feet, ran out, back down the stairs to the restaurant, pushing one of the notes into the man's hand, considerably more than a single bottle was worth.

—*Where is she?*

—*She left a couple of hours ago. She was carrying her case.*

—*Where was she going?*

—*She didn't speak to me. I didn't speak to her.*

—*How long ago, exactly how long ago?*

—*Two or three hours . . .*

Three hours – that meant she was gone, not just out of the restaurant but quite possibly out of the town. Leo couldn't guess where she might be heading or which direction she'd be travelling.

Feeling generous after his substantial reward, Basarov volunteered a little extra information.

—*It's unlikely she made it in time for the late afternoon train. As far as I remember there isn't another train till right about now.*

—*What time?*

—*Seven thirty . . .*

Leo had ten minutes.

Ignoring his tiredness, he ran as fast as he could. But desperation choked him. Short of breath, he had only the roughest idea where the station was. He was running blindly, trying to recall the route the car had driven. His uniform was soaked with spray from the icy slush on the street, the cheap material getting heavier and heavier. His blisters rubbed and burst, his toes were bleeding again, his shoes filling with blood. Each step sent a searing pain through his legs.

He turned the corner only to be confronted by a dead end – a line of wooden houses. He was lost. It was too late. His wife was gone; there was nothing he could do. Hunched over, trying to catch his breath, he remembered these ramshackle timber houses, the stench of human effluent. He was close to the station; he was sure of it. Rather than retrace his steps he ran forward, entering the back of one of the huts, stepping into a family seated on the floor, in the middle of a meal. Huddled around a stove, they stared up at him, silent, afraid at the sight of his uniform. Without saying a word he stepped over the children and ran out, entering onto the main street; the street they'd driven down on their arrival. The station was within sight. He tried to run faster but he was slowing. Adrenaline could no longer compensate for exhaustion. He had nothing in reserve.

He barged into the station doors, knocking them open with his shoulder. The clock showed it was seven forty-five. He was fifteen minutes too late. The realization that she was gone, probably forever, began to crash across his mind. Leo clung to the groundless hope that somehow she'd be on the platform, somehow she hadn't got on the train. He stepped out: looking right and left. He couldn't see his wife, he couldn't see the train. He felt weak. He leant forward, his hands on his knees, sweat running down the side of his face. Out of the corner of his eye he saw a man sitting on a bench. Why would a man still be on the platform? Was he waiting for a train? Leo straightened up.

Raisa was at the far end of the platform, hidden in the gloom. It took an enormous effort not to run and grab her hands. Catching his breath, he was trying to think of what to say. He glanced at himself – he was a mess, sweating, filthy. But she wasn't even looking at him: she was looking over his shoulder. Leo turned around. Thick bursts of smoke were rising over the tree tops. The delayed train was approaching.

Leo had imagined taking time over his apology, finding the correct words, being eloquent. However, right now he had a matter of seconds to convince her. His words stumbled out.

—I'm sorry, I wasn't thinking. I grabbed you but that wasn't me – or it wasn't the person I want to be.

Hopeless – he had to do better. Slow down, concentrate – he'd get one shot at this.

—Raisa, you want to leave me. You're right to want to leave me. I could tell you how difficult it would be on your own. How you might get stopped, questioned, arrested. How you don't have the right paperwork. You'd be a vagrant. But that's not a reason to stay with me. I know that you'd rather take your chances.

—Paperwork can be faked, Leo. I'd rather fake that than this marriage.

There it was. The marriage was a sham. All Leo's words dried up. The train came to a halt alongside them. Raisa's face was impassive. Leo stepped out of her way. She moved towards the carriage. Could he let her go? Over the sound of grinding brakes, Leo raised his voice:

—The reason I didn't denounce you wasn't because I believed you were pregnant and it had nothing to do with me being a good person. I did it because my family is the only part of my life that I'm not ashamed of.

To Leo's surprise Raisa turned around.

—Where does it come from, this overnight enlightenment? It feels cheap. Having been stripped of your uniform, your office, your power, you now have to make do with me. Is that it? Something which was never very important to you before – us – becomes important because you find yourself with nothing else?

—You don't love me, I know that. But there was a reason we got married, there was something between us, some connection. We've lost that. I've lost that. We can find it again.

Carriage doors were opening, a handful of passengers were disembarking. Time was running out. Raisa looked at the carriage, weighing up her choices. They were pitiful. She had no friends to run to, no family who could shelter her, no money and no means of supporting herself. She didn't even have a ticket. Leo was right in his analysis. If she left, she'd probably get picked up by the authorities. She felt exhausted at the thought of it. She looked at her husband. They had nothing except each other, whether they liked each other or not.

She put down her case. Leo smiled, obviously believing them to be reconciled. Annoyed with this idiotic interpretation, she raised her hand, cutting short his smile.

—*I married you because I was scared, scared that if I rejected your advances I'd be arrested, maybe not immediately but at some point, on some pretext. I was young, Leo, and you were powerful. That is the reason we got married. That story you tell about me pretending that my name was Lena? You find that story funny, romantic? I gave you a false name because I was worried you'd track me down. What you took for seduction, I took for surveillance. Our relationship was built out of fear. Maybe not from your point of view – you have no reason to fear me, what power did I have? What power have I ever had? You asked me to marry you and I acquiesced because that's what people do. They put up with things; they tolerate in order to survive. You never hit me or shouted at me, you were never drunk. So, on balance, I reckoned that I was luckier than most. When you grabbed my neck, Leo, you removed the only reason I had for staying with you.*

The train pulled out. Leo watched it go, trying to digest what she'd said. But she gave him no pause, speaking as though these words had been forming in her head over many years. Now, tapped, they were flowing freely.

—*The problem with becoming powerless, as you are now, is that people start telling you the truth. You're not used to it, you've lived in a world protected by the fear you inspire. But if we're going to stay together, let's cut the deluded romanticism. Circumstance is the glue between us. I have you. You have me. We don't have very much else. And if we're going to stay together, from now on I tell you the truth, no comfortable lies – we're equal as we have never been equal before. You can take it or I can wait for the next train.*

Leo had no reply. He was unprepared, outgunned, outspoken. In the past he'd used his position to get better accommodation, better food. He hadn't imagined he'd used it to get a wife too. Her voice softened a little.

—There are so many things to be afraid of. You can't be one of them.

—I never will again.

—I'm cold, Leo. I've been standing on this platform for three hours. I'm going back to our room. Are you coming?

No, he didn't feel like walking back, side by side, a chasm between them.

—I'm going to stay here for a bit. I'll see you back there.

Carrying her case, Raisa returned to the station building. Leo sat on the bench, staring into the forest. He shuffled through the memories of their relationship, re-examining each one, adjusting his understanding, rewriting his past.

He'd been sitting there for he didn't know how long when he became aware of someone standing to the side of him. He looked up. It was the man from the ticket office, a youngish man, the man they'd met on their arrival.

—Sir, there are no more trains tonight.

—Do you have a cigarette?

—I don't smoke. I could get you one from our apartment. It's just upstairs.

—No, that's OK. Thank you anyway.

—*I'm Aleksandr.*

—*Leo. Do you mind if I stay here for a bit?*

—*Not at all, let me get you that cigarette.*

Before Leo could answer, the young man had hurried off.

Leo sat back and waited. He saw a wooden hut set back from the tracks. That was the place where the girl's body had been found. He could make out the edge of the forest, the crime scene – snow trampled down by detectives, photographers, investigative lawyers – all studying that dead girl, her mouth open, stuffed with soil.

Struck by a thought Leo stood up, hurried forward, lowering himself off the platform, crossing the tracks and heading towards the trees. Behind him a voice called out:

—*What are you doing?*

He turned around and saw Aleksandr standing on the edge of the platform, holding a cigarette. He gestured for him to follow.

Leo reached the area where the snow had been trodden down. There were criss-crossing boot tracks in all directions. He entered the forest, walking for a couple of minutes, arriving at roughly the area where he supposed the body must have laid. He crouched down. Aleksandr caught up with him. Leo looked up.

—*You know what happened here?*

—*I was the one who saw Ilinaya running to the station. She was badly beaten up, shaking – she couldn't speak for a while. I called the militia.*

—*Ilinaya?*

—*She found the body, stumbled across it. Her and the man she was with.*

The couple in the forest – Leo had known there was something wrong.

—*Why was she beaten up?*

Aleksandr looked nervous.

—*She's a prostitute. The man she was with that night is an important Party official. Please, don't ask me any more.*

Leo understood. This official wanted his name kept out of all the paperwork. But could he be a suspect in the murder of the young girl? Leo nodded at the young man, trying to reassure him.

—*I won't mention you, I promise.*

Leo's hand pushed through the thin sheet of snow.

—*The girl's mouth was filled with soil, loose soil. Imagine I was struggling with you, right here, and I reached out to grab something to stuff into your mouth because I'm afraid you're going to scream, I'm afraid someone's going to hear you.*

Leo's fingers hit the ground. It was hard, like the surface of a stone. He tried another place, then another and another. There was no loose soil. The ground was frozen solid.

18 March

Standing outside Hospital 379, Leo reread the autopsy report, the main points of which he'd copied longhand from the original:

> *Multiple stab wounds*
> *Blade indeterminate length*
> *Extensive damage to the torso and internal organs*
> *Raped either before or after death*
> *Mouth was full of soil but she did not suffocate, her nasal passage was clear. The soil was to some other purpose – to silence her?*

Leo had circled the last point. Since the ground was frozen the killer must have brought the soil with him. He must have planned the murder. There was intention, preparation. But why bring soil at all? It was a cumbersome means to silence someone, a rag, or cloth or even a hand would have been far easier. With no answers Leo had decided to belatedly take Fyodor's advice. He was going to see the body for himself.

When he'd asked where her body was being kept he'd been told to go to Hospital 379. Leo hadn't expected forensic laboratories, pathologists or a dedicated morgue. He knew there was no specialized apparatus for dealing with wrongful death. How could there be when there was no wrongful death? In the hospital the militia were forced to canvass for a doctor's spare moment, such as a meal break or ten minutes before surgery. These doctors, with no training beyond their own medical qualifications, would take an educated guess at what might have happened to the victim. The autopsy report Leo had read was based on notes taken during one of these snatched sessions with a doctor. The notes would have been typed up several days later by a different person altogether. There could be little doubt that much of the truth had been lost along the way.

379 was one of the most famous hospitals in the country and reportedly one of the finest free-to-all hospitals in the world. Situated at the end of Chkalova Street, the hospital was spread over several hectares with landscaped grounds stretching into the forest. Leo was impressed. This was no mere propaganda project. Plenty of money had been invested in these facilities and he could understand why dignitaries reportedly travelled many kilometres to recuperate in the picturesque surroundings. He presumed that the lavish funding was primarily intended to ensure that the Volga's workforce was kept healthy and productive.

At reception he asked if he could speak to a doctor, explaining that he needed help with the examination of a murder victim, a young girl they had in their morgue. The receptionist seemed uncomfortable with the request, asking if it was urgent and wondering if he couldn't come back at a less busy time. Leo understood: this man wanted nothing to do with the case.

—*It's urgent.*

The man reluctantly moved off to see who was available.

Leo's fingers tapped against the front desk. He was uneasy, glancing over his shoulder at the entrance. His visit was unauthorized, independent. What did he hope to achieve? His job was to find evidence confirming a suspect's guilt, not question the guilt itself. Though he'd been exiled from the prestigious world of political crime to the dirty secret of conventional crime, the process was much the same. He'd dismissed the death of Fyodor's little boy as an accident not because of any evidence but because the Party line necessitated a dismissal. He'd made arrests based upon a list of names given to him, names drawn up behind closed doors. That had been his method. Leo wasn't naive enough to think that he could change the direction of the investigation. He had no authority. Even if he'd been the top-ranking officer he couldn't reverse the proceedings. A course had been set, a suspect chosen. It was inevitable that Babinich was going to be found guilty and inevitable that he was going to die. The system didn't allow for deviation or admissions of fallibility. Apparent efficiency was far more important than the truth.

And what did it have to do with him, anyway? This wasn't his town. These weren't his people. He hadn't pledged to the girl's parents that he'd find the killer. He hadn't known the girl or been touched by the story of her life. What's more, the suspect was a danger to society – he'd taken a baby. These were excellent reasons for doing nothing and there was one more reason besides:

What difference can I make?

The receptionist returned with a man in his early forties, Dr Tyapkin, who agreed to show Leo down to the morgue as long as it didn't involve any paperwork and on the condition that his name didn't show up on any documents.

As they walked the doctor expressed doubts as to whether the girl's body was still there.

—*We don't keep them for long unless we're asked to. We were under the impression the militia had all the information they required.*

—Did you carry out the initial examination?

—No. But I've heard about the murder. I thought you'd already caught the man responsible.

—Yes, it's possible.

—I hope you don't mind me asking but I haven't seen you before.

—I arrived recently.

—Where are you from?

—Moscow.

—Transferred here?

—Yes.

—I was sent here three years ago, also from Moscow. No doubt you're disappointed to be here?

Leo remained silent.

—Yes, don't answer. At the time I was disappointed. I had a reputation, acquaintances, family. I was good friends with Professor Vovsi. I felt coming here was a demotion. Of course, it turned out to be a blessing.

Leo recognized the name – Professor Vovsi was one of many leading Jewish doctors arrested. His arrest and the arrest of his colleagues had marked the acceleration of a Jewish purge driven by Stalin. Plans had been drawn up. Leo had seen the papers. The removal of key Jewish figures within influential spheres was to be followed by wider purge, targeting any Jewish citizens whether they were prominent or not, plans cut short by Stalin's death.

Unaware of his companion's train of thought, Tyapkin blithely continued.

—I was worried I was being sent to some rural health clinic. But 379 has become the envy of the region. If anything it's a little too successful. Many of the mill-workers prefer a night in our clean beds with inside toilets and running water to their own homes. We got wise to the fact that not everyone was as ill as they claimed.

Some of them went as far as cutting off part of a finger in order to guarantee a week in here. The only solution was to have MGB officers police the wards. It wasn't that we didn't sympathize with the mill-workers. We've all seen their homes. But if overall productivity fell due to illness then we'd be accused of neglect. Keeping people healthy has become a matter of life and death not just for the patients but for us doctors as well.

—I understand.

—*Were you a member of the Moscow militia?*

Should Leo admit to being a member of the MGB or lie and pretend he was merely a member of the militia? A lie would be easier. He didn't want to ruin the doctor's talkative mood.

—*Yes, I was.*

The morgue was in the basement, built deep into ground that was frozen throughout the long winter. As a result the corridors were naturally cold. Tyapkin led Leo to a large room with a tiled floor and a low ceiling. On one side there was a rectangular vat, shaped like a small swimming pool. On the far side of the room there was a steel door which led through to the morgue itself.

—*Unless relatives can make arrangements we incinerate bodies within twelve hours. The TB victims are incinerated within an hour. We don't have much need for storage. Wait here, I'll be back.*

The doctor unlocked the steel door and entered the morgue. Waiting, Leo approached the vat, peering over the edge. It was filled with a dark, gelatinous liquid. He was unable to see anything except his own reflection. The surface was still, black, although from the stains on the concrete sides he could see it was in fact dark orange. On the side there was a hook, a long metal pole with a barbed prong on the end. He picked it up, tentatively prodding the surface. Like syrup, it broke and then re-formed, becoming smooth once again. Leo sunk the hook deeper, this time feeling something move — something heavy. He pushed down harder. A naked body rose to the surface, slowly rotating one hundred and eighty degrees, before sinking again. Tyapkin emerged from the morgue pushing a gurney.

—*Those bodies are going to be packed in ice and shipped to Sverdlovsk for dissection. They have a medical college there. I've found your girl.*

Larisa Petrova lay on her back. Her skin was pale, criss-crossed with blue veins as thin as spider's web. Her hair was blonde. A large part of the fringe had been unevenly cut off: the part Varlam had taken. Her mouth was no longer stuffed with soil — that had been removed — but her jaw was still open, locked in the same position. Her teeth and tongue were dirty, stained brown with the remnants of earth that had been forced in.

—*There was soil in her mouth.*

—*Was there? I'm sorry, this is the first time I've seen her body.*

—*Her mouth was stuffed with soil.*

—*Perhaps the doctor washed it out in order to examine her throat.*

—*It hasn't been kept?*

—*I would think it very unlikely.*

The girl's eyes were open. They were blue. Perhaps her mother had been transferred from a town near the Finnish border, from one of the Baltic regions. Recalling the superstition that the face of a murderer was captured on the surface of a victim's eye Leo leaned closer, studying the pale blue eyes. Suddenly embarrassed, he stood up straight. Tyapkin smiled.

—*We all check — doctors and detectives alike. It doesn't matter if our brains tell us that there'll be nothing there, we all want to make sure. Of course it would make your job a whole lot easier if it was true.*

—If it was true then murderers would always cut out their victims' eyes.

Having never studied a dead body before, at least with any forensic interest, Leo was unsure how to proceed. To his mind the mutilation was so frenzied it could only be the work of someone insane. Her torso had been ripped apart. He'd seen enough. Varlam Babinich fitted the bill. He must have brought the soil for his own incomprehensible reasons.

Leo was ready to leave but Tyapkin, having come all the way down to the basement, seemed to be in no hurry. He leaned closer, staring at what appeared to be nothing more than a savaged mess of flesh and tissue. Using the tip of his pen he probed into the mangled midriff, examining the wounds.

—Can you tell me what the report said?

Leo took out his notes and read them aloud. Tyapkin continued his examination.

—That fails to mention her stomach is missing. It's been cut out, severed from the oesophagus.

—How precise, I mean in terms of . . .

—You mean did a doctor do this?

The doctor smiled, remarking:

—Possibly but the cuts are ragged, not surgical. Not skilled. Although I would be surprised if this was the first time they'd handled a knife, at least to cut flesh. The cuts aren't skilful but they are confident. They're targeted, not random.

—This might not be the first child that he's killed?

—I'd be surprised.

Leo touched his forehead and found that despite the cold he was sweating. How could the two deaths – Fyodor's little boy and this girl – have anything to do with each other?

—How large would her stomach have been?

Above the girl's torso Tyapkin indicated a rough outline of a stomach's shape with his pen tip. He asked:

—*Was it not found nearby?*

—*No.*

It was either missed in the search which seemed unlikely or it had been taken away by the killer.

Leo remained silent for a moment then asked:

—*Was she raped?*

Tyapkin examined the girl's vagina.

—*She wasn't a virgin.*

—*But that doesn't mean she was raped.*

—*She'd had previous sexual encounters?*

—*That's what I'm told.*

—*There's no trauma to her genitals. No bruising, no incisions. Also notice that the injuries weren't targeted at her sexual organs. There are no cuts to the breasts or to her face. The man who did this was interested in a narrow band below her ribcage and above her vagina, her guts – her digestive organs. It looks savage but actually it's quite controlled.*

Leo had rushed to the conclusion that this was a frenzied attack. The blood and mutilation represented chaos to his mind. But it was no such thing. It was ordered, precise, planned.

—*Do you label the bodies when you bring them in – for identification purposes?*

—*Not that I'm aware.*

—*What is that?*

Around the girl's ankle was a loop of string. It had been tied in a tight noose and a small length drooped down off the gurney. It looked like a pauper's anklet. There were burn marks where the string had rubbed against the skin.

Tyapkin saw him first. General Nesterov was standing at the

door. It was impossible to say how long he'd been there, watching them. Leo stepped away from the body.

—*I came here to familiarize myself with procedure.*

Nesterov addressed Tyapkin.

—*Would you excuse us?*

—*Yes, of course.*

Tyapkin glanced at Leo, as though wishing him luck, before moving away. Nesterov approached. As a crude way of deflecting attention, Leo began summarizing the recent observations.

—*The original report doesn't mention that her stomach has been removed. We have a specific question to put to Varlam: why did he cut out her stomach and what did he do with it afterwards?*

—*What are you doing in Voualsk?*

Nesterov was now standing opposite Leo. The girl's body was in between them.

—*I was transferred here.*

—*Why?*

—*I can't say.*

—*I think you're still MGB.*

Leo remained silent. Nesterov continued.

—*That doesn't explain why you'd be so interested in this murder. We released Mikoyan without charge, as we were instructed to.*

Leo had no idea who Mikoyan was.

—*Yes, I know.*

—*He had nothing to do with this girl's murder.*

Mikoyan must be the name of the Party official. He'd been protected. But was a man who beat a prostitute the same man who murdered this young girl? Leo didn't think it likely. Nesterov continued.

—*I haven't arrested Varlam because he said the wrong thing, or forgot to attend a march in Red Square. I arrested him because he killed that girl, because he's dangerous and because this town is safer with him in custody.*

—*He didn't do it.*

Nesterov scratched the side of his face.

—*Whatever it is that you've been sent here to do, remember that you're not in Moscow anymore. Here, we have an arrangement. My men are safe. None of them have ever or will ever be arrested. If you do anything to endanger my team, if you report anything which undermines my authority, if you disobey an order, if you derail a prosecution, if you portray my officers as incompetent, if you make any denouncements regarding my men: if you do any of these things, I'll kill you.*

20 March

Raisa touched the window frame. The nails that had been hammered in to keep the bedroom window shut had all been prised out. She turned around, moving to the door and opening it. In the hallway she could hear noise from the restaurant downstairs but there was no sign of Basarov. It was late in the evening, his busiest time. Shutting the door and locking it, Raisa returned to the window, opening it and glancing down. Directly below was a sloping roof, part of the kitchen. The snow had been disturbed where Leo had climbed down. She was furious. Having survived by the thinnest of margins, he was now gambling with both their lives.

Today had been Raisa's second day at Secondary School 151. The school's director, Vitali Kozlovich Kapler, a man in his late forties, had been more than happy with Raisa joining his staff since she'd be taking over many of his lessons enabling him, he'd claimed, to catch up with his paperwork. Whether her arrival was actually freeing him up to do other work or just allowing him to do less work, Raisa couldn't say for sure. On the basis of first impressions he seemed like a man who preferred bookwork to teaching. But she'd been more than happy to start work immediately. From the handful of classes she'd taught so far she'd found the children less politically savvy than students in Moscow. They didn't break into applause at the mention of key Party figures, they weren't fiercely competitive about proving their loyalty to the Party and generally they seemed much more like children. They were made up of a patchwork of different backgrounds, families plucked from all corners of the country — their collective experiences wildly contrasting. The same was true of the staff. Almost all of the teachers had been transferred to Voualsk from different regions. Having experienced a similar upheaval to the one she'd just gone through they treated her nicely enough. They were suspicious of her, of course. Who was she? Why was she here? Was she all that she seemed? But she didn't mind, these were questions everyone asked of each other. For the first time since arriving in this town Raisa could imagine creating a life here.

She'd lingered at the school until late in the evening, reading, preparing for her lessons. School 151 was considerably more comfortable than a noisy room above a stinking restaurant. The shabby conditions had been intended as a punishment and while they bothered Leo they were an ineffective weapon against her. Above all else she was supremely adaptable. She had no attachment to buildings or cities or belongings. These sentiments had been taken from her, stripped out the day she'd witnessed the destruction of her childhood home. During the first years of the war, seventeen years old, she'd been foraging in the forest, mushrooms in one pocket, berries in the other, when shells had begun to fall. They'd landed not near her but in the distance. Climbing the tallest tree, feeling the vibrations through the trunk, she'd perched on a high branch, like a bird, watching as several kilometres away her home town had been transformed into brick dust and smoke, a town literally flung up into the sky. The horizon had disappeared beneath a man-made fog, beaten up from the ground. The destruction was too swift, too widespread, too complete for her to have felt even the slightest hope for her family. After the shelling had finished she'd climbed down from the tree and walked back through the forest in a state of shock, her right pocket dripping juice from the crushed berries. Her eyes had streamed: not tears of sadness, for she hadn't cried then or since, but a reaction to the dust. Coughing on an acrid cloud, all that remained of her home and family, she'd realized that the shells hadn't been fired from the German line, they'd whistled overhead, direct from the Russian front line. Later, as a refugee, she'd heard confirmation that their country's army had instructions to destroy any towns and villages which might fall into German hands. The complete annihilation of her childhood home had been a:

Precautionary measure.

With those words any deaths could be justified. Better to destroy your own people than there be a chance a German soldier might find a loaf of bread. There were no qualms, no apologies and no questions allowed. To object to the killings was treason. And the lessons her parents had taught her about love and affection, the lessons a child learns from watching and listening and living around two people in love, were pushed to the back of her mind. That behaviour belonged to a different time. Having a home – a sense of place: only children held onto such dreams.

Stepping back from the window, Raisa was struggling to remain calm. Leo had begged her to stay with him, detailing the risks in leaving. She had agreed for no other reason than this was her best bet, not much of one, but the best all the same. And now he was jeopardizing their second chance. If they were to survive in this new town they had to remain inconspicuous, do nothing out of the ordinary – say nothing and provoke no one. They were almost certainly under observation. Basarov was almost certainly an informer. Vasili would most probably have agents in the town spying on them, just waiting for a reason to go the extra distance, to upgrade their punishment from exile to internment to execution.

Raisa turned the light off. In the dark she stood, staring out of the window. She could see no one outside. If there were agents working surveillance they'd almost certainly be downstairs. Maybe that's why the window had been secured. She would have to make sure Leo brought back the nails so they could be replaced. Basarov might check them when they were at work. She put on her gloves and coat and climbed out of the window, lowering herself onto the icy roof, trying not to make a sound. She closed the window behind her and clambered down to the ground. She had made Leo swear to one condition — they were to be equals as they'd never been equals before. Yet he'd already gone back on his word. If he thought that she would silently stand by him — the obedient, supportive wife — while he endangered her life for his own personal reasons, he was mistaken.

Same Day

An area with a radius of roughly five hundred metres from the point where Larisa's body had been found had been searched as part of the official investigation. Even without any experience in murder investigations that area seemed small to Leo. Nothing had been discovered except the girl's clothes, discarded some forty or so paces from the body deeper into the forest. Why were her clothes – her shirt, skirt, hat, jacket and gloves – located in a neat pile so far from her body? The clothes showed no trace of blood, they bore no knife marks, no slashes or cuts. Larisa Petrova had either been undressed or she'd undressed herself. Perhaps she'd tried to run away, towards the edge of the forest, only to be caught just before the clearing. If that was true she'd been running naked. The killer must have persuaded her to accompany him, maybe offering money for sex. Once hidden in the relative depths of the forest, once she'd taken her clothes off, he'd attacked. But Leo was finding it difficult to apply logic to this crime. The incomprehensible details – the soil, the removal of the stomach, the string – were alien to him and yet at the same time he couldn't stop thinking about them.

There was little chance of finding anything new regarding Larisa's death, even allowing for incompetence and oversight. Therefore Leo was in the conflicted position of needing to find a second body. During the winter these forests would be deserted, a body could lie here for months, preserved as Larisa's body had been preserved. Leo had reason to believe she wasn't the first victim. The doctor had suggested the killer knew what he was doing, that he had a competence and assuredness that came from practice. The method suggested a routine, a routine suggested a sequence. And then, of course, there was the death of Arkady – a fact that Leo held in abeyance at this time.

Searching by a combination of moonlight and discreet use of his flashlight, Leo's life depended on being undetected. He believed the general's death threat absolutely. However, his need for secrecy had received a setback when the man working in the train station, Aleksandr, had seen him walking into the woods. He had called out and Leo, unable to think of a plausible lie, was forced to tell the truth, saying that he was collecting evidence regarding the young girl's murder. He'd then asked Aleksandr not to mention this to anyone, claiming that it would compromise the investigation. Aleksandr had agreed and wished him luck, remarking that he'd always presumed the killer had been on a train journey. Why else was the body so near the station? Someone who lived in the town would know far more secluded areas of forest. Leo had agreed that the location was suggestive, making a mental note to himself to check up on this man. Though he seemed nice enough the appearance of innocence counted for little. Although, Leo mused, innocence didn't count for much either.

Using a map stolen from the militia's office, Leo had divided the forests surrounding the railway station into four areas. He found nothing in the first area, which was where the victim's body had been found. Much of the ground had been trampled under hundreds of boots. Not even the bloody snow remained, removed no doubt as part of the effort to erase all trace of this crime. As far as

Leo could tell, the remaining three areas hadn't been searched: the snow was untouched. It had taken him an hour or so to cover the second grid, by which time his fingers were numb with cold. However, the advantage of the snow was that he could move relatively quickly, scanning large sweeps of ground for footprints, using his own tracks to mark sections that he'd covered.

Having almost finished the third area he paused. He could hear footsteps – the crunch of snow. Turning the flashlight off, he moved behind a tree, crouching down. But he couldn't hide – they seemed to be following his tracks. Should he run? That was his only chance.

—*Leo?*

He stood up, turning on his flashlight. It was Raisa.

Leo lowered the beam out of her face.

—*Were you followed?*

—*No.*

—*Why are you here?*

—*I'm here to ask you that question.*

—*I told you. A little girl was murdered, they have a suspect but I don't think—*

Raisa interrupted, impatient, abrupt.

—*You don't think he's guilty?*

—*No.*

—*And since when has that mattered to you?*

—*Raisa, I'm just trying—*

—*Leo, stop, because I don't think I can stomach you telling me you're here doing the right thing, motivated by the principles of justice, or honour. Let's be blunt. This is going to end badly and when it ends badly for you, it ends badly for me.*

—*You want me to do nothing?*

Raisa became angry.

*—I'm supposed to bow down to this personal investigation of
yours? There are innocent people suffering all across this country and
there's nothing I can do about it except try and not be one of them.*

*—You believe that keeping our heads down, doing nothing wrong,
that protects us? You did nothing wrong before, they wanted to
execute you as a traitor. Doing nothing is no guarantee we won't
be arrested anyway – I've learnt that lesson.*

*—But you're like a child with a new fact. Everyone knows there
are no guarantees. It's about risk. And this is an unacceptable one.
You think if you can catch one genuinely guilty person all those
innocent men and women you've arrested will just fade away? This
isn't about any little girl, it's about you.*

*—You hate me when I toe the line. You hate me when I do the
right thing.*

Leo turned the flashlight off. He didn't want her to see him
upset. Of course, she was correct, everything she said was true.
Their fates were stitched together; he had no right to embark on
this investigation without her approval. And he was in no position
to argue morality.

*—Raisa, I don't believe they'll ever leave us alone. At a guess
they'll wait a couple of months, maybe a year, between my arrival
here and my arrest.*

—You don't know that.

*—They don't leave people alone. Perhaps they need to construct
a case against me. Perhaps they just want me to rot in obscurity
before finishing me off. But I don't have long. And this is how
I want to spend that time, trying to find the man who did this.
He needs to be caught. I appreciate that doesn't help you. However,
there's a way for you to survive. Just before I'm arrested they'll
double the surveillance. At this point, you should go to them, feed
them some story about me, make a show of betraying me.*

—*What am I supposed to do until then? Sit in that room and wait? Lie for you? Cover for you?*

—*I'm sorry.*

Raisa shook her head, turned around and walked back towards town. Alone, Leo switched the flashlight on. His energy was sapped, his movements sluggish – his thoughts were no longer on the case. Was this nothing but a selfish, futile enterprise? He hadn't gone far when he once more heard the sound of footsteps in the snow. Raisa had returned.

—*You're sure this man's killed before?*

—*Yes. And if we find another victim the case reopens. The evidence against Varlam Babinich is specific to this girl. If there's a second murder, the case against him falls apart.*

—*You said this boy Varlam had learning difficulties. Sounds like a perfect person to blame for any crime. They might just blame him for both murders.*

—*You're right. That is a risk. But a second body is the only chance I have of reopening this case.*

—*So, if we find another body, you have an investigation. If we don't, if we find nothing, you promise to let this drop.*

—*Yes.*

—*All right, then. You lead.*

Awkward, uncertain, they set off, deeper into the forest.

After almost thirty minutes, walking alongside each other, Raisa pointed ahead. Crossing their path were two sets of tracks, an adult's and a child's, side by side. There was no sign of any disturbance. The child hadn't been pulled along. The adult's boot prints were enormous and deep. He was a tall, heavy man. The child's footsteps were faint. The child was small, young.

Raisa turned to Leo.

—*These might continue all the way to some rural village.*

—*They might.*

She understood. Leo was going to follow them to their end.

They'd been walking for some time, following the tracks, with no sign of anything being amiss. Leo had begun to wonder if Raisa was right. Maybe there was an innocent explanation. Suddenly he stopped walking. Up ahead an area of snow had been flattened, as though someone had lain down. Leo moved forward. The footprints became confused, as if there'd been a struggle. The adult had walked away from the disturbance while the child's tracks went off in the opposite direction, their footsteps unevenly spaced, ragged – the child had been running. From the impressions in the snow it was clear that the child had fallen over, there was a single hand print. But the child had got up and continued to run before falling again. Again the child had struggled on the ground although it was impossible to work out with whom or what they'd been struggling. There were no other footsteps. Whatever had happened here, the child had managed to get up, running once more. Desperation could be read on the snow. However, the adult's footsteps were still nowhere to be seen. Then, several metres up ahead, they reappeared. Deep boot prints emerged out of the trees. Yet something was odd – the adult was running in zigzags, this way and that, inaccurately converging on the child's position. None of it made any sense. Having walked away from the child the man had changed his mind and run erratically back towards him. Judging from the angles of the footprints he had caught up at some point past the next tree.

Raisa stopped, staring ahead at the point where the tracks would meet. Leo touched her on the shoulder.

—*Stay here.*

Leo moved forward, stepping around the tree. He saw the bloody snow first, then the bare legs, the mutilated torso. It was a young boy, maybe no more than thirteen or fourteen years old. He was small, slight. Just as the girl had been on her back, so was he, staring up at the sky. There was something in his mouth. Out of the corner of his eye Leo caught sight of movement. He turned to see Raisa standing behind him, staring down at the boy's body.

—*Are you OK?*

Slowly, Raisa raised her hand to her mouth. She gave Leo the smallest of nods.

Leo knelt down beside the boy. Tied around his ankle was string. The string had been cut: only a short length trailed in the snow. The boy's skin was red where the string had rubbed, cutting into his flesh. Steeling himself, Leo turned to look at the boy's face. His mouth had been stuffed with soil. It gave him the appearance of screaming. Unlike Larisa there was no layer of snow over his body. He'd been killed after her, maybe within the last couple of weeks. Leo leant over, reaching towards the boy's mouth and taking a pinch of the dark soil. He rubbed it between his finger and thumb. It was coarse and dry. The texture wasn't like earth. There were large, uneven chunks. Under the pressure of his fingers the fragments broke apart. It wasn't soil at all. It was bark from the trunk of a tree.

22 March

Some thirty-six hours after he and Raisa had found the boy's body, Leo still hadn't reported the discovery. Raisa was right. Instead of throwing the case open the second murder could be blamed on Varlam Babinich. The boy had no sense of self-preservation, he was open to suggestion – whisper something in his ear and he was likely to go along with it. He offered a convenient and swift solution to two horrific murders. Why look for a second suspect when there was one already in custody? It was unlikely Babinich would have an alibi, given that staff working at the *internat* wouldn't remember his movements or be prepared to vouch for him. The charges would almost certainly jump from one count of murder to two.

Leo couldn't simply announce the discovery of the young boy's body. First he had to establish that Varlam Babinich knew nothing about it. That was the only way to save him: to collapse the proceedings against the militia's prime suspect – their only suspect. However, this was exactly what Nesterov had warned Leo against doing. It would mean that a criminal case would be opened without any suspect: a criminal case against persons unknown. The problem was exacerbated by the fact that Babinich had already confessed. Local MGB operatives would almost certainly become involved if they heard that a confession had been discredited by the militia. Confessions were the bedrock of the judicial system and their sanctity needed to be protected at all costs. If anyone else found out about the second murder before Leo could establish Babinich's ignorance, they might decide that it was far easier, simpler and safer for everyone involved to amend the confession and spoon-feed the suspect the necessary details — thirteen-year-old boy stabbed in the woods, on the opposite side of the tracks, several weeks ago. This solution was neat, efficient and upset no one, not even Babinich himself since he probably wouldn't understand what was going on. There was only one way to guarantee that news of the second body didn't filter through and that had been for Leo to remain silent. On returning to the train station he hadn't raised the alarm or called his superior officers. He hadn't reported the murder or set up a crime scene. He'd done nothing. To Raisa's bewilderment he'd asked her not to say anything, explaining that he couldn't get access to Babinich until the following morning, which meant leaving the body out in the woods for the night. If the boy was to have a chance at justice then he couldn't see that there was any other option.

Babinich was no longer in the militia's care — he'd been handed over to the lawyers from procurator's office. A team of *sledovatyel* had already obtained a confession to the murder of Larisa Petrova. Leo had read the document. There were differences between the confession obtained by the militia and the one obtained by the *sledovatyel* but this hardly mattered: they were broadly the same — he was guilty. In any case, the militia's document wasn't official and wouldn't be referred to in court: their job had only been to point out the most likely suspect. By the time Leo had made his request to speak to the prisoner the investigation had all but been completed. They were ready to go to trial.

Leo had been forced to argue that the suspect might have killed more girls and that before he was taken to trial the militia and *sledovatyel* should jointly question him in order to establish if there were any more victims. Nesterov had cautiously agreed: it was something they should've done already. He had insisted upon joining the interrogation, which had suited Leo fine; the more witnesses the better. With two *sledovatyel* and two militia officers present Babinich had denied knowing anything about any other victims. Afterwards the team had agreed that it was unlikely the accused had killed anyone else. As far as they were aware, there were no other missing girls with blonde hair, which was the motive in this case. Having achieved mutual agreement that Babinich was unlikely to have killed anyone else, Leo had feigned uncertainty, claiming they should search the forests just in case, widening the search to include any part of the forests within a thirty-minute walk of the town's perimeter. Sensing that Leo had an agenda, Nesterov's uneasiness had grown. In ordinary circumstances, had Leo not been connected to the MGB, his request would've been dismissed. The idea that the militia's resources should be spent actively looking for a crime was ridiculous. But as much as Nesterov mistrusted Leo he'd seemed afraid to oppose the suggestion, afraid that to do so would be dangerous since the order might be coming from Moscow. The search had been arranged to take place today: thirty-six hours after Leo and Raisa had found the boy's body.

During these past hours the memory of the boy lying in the snow had dominated Leo's thoughts. He'd suffered nightmares where a boy in the middle of the forest, naked, disembowelled, had asked why they'd abandoned him.

Why did you leave me?

The boy in the nightmare was Arkady — Fyodor's son.

Raisa had told Leo that she found it hard concentrating at school knowing there was a dead child in the woods and pretending nothing was wrong. She felt an overwhelming urge to warn the children, somehow alert the town — the parents knew nothing of the danger. None of them had reported a child missing. The school records showed no unexplained absences. Who was the boy in the woods? She wanted to name him, find his family. All Leo could do was to ask her to wait. Despite her unease she'd deferred to Leo's judgement that this was the only way to free an innocent young man and initiate a hunt for the person responsible. The ludicrousness of the reasoning made it sound entirely plausible.

*

Having recruited workers from the lumber mills to make up the search teams, Nesterov split the men and women into seven groups of ten. Leo was assigned to a group searching the forests beside State Hospital 379, on the opposite side of town from where the body was located. This was ideal since it would be better if he didn't make the discovery. There was also a possibility that there were more bodies to be found. He was convinced that these victims weren't the first.

The ten members of Leo's team broke down into two groups of three and one group of four. Leo was working with Nesterov's deputy, a man instructed, no doubt, to keep an eye on him. They were joined by a woman, a mill worker. It took them the entire day to complete their portion of the search, several square kilometres through difficult snow drifts which needed to be prodded with sticks to make sure there was nothing underneath them. They found no body. Reassembling back at the hospital, none of the other two teams had found anything either. These forests were empty. Leo was impatient to know what was happening on the other side of town.

*

Nesterov was standing by the edge of the forest, near the railway maintenance cabin which had been commandeered and turned into a temporary headquarters. Leo approached, trying to seem unhurried and indifferent. Nesterov asked:

—*What have you found?*

—*Nothing.*

And after a calculated pause Leo added:

—*What about here?*

—*No, nothing, nothing at all.*

Leo's poise of cool indifference fell away from him. Aware that his reaction was being watched, he turned away trying to work out what could have gone wrong. How had they missed the body? Was it still there? The tracks were clearly visible. It was possible that the search perimeter hadn't stretched as far as the body but it must have stretched as far as the tracks. Was it that the team hadn't followed them to their end? If they were unmotivated, then they might have given up once the tracks continued past the edge of their designated search area. Most of the teams were returning: there wasn't much time before the entire operation would be concluded with the boy's body still in the woods.

Leo began questioning the returning men. Two militia officers, neither of them much older than eighteen, had been part of the team searching the area of the forests closest to where the body lay. They admitted there'd been tracks but they'd appeared to be innocent since they were four sets of prints rather than two: they'd presumed that they were nothing more than a family on an expedition. Leo had neglected to take into consideration that he and Raisa had made an additional set of tracks running parallel to those of the victim and the murderer. Fighting back his exasperation he forgot that he no longer had any authority and ordered the two men back into the woods to follow the tracks to their conclusion. The officers weren't convinced. The tracks might go on for kilometres. And more to the point: who was Leo to give orders?

Leo had no option but to go to Nesterov, illustrating with the use of a map that there were no nearby villages in that direction, arguing that the tracks were suspicious. But Nesterov agreed with the two young officers. The fact there were four sets of prints made it an unlikely trail and not worth following. Unable to contain his frustration, Leo said:

—*I'll go alone, then.*

Nesterov stared at him.

—*We'll both go.*

Leo was following his own footsteps deeper and deeper into the forests, accompanied only by Nesterov. Belatedly he realized that he was in danger, unarmed and alone with this man who wanted him dead. If he was going to be killed this was a good place. Nesterov seemed calm. He was smoking.

—*Tell me, Leo, what are we going to find at the end of these tracks?*

—*I have no idea.*

—*But these are your footprints.*

Nesterov pointed to the tracks in front of them and then at the tracks Leo had just made. They were identical.

—*We're going to find the body of a dead child.*

—*Which you've already discovered?*

—*Two days ago.*

—*But you didn't report it?*

—*I wanted to establish that Varlam Babinich knew nothing about this murder.*

—*You were worried we'd blame him for the murder?*

—*I'm still worried.*

Was Nesterov going to draw his gun? Leo waited. Nesterov finished his cigarette and continued walking. They said nothing more until they reached the body. The boy lay exactly as Leo remembered, on his back, naked, his mouth full of bark, his torso a savaged mess. Leo stood back, watching as Nesterov made an examination. He took his time. Leo could see that his superior officer was outraged by the crime. That was of some comfort.

Finally, Nesterov approached Leo:

—*I want you to go back, call the procurator's officer. I'm going to stay here with the body.*

Remembering Leo's concerns, Nesterov added:

—*It's obvious that Varlam Babinich had nothing to do with this murder.*

—*I agree.*

—*These are two separate cases.*

Leo stared blankly, bewildered by the assertion.

—*But these children were murdered by the same man.*

—*A girl has been sexually assaulted and murdered. A boy has been sexually assaulted and murdered. These are different crimes. These are different depravities.*

—*We don't know the boy was sexually assaulted.*

—*Look at him!*

—*I don't believe, nor does the doctor I spoke to, that the girl was sexually assaulted.*

—*She was naked.*

—*But they both had bark, tree bark, ground-up tree bark stuffed into their mouths.*

—Larisa's mouth was stuffed with soil.

—That's wrong.

—Varlam Babinich has admitted stuffing her mouth with soil.

—Which is why he can't have killed her – the ground is frozen. If it was soil where did he get it from? Her mouth was stuffed with bark just as this boy's mouth was stuffed with bark. The bark was prepared in advance, I don't know why.

—Babinich has confessed.

—He'd admit anything if you asked him enough times.

—Why are you so sure this is the same killer? One child was murdered close to the station: careless, reckless, barely out of sight. The screams could have been heard by the passengers. It was an idiot's crime and an idiot has confessed. But this child has been led almost an hour's walk into the forest. Care has been taken, so that no one could interrupt him. This is a different man.

—Who knows what happened with the girl, maybe he wanted to walk further into the woods and she changed her mind so he had to kill her there. Why do they both have string around their ankles?

—This is a different crime.

—Tell me you're not so desperate to prosecute that you'll say and believe anything.

—You tell me what kind of person rapes a girl, kills her, and then rapes a boy and kills him? Who is this person? I've worked in the militia for twenty years. I've never encountered such a person. I've never heard of such a person. Can you give me one example?

—The girl wasn't raped.

—You're right. There was a reason the girl was killed – she was killed for her blonde hair. She was killed by a sick man. There was a reason this boy was killed. He was killed by a different man, with a different sickness.

23 March

Aleksandr closed the ticket office, lowering the blind and sitting back in his chair. Although the office was small, no more than a couple of square metres, he liked the fact that it was his. He didn't share it with anyone nor did he have anyone overseeing his work. He had a kind of freedom, unburdened by quotas or productivity reviews. There was just one downside to having this job. Everyone who knew him presumed that he must be disappointed with how life had turned out.

Five years ago Aleksandr had been the fastest sprinter at Secondary School 151. People had believed he was destined for success on a national level, perhaps even an international one if the Soviet Union were to compete in the Olympics. Instead, he'd ended up in a sedentary job manning a ticket office, watching other people embark on journeys while he went nowhere. He'd spent years following a punishing exercise regime, winning regional competitions. And to what end? Timetables and tickets: work which could be done by anyone. He remembered the exact moment the dream came to nothing. He and his father had taken a train to Moscow, attending the selection process at the Central Army Sports Club, the CSKA – part of the Ministry of Defence. The CSKA was renowned for selecting the best athletes from all over the country and pushing them to become exceptional.

Ninety per cent of applicants were rejected. Aleksandr had raced until he was sick by the side of the track. He'd run faster than he'd ever run before, beating his personal best. He hadn't made the cut. On the return trip home his father had tried to put a positive slant on the rejection. It would motivate them to train harder, he'd make the cut next year for certain and he'd be the stronger for having been made to fight for his dream. But Aleksandr had given everything and it hadn't been enough. There'd be no next year. Though his father had continued to press, Aleksandr's heart wasn't in it and soon his father's heart wasn't in it either. Aleksandr had left school, begun work, settling into an easy routine.

It was eight in the evening by the time he finished. He left the ticket office, locking it behind him. He didn't have far to walk as he and his parents lived in an annexe built above the station. Technically speaking, his father was in charge of the station. However, his father wasn't well. No one at the hospital could say what was wrong with him except that he was overweight and drank too much. His mother was in good health and, her husband's illness aside, generally cheerful. She had reason to be – they were a fortunate family. The pay for working on the State railway was modest, the amount of *blat*, influence, relatively small. But the real advantage was the accommodation. Instead of having to share with another family they had sole use of an apartment with plumbing, hot water and insulation – as new as the station itself. In exchange they were expected to be on call twenty-four hours a day. There was a bell which could be rung from the station wired directly to the apartment. If there was a night train or an early morning train they had to be on hand. But these were small inconveniences which, shared across the family, were more than offset by the relative comforts they enjoyed. They had an apartment easily big enough for two families. Aleksandr's sister had married a cleaner who worked at the car assembly plant, where she also worked, and they'd moved into a new apartment in a good district. They were expecting their first child. This meant that Aleksandr, at twenty-two years old, had nothing to worry about. One day he'd take over the running of the station and the annexe would be his.

In his bedroom he changed out of his uniform, put on casual clothes and sat down to eat with his parents: pea-haddock soup followed by fried *kasha*. His father was eating a small portion of cow's liver. Though expensive and extraordinarily difficult to come by, liver had been recommended by the doctors. Aleksandr's father was on a strict diet, including no alcohol, which he was convinced was making him worse. They didn't speak over dinner. His father appeared to be in some discomfort. He hardly ate. After washing the plates Aleksandr excused himself: he was going to the cinema. By this stage his father was lying down. Aleksandr kissed him goodnight, telling him not to worry, he'd get up to deal with the arrival of the first train.

There was only one cinema in Voualsk. Until three years ago there'd been none. A church had been transformed into a six-hundred-seat auditorium where a backlog of State-sponsored films were shown, many of which had been missed by the town's population. These included *The Fighters*, *Guilty Without Guilt*, *Secrets of Counter-Espionage* and *Meeting on the Elbe*, some of the most successful movies of the last ten years, all of which Aleksandr had seen several times. Since the cinema's opening it had quickly become his favourite pastime. Because of his running he'd never developed an interest in drink and he wasn't particularly social. Arriving at the foyer he saw that *Nezabyaemy God* was showing. Aleksandr had seen the movie only a couple of nights ago and numerous occasions before that. He'd found it fascinating, not the film itself particularly, but the idea of an actor playing Stalin. He wondered whether Stalin had been involved in the casting. He wondered what it must be like watching another man pretend to be you, instructing them what they were doing right and what they were doing wrong. Aleksandr walked past the foyer. He didn't join the queue, heading instead towards the park.

At the centre of Victory Park there was a statue of three bronze soldiers, fists clenched to the sky, rifles slung over their shoulders. Officially the park was closed at night. But there was no fence and the rule was never enforced. Aleksandr knew the route to take: a path away from the streets and largely out of view, hidden by the trees and the bushes. He could feel his heartbeat quicken in anticipation, as it always did, as he took a slow lap around the perimeter. It seemed that he was alone tonight and after the second lap he considered going home.

There was a man up ahead. Aleksandr stopped. The man turned to face him. A nervous pause communicated that they were both here for the same reason. Aleksandr continued forward and the man remained where he was, waiting for him to catch up. Side by side both of them glanced around, making sure they were alone, before looking at each other. The man was younger than Aleksandr, perhaps only nineteen or twenty. He appeared uncertain and at a guess Aleksandr supposed that this was his first time. Aleksandr broke the silence.

—*I know somewhere we can go.*

The young man looked around once more and then nodded, saying nothing. Aleksandr continued:

—*Follow me, keep at a distance.*

They walked separately. Aleksandr took the lead, getting a couple of hundred paces ahead. He checked. The other man was still following.

Arriving back at the train station, he checked his parents weren't at the window of their apartment. Unseen, he entered the main station building, as though he were about to catch a train. Without turning on the lights he unlocked the ticket office, going inside and leaving the door open. He pushed the chair aside. There wasn't much space but there was enough. He waited, checking his watch, wondering why the man was taking so long, before remembering that he walked fast. Finally, he heard someone enter the station. The door to the ticket booth was pushed opened. The man stepped inside and the two of them looked at each other properly for the first time. Aleksandr stepped forward to shut the door. The sound of the lock excited him. It meant they were safe. They were almost touching and yet not quite, neither of them sure who should make the first move. Aleksandr liked this moment and he waited for as long as he could bear it before leaning forward to kiss him.

Someone was hammering on the door. Aleksandr's first thought was that it must be his father – he must have seen, he must have known all along. But then he realized it wasn't coming from outside. It was this man, hammering on the door, calling out. Had he changed his mind? Who was he speaking to? Aleksandr was confused. He could hear voices outside the office. The man was no longer meek and nervous. A transformation had occurred. He was angry, disgusted. He spat in Aleksandr's face. The glob of phlegm hung on his cheek. Aleksandr wiped it away. Without thinking, without understanding what was happening, he punched the man, knocking him to the floor.

The door handle rattled. Outside a voice called:

—*Aleksandr, this is General Nesterov, the man you're with is a militia officer. I'm ordering you to open the door. Either you obey or I call your parents and bring them down here to watch as I arrest you. Your father's ill, isn't he? It would kill him to discover your crime.*

He was right – it would kill his father. Hurrying, Aleksandr tried to open the door but the office was so small that the man's slumped body was blocking the way. He had to drag him to the side before he could unlock and open the door. As soon as the door was open hands reached in, grabbing him, pulling him out of the office onto the concourse.

Leo looked at Aleksandr, the first person he'd encountered after getting off the train from Moscow, the man who'd fetched him a cigarette, the man who'd helped search the woods. There was nothing he could to do to help him.

Nesterov peered into the ticket office, staring down at his officer, still dazed on the floor, embarrassed by the fact that he'd been overpowered.

—*Get him out of there.*

Two officers went in and helped the injured officer to a car outside. Seeing what he'd done to one of his men, Nesterov's deputy cracked a blow across Aleksandr's face. Before he could hit him again Nesterov intervened.

—*That's enough.*

He circled the suspect, weighing up his words.

—*I'm disappointed to catch you doing this. I would never have thought it of you.*

Aleksandr spat blood on the floor but he didn't reply. Nesterov continued.

—*Tell me why.*

—*Why? I don't know why.*

—*You've committed a very serious crime. A judge would give you five years minimum and he wouldn't care how many times you said you were sorry.*

—*I haven't said sorry.*

—*Brave, Aleksandr, but would you be so brave if everyone found out? You'd be humiliated, disgraced. Even after serving your five years in prison you wouldn't be able to live or work here. You'd lose everything.*

Leo stepped forward.

—*Just ask him.*

—*There is a way to avoid this shame. We need a list of every man in this town who has sex with other men, men who have sex with younger men, men who have sex with boys. You will help us create this list.*

—*I don't know any others. This is my first time . . .*

—*If you choose not to help us we'll arrest you, put you on trial and invite your parents to court. Are they getting ready for bed right now? I could send one of my men to find out, bring them down.*

—*No.*

—*Work for us and maybe we won't need to mention anything to your parents. Work for us and maybe you won't need to go to trial. Maybe this disgrace can stay a secret.*

—*What is this about?*

—*The murder of a young boy. You'll be doing a public service and making amends for your crime. Will you make this list?*

Aleksandr touched the blood running out of his mouth.

—*What will happen to the men on the list?*

29 March

Leo sat on the edge of his bed contemplating how his attempt to re-launch an investigation had instead precipitated a city-wide pogrom. Over the past week the militia had rounded up one hundred and fifty homosexuals. Today alone Leo had arrested six men, bringing his count to twenty. Some had been taken from their place of work, escorted out in handcuffs while their colleagues watched. Others had been taken from their homes, their apartments, taken from their families – their wives pleading, convinced that there must be some mistake, unable to comprehend the charges.

Nesterov had reason to be pleased. Quite by chance he'd found a second undesirable: a suspect he could call *murderer* without upsetting the social theory. Murder was an aberration. These men were an aberration. It was a perfect fit. He'd been able to announce that they were now instigating the largest murder hunt ever launched by the Voualsk militia, a claim that would've cost him his career if he hadn't been targeting such an unacceptable subgroup. Short of space, offices had been converted into makeshift holding cells and interrogation rooms. Even with these improvised measures it had been necessary to lock several men in each cell with guards given clear instructions that the men needed to be watched at all times. The cause for concern had been the possibility of spontaneous incidents of sexual deviancy. No one quite knew what they were dealing with. But they were certain that were such sexual activities to take place within the militia headquarters they would undermine the establishment. It would be an affront to the principles of justice. In addition to this high level of scrutiny every officer had been timetabled to work twelve-hour shifts, with suspects questioned constantly, twenty-four hours a day. Leo had been obliged to ask the same questions again and again, picking through answers for even the smallest variation. He'd carried out this task like a dull automaton, convinced even before they'd made a single arrest that these men were innocent.

Aleksandr's list had been trawled through name by name. On producing the list he'd explained that he could create it not because he'd been promiscuous, at least not to the extent of having sexual encounters with a hundred or so men. In fact, many of the names on the list were people he'd never even met. His information came from conversations with the ten or so that he'd had sex with. Each man recounted liaisons with different men so that, added together, it was possible to draw a sexual constellation with each man knowing his place in relation to each other. Leo had listened to this explanation, a hidden world opening up, a hermetically sealed existence constructed within society at large. The integrity of the seals was critical. Aleksandr had described how men on the list met by chance in routine situations, standing in a food line buying bread, eating at the same table in a factory canteen. In these everyday surroundings casual conversation was forbidden, a glance was the most that was allowed and even that needed to be disguised. These were rules that had come about not by agreement or decree, no one needed to be told them, they arose out of self-preservation.

As soon as the first wave of arrests had begun, news of a purge must have spread throughout their ranks. The secret meeting places – no longer a secret – were abandoned. But this desperate counter-measure had been to no avail. There was the list. The seals around the world had broken. Nesterov didn't need to catch anyone in a sexually compromising act. Seeing their names in print, one after the after, and realizing that their ranks had been broken, most of the men succumbed to the pressure of this betrayal. Like U-boats which had for so long remained unseen under the water's surface, suddenly they found all their positions had been given away. As they were forced to the surface they were presented with a choice, not much of a choice but a choice all the same: they could reject the charges of sodomy and face public prosecution, certain conviction, imprisonment, etc. Or they could identify the homosexual among them responsible for this terrible crime, the murder of a young boy.

As far as Leo could ascertain, Nesterov seemed to believe that all these men suffered from a sickness of some kind. While some were sick in the mildest sense, plagued by feelings for other men as a normal person might be racked by persistent headaches, others were dangerously ill, symptoms which expressed themselves in the need for young boys. This was homosexuality in its most extreme form. The murderer was one such man.

When Leo had shown photos of the crime scene, photos of the young boy with his guts cut open, all the suspects had reacted in exactly the same way – they were horrified – or at least they appeared to be. Who could've done such a thing? It wasn't one of them, it wasn't anyone they knew. None of them had any interest in boys. Many of them had children of their own and so on the answers had gone. Every man was resolute: they knew of no killer amongst them and they wouldn't protect him if they did.

Nesterov had expected a prime suspect within a week. After a week they had nothing to show for their work except a longer list. More names were added, some merely out of spite. The list had become a brutally effective weapon. Members of the militia were adding the names of their enemies onto it, claiming the person had been mentioned in confession. Once a name was on the list it was impossible to claim innocence. So the number in custody had grown from a hundred to nearly one hundred and fifty men.

Frustrated with the lack of progress, the local MGB had suggested they take over the interrogations, shorthand for the use of torture. To Leo's dismay Nesterov had agreed. Despite floors flecked with blood there'd been no breakthrough. Nesterov had been left with little choice but to initiate prosecutions against all one hundred and fifty men, hoping this would make one of them speak. It wasn't enough that they were humiliated and disgraced and tortured: they needed to understand that they would lose their lives. They would, if the judge was so instructed, receive twenty-five years for political subversion rather than a mere five years for sodomy. Their sexuality was considered a crime against the very fabric of the nation. Faced with this prospect three men had cracked and begun pointing the finger. However, none of them had picked the same person. Refusing to accept that his line of investigation was flawed, Nesterov considered himself up against a kind of perverse, criminal solidarity – honour amongst deviants.

Exasperated, Leo had approached his superior officer.

—*These men are innocent.*

Nesterov had stared at him, puzzled.

—*All these men are guilty. The question is which one is also guilty of murder.*

*

Raisa watched as Leo kicked the heels of his boots together. Dirty chunks of snow fell to the floor. He stared down, unaware that she was in the room. She found his disappointment impossible to bear. He'd believed, sincerely believed, that his investigation stood a chance. He'd pinned his hopes on a fanciful dream of redemption: a final act of justice. It was an idea she'd mocked that night in the forest. But it had been mocked far more cruelly by the turn of events. In the pursuit of justice he'd unleashed terror. In the pursuit of a killer, one hundred and fifty men would lose their lives, if not literally, then on every other level – they'd lose their families, their homes. And she realized, seeing her husband's hunched shoulders and drawn face, that he never did anything without believing in it. There was nothing cynical or calculating about him. If this was true then he must also have believed in their marriage: he must have believed it was built on love. Steadily all the fantasies he'd created – about the State, about their relationship – had been shattered. Raisa was envious of him. Even now, even after everything that had happened, he was still able to hope. He still wanted to believe in something. She stepped forward, sitting beside him on the bed. Tentatively, she took his hand. Surprised, he looked at her but said nothing, accepting the gesture. And together they watched as the snow began to melt.

30 March

Orphanage 80 was a five-storey brick building with faded white lettering painted on the side: WORK HARD LIVE LONG. On the roof there was a long line of chimney stacks. The orphanage had once been a small factory. Dirty rags hung across the barred windows, making it impossible to see inside. Leo knocked on the door. No response; he tried the handle. It was locked. Moving to the windows he tapped on the glass. The rags were jerked back. The face of a young girl appeared for little more than a second, an apparition of filth, before the rags fell back into place. Leo was accompanied by Moiseyev, a militia officer who Leo had pegged as little more than a uniformed thug. After a long wait the main door opened. An elderly man with a fist full of brass keys stared at the two officers. Seeing their uniforms his expression changed from irritation to deference. He dropped his head slightly.

—*What can I do for you?*

—*We're here about the murdered boy.*

The main hall of the orphanage had once been the factory floor. All the machinery had been cleared and it had been converted into a dining room, not by the addition of tables and chairs, for there were none, but by the fact that the entire floor was covered with children sitting cross-legged, pressed up against each other and

261

trying to eat. Every child clutched a wooden bowl filled with what appeared to be a watery cabbage soup. However, it seemed only the eldest children had spoons. The rest either sat waiting for a spoon or drank straight from the bowl. Once a child had finished, they licked the spoon from top to bottom before passing it onto the next child.

This was Leo's first experience of a State orphanage. He stepped closer, surveying the room. It was difficult to guess how many children there were — two hundred, three hundred, aged from four to fourteen. None of the children paid Leo any attention: they were too busy eating or watching their neighbours, waiting for a spoon. No one spoke. All that could be heard was the scraping of bowls and slurping. Leo turned to the elderly man.

—*Are you the director of this institution?*

The director's office was on the first floor, looking out over a factory floor covered with children as though they were being mass-produced. In the office were several teenage boys, older than the children downstairs. They were playing cards on the director's desk. The director clapped his hands.

—*Continue this in your room, please.*

The boys stared at Leo and Moiseyev. Leo could only suppose that their irritation came from being told what to do. They had intelligent eyes, experience beyond their years. Without a word they moved together, like a pack of wild dogs, collecting up their cards, their matches —used as chips — and filed out.

Once they'd left, the director poured himself a drink and gestured for Leo and Moiseyev to take a seat. Moiseyev sat down. Leo remained standing, studying the room. There was a single metal filing cabinet. The bottom drawer had been dented by a kick. The top drawer was partially open and crumpled documents jutted out at all angles.

—*There was a young boy murdered in the forest. You've heard about this?*

—*Some other officers were here showing me photos of the boy, asking if I knew who he was. I'm afraid I don't.*

—*But you couldn't say for sure if you were missing any children?*

The director scratched his ear.

—*There are four of us looking after three hundred or so children. The children come and go. New ones arrive all the time. You must forgive our failings regarding the paperwork.*

—*Do any of the children in this facility resort to prostitution?*

—*The older ones do whatever they want. I can't keep tabs on them. Do they get drunk? Yes. Do they prostitute themselves? Quite possibly, although I don't sanction it, I'm not involved in it and I certainly don't profit from it. My job is to make sure they have something to eat and somewhere to sleep. And considering my resources I do that very well. Not that I expect any praise.*

The director showed them upstairs towards the sleeping areas. As they passed a shower room he commented:

—*You think that I'm indifferent to the children's welfare? I'm not, I do my best. I make sure they wash once a week, I make sure they're shaved and deloused once a month. I boil all their clothes. I will not have lice in my orphanage. You go to any other orphanage and the children's hair will be alive with them, their eyebrows thick with them. It's disgusting. Not here. Not that they thank me for it.*

—*Would it be possible to speak to the children on our own? They might be intimidated by your presence.*

The director smiled.

—*They won't be intimidated by me. But by all means . . .*

He gestured to the flight of stairs.

—*The older ones live on the top floor. It's very much their fiefdom up there.*

The upstairs bedrooms, tucked under the roof, contained no bed frames, just the occasional thin mattress on the floor. The older children evidently took their lunch at a time which suited them; no doubt they'd already eaten and taken the best of the food.

Leo stepped into the first room on the landing. He caught sight of a girl hiding behind the door and saw a glint of metal. She was armed with a knife. Seeing his uniform she slipped the knife away, the blade disappearing into the folds of her dress.

—*We thought you were the boys. They're not allowed in here.*

Some twenty girls, at a guess aged between fourteen and sixteen, stared at Leo with hardened faces. Leo's mind was thrown back to his promise to Anatoly Brodsky that the two daughters were safe in the care of a Moscow orphanage. It had been an empty, ignorant assurance. Leo understood that now. Brodsky had been right. Those two girls would've been better on their own, looking after each other.

—*Where do the boys sleep?*

The older boys, some of whom had been in the director's office, were huddled at the back of their room, waiting, expecting them. Leo entered the room and knelt down, placing an album of photographs on the floor in front of them.

—*I'd like you to look through these photos, tell me if any of these men have ever approached you, offered you money in return for sexual favours.*

None of the boys moved or gave any indication that his supposition was correct.

—*You haven't done anything wrong. We need your help.*

Leo opened the album, slowly turning the pages of photographs. He reached the end. The audience of teenagers had stared at the photos but given no reaction. He turned back through the pages. There was still no reaction from the boys. He was about to shut the album when a boy from the back of the group reached out and touched one of the photos.

—*This man propositioned you?*

—*Pay me.*

—*He paid you?*

—*No, you pay me and I'll tell you.*

Leo and Moiseyev clubbed together, offering the boy three roubles. The boy flicked through the album, stopping at a page and pointing to one of the photos.

—*The man looked like that man.*

—*So it wasn't this man?*

—*No, but similar.*

—*Do you know his name?*

—*No.*

—*Can you tell us anything about him?*

—*Pay me.*

Moiseyev shook his head, refusing to pay any more.

—*We could arrest you for profiteering.*

Cutting the threat short, Leo took out the last of his money, giving it to the boy.

—*That's all I have.*

—*He works at the hospital.*

Same Day

Leo drew his gun. They were on the top floor of Apartment Building 7: apartment 14 was at the end of the corridor. They'd been given the address by staff at the hospital. The suspect was off sick and had been for the past week, a length of time which would have meant, if all the MGB officers hadn't been busy with their interrogations, that he would've almost certainly been questioned. It turned out that the beginning of his sickness corresponded with the first wave of arrests against the town's homosexual population.

Leo knocked on the door. There was no response. He called out, stating their name and rank. There was no reply. Moiseyev lifted his boot, ready to kick at the lock. The door opened.

Seeing the guns pointed at him, Dr Tyapkin raised his hands and stepped back. Leo barely recognized him. This was the same man who'd helped him with the examination of the girl's body, the prestigious doctor transferred from Moscow. His hair and eyes were wild. He'd lost weight. His clothes were rumpled. Leo had seen men broken by worry; he'd seen how their muscles lost shape and strength, as if they'd been eaten up by fear.

Leo pushed the door open with his foot, surveying the apartment.

—*Are you alone?*

—*My youngest son's here. But he's asleep.*

—*How old is he?*

—Four months.

Moiseyev stepped in, smashing the metal butt of his gun against Tyapkin's nose. Tyapkin dropped to his knees, blood running into his cupped hands. Moiseyev ordered Leo.

—Search him.

Moiseyev began searching the apartment. Leo crouched down, helping Tyapkin to his feet, bringing him into the kitchen, where he sat him down on a chair.

—Where's your wife?

—Buying food . . . she'll be back soon.

—The hospital said you were sick.

—That's true, in a way. I heard about the arrests. I knew it was only a matter of time before you came to me.

—Tell me what happened.

—I was mad, there's no other explanation for it. I didn't know his age. He was young. Maybe fifteen or sixteen, I didn't want someone who'd talk to me or someone who'd tell anyone else about me. I didn't want to have to meet them again. Or see them. Or speak to them. I wanted anonymity. I reasoned no one would ever listen to an orphan. His word would count for nothing. I could give him a little money and that would be the end. I wanted someone invisible – can you understand?

Having completed a cursory search, Moiseyev re-entered the room and holstered his gun. He grabbed Tyapkin's broken nose, twisting the fractured bone right and left, causing him to scream in pain. A baby awoke in a nearby room and began to cry.

—You fuck these boys then kill them?

Moiseyev let go of Tyapkin's nose. The doctor dropped to the floor, curling up into a ball. It was some time before he could manage to speak.

—I didn't have sex with him. I didn't go through with it. I

couldn't go through with it. I asked him, I paid him, but I couldn't do it. I walked away.

—*Get to your feet. We're leaving.*

—*We have to wait till my wife comes back – we can't leave my son alone.*

—*The kid will survive. Get to your feet.*

—*At least let me stop the bleeding.*

Moiseyev nodded.

—*Leave the bathroom door open.*

Tyapkin left the kitchen and lurched to the bathroom, leaving a bloody hand print on the door, which remained open as instructed. Moiseyev surveyed the apartment. Leo could tell he was jealous. The doctor had a pleasant home. Tyapkin ran the water in the sink, pressing a towel against his nose and speaking, his back turned to them.

—*I'm very sorry for what I did. But I never killed anyone. You must believe me. Not because I think my reputation can be salvaged. I know I'm ruined. But someone else murdered that boy, someone who must be caught.*

Moiseyev was becoming impatient.

—*Come on.*

—*I wish you the best of luck.*

Hearing those words Leo ran into the room, spinning Tyapkin round. Embedded in his arm was a syringe. Tyapkin's legs went slack. He fell. Leo caught him, laying him down on the floor, pulling the syringe out of his arm. He checked his pulse. Tyapkin was dead. Moiseyev stared down at the body.

—*That makes our job easier.*

Leo looked up. Tyapkin's wife had returned. She was standing at the entrance to the apartment, holding her family's groceries.

1 April

Aleksandr closed the ticket office. As far as he was aware Nesterov had been true to his word. The secret of his sexual activities had been contained. None of the customers glanced at him oddly. None of them whispered about him. His family hadn't shunned him. His mother still loved him. His father still thanked him for his hard work. They were both still proud of him. The price for this status quo had been the names of over one hundred men, men who'd been rounded up while Aleksandr continued selling tickets, answering passenger queries and dealing with the day-to-day running of a station. His life had returned to normal. His routine was almost identical. He ate dinner with his parents, took his father to hospital. He cleaned the station, read the papers. However, he no longer went to the movies. In fact, he no longer went into the centre of town at all. He was fearful of who he might meet; perhaps a militia officer who would smirk knowingly at him. His world had shrunk. But it had shrunk when he'd given up his dream of being an athlete and he told himself he'd adjust just as he'd adjusted before.

The truth is that he spent every moment wondering if the men had guessed he'd betrayed them. Maybe they'd been told. The sheer number of arrests meant that they were probably forced into cells with each other. What else would they have spent their time doing except speculate on who'd written the list? It was the first time in their life they no longer had anything to hide. And as he thought about those men he'd found himself wishing that he could swap his freedom for the public humiliation of one those cells. However, he wouldn't be welcome there. He had nowhere, neither this world, nor their world.

He shut the door to the ticket office, locking it behind him and checking the clock which hung over the concourse. He put the keys into his pocket and walked onto the platform. A couple were waiting for the train. He recognized them by sight although not by name. They waved to him and he waved back, walking to the end of the platform, watching as the train approached. This train was on time. Aleksandr stepped off the platform and positioned himself across one of the tracks, staring up at the night sky.

He hoped his parents would believe the note he'd left behind. In the note he'd explained that he'd never been able to recover from the disappointment of failing to become a long-distance runner. And he'd never forgiven himself for letting his father down.

Same Day

Nesterov had spent the last four years promising his family a better place to live, a promise that until recently he used to repeat regularly. He no longer believed that they would be designated a better residence; no longer believed if he worked hard, if his wife worked hard, their labour would be translated into material benefit. They lived on Kropotkinsky Street, on the outskirts of town, close to the lumber mills. The houses on this street had been built haphazardly; all of them were different shapes and sizes. Nesterov spent much of his free time making home improvements. He was a competent carpenter and had replaced the window frames, the doors. But over the years the foundations had sunk and the front of the house was now tilting forward, slanting at an angle so that the door could only open so far before it became wedged into the ground. Some years ago he'd built a small extension which he used as a workshop. He and his wife, Inessa, crafted tables and chairs and fixed up the house, making whatever they needed. They did this not just for their own family but for any of the families on the street. All a person had to do was bring them the raw materials and perhaps, as a gesture, some item of food or drink.

Yet in the end no amount of tinkering could compensate for the property's shortcomings. There was no running water – the nearest well was a ten-minute walk. There was no plumbing –

there was a pit toilet at the back of the house. When they'd moved in the pit toilet was filthy and falling apart. It had been far too shallow and it was impossible to go in without gagging at the smell. Nesterov had constructed a new one, in a separate location, working through the night to finish. It had decent walls and a much deeper hole with a barrel of sawdust to throw in afterwards. Even so, he was aware that his family lived cut off from the advancements in comfort and hygiene, with no promise of a better future. He was forty years old. His pay was less than many of the twenty-something workers at the car assembly plant. His aspiration – to provide a decent home – had come to nothing.

There was a knock on the front door. It was late. Nesterov, still wearing his uniform, could hear Inessa answer the door. A moment later she appeared in the kitchen.

—*It's someone for you. He's from your work. I don't recognize him.*

Nesterov walked into the hallway. Leo was standing outside. Nesterov turned to his wife.

—*I'll deal with this.*

—*Will he be coming inside?*

—*No, this won't take long.*

Inessa glanced at Leo and then left. Nesterov stepped outside, shutting the door.

Leo had run all the way here. The news of Aleksandr's death had wiped out any sense of discretion. He no longer felt the disappointment and melancholy that had wracked him all week. He felt unhinged, part of a horrific, absurd charade, a player in a grotesque farce – the naive dreamer, striving for justice but leaving a trail of destruction in his wake. His aspiration – that a killer be caught – had been answered with bloodshed. Raisa had known all along, she'd known in the forest, she'd known two nights ago, she'd tried to warn him and yet he'd pressed on, like a child on an adventure.

What could one man achieve?

He had his reply: the ruin of two hundred lives, the suicide of a young man and the death of a doctor. A young man's body cut in two by a train: this was the fruit of his labour. This was what he'd risked his life for; this was what he'd risked Raisa's life for. This was his redemption.

—*Aleksandr is dead. He killed himself, threw himself under a train.*

Nesterov dropped his head.

—*I'm sorry to hear that. We gave him a chance to sort himself out. Maybe he couldn't. Maybe he was too sick.*

—*We're responsible for his death.*

—*No, he was ill.*

—*He was twenty-two years old. He had a mother and a father and he liked going to the cinema. And now he's dead. But the good thing is if we find another dead child we can just blame it on Aleksandr, solve the case in record time.*

—*That's enough.*

—*What are you doing this for? Because you're not doing it for the money or the perks!*

Leo stared at Nesterov's lopsided house. Nesterov replied:

—*Tyapkin killed himself because he was guilty.*

—*As soon as we started arresting those men he knew we'd question those children, he knew we'd track him down.*

—*He had the surgical skill necessary to cut out a child's stomach. He gave a false testimony to you regarding the girl's murder to confuse us. He was devious, cunning.*

—He told me the truth. That little girl's stomach was cut out. Her mouth was stuffed with bark just as the boy's stomach was cut out and his mouth was stuffed with bark. She had string tied around her ankle and so did the boy. They were killed by the same man. And it wasn't Dr Tyapkin and it wasn't that teenager Varlam Babinich.

—Go home.

—There was a body in Moscow. A young boy, called Arkady, not even five years old. I didn't see his body but I was told that he was found naked, his stomach cut open, his mouth stuffed with dirt. I suspect his mouth was stuffed with bark.

—Suddenly there's a murdered child in Moscow? That's very convenient, Leo. I don't believe it.

—I didn't believe it either. I had the grieving family in front of me, telling me their son had been murdered, and I didn't believe it. I told them it wasn't true. How many other incidents have been covered up? We have no way of knowing, no way of finding out. Our system is perfectly arranged to allow this man to kill as many times as he likes. And he's going to kill again and again, and we're going to keep arresting the wrong people, innocent people, people we don't like, or people we don't approve of, and he's going to kill again and again.

Nesterov didn't trust this man. He'd never trusted him and he certainly wasn't going to be drawn into making criticisms about the State. He turned his back on Leo, reaching for the front door.

Leo grabbed him by the shoulder, turning him so they were face to face again. The intention had been to make another point, to drive home his argument with reasoning and logic but instead, stumped for words, Leo punched him. It was a good punch, solid. Nesterov's head cracked to the side. He remained in that position, head to one side. Then, slowly, he turned to face his junior officer. Leo tried to keep his voice steady.

—*We've solved nothing.*

Nesterov's punch lifted Leo off his feet. He landed on the ground, on his back. It didn't hurt, not yet. Nesterov stared down at him, touching his own jaw.

—*Go home.*

Leo got to his feet.

—*We've solved nothing.*

He threw a punch. Nesterov blocked, throwing one back. Leo ducked. He was a good fighter: trained, skilled. But Nesterov was larger and quick despite his size. Punched in the stomach, Leo doubled up. Nesterov brought a second blow down across the exposed side of his face, dropping him to his knees and splitting open the skin on his cheek. With his vision blurred Leo toppled forward, falling. He rolled onto his back, gasping. Nesterov stood over him.

—*Go home.*

In reply Leo kicked him squarely in the groin. He scuttled back, hunched over. Leo staggered to his feet.

—*We've solved—*

Before he could finish Nesterov ran forward, crashing into Leo, knocking him to the ground, landing on top of him. He punched him in the stomach, the face, the stomach, the face. Leo lay there, taking blow after blow, unable to get free. Nesterov's knuckles were bloody. Catching his breath, he stopped. Leo wasn't moving. His eyes were closed – a pool of blood collecting in his right eye, fed by a cut to his brow. Nesterov got to his feet, shaking his head at the sight. He moved towards the front door, wiping the blood on his trousers. As he reached for the handle he heard a sound behind him.

Wincing in pain, Leo pulled himself up. Unsteady on his feet, he raised his hands, as though ready to fight. He rocked from side to side, as if standing on a boat out at sea. He had only a vague idea where Nesterov was. His voice was a whisper.

—*We've . . . solved . . . nothing.*

Nesterov watched as Leo swayed. He walked towards him, fists clenched, ready to knock him down. Leo swung a hopeless, pitiful punch – Nesterov sidestepped and caught Leo under the arm just as his legs gave way.

*

Leo sat at the kitchen table. Inessa had warmed some water on the fire. She poured it into a bowl. Nesterov dropped a cloth in the water and Leo was left to clean his face. His lip had been split. His eyebrow was bleeding. The pain in his stomach had subsided. Pressing a finger over his chest and ribs, nothing felt broken. His right eye was swollen. He couldn't open it. None the less, it was a relatively cheap price for getting Nesterov's attention. Leo wondered if his case would sound any more convincing inside than outside and if Nesterov could be so dismissive in front of his wife, with their children sleeping in the room next door.

—*How many children do you have?*

Inessa replied:

—*We have two boys.*

—*Do they walk through the woods on their way to school?*

—*They used to walk that way.*

—*Not any more?*

—*We make them walk through the town. It takes longer and they complain. I have to walk with them to make sure they don't slip into the forest. On the way back there's nothing we can do but trust them. We're both at work.*

—*Will they be walking through the forests tomorrow? Now the killer has been caught?*

Nesterov stood up, pouring tea and putting a glass down in front of Leo.

—*Would you like something stronger?*

—*If you have it.*

Nesterov took out a half-empty bottle of vodka, pouring three glasses, one for himself, one for his wife and one for Leo.

The alcohol stung the gash on the inside of Leo's mouth. Perhaps that would do it good. Nesterov sat down, refilling Leo's glass.

—*Why are you in Voualsk?*

Leo dropped the bloody cloth into the bowl of water, rinsing it and placing it against his eye.

—*I'm here to investigate the murder of these children.*

—*That's a lie.*

Leo had to win this man's trust. Without his help, there was nothing else he could do.

—*You're right. But there was a murder in Moscow. I wasn't ordered to investigate it. I was ordered to sweep the matter aside. I did my duty in that respect. Where I failed was in refusing to denounce my wife as a spy. I was considered compromised. As a punishment I was sent here.*

—*So you really are a disgraced officer?*

—*Yes.*

—*Then why are you doing this?*

—*Because three children have been murdered.*

—*You don't believe Varlam killed Larisa because you're sure that Larisa wasn't this killer's first victim. Am I right?*

—*Larisa wasn't the first victim. She couldn't have been. He'd done it before. There's a chance the boy in Moscow wasn't the first victim either.*

—*Larisa is the first murdered child we've had in this town. That's the truth, I swear it.*

—*The killer doesn't live in Voualsk. The murders were by the train station. He travels.*

—*He travels? He murders children? What kind of man is this?*

—*I don't know. But there's a woman in Moscow who's seen him. She saw him with the victim. An eyewitness can describe this man to us. But we need the murder records from every major town from Sverdlovsk to Leningrad.*

—*There are no centralized records.*

—*That's why you have to visit each town and collect their case files one by one. You're going to have to persuade them and if they refuse, you're going to have to talk to the people living there. Find out from them.*

The idea was outlandish. Nesterov should've laughed. He should've arrested Leo. Instead, he asked:

—*Why would I do that for you?*

—*Not for me. You've seen what he does to these children. Do it for the people we live with. Our neighbours, the people we sit next to on the train, do it for the children we don't know and will never meet. I don't have the authority to request those files. I don't know anyone in the militia. You do: you know these men – they trust you. You can get those files. You'll be looking for incidents of murdered children: the cases can be solved or unsolved. There'll be a pattern: their mouths stuffed with bark and their stomachs missing. Their bodies will probably have been found in public spaces: the woods, or rivers, maybe near train stations. They'll have string tied around their ankles.*

—*What if I find nothing?*

—*If there are three, which I've stumbled across by chance, there will be more.*

—*I'd be taking a great risk.*

—*Yes, you would. And you'd have to lie. You couldn't tell*

anyone the real reason. You couldn't tell any of your officers. You can trust no one. And in return for your bravery, your family might end up in the Gulag. And you might end up dead. That is my offer.

Leo stretched out his hand across the table.

—Will you help me?

Nesterov moved to the window, standing beside his wife. She didn't look at him, swirling the vodka at the bottom of her glass. Would he risk his family, his home, everything he'd worked for?

—No.

South-Eastern Rostov Oblast
West of the Town of Gukovo

2 April

Petya was awake before dawn. Sitting on the cold stone steps of their farmhouse, he waited impatiently for sunrise so that he might ask his parents' permission to walk into town. After months of saving he had enough to buy another stamp which would bring him to the last page of his album. On his fifth birthday he'd been given his first set of stamps by his father. He hadn't asked for them but he'd taken to the hobby, cautiously at first and then more and more doggedly until it had become an obsession. Over the past two years he'd collected stamps from other families working on the *kolkhoz* – Collective Farm 12, the farm his parents had been assigned. He'd even struck up casual acquaintances in Gukovo, the nearest town, in the hope of obtaining their stamps. As his collection had grown he'd bought a cheap paper album in which he stuck the stamps, gluing them in neat rows. He kept this album inside a wooden box which his father had built for him with the express purpose of protecting it from mishap. Such a box had been necessary since Petya had been unable to sleep at night, constantly checking that water wasn't leaking in through the roof or that rats hadn't eaten the precious pages. And of all the stamps he'd collected he loved the first four that his father had given him the most.

Every now and then his parents gave him the occasional *kopek* — not a spare *kopek*, since he was old enough to realize there was no money to spare. In exchange he always made sure he did a little extra work around the farm. It took so long to save up that months went by and all he could do was contemplate which stamps to buy next. Last night he'd been given another *kopek*, the timing of which his mother had considered unwise, not because she was opposed to him buying stamps, but because she knew it meant that there was no chance he'd sleep that night. She'd been right.

As the sun began to rise Petya hurried inside. His mother insisted that he eat a bowl of oatmeal before going anywhere. He ate it as fast as he could, ignoring her concerns that he'd get a stomach ache. Finished, he ran out of the house, reaching the track that snaked through the fields on its way towards town. He slowed to a brisk pace. The shops wouldn't be open yet. He might as well enjoy the anticipation.

In Gukovo the kiosk which sold stamps and newspapers was still closed. Petya didn't have a watch. He didn't know when it would open exactly but he didn't mind waiting. It was exciting being in town knowing that he had enough money for a new stamp and he wandered the streets without any particular destination. He stopped by the *elektrichka* station, knowing that there was a clock inside. The time was seven fifty. A train was due to leave and he decided to watch it, walking onto the platform and sitting down. He'd travelled on the *elektrichka* before. It was a slow train which stopped at every destination on the way to the city of Rostov. Though he'd only ever been as far as Rostov with his parents, he and some of his school friends occasionally boarded the train for no reason other than they knew they could do so for free. Tickets were rarely checked.

He was almost ready to return to the kiosk and buy his stamp when a man sat down beside him. The man was smartly dressed and had a black case, which he put on the ground between his legs as though he was afraid someone might run off with it. Petya looked up at his face. He had thick square glasses, neat black hair. He was wearing a suit. Petya couldn't tell how old the man was. He wasn't properly old, with grey hair. But then again he wasn't properly young either. He seemed unaware of Petya's presence. Petya was about to stand and leave when, quite suddenly, the man turned and smiled.

—*Where are you travelling to today?*

—*I'm not going anywhere, sir. Not on a train, I mean. I'm just sitting here.*

Petya had been taught to be polite and respectful towards elders.

—*It's an odd place to be sitting for no reason.*

—*I'm waiting to buy some stamps but the kiosk isn't open yet. Although it might be open now, I should go and check.*

Upon hearing this, the man turned his whole body towards Petya.

—*You collect stamps?*

—*Yes, sir.*

—*I used to be a stamp collector when I was your age.*

Petya sat back, relaxing – he didn't know anyone else who collected stamps.

—*Did you collect new stamps or used stamps? I collect both.*

—*All of mine were new. I bought them from a kiosk. Just like you.*

—I wish all mine were new. But they're mostly used. I cut them off old envelopes.

Petya reached into his pocket, pulling out his handful of copper *kopeks* and showing them to the man.

—I had to save for three months.

The man glanced at the small heap of coins.

—Such a long time for not very much.

Petya looked down at his coins. The man was right. He didn't have very much. And he realized that he'd never have very much. His excitement was tainted. He'd never have a great collection. Other people would always have more than him: it didn't matter how hard he worked, he could never catch up. His spirits dampened, he wanted to leave and was about to stand when the man asked:

—Are you a tidy boy?

—Yes, sir.

—Do you look after your stamps?

—I take good care of them. I put them in an album. And my dad has made me a wooden box. That's to keep the album safe. Our roof leaks sometimes. And there are rats sometimes too.

—That's sensible to put your album somewhere safe. I did a similar thing when I was your age. I kept mine in a drawer.

The man seemed to weigh something up in his mind.

—Listen, I have children of my own. Two young daughters and neither of them are interested in stamps. They're messy children. As for me, I no longer have time for stamps – I'm busy with my work. You can understand that? I'm sure your parents are also busy.

—All the time, sir, they work very hard.

—They don't have time to collect stamps, do they?

—No, sir.

—I'm in the same situation as them. Here's my idea: I would

like my collection to go to a person who'd appreciate it, a person who'd take care of it, a person just like you.

Petya considered the prospect of an entire book filled with new stamps. They would date back for as long as this man had been collecting. It would be the collection he'd always dreamed of. He said nothing, unable to believe his luck.

—*Well? Would that interest you?*

—*Yes, sir, I could put it in my wooden box and it would be safe.*

The man didn't seem so sure, shaking his head.

—*But my book is so full of stamps it might be too big for your little box.*

—*Then my father will make me another one. He's clever like that. And he wouldn't mind at all. He likes making things. He's skilful.*

—*And you're sure you'd look after the stamps?*

—*Yes, sir.*

—*Promise me.*

—*I promise, sir.*

The man smiled.

—*You've convinced me. You can have it. I only live three stops away. Come on, I'll buy you a ticket.*

Petya was about to say that a ticket was unnecessary but he swallowed the words. He didn't want to admit to breaking the rules. Until he got the stamps he needed to maintain this man's good opinion.

*

Sitting on the wooden seats of the *elektrichka*, staring out the window at the forests, Petya swung his legs backwards and forwards, his shoes almost touching the floor. There was now the question of whether he should spend his *kopeks* on a new stamp. It seemed unnecessary considering all the stamps he was about to acquire and he decided that he'd return the money to his parents. It would be nice if they could share in his good fortune. The man interrupted his thoughts by tapping him lightly on the shoulder.

—*We're here.*

The *elektrichka* had stopped at a station in the middle of the woods, long before the town of Shakhty. Petya was confused. This was a leisure stop for people wanting to get away from the towns. There were paths through the undergrowth, trodden down by walkers. But this wasn't a good time for walking. The snows had only recently melted. The woods were bleak and unwelcoming. Petya turned to his companion, looking at his smart shoes and black case.

—*You live here?*

The man shook his head.

—*My* dacha *is here. I can't keep my stamps at home. I'm too worried that my children will find them and touch them with their dirty fingers. But I'm going to have to sell this* dacha, *you see. So I have nowhere to keep this collection any more.*

He got off the train. Petya followed, stepping down onto the platform. No one else had disembarked.

The man walked into the woods, Petya just behind. Having a *dacha* made a kind of sense. Petya didn't know anyone rich enough to have a summer home, but he knew they were often situated in woods or by lakes or by the sea. While walking the man continued to talk.

—*Of course it would have been nice if my children took an interest in stamps but they just don't care for them.*

Petya considered telling this man that perhaps his children needed a little time. It had taken him time to become a careful collector. But he was canny enough to understand that it was in his advantage that this man's children were uninterested in stamps. And so he said nothing.

The man stepped off the path, walking through the under-growth with quite some speed. Petya struggled to keep up. The man took long strides. Petya almost had to run.

—*Sir, what's your name? I'd like to be able tell my parents the name of the man who gave me the stamps in case they don't believe me.*

—*Don't worry about your parents. I'll write them a note explaining exactly how you came into possession of the album. I'll even give them my address in case they want to check.*

—*Thank you very much, sir.*

—*Call me Andrei.*

After some time the man stopped walking and bent down, opening his case. Petya also stopped, looking around for some sign of this *dacha*. He couldn't see one. Maybe they had a bit further to go. Catching his breath, he stared up at the leafless branches of the tall trees that criss-crossed the grey sky.

*

Andrei stared down at the boy's body. Blood ran down the boy's head, across the side of his face. Andrei knelt, placing a finger on the boy's neck, feeling for a pulse. He was alive. That was good. He rolled the boy onto his back and began undressing him as though he were a doll. He took off the boy's coat, his shirt, then his shoes and his socks. Finally he took his trousers and under-wear. He gathered the clothes in a bundle, picked up his case, walking away from the child. After about twenty paces he stopped beside a fallen tree. He dropped the clothes, a small pile of cheap garments. He put his case on the ground, opened it and pulled out a long piece of coarse string. He returned to the boy, tying one end of the string around his ankle. He made a tight knot, testing it by pulling the boy's leg. It held fast. Walking backwards, he carefully unwound the string as though laying the fuse to a stack of dynamite. He reached the fallen tree, hid behind it and lay down on the ground.

He'd chosen a good spot. The position of the tree meant that when the boy awoke he'd be out of sight. His eyes followed the line of string from his hand, across the ground all the way to the boy's ankle. There was still plenty of string left in his hand, plenty of slack, at least another fifteen or so paces' worth. Set up, ready, he was so excited he wanted to pee. Afraid he might miss the moment the boy woke up, he rolled onto his side, unbuttoned his flies and still lying on the ground emptied himself. Done, he shuffled away from the damp soil, adjusting his position slightly. The boy was still unconscious. Time for the last of the preparations. Andrei took off his glasses, putting them in his glasses case and slipping them into his jacket pocket. Now, looking back, the child was just a blur. Squinting hard, all Andrei could see was an outline, an indistinct splash of pink skin contrasting with the ground. Andrei reached out, snapped a twig off a nearby tree and began to chew the bark, his teeth turning coarse and brown.

*

Petya opened his eyes, focusing on the grey sky and the branches of leafless trees. His head was sticky with blood. He touched it and looked at his fingers, beginning to cry. He was cold. He was naked. What had happened? Confused, he didn't dare sit up for fear of seeing that man beside him. He was certain the man was close. Right now all he could see was the sky. But he couldn't stay here, naked on the ground. He wanted to be at home with his parents. He loved his parents so much and he was sure they loved him. His lips trembling, his whole body trembling, he sat up – looking right and left, hardly daring to breathe. He couldn't see the man anywhere. He looked behind him, to the side. The man was gone. Petya raised himself into a crouching position, staring into the forests. He was alone, abandoned. He breathed deeply, relieved. He didn't understand. But he didn't want to understand.

He peered around for his clothes. They were gone. They weren't important. He jumped and began to run, running as fast as he could, his feet crunching across fallen branches, the soil wet from rain and snow melt. His bare feet, when they weren't crunching branches, made a slapping noise. He wasn't sure if he was running in the right direction. All he knew was that he had to get away.

Suddenly his right foot was pulled back as though a hand had grabbed his ankle. Unable to keep his balance he toppled forward, falling to the ground. Without waiting to catch his breath he rolled onto his back, looking behind him. He couldn't see anyone. He must have tripped and he was about to stand again when he caught sight of the string tied around his right ankle. His eyes followed its trail into the forests where he could see it stretching across the ground like a fishing line. The string continued all the way to a fallen tree some forty paces away.

He grabbed the string, trying to pull it down over his ankle and off his foot. But it was so tight it dug into his skin. The string was pulled again, harder this time. Petya was wrenched across the ground, his back covered with mud, before coming to a stop. He looked up. There he was, that man, standing up behind the tree, reeling him in. Petya clutched branches, handfuls of soil. But it was no good: he was being pulled closer and closer. He concentrated on the knot. He couldn't undo it. He couldn't break the string. He had no choice but to tug it down, scraping the skin around his ankle. The string was pulled again, this time sinking into his flesh.

He gritted his teeth, refusing to scream. He grabbed a handful of wet mud, lubricating the string. Just as the man pulled again, Petya freed himself from the noose. He leapt to his feet and ran.

The string was slack in Andrei's hands. There was nothing at the end of it. He tugged again, feeling his face flush red. He squinted but the distance was too far, he couldn't see anything, he'd always relied on the string. Should he put his glasses on? No, he'd never had that option as a child.

He'd been stuck like this – nearly blind, alone, stumbling through the forests.

He's leaving you behind.

Andrei jumped up, climbing over the fallen tree. With his nose close to the ground he followed the string.

Petya ran as fast as he'd ever run before. He'd reach the station – the train would be there. He'd get on. And it would move off before the man arrived. He'd survive.

I can do it.

He turned around. The man was behind him, running, but with his head close to the ground, as though looking for something he'd dropped. What's more, he was going in the wrong direction. The distance between them was growing. Petya was going to make it, he was going to escape.

Reaching the end of the string, the noose, his heart beating fast – Andrei stopped and stared all around, squinting hard. He felt tears forming; he couldn't see him. The boy was gone. Andrei was alone, abandoned. Then, there, to the right, movement – a light colour, the colour of skin, a boy.

Petya checked behind him, hopeful that the distance between them had grown even more. This time he saw the man running very fast and heading in his direction. He was taking long strides, his jacket flapping about his sides. He was smiling wildly. Petya could see that his teeth were for some reason completely brown and he stopped, understanding that there was no escape. Feeling weak, all the blood had left his legs. He raised his arms to his head, as if this could protect him, and closed his eyes, imagining himself back in his parents' arms.

Andrei collided with the boy at such speed that they both fell to the ground. Andrei was on top, the boy wriggling underneath; scratching and biting his jacket. Keeping himself flat on the boy to stop him escaping Andrei muttered:

—*It's still alive!*

He pulled out the long hunting knife attached to his belt. Closing his eyes, he jabbed the blade underneath him, cautious jabs at first, stabbing only with the tip, small stabs, listening to its screams. He waited, savouring this moment, feeling the vibrations of the struggle in his stomach. What a feeling! Excited, the blade went in further and faster, further and faster until finally the blade went in all the way up to the hilt. At this point the child was no longer moving.

THREE MONTHS LATER

South-Eastern Rostov Oblast
The Sea of Azov

4 July

Nesterov sat with his toes buried in the sand. This stretch of beach was popular with people living in the nearby city of Rostov-on-Don, some forty or so kilometres to the north-east. Today was no exception. The beach was crowded. As if the inhabitants of the town had emerged from hibernation, their bodies were drained of colour by the long winter. Could he guess what kind of jobs people held from the shapes of their bodies? The fatter men were important in some way. Perhaps they were factory managers or Party officials or high-ranking State Security officers, not the kind who kicked down doors but the kind who signed forms. Nesterov was careful not to catch their eye. He concentrated on his family. His two sons were playing in the shallow water, his wife lay beside him, sleeping on her side – her eyes closed, her hands tucked under her head. At a glance they seemed content: a perfect Soviet family. They had every reason to be relaxed – they were on holiday, allowed the use of an official militia car, with a State voucher for fuel, as a reward for the successful, discreet and efficient handling of the two separate murder investigations. He'd been told to take it easy. Those had been his orders. He repeated the words in his head, sucking on their irony.

The trial of Varlam Babinich had lasted two days with his defence lawyer entering a plea of insanity. According to procedure the defence were forced to rely upon the testimony of the same experts used by the prosecution. They couldn't call their own independent witnesses. Nesterov was no lawyer and didn't need to be in order to understand the enormous advantage this set-up handed to the prosecution. In Babinich's case the defence had to prove insanity without being able to call a witness who hadn't first been groomed by the prosecution. Since there were no psychiatrists working at Hospital 379 a doctor with no specialist training had been selected by the prosecution and called to make a judgement. This doctor had stated that he believed Varlam Babinich understood the difference between right and wrong and knew murder was wrong; the defendant's intelligence was limited certainly but sufficient to grasp concepts such as criminality, after all he'd said upon arrest:

I'm in so much trouble.

The defence then had no choice but to call the same doctor and attempt to argue a contradictory point of view. Varlam Babinich had been found guilty. Nesterov had received a typed letter confirming that the seventeen-year-old had died on his knees, shot in the back of the head.

Dr Tyapkin's case had taken less time, barely a day. His wife had testified that he was violent, describing his sick fantasies and claiming that the only reason she hadn't come forward before was because she'd feared for her own life and for the life of her baby. She'd also told the judge that she renounced her religion –

Judaism. She would bring her children up to be loyal Communists. In exchange for this testimony she'd been transferred to Shakhty, a town in the Ukraine, where she could continue her life without the stigma of her husband's crime. Since no one outside Voualsk had heard of the crime, there wasn't even any need to change her name.

With these two cases concluded, the court had processed close to two hundred cases against men accused of anti-Soviet behaviour. These homosexuals had received hard-labour sentences of between five and twenty-five years. In order to deal with the sheer number of cases swiftly the judge had devised a formula for sentencing which depended upon their employment record, the number of children they had and finally the quantity of perverse sexual encounters they'd been alleged to have experienced. Being a member of the Party was counted as a strike against the accused since they'd brought the Party into disrepute. They should have known better and their membership was stripped from them. Despite the repetitive nature of these sessions Nesterov had sat through all of them, all one hundred and fifty or so. After the last man had been sentenced he'd left the court only to find himself being congratulated by local Party officials. He'd done well. It was almost certain he'd have a new apartment within the next couple of months, or if not then by the end of the year.

Several nights after the conclusion of the trials, as he'd lain awake, his wife had told him it was only a matter of time before he agreed to help Leo. She wished he'd just get on and do it. Had he been waiting for her permission? Perhaps he had. He was gambling with not only his own life but with those of his family. It wasn't that he was doing anything technically wrong by asking questions and making enquiries, but he was acting on his own. Independent action was always a risk since it implied that the structures put in place by the State had failed: that the individual could somehow achieve something the State could not. All the same he was confident that he could begin a quiet kind of investigation, a casual investigation which would appear to be no more than conversations between colleagues. If he discovered that there were no similar cases, no other murdered children, then he could be sure that the brutal punishments he'd been instrumental in bringing about had been fair, just and appropriate. Though he mistrusted Leo and resented the doubt he'd stirred up, there was no escaping that the man had posited a very simple question. Did his work have meaning or was it merely a means to survive? There was nothing shameful about trying to survive – it was the occupation of the majority. However, was it enough to live in squalor and not even be rewarded with a sense of pride, not even to be sustained by a sense that what he did served some purpose?

For the past ten weeks Nesterov had operated on his own without any discussion or collaboration with Leo. Since Leo was almost certainly under surveillance the less contact between them the better. All he'd done was to scribble Leo a short note – *I'll help* – including instructions to destroy the note immediately.

There was no easy way of accessing regional criminal files. He'd made phone calls and written letters. In both forms of communication he'd mentioned the subject only in passing, praising the efficiency of his department for the swift resolution of their two cases in an attempt to provoke similar boasts. As the replies began to arrive he'd been forced to make several off-duty train journeys, arriving in towns and meeting with his colleagues, drinking with them, discussing relevant cases for no more than a fraction of a minute before boasting about other things. It was an extraordinarily inefficient means of collecting information. Three hours of drinking might provide two minutes of useful conversation. After eight weeks Nesterov hadn't unearthed a single unsolved crime. At this point he'd called Leo into his office.

Leo had entered the office, shut the door and sat down. Nesterov had double-checked the corridors before returning, locking the office door and reaching under his desk. He'd taken out a map of the Soviet Union, which he'd spread across the desk, weighing down the corners with books. He'd then picked up a handful of pins. He'd stuck two into the map at Voualsk, two in Molotov, two in Vyatka, two in Gorky and two in Kazan. These pins formed a row of towns which followed the train line west towards Moscow. Nesterov hadn't been to Moscow, deliberately avoiding its militia officers who he'd feared were likely to be suspicious of any enquiries. West of Moscow, Nesterov had been less successful in gathering information, but he'd found one possible incident in Tver. Moving south, he stuck three pins in the city of Tula, two in the town of Orel and two in Belgorod. Now into the Ukraine, he picked up the box of pins, shaking at least twenty into his hand. He continued: three pins in the towns of Kharkov and Gorlovka, four in the city of Zaporoshy, three in the town of Kramatorsk and one in Kiev. Moving out of the Ukraine, there were five pins in Taganrog and finally six pins in and around the city of Rostov.

Nesterov had understood Leo's reaction – stunned silence. In many ways he had collected this information in a comparable frame of mind. At first he'd tried to dismiss the similarities: the ground-up material stuffed into the children's mouths, whether officers called it soil or dirt, the mutilated torsos. But the points of similarity were too striking. There was the string around the ankles. The bodies were always naked, the clothes left in a pile some distance away. The crime scenes were in forests or parks and often near train stations, never household crimes, never interior.

Not one town had spoken to another even though some crimes had occurred less than fifty kilometres apart. No connecting line had been traced, joining up these pins. They'd been solved by blaming drunks or thieves or convicted rapists – undesirables, to whom any allegation would stick.

By his count there were forty-three in total. Nesterov had reached over, taken another pin from the box and stuck it into the centre of Moscow, making Arkady child 44.

*

Nesterov awoke to find the side of his face pressed against the sand, his mouth open. He sat up, brushing the sand off. The sun had disappeared behind a sheet of cloud. He looked for his children, searching the stretch of beach, the people playing. His eldest son, Efim, seven years old, sat near the water's edge. But his youngest son – only five years old – was nowhere to be seen. Nesterov turned to his wife. She was cutting slices of dried meat, ready for their lunch.

—*Where's Vadim?*

Inessa looked up, her eyes immediately finding their eldest son but not their youngest. Still holding the knife, she got up, turning around, checking behind her. Unable to see him, she dropped the knife. They both moved forward, arriving by Efim, kneeling down beside him, one on either side.

—*Where's your brother?*

—*He said he was going back to you.*

—*When?*

—*I don't know.*

—*Think.*

—*Not long ago. I'm not sure.*

—*We told you to stay together.*

—*He said he was going back to you!*

—*He didn't go out into the water?*

—*He went that way, towards you.*

Nesterov stood again, staring into the water. Vadim hadn't gone out into the sea, he hadn't wanted to swim. He was on the beach, somewhere amongst these hundreds of people. Images from the case files rose into his mind. One young girl had been murdered off a popular riverside trail. Another young girl had been murdered in a park, behind a monument, one hundred yards from her house. He crouched beside his son:

—*Go back to the blankets. Stay there no matter who talks to you, no matter what they say. Even if they're your elders and demand your respect, you remain in the same place.*

Remembering how many children had been persuaded into disappearing into the forest he changed his mind, taking his son's hand.

—*Come with me. We'll both look for your brother.*

His wife went up the beach, in the opposite direction, while Nesterov walked down, weaving in and out of people, walking at a brisk pace, too quick for Efim so he picked his son up, carrying him. The beach came to an end, tapering off into long grass and reeds. Vadim was nowhere to be seen.

Efim knew a little about his father's work. He knew about the two murdered children in his home town because his parents had spoken to him about them, although they'd made him swear not to mention the murders to anyone. No one was supposed to be worried about them. They were meant to be solved. Efim knew his little brother was in danger. He was a talkative, friendly boy. He'd find it difficult to be rude to anyone. Efim should've kept a better watch on him and realizing he was to blame he began to cry.

At the other end of the beach Inessa called for her son. She'd read the documents pertaining to her husband's investigation. She knew exactly what had happened to these missing children. Panicking, she blamed herself entirely. She'd told her husband to help Leo. She'd encouraged him, advising on basic precautions to keep the investigation a secret. He was by nature blunt and this work needed caution. She'd read his letters before they were posted, suggesting the insertion of certain phrases should the letters be intercepted. When he'd shown her the map marked with pins; she'd touched each pin individually. It was an impossible number and that night she'd slept in the same bed as her sons. Tying their holiday into the investigation had been her idea. Since the greatest concentration of murders had taken place in the south of the country, the only way Nesterov could make a substantial expedition unnoticed would be to use his family holiday as a cover. Only now did she fully understand that she'd put her children in danger. She'd taken them into the heartland of this mysterious evil. She'd underestimated the power of this thing they were searching for. No child was safe. They were seemingly taken at will, murdered only metres from their homes. Now it had taken her youngest son.

Short of breath, shouting for her son, calling his name into the face of the bathers, her eyes filled with tears. People circled her with their dumb, unconcerned eyes. She begged them to help her.

—*He's only five years old. He's been taken. We have to find him.*

A stern-looking woman tried to take hold of her.

—*He'll be here somewhere.*

—*You don't understand: he's in terrible danger.*

—*From what?*

She pushed the woman out of the way, turning around and around, calling his name. Suddenly she felt a man's strong hands on her arms.

—My little boy's been taken. Please help me look for him.

—Why don't you calm down?

—No, he'll be killed. He'll be murdered. You have to help me find him.

The man laughed.

—No one is going to be killed. He's quite safe.

She began to struggle but the man wouldn't let her go. Surrounded by pitying faces, she tried to break free.

—Let go of me! I need to find my son.

Nesterov pushed through the crowd, breaking through to his wife. He'd found his youngest son playing in the tall reeds and was now carrying both his children. The man let go of his Inessa's arm. She took hold of Vadim, clutching his head as though it were fragile and might break. They stood together as a family, surrounded, hostile faces all around. Why had they behaved like that? What was wrong with them? Efim whispered:

—Let's go.

They left the crowd, hurriedly collecting their stuff and heading to the car. There were only four other cars parked by the dirt road. The rest of the bathers had arrived by tram. Nesterov started the engine, driving off.

*

On the beach a thin woman with a touch of grey in her hair watched as the car disappeared. She'd made a note of the number plate, having decided this was a family that needed investigating.

Moscow

5 July

Until yesterday, if Leo had been arrested, there was nothing directly linking Raisa to his unauthorized investigation. She could have denounced him and there might have been a chance she'd survive. That was no longer true. On a train nearing Moscow, travelling under false papers, their guilt was indivisible.

Why had Raisa boarded the train, accompanying Leo? It went against her governing principle – survival. She was accepting an immeasurable risk when an alternative presented itself to her. She could've stayed in Voualsk and done nothing or, to be safer still, she could've betrayed Leo and hoped that this betrayal would have secured her future. It was an unpleasant strategy, hypocritical and despicable, but she'd done many unpleasant things in the name of survival, including marrying Leo, a man she'd loathed. What had changed? This wasn't about love. Leo was now her partner, not in the straightforward marital sense. They were partners in this investigation. He trusted her, listened to her – not as a courtesy but as an equal. They were a team, sharing a common goal, united behind a purpose more important than either of their lives. Energized, excited, she didn't want to return to her former subsistence existence, wondering how much of her soul she'd have to slice off and sell in order to survive.

The train came to a stop at Yaroslavski Vokzal. Leo was all too aware of the significance of returning here, travelling across the very train tracks where Arkady's body had been found. They were returning to Moscow for the first time since their exile four months ago. They had no official business here. Their lives and investigation depended on being undiscovered. If they were caught they would die. The reason for their venture was a woman called Galina Shaporina, a woman who'd seen the killer, an eye-witness who could describe this man, put an age on him, flesh him out – make him real. Currently neither Leo nor Raisa had any idea of what kind of man they were searching for. They were clueless as to whether he was old or young, lean or heavy, scruffy or well dressed. In short, he could be almost anyone.

In addition to speaking to Galina, Raisa had proposed talking to Ivan, her colleague from school. He was well read in censored Western material and had access to restricted publications, magazine articles, newspapers and unauthorized translations. He might be aware of case studies about comparable crimes from abroad: random, multiple, ritualized murders. Raisa knew only about such crimes in the barest of detail. She'd heard about an American, Albert Fish, who'd murdered children and eaten them. She'd heard stories about a Frenchman, Dr Pettiot, who, during the Great Patriotic War, had lured Jews to his cellar offering safety, and then killed them, burning their bodies. She had no idea whether this was merely Soviet propaganda about the decay of Western civilization, killers depicted as products of a flawed society and perverse politics. From the point of view of their investigation a determinist theory was useless. It meant that the only suspect they could be looking for was a foreigner, someone whose character had been determined by living in a capitalist society. But clearly the killer was moving around the country with ease; he spoke Russian and charmed children. This was a killer operating within the fabric of their country. Everything they knew or had been told about this type of crime was either false or irrelevant. They had to unlearn every presumption and start afresh. And Raisa believed that Ivan's access to sensitive information was crucial to re-educating themselves.

Leo appreciated that such material would be of benefit but equally he was also keen to reduce their interaction to as few people as possible. Their primary objective was speaking to Galina Shaporina, Ivan was secondary. Leo wasn't entirely convinced that he was worth the risk. However, he was aware that his evaluation was tainted by personal factors. Was he jealous of Ivan's relationship with his wife? Yes, he was. Did he want to share their investigation with Ivan? Not for a second.

Leo glanced out of the window, waiting for everyone to disembark. Train stations were patrolled by undercover and uniformed agents. All major transport junctions were deemed to be vulnerable as points of infiltration. There were armed checkpoints on the roads. Ports and harbours were under constant surveillance. Nowhere was layered in more levels of protection than Moscow. They were attempting to sneak into the most heavily policed city in the country. Their only advantage was that Vasili had little reason to suppose they'd be reckless enough to embark on such a venture. About to step off the train, Leo turned to Raisa.

—*If you happen to catch their eye, a guard or anyone else, even someone who appears to be a civilian, don't immediately look away. Don't smile or make any gestures. Just hold eye contact and then look at something else.*

They stepped down onto the platform, neither of them

carrying much luggage. Large bags were more likely to draw attention. Walking briskly, they had to stop themselves from rushing. Leo was thankful that the station was busy. All the same he could feel his shirt collar becoming damp with sweat. He tried to reassure himself that there was almost no chance any of the agents here were looking for them. They'd already been careful to shake any possible surveillance back at Voualsk. They'd established that they were going on a walking holiday in the mountains. Applications had to be made for vacations. Because of their limited status they'd only been able to get a couple of days. Under extreme time pressure, they'd set off into the forest, trekking in a loop, making sure they weren't being followed. Once they were confident they were alone they'd returned to the forest near the station. They'd changed out of their muddy clothes, buried them and their camping equipment, and sat waiting for the train to Moscow to arrive. They'd boarded it at the last minute. Should all go according to plan they'd collect the eyewitness report, return to Voualsk, slip into the forest, retrieve their equipment and change back into their muddy clothes. They'd re-enter the town from one of the northern forest trails.

They were almost at the exit when a man behind them called out:

—*Papers*.

Without hesitating, Leo turned. He didn't smile or try to appear relaxed. The officer they were dealing with was State Security. But Leo didn't recognize him. That was fortunate. He handed over his papers. Raisa handed over hers.

Leo studied the man's face. He was tall, stocky. His eyes were slow, his movements sluggish. This was nothing more a routine stop and search. However, routine or not, the papers he now examined were fake and at best only a passable imitation. In his days as an agent Leo would never have been fooled by them. Nesterov had helped provide them, doctoring them with Leo's assistance. They'd worked hard but the more they'd worked the more he'd become conscious of their weakness: the scratches on the paper, the points where the ink bled, the double lines where it had been stamped twice. He now wondered how he could've put his faith in these documents and realized he hadn't — he'd hoped they wouldn't be checked.

Raisa watched the agent pore over the writing and realized the man could barely read. He was trying to hide this fact by pretending to be extremely thorough. But she'd seen too many children struggle with the same problem not to be able to spot the signs. The man's lips moved as his eyes scanned the lines. Aware that if she gave any indication of knowing his weakness he'd almost certainly lash out, she maintained her look of fear. She reasoned he'd appreciate being feared: it would soothe any anxiety that he might be feeling. Sure enough the agent checked on their expressions, not because he had some suspicion regarding the document but because he was worried they'd become less afraid of him. Satisfied that he was still a man to be feared, he slapped the documents against the palm of his hand, making it clear that he was weighing them up, that he still had power over their lives.

—*Let me see your bags.*

Leo and Raisa opened their small bags. They carried nothing more than a change of clothes and some basic essentials. The officer was becoming bored. He shrugged. In reply they nodded reverentially at him, moving towards the exit, trying not to walk too fast.

Same Day

Having quashed Fyodor's own investigation into the murder of his son, cajoled and bullied him into silence, Leo was about to ask for his help with the same subject. He needed Fyodor to take him to Galina Shaporina's apartment since he'd been unable to find the address. Indeed, it was possible that he couldn't even remember her name correctly. He hadn't been paying much attention at the time and so much had happened since then. Without Fyodor there was little hope of finding this witness.

Leo was prepared for humiliation, the loss of face; he was braced for scorn and contempt, just as long as he secured that eyewitness account. Although Fyodor was an MGB agent, Leo was banking on the fact that his loyalty would be to the memory of his son. No matter how much hatred Fyodor felt towards Leo, surely his desire for justice would force them into an alliance? With that said Leo's assessment of the situation four months ago had been correct. An unauthorized investigation into the death of his son would put his entire family at risk. Perhaps Fyodor had come to terms with that assessment. Better to protect the living, better to turn Leo over to the State, that way he benefited from both safety and revenge. What would he decide? Leo knocked on the door. He was about to find out.

Apartment Block 18, fourth floor, an elderly woman opened

the door — the woman who'd stood up to him, the woman who'd dared to call a murder by its name.

—*My name is Leo, this is my wife, Raisa.*

The old woman stared at Leo, remembering him, hating him. She glanced at Raisa.

—*What do you want?*

Raisa answered, her voice low:

—*We're here about the murder of Arkady.*

There was a long silence, the old woman studying both their faces before replying:

—*You've come to the wrong address. No boy was murdered here.*

As she went to close the door, Leo put his foot forward.

—*You were right.*

*

Leo expected anger. But instead the elderly woman began to cry.

Fyodor, his wife and the elderly woman, Fyodor's mother, stood together, a civilian *troika* — a citizen's tribunal — watching as Leo took off his coat, dropping it on the chair. He pulled off his jumper and began unbuttoning his shirt. Underneath, taped to his body, were the details of the murders — photos, descriptions, statements, maps showing the geographical spread of the crimes: the most important pieces of evidence that they'd accumulated.

—*I had to take certain precautions in carrying this material around. These are the details of over forty murders, children, both boys and girls, murdered across the western half of our country. They've been killed in almost exactly the same way, the same way as I now believe your son was killed.*

Leo pulled the papers free from his chest: the ones closest to his skin were damp with sweat. Fyodor took hold of them, glancing through. His wife stepped forward, as did his mother. Soon all three were reading the documents, passing them between each other. Fyodor's wife spoke first.

—*And if you catch him, what will you do?*

Remarkably, it was the first time Leo had been asked that question. Until now they'd concentrated on whether it was even possible to catch him.

—*I'll kill him.*

Once Leo had explained the nature of his personal investigation, Fyodor wasted no time with insults or recriminations. It evidently didn't cross his mind to refuse them assistance or doubt their sincerity or worry about the repercussions. Nor did those thoughts occur to Fyodor's wife or his mother, at least not in any significant way. Fyodor would take them to Galina's apartment immediately.

The shortest route there involved crossing the railway tracks, where Arkady had been found. There were several train tracks running parallel, a wide space, lined with ragged shrubs and trees. With the fading evening light, Leo appreciated the appeal of this secluded no man's land. In the heart of the city it felt eerily empty. Had the boy run across these sleepers, chased by that man? Had he fallen to the ground, desperate to get away? In the dark, had a train raced past, indifferent? Leo was glad to get off the tracks.

Nearing the apartment, Fyodor argued that Leo should remain outside. Galina had been terrified by him before: they couldn't risk him scaring her into silence again. Leo agreed. It would just be Raisa and Fyodor.

Raisa followed Fyodor up the stairs, reaching the apartment door and knocking. She could hear the sound of children playing inside. She was pleased. Of course she didn't believe a woman had to be a mother to appreciate the gravity of this case but the fact that Galina's own children were in danger should make her easy to enlist.

The door was opened by a gaunt woman in her thirties. She was wrapped up as though it was the middle of winter. She appeared ill. Her eyes were nervous, taking in every detail of Raisa's and Fyodor's appearance. Fyodor seemed to recognize her.

—*Galina, you remember me? I'm Fyodor, father of Arkady, the little boy who was murdered. This is my friend Raisa. She lives in Voualsk, a town near the Urals. Galina, the reason we're here is because the man who murdered my son is murdering other children, in other towns. That is why Raisa has travelled to Moscow, so that we can work together. We need your help.*

Galina's voice was soft, barely a whisper.

—*How can I help? I don't know anything.*

Expecting such a reply, Raisa pointed out:

—*Fyodor isn't here as an officer of the MGB. We're a group made of fathers and mothers, any citizens outraged at these crimes. Your name won't appear in any documents; there are no documents. You'll never see or hear from us again. All we need to know is what he looks like. How old is he? Is he tall? What colour is his hair? Were his clothes expensive or cheap?*

—*But the man I saw wasn't with a child. I told you that.*

Fyodor answered:

—*Please, Galina, let us in for a second. Let's talk out of the hallway.*

She shook her head.

—*I can't help you. I don't know anything.*

Fyodor was becoming agitated. Raisa touched his arm, silencing him. They had to remain calm, they couldn't bully her. Patience was the key.

—*OK, that's OK, Galina. You didn't see a man with a child. Fyodor explained that you saw a man with a tool bag, is that right?*

She nodded.

—*Can you describe him for us?*

—*But he didn't have a child with him.*

—*We understand. He didn't have a child with him. You've been clear about that. He just had a tool bag. But what did he look like?*

Galina considered. Raisa held her breath, sensing she was about to break. They didn't need the information written down. They didn't need a signed testimony. They just needed a description, thrown away, deniable. Thirty seconds, that was all it would take.

Suddenly Fyodor cut through the silence, saying:

—*There's no harm in telling us what a man with tool bag looked like. No one can get in trouble for describing a railway worker.*

Raisa stared at Fyodor. He'd made a mistake. People could get in trouble for describing a railway worker. They could get in trouble for much less. The safest course of action was always to do nothing. Galina shook her head, stepping back from them.

—*I'm sorry, it was dark. I didn't see him. He had a bag, that's all I remember.*

Fyodor put his hand on the door.

—*No, Galina, please . . .*

Galina shook her head.

—*Leave.*

—*Please, please . . .*

Like a panicked animal, her voice became shrill with worry:

—*Leave!*

There was silence. The noise of the children playing stopped. Galina's husband appeared.

—*What's going on?*

In the corridor apartment doors opened, people were staring, observing, pointing: alarming Galina further. Sensing that they were losing control of the situation, that they were about to lose their eyewitness, Raisa moved forward, hugging Galina, as if saying goodbye.

—*What did he look like?*

Cheek to cheek, Raisa waited, closing her eyes, hoping. She could feel Galina's breath. But Galina did not reply.

Rostov-on-Don

Same Day

The cat perched on the window ledge, its tail flicking from side to side, its cool green eyes following Nadya around the room as if it were considering pouncing on her, as if she were nothing more an over-sized rat. The cat was older than her. She was six years old; the cat was eight or nine. That fact might go some way to explain why it had such a superior attitude. According to her father the area they lived in had a problem with rats and therefore cats were essential. Well, that was partly true: Nadya had seen plenty of rats, big rats and bold too. But she'd never seen this cat do anything useful about them. It was a lazy cat, spoilt rotten by her father. How could a cat think itself more important than her? It never allowed her to touch it. Once, as it had happened to pass by, she'd stroked its back, to which it had replied by twisting around, hissing, before bolting to the corner with its fur stuck out as though she'd committed some sort of crime. At that point she'd given up trying to befriend it. If the cat wanted to hate her, she'd hate it back twice as much.

Unable to remain in the house any longer with the cat staring at her, Nadya set off, even though it was late and the rest of her family were in the kitchen, preparing *uzhin*. Knowing that she'd be refused permission to go for a walk she didn't bother asking, slipping on her shoes and sneaking out of the front door.

They lived on a bank of the river Don, her younger sister, her mother and father, in a neighbourhood on the outskirts, cratered streets and brick hut-houses. The city's sewage and factory waste fed into the river just upstream and Nadya would sometimes sit and watch the patterns of oils, filth and chemicals on the water's surface. There was a well-trodden path along the riverbank which ran in both directions. Nadya turned downstream, out towards the countryside. Even though there was very little light she was confident of the route. She had a good sense of direction and as far as she could remember she'd never been lost, not once. She wondered what kind of jobs a girl with a good sense of direction might get when she grew up. Maybe she'd become a fighter pilot. There was no point becoming a train driver since they never had to think about where they were going: a train could hardly get lost. Her father had told her stories about female bomber pilots during the war. That sounded good to her, she wanted to be one of them, her face on the front of a newspaper, awarded the Order of Lenin. That would get her father's attention; that would make him proud of her. That would distract him from his stupid cat.

She'd been walking for a little while, humming to herself, pleased to be out of the house and away from that cat, when suddenly she came to a stop. Up ahead she could see the outline of a man walking towards her. He was a tall man but in the gloom she couldn't tell much else about him. He was carrying some kind of case. Normally the sight of a stranger wouldn't have bothered her in the least. Why would it? But her mother had recently done a peculiar thing: she'd sat Nadya and her sister down and warned them not to talk to any strangers. She'd even gone as far as telling them it would be better to be impolite than to obey a stranger's request. Nadya looked back towards her house. She wasn't all that far from home; if she ran she could get back in less than ten minutes. The thing was, she really wanted to walk to her favourite tree further downstream. She liked to climb up and sit in it and dream. Until she'd done that, until she'd reached that tree, she didn't feel like the walk had been a success. She imagined that this was her military mission: to reach the tree and she couldn't fail. Making a snap decision, she decided she wouldn't talk to this man: she'd just walk straight past him and if he spoke to her, she'd say *good evening* but not stop walking.

She continued along the path with the man getting nearer. Was he walking faster? He seemed to be. It was too dark to see his face. He was wearing some sort of hat. She moved up the edge of the path, giving him plenty of room to pass by. They were only a couple of metres apart. Nadya felt afraid, an inexplicable urge to hurry past him. She didn't understand why. She blamed her mother. Bomber pilots were never afraid. She broke into a run. Concerned this would insult the gentleman, she called out:

—*Good evening.*

With his free arm, Andrei grabbed her around the waist, lifting her small frame clear off the ground, bringing her face close to his, staring into her eyes. She was terrified, holding her breath, her little body rigid with tension.

And then Nadya began to laugh. Recovering from her surprise, she put her arms around her father's neck and hugged him.

—*You scared me.*

—*Why are you out so late?*

—*I wanted to walk.*

—*Does your mother know you're outside?*

—*Yes.*

—You're lying.

—No, I'm not. Why are you coming from this direction? You never come from this direction. Where have you been?

—I've been working. I had some business in one of the villages just outside the city. There was no way to get back except to walk. It was only a couple of hours.

—You must be tired.

—Yes, I am.

—Can I carry your case?

—But I'm carrying you so even if I gave you my case I'd still be carrying its weight.

—I could walk by myself and carry your case.

—I think I can manage.

—Father, I'm glad you're home.

Still carrying his daughter, he used the base of his case to push open their door. He stepped into the kitchen. There was affection from his youngest daughter who ran over to greet him. He watched his family's pleasure at his return. They took it for granted that when he went away, he'd come back.

Nadya had her eye on the cat. Evidently jealous of the attention she was getting from her father, the cat jumped down from the window, joining the family reunion, rubbing itself against her father's leg. As Andrei lowered her to the floor she *accidentally* dropped her foot onto the cat's paw, causing it to screech and dart away. Before she could enjoy any small sense of satisfaction her father took hold of her wrist, crouched down, staring at her through his thick square glasses, his face trembling with anger.

—Don't ever touch her.

Nadya wanted to cry. She bit her lip instead. She'd already learned that crying made no impression on her father.

Andrei let go of his daughter's wrist, standing up straight. He felt flustered and hot. He looked at his wife. She hadn't moved forward, but she smiled at him.

—*Have you eaten?*

—*I have to put my things away. I don't want anything to eat.*

He wife didn't attempt to hug or kiss him, not in front of the children. He was strict about these things. She understood.

—*Was your work successful?*

—*They want me to go away again in a couple of days. I'm not sure for how long.*

Without waiting for a reply, he was already feeling claustrophobic, he moved to the door that led to the basement. The cat followed him, its tail up high, excited.

He locked the door behind him, descending the stairs, immediately feeling better now that he was on his own. An elderly couple had previously occupied this downstairs space but the woman had died and the man had moved into his son's apartment. The housing bureau hadn't sent another couple to replace them. It wasn't a nice room: a basement sunk into the riverbank. The bricks were always wet. In winter the room was freezing. There was a *burzhuika*, a wood-fired stove, which the elderly couple had been forced to keep running for eight months of the year. Despite the basement's many disadvantages it had one advantage. It was his space. He had a chair in one corner and a slender bed which had belonged to the elderly couple. He occasionally slept down here when the conditions were tolerable. He lit the gas lamp and before long another cat had entered through the space in the wall where the pipes from the *burzhuika* ran outside.

He opened his case. Amongst his papers and the remains of his lunch there was a glass jar with a screw-top lid. He unscrewed the lid. Inside the jar, wrapped in an old issue of *Pravda*, sodden with blood, was the stomach of the girl he'd murdered some hours ago.

He peeled the paper away, carefully making sure no paper was stuck to the flesh. He put the stomach on a tin plate, slicing it into strips then again into cubes. Once he'd finished he fired up the stove. By the time it was hot enough to cook the meat there were six cats circling him. He fried the meat, waiting till it had turned brown before tipping it back onto the tin plate. Andrei stood watching the cats around his feet, enjoying the spectacle of their hunger, holding the food, teasing them, watching them yelp. They were desperately hungry, frenzied by the smell of cooked meat.

After he'd had his fill of teasing them he put the food down. The cats squeezed together in a circle around the plate and began to eat, purring with delight.

*

Upstairs, Nadya stared at the basement door, wondering what kind of father preferred cats to children. He was only going to be home for two days. No, she was wrong to be angry with her father. She refused to blame him, the cats were to blame. A thought came into her mind. It wouldn't be all that difficult to kill a cat. The hard part would be getting away with it.

Same Day

On Vorovski Street, Leo and Raisa joined the back of the grocery-store queue. The queue would take several hours before it reached inside, where each person would place their order before being made to wait in a second queue to pay for the item. After those two queues there was a third queue to collect the item. They could easily remain in these various lines for up to four hours, waiting inconspicuously for Ivan to come home.

Having failed to persuade Galina Shaporina to speak, they were in danger of coming away from Moscow with nothing. Raisa had been pushed out of the apartment, the door shut in her face. Standing in the hallway, surrounded by staring neighbours, many of whom might be informers, there was no way they could try again. It was possible that Galina and her husband had already notified the State Security forces. Leo didn't think that was likely. Galina clearly believed that doing as little as possible was the safest course of action; if she tried to inform there was a possibility she'd be incriminating herself, drawing attention to herself. That was a small consolation. Their only achievement so far was to recruit Fyodor and his family into their investigation. Leo had instructed Fyodor to send any information he might be able to discover to Nesterov since mail addressed to Leo was being intercepted. Even so, they were no closer to identifying the kind of man they were looking for.

In these circumstances Raisa had pushed hard to speak to Ivan. What other options did they have except to leave the city empty-handed? Leo had reluctantly agreed. Raisa hadn't been able to get a message to Ivan. There was no way they could post a letter or make a call. She'd taken a calculated risk hoping that he'd be here. But she knew he rarely left Moscow, certainly not for any length of time. He didn't holiday, had no interest in the countryside. The only reason she could think that he wouldn't be at home was if he'd been arrested. On that front she could only hope that he was safe. Even though she was looking forward to seeing him again she was under no illusions – this was going to be an awkward encounter. She was with Leo, a man Ivan hated as he hated all officers of the MGB, a rule to which he made no exceptions. There were no *good ones*. However, it wasn't his dislike for Leo which worried her most. Rather, it was her affection for Ivan. Though she'd never cheated on Leo sexually, she'd cheated on him with Ivan in almost every other way, intellectually, emotionally, criticizing him behind his back. She'd struck up a friendship with a man defined by being against everything Leo had stood for. There was something awful about bringing these two men together. She wanted to tell Ivan as quickly as possible that Leo wasn't the same man and that he'd changed, that his blind faith in the State had been broken, smashed. She wanted to explain that she'd been wrong about her husband. She wanted them both to see that the differences between them were smaller than they'd ever realized. But there was little hope of that.

Leo wasn't looking forward to meeting Ivan – Raisa's kindred spirit. He'd be forced to watch as the connection sparked between them, forced to see up close the kind of man Raisa would've married had she been free to choose. That still hurt him, more than his loss of status, more than his loss of faith in the State. He'd blindly believed in love. Perhaps he'd clung to the notion as a way of counteracting the nature of his work. Perhaps subconsciously he needed to believe in love as a way of humanizing himself. That would explain the extreme justifications he'd created to rationalize her coldness to him. He'd refused to contemplate the possibility that she hated him. Instead, he'd closed his eyes and congratulated himself on having everything. He'd told his parents that she was the wife he'd always dreamt of. He'd been right – that was all she'd been, a dream, a fantasy and she'd shrewdly agreed to play along, all the time being terrified for her own safety, confiding in Ivan her true feelings.

This fantasy had been shattered months ago. Yet why wouldn't the wounds heal? Why couldn't he move on as he'd moved on from his devotion to the MGB? He'd been able to swap devotion to the MGB with another cause, devotion to this investigation. But he had no one else to love; there'd never been anyone else. The truth was that he couldn't let go of the small hope, the fantastical notion that maybe, just maybe she could love him for real. Although he was reluctant to trust his emotions since he'd been so categorically wrong before, he felt that he and Raisa were closer than they'd ever been. Was that merely as a result of their working together? It was true they no longer kissed or had sex. Since Raisa had told him the truth about their history it hadn't felt right. He'd been forced to accept that all their previous sexual experiences had meant nothing to her – or worse, they'd been unpleasant. Yet far from circumstance being the only thing keeping them together – *You have me. I have you.* – Leo preferred to think that circumstance had been keeping them apart. Leo had been a symbol of the State and one that Raisa had loathed. But now he no longer represented anything other than himself, divested of authority and stripped out of the system she so hated.

They were almost at the shop door when they saw Ivan approach from the other end of the street. They didn't call out or draw attention to themselves, they didn't move from the line, watching as he entered his apartment building. Raisa was about to leave the queue when Leo touched her arm, stopping her. They were dealing with a dissident: it was possible he was under surveillance. It occurred to Leo that maybe the hollow coin had belonged to Ivan: maybe he'd been the spy. What was it doing in amongst Raisa's clothes? Had she undressed in Ivan's apartment, picked up the coin by mistake? Leo pushed the thoughts aside, aware that his jealousy was playing tricks on him.

Leo checked the street. He couldn't see any agents taking position around the apartment. There were several obvious places – the foyer to the cinema, this grocery queue, sheltered doorways. No matter how well trained the agents might be, keeping watch on a building was difficult since it was such an unnatural action: remaining stationary, alone, doing nothing at all. After several minutes he was confident there was no one following Ivan. Without bothering to give a reason or make a pantomime of having forgotten a wallet, they left the queue exactly at the point when they were finally about to enter the shop. It was suspicious but Leo could count on the fact that most people were smart enough to mind their own business.

They entered the apartment building, walking up the stairs. Raisa knocked on the door. Footsteps could be heard inside. A voice, nervous, asked through the door.

—*Yes?*

—*Ivan, it's Raisa.*

A bolt was pulled back. Ivan cautiously opened the door. Upon seeing Raisa his suspicions dropped away and he smiled. She smiled in reply.

A couple of steps back Leo watched their reunion in the gloom of the hallway. She was pleased to see him, they were easy together. Ivan opened the door, moving forward, hugging her, relieved that she was still alive.

Ivan noticed Leo for the first time. His smile fell away like a picture falling off a wall. He let go of Raisa suddenly unsure, glancing at her expression, checking that this wasn't a betrayal of some kind. Sensing his unease, she remarked:

—*We have a lot to explain.*

—*Why are you here?*

—*It would be better to speak inside.*

Ivan didn't seem convinced. Raisa touched his arm.

—*Please, trust me.*

The apartment was small, well furnished, polished-wood floors. There were books: at a glance they all seemed to be authorized texts, Gorky, political tracts, Marx. The door to the bedroom was shut and there was no bed in the main room. Leo asked:

—*Are we alone?*

—*My children are with my parents. My wife is in hospital. She has tuberculosis.*

Raisa touched his arm again.

—*Ivan, I'm so sorry.*

—*We thought you'd been arrested. I feared the worst.*

—*We were lucky. We've been relocated to a town just west of the Urals. Leo refused to denounce me.*

Ivan couldn't keep the surprise from his face, as if such a thing were remarkable. Stung, Leo held his tongue as Ivan stared at him, evaluating.

—*Why did you refuse?*

—*She isn't a spy.*

—*Since when has the truth stopped you?*

Raisa interrupted:

—*Let's not get into that now.*

—*But it matters. Are you still MGB?*

—*No, I was demoted to the militia.*

—*Demoted? You escaped lightly.*

It was a question, accusatory.

—*It's only a temporary reprieve, demotion, exile – a prolonged punishment in obscurity.*

Seeking to comfort him, Raisa added:

—*We weren't followed here. We're sure of that.*

—*You've travelled all the way to Moscow? Why?*

—*We need help.*

At this, he was puzzled.

—*What could I possibly help you with?*

Leo took off his coat, his jumper, his shirt – retrieving the files taped to his body. He summarized the case, offering the papers to Ivan. Ivan accepted the papers but didn't look at them, sitting down on a chair and placing the evidence on the table beside him. After a moment he stood again, collecting a pipe, carefully filling it.

—*I take it the militia itself isn't investigating these murders?*

—*All these murders have been solved incorrectly, covered up or blamed on the mentally ill, some political enemy, a drunk, a vagrant. No connection has been drawn between them.*

—*And you two are working together now . . . ?*

Raisa blushed.

—*Yes, we're working together.*

—*You trust him?*

—*Yes, I trust him.*

Leo was forced to remain silent as Ivan questioned his wife, scrutinizing the integrity of their relationship in front of him.

—And together you plan to solve this crime?

Leo answered:

—If the State won't, then the people will have to.

—Spoken like a true revolutionary. Except, Leo, you've spent your entire life murdering for the State – whether in war or peace, whether they be Germans or Russians, or whoever else the State tells you it hates. Now I'm supposed to believe you're bucking the official line and thinking for yourself? I don't believe it. I think this is a trap. I'm sorry Raisa, I think he's trying to win his way back into the MGB. He's duped you, and now he wants to hand them me.

—He's not, Ivan. Look at the evidence. This is real, not some trick.

—I haven't trusted paper evidence for a long time, nor should you.

—I've seen one of these bodies, a young boy, his stomach cut open, his mouth filled with bark. I've seen it, Ivan. I was there. Someone did this to a child, someone enjoyed doing this and they're not going to stop. And they're not going to get caught by the militia. I know you have every right to be suspicious of us. But I can't prove it to you. If you can't trust me, then I'm sorry for coming here.

Leo stepped forward, ready to collect up the files. Ivan put his hand on top of them.

—I'll take a look. Close the curtains. And both of you sit down, you're making me nervous.

With the room cut off from the world outside, Leo and Raisa sat beside Ivan and narrated the specifics of the case, reciting as much information as they thought was useful. Leo summed up his own conclusions.

—He persuades these children to come with him. The footprints

in the snow were side by side, the boy had agreed to walk into the forests. Even though this crime seems insane, an obviously insane man would ramble, make no sense, an obviously insane man would scare these children.

Ivan nodded.

—*Yes, I agree.*

—*Since it's very difficult to move about this country without a designated reason, he must have a job, one that involves travel. He must have papers, documents. He must be integrated into our society; he must be acceptable, respectable. The question we can't answer is—*

—*Why does he do it?*

—*How can I catch him if I don't understand why? I have no image of him in my mind. What kind of man is he? Is he young or old? Is he rich or poor? We simply have no idea what kind of person we're looking for – beyond the basics, that he has a job and must appear on the outside at least, to be sane. But that is almost everyone.*

Ivan was smoking his pipe, absorbing everything Leo had said.

—*I'm afraid I cannot help you.*

Raisa sat forward.

—*But you have Western articles about these kinds of crime, murders that aren't conventionally motivated?*

—*What will they tell you? I might be able to get together a couple of articles. But they wouldn't be enough to give you an image of this man. You can't build a picture of him from two or three sensational pieces of Western journalism.*

Leo sat back: this had been a wasted journey. More worrying than that: had they set themselves an impossible task? They were hopelessly ill-equipped both materially and intellectually to tackle these crimes.

Ivan drew on his pipe, watching their reactions.

—However, I know a man who might be able to help. His name is Professor Zauzayez, a retired psychiatrist, a former MGB interrogator. He lost his sight. Going blind gave him a change of heart, an epiphany, just like you, Leo. He's now quite active in underground circles. You could tell him what you've told me. He might be able to help.

—Can we trust him?

—As much as you can trust anyone.

—What exactly can he do?

—You'll read him these documents, describe the photos: perhaps he'll be able to shed some light on the kind of person who'd do this such as his age, his background – that kind of thing.

—Where does he live?

—He won't allow you to go to his apartment. He's very cautious. He'll come here, if he'll come at all. I'll do my best to convince him, but I can make no guarantees.

Raisa smiled.

—Thank you.

Leo was pleased: an expert was certainly better than some journalistic scraps. Ivan stood up, putting his pipe down, moving to the side cabinet, the telephone.

The telephone.

This man had a telephone, in his apartment, his tidy, well-furnished apartment. Leo took in the details of the room. Something was wrong. This was no family apartment. Why did he live in such comparative luxury? And how had he managed to escape arrest? After their exile he should've been taken in. After all, the MGB had a file on him: Vasili had showed Leo the photos. How had he evaded the authorities?

The call had been set up. Ivan was now speaking on the phone.

—*Professor Zauzayez, Ivan Sukov here. I have an interesting task I need your help with. I can't speak about it on the phone. Are you free at the moment? Could you to come to my apartment? Yes, immediately if that's possible.*

Leo's body tensed. Why did he call him *professor* – if they were so close? Why call him that unless it was for their benefit? This was wrong. Everything was wrong.

Leo leapt up, his chair flying back. He was across the room before Ivan had a chance to react, grabbing the phone and twisting its cord tight around Ivan's neck. Leo was behind him now, back pressed up against the corner of the room, throttling him, tightening the cord. Ivan's legs were slipping on the polished floor, he gasped, unable to speak. Stunned, Raisa got out of her chair.

—*Leo!*

Leo raised his finger, indicating that she remain silent. With the cord still wrapped around Ivan's neck he lifted the receiver to his ear.

—*Professor Zauzayez?*

The phone went dead. They'd hung up. They were on their way.

—*Leo, let him go!*

But Leo tightened the cord. Ivan's face was turning red.

—*He's an operative, he's under cover. Look at how he lives. Look at his home. There is no Professor Zauzayez. That was his State Security contact; he's on his way to arrest us.*

—*Leo, you're making a mistake. I know this man.*

—*He's a fake dissident, placed underground, flushing out other anti-authority figures, accumulating evidence against them.*

—*Leo, you're wrong.*

—*There is no professor. They're on their way. Raisa, we don't have much time!*

Ivan's fingers were frantically clasping at the cord. Raisa shook her head, prising her fingers under the cord, relieving the pressure on his neck.

—*Leo, let him go, let him prove himself.*

—*Haven't all your friends been arrested, every one, except for him? That woman Zoya, where do you think the MGB got her name from? They didn't arrest on her on the basis of her prayers. That was just their excuse.*

Unable to get free, Ivan's legs began slipping across the floor, forcing Leo to take his full weight. Leo couldn't hold him for much longer.

—*Raisa, you never spoke to me about your friends. You never trusted me. Who did you confide in? Think!*

Raisa stared at Leo then at Ivan. It was true: all her friends were dead or arrested, all except him. She shook her head, refusing to believe it – it was the paranoia of today, the paranoia created by the State that any allegation no matter how far-fetched was enough to kill a man. She caught sight of Ivan's hand reaching for the cabinet drawer. She let go of the cord.

—*Leo, wait!*

—*We don't have time!*

—*Wait!*

She opened the drawer, riffling through. Inside was a letter-opener, sharp – the item Ivan was reaching for to defend himself. She could hardly blame him for that. Behind that was a book, his copy of *For Whom the Bell Tolls*. Why was it not hidden? She picked it up. A sheet of paper was inside it. On it was written a list of names: people the book had been loaned to. Some of the names were scored through. Her name had been scored through. On the other side of the page was a list of people he intended to loan the book to.

She turned to Ivan, raising the sheet of paper to his face, her hand shaking. Was there an innocent explanation? No, she already knew there wasn't. No dissident would be foolish enough to write down a list of names. He loaned the book to incriminate.

Leo was struggling to hold Ivan.

—*Raisa, turn away.*

She obeyed, walking to the other side of the room, the book still in her hand, listening as Ivan's legs kicked the furniture.

Same Day

Since he was a State Security operative, Ivan's death would immediately be catagorized as murder, an outrage that must have been committed by someone opposed to the system, an anti-Soviet element. The culprit was an outsider, a non-believer, so legitimizing the launch of a comprehensive investigation. There was no need to cover it up. Fortunately for Leo and Raisa, Ivan must have had many enemies. He was a man who'd lived his life betraying intrigued citizens, attracting them with the promise of censored material as a predator might attract its prey with alluring bait. The censored material had been provided to him by the State.

Before leaving the apartment, Raisa had taken the list of names, crumpling the paper into her pocket. Leo had hurriedly gathered together the case file. They had no idea how long it would take the State Security to respond to Ivan's call. They'd opened the front door, running down the stairs before approximating calmness as they walked away. As they'd reached the end of the street they'd glanced back. Agents were entering the building.

No one in Moscow had any reason to believe Leo and Raisa had returned. They wouldn't be immediate suspects. The officers in charge of the investigation, if the connection even occurred to him, would check with the MGB in Voualsk and discover that they were on a walking holiday. That excuse might hold unless a witness identified a man and a woman entering the apartment building. If that happened then their alibi would come under closer scrutiny. But Leo knew all of these facts were of only the slightest importance. Even if there was no evidence, even if they really had been on a walking holiday, this murder could be used as a pretext to arrest them. The weight of evidence was totally irrelevant.

In their current predicament trying to see his parents was an act of sheer brazenness. But there was no train back to Voualsk until five in the morning and more to the point Leo understood this would be his last chance to speak to them. Although he'd been refused contact with them since leaving Moscow and been given no details of their whereabouts, he had acquired the address several weeks ago. Knowing that the State departments tended to operate in autonomy, he'd felt there was a chance that an enquiry to the Department of Housing about Stepan and Anna wouldn't be automatically flagged up and passed on to the MGB. As a precaution he'd given a false name and tried to make his request seem as though it was official business, asking for a selection of names, including Galina Shaporina. Although all the other names had drawn a blank he'd managed to locate his parents. Vasili might have been expecting such an attempt; indeed, he might even have given orders for the address to be released. He knew Leo's weakness in exile would be his parents. If he wanted to catch him violating orders then his parents were the perfect trap. But it seemed unlikely that his parents would be under permanent surveillance for as long as four months. More probable was that the family they were forced to share with were also doubling as informers. He had to reach his parents without the other family seeing or hearing or knowing. His parents' safety depended upon this secrecy as much as their own. If they were caught, they'd be tied to Ivan's murder and Leo's entire family would die, perhaps even before the night was over. Leo was prepared to take the risk. He had to say goodbye.

They'd arrived on Ulitsa Vorontsovskaya. The house in question was an old building, pre-Revolutionary – the kind that had been sliced into a hundred tiny apartments, partitioned by nothing more than dirty sheets hanging off lengths of rope. There would be no amenities, no running water and no indoor toilets. Leo could see pipes jutting out of the windows to release the smoke from the wood stoves, the cheapest and dirtiest form of heating available. Surveying the property from a safe distance, they waited. Mosquitoes landed on their necks forcing them to continually slap their skin until their hands were spotted with their own blood. Leo knew no matter how long he stood here there was no way he could ascertain if this was a trap. He'd have to go in. He turned to Raisa. Before he could speak, she said:

—*I'll wait here.*

Raisa felt ashamed. She'd trusted Ivan; her opinion of him had been based solely on the trappings of his books and papers, his musings on Western culture, his alleged plans to help key dissident writers smuggle their works out to the West. Lies: all of it – how many writers and opponents of the regime had he snared? How many manuscripts had he burnt so that they were lost to the world? How many artists and free-thinkers had he directed the *Chekists* to arrest? She'd fallen for him because of his obvious differences to Leo. The difference had been a disguise. The dissident had been the policeman and the policeman had become the counter-revolutionary. The dissident had betrayed her, the policeman saved her. She could hardly say goodbye to Leo's parents, side by side with her husband, as though she'd been a loyal, loving wife. Leo took her hand.

—*I'd like you to come with me.*

The communal door was unlocked. The air inside was hot, stale and they immediately began to sweat: their clothes clung to their backs. Upstairs, apartment 27, the door was locked. Leo had broken into many properties. The older locks were normally more difficult to pick than the modern ones. Using the tip of a flick knife, he unscrewed the plate, revealing the lock mechanism. He inserted the blade but the lock refused to open. He wiped the sweat from his face, stopping for a moment, breathing deeply, closing his eyes. He dried his hands on his trousers, ignoring the mosquitoes – let them have their fill. He opened his eyes. *Concentrate.* The lock clicked open.

The only light came from the window facing the street. The room stank of sleeping bodies. Leo and Raisa waited by the door, adjusting to the gloom. They could distinguish the outline of three beds: two of the beds contained adult couples. A smaller bed appeared to have three children sleeping in it. In the kitchen area two small children slept on rugs on the floor like dogs under a table. Leo moved towards the sleeping adults. Neither of them were his parents. Had he been given the wrong address? Such incompetence was commonplace. Maybe the wrong address had been given to him deliberately?

Seeing the outline of another door, he moved towards it, the floorboards straining under each step. Raisa was just behind and of much lighter tread. The couple in the nearest bed began to stir. Leo paused, waiting for them to settle down. The couple remained asleep. Leo continued, Raisa following. He reached out, taking hold of the door handle.

There were no windows in this room, no light whatsoever. Leo had to keep the door open in order to see anything. He could make out that there were two beds and barely a gap between them. Not even a dirty sheet partitioned them. One bed contained two children. In the other bed there was an adult couple. He moved closer. These were his parents, sleeping pressed against each other, in a narrow single bed. Leo stood up, returning to Raisa and whispering:

—*Shut the door.*

Forced to move in total darkness, Leo felt his way along the bed until he was crouched on the floor beside his parents. He listened to them sleep, glad it was dark. He was crying. The room they'd been forced into was smaller than the bathroom of their previous apartment. They had no space of their own and no way of cutting themselves off from this family. They'd been sent here to die in parallel to their son's intended demise: humiliated.

At exactly the same time he placed his hands over their mouths. He could feel them waking, startled, tense. To stop them from calling out he whispered:

—*It's me. Leo. Don't make a noise.*

The tension in their bodies disappeared. He removed his hands from their mouths. He could hear them sitting up. He felt his mother's hands on his face. Blind, in this darkness, she was touching him. Her fingers stopped moving when they felt his tears. He heard her voice, barely a whisper:

—*Leo . . .*

His father's hands joined hers. Leo pressed their hands against his face. He'd sworn to look after them and he'd failed. All he could do was mutter:

—*I'm sorry.*

His father replied:

—*You've nothing to apologize for. We would've lived like this all of our life had it not been for you.*

His mother interrupted, her mind catching up with all the questions she wanted to ask:

—We thought you were dead. We were told you'd both been arrested.

—They lied. We've been sent to Voualsk. I was demoted, not imprisoned. I'm now working for the militia. I wrote to you many times, asking the letters be forwarded to you but they must have been intercepted and destroyed.

The children in the nearby bed stirred, their bed frame creaking. Everyone fell silent. Leo waited until he could hear the children's deep, slow breathing.

—Raisa is here.

He guided their hands to her. All four of them held hands. His mother asked.

—The baby?

—No.

Leo added, not wanting to complicate this reunion:

—Miscarriage.

Raisa spoke again, her voice broken with emotion.

—I'm sorry.

—This is not your fault.

Anna added:

—How long are you in Moscow for? Can we meet tomorrow?

—No, we shouldn't be here at all. If we're caught we'll be imprisoned and you will be too. We leave first thing in the morning.

—Shall we come outside so we can talk?

Leo thought about this. There was no way they'd all be able to leave the apartment without waking some of the family.

—We can't risk waking them. We have to talk here.

No one spoke for a while, four sets of hands clasped together in the darkness. Eventually Leo said:

—I have to get you a better place to live.

—No, Leo. Listen to me. You've often behaved as if our love was

dependent on the things you could do for us. Even as a child. That is not true. You must concentrate on your lives. We're old. It doesn't matter where we live any more. The only thing that has kept us alive is waiting for some news from you. We must accept that this will be the last time we meet. We mustn't make futile plans. We must say goodbye while we have the chance. Leo, I love you and I'm proud of you. I wish you could've had a better government to serve.

Anna's voice was now quite calm.

—You have each other, you love each other. You will have a good life, I believe that. Things will be different for you and for your children. Russia will be different. I feel very hopeful.

A fantasy, but she enjoyed believing it and Leo said nothing to contradict it.

Stepan took hold of Leo's hand, placing in it an envelope.

—This is a letter I wrote to you many months ago. I never had the chance to give it to you because you were sent away. I didn't want to post it. Read this when you're safely on the train. Promise me not to read it earlier. Promise me.

—What is it?

—Your mother and I considered very carefully the contents of this letter. It contains everything we wanted to say to you but were unable to for one reason or another. It contains all the things we should've spoken about a long time ago.

—Father . . .

—Take it, Leo, for us.

Leo accepted the letter and in the darkness the four of them hugged for the last time.

6 July

Leo approached the train, Raisa beside him. Were there more officers than usual on the platform? Was it possible they were already looking for them? Raisa was walking too fast: he took hold of her hand, briefly, and she slowed. The letter written by his parents had been stashed with the case file attached to his chest. They were almost at their carriage.

They boarded the crowded train. Leo whispered to Raisa.

—*Stay here.*

She nodded. He entered the cramped toilet, locking the door behind him, dropping the toilet lid to reduce the smell. Taking off his jacket, unbuttoning his shirt, he removed the thin cotton bag he'd stitched to hold the case file. It was soaked with sweat and the ink from the typed documents had made an impression on his skin, writing printed across his chest.

He found the letter, turning it over in his hand. No name on the envelope, it was crumpled, dirty. He wondered how his parents had managed to keep it a secret from the other family, who inevitably would've searched through their belongings. One of them must have kept the letter on their person at all times, morning and night.

The train began to move, leaving Moscow. He'd kept his promise. He was now allowed to read it. He waited until they'd left the station before opening the envelope and unfolding the letter. It was his father's handwriting.

Leo, neither your mother nor I have any regrets. We love you. We always expected there would come a day when we'd talk to you about this matter. To our surprise that day never came. We thought you would raise it when you were ready. But you never did, you've always acted as though it never happened. Perhaps it was easier to teach yourself to forget? This is why we said nothing. We thought this was your way of dealing with the past. We were afraid that you'd blanked it out and that bringing it up again would only cause hurt and pain. In short, we were happy together and we didn't want to ruin that. That was cowardly of us.

I say once again, both I and your mother love you very much, and neither of us have any regrets.

Leo—

Leo stopped reading, turning his head away. Yes, he remembered what had happened. He knew what the letter would go on to say. And yes, he'd spent his whole life trying to forget. He folded the letter before carefully ripping it into small pieces. He stood up, opening the small window, throwing the fragments out. Caught in the wind, the uneven squares of paper rose up into the air and disappeared out of view.

South-Eastern Rostov Oblast
Sixteen Kilometres North of
Rostov-on-Don

Same Day

Nesterov had spent his last day in the oblast visiting the town of Gukovo. He was now on the *elektrichka*, travelling back towards Rostov. Though the newspapers made no mention of these crimes, the incidents of murdered children had entered the public domain in the form of whispers and rumour. So far the militia in their closed localities had refused to see each murder as anything other than an isolated occurrence. But people outside of the militia, unburdened by any theory regarding the nature of crime, had begun to thread together these deaths. Unofficial explanations had begun to circulate. Nesterov had heard it stated that there was a wild beast murdering children in the forests around Shakhty. Different places had conjured different beasts, and supernatural explanations of one kind or another were being repeated all across the oblast. He'd heard a fearful mother claim the beast was part man part animal, a child brought up by bears who now hated all normal children, making them its food source. One village had been sure it was a vengeful forest spirit, the inhabitants performing elaborate ceremonies in an attempt to mollify this demon.

The people living in the Rostov oblast had no idea that there were similar crimes hundreds of kilometres away. They believed this was their blight, an evil that plagued them. In a way Nesterov agreed with them. There was no doubt in his mind that he was in the heartland of these crimes. The concentration of murders was far higher here than anywhere else. While he had no inclination to believe the supernatural explanations, he was in part seduced by the most persuasive and widespread of the theories, the notion that Nazi soldiers had been left behind as Hitler's final act of revenge: soldiers whose last orders were to murder Russia's children. These Nazi soldiers had been trained in the Russian way of life, blending in, while systematically murdering children according to a predetermined ritual. It would explain the scale of the murders, the geographical scope, the savagery but also the absence of any sexual interference. There wasn't one killer but many, perhaps as many as ten or twelve, each acting independently, travelling to towns and killing indiscriminately. This theory had developed such momentum that some local militia, who'd paradoxically claimed to have solved all the crimes, began questioning any man who could speak German.

Nesterov stood up, stretching his legs. He'd been on the *elektrichka* for three hours. It was slow and uncomfortable and he wasn't used to sitting still for so long. He walked the length of the carriage, opening the window, watching the lights of the city approach. Having heard about the murder of a boy named Petya living on a collective farm near Gukovo he'd travelled there this morning. Without too much difficulty he'd found the parents of the boy concerned. Though he'd given a false name he'd truthfully explained that he was working on an investigation involving the similar murders of a number of children. The boy's parents had been staunch advocates of the Nazi-soldier theory, explaining that the Germans might even have been helped by traitorous Ukrainians, assisting them to integrate into society before murdering at random. The boy's father had shown Nesterov Petya's book of stamps, which the couple kept in its wooden box under their bed, a shrine to their dead son. Neither of them could look at the stamps without crying. Both parents had been refused access to their boy's body. But they'd heard what had been done to him. He'd been savaged as if by an animal, dirt thrust in his mouth as if to spite them further. The father, who'd fought in the Great Patriotic War, knew that the Nazi soldiers were given drugs to ensure they were vicious, amoral and merciless. He was sure that these killers were the products of some such Nazi-created drug. Maybe they'd been made addicted to children's blood, without which they'd die. How else could these men commit such crimes? Nesterov had no words of consolation except a promise that the culprit would be caught.

The *elektrichka* arrived at Rostov. Nesterov disembarked, confident only that he'd found the centre of these crimes. Having once been a member of the militia in Rostov before being transferred to Voualsk four years ago he'd had little difficulty gathering information. According to his most recent count fifty-seven children had been killed in what he considered to be comparable circumstances. A high portion of those murders had taken place in this oblast. Was it possible that across the entire western half of the country Nazi infiltrators had been left behind? An enormous stretch of land had been occupied by the Wehrmacht. He himself had fought in the Ukraine and encountered first-hand the rape and murder by the retreating army. Deciding not to commit himself to one theory or another, he pushed these explanations to one side. Leo's mission in Moscow would be crucial to bring some kind of professionalism to the speculation of the killer's identity. Nesterov had been tasked with the accumulation of facts regarding the killer's location.

During their vacation his family had been staying in his mother's apartment in the New Settlement, built during one of the postwar accommodation programmes with all the usual characteristics: constructed to fulfil a quota rather than to be lived in. They were already in a state of decay: they'd been in a state of decay before they were even finished. With no running water or central plumbing, they were similar to his home back in Voualsk. He and Inessa had agreed to lie to his mother, assuring her that they were now living in a new apartment. His mother had been comforted by the lie as though she herself was now living in that new apartment too. Approaching his mother's house Nesterov checked his watch. He'd left at six this morning and it was now coming up to nine in the evening. Fifteen hours had been spent for the gain of no real information. His time was up. Tomorrow they were returning home.

He entered the courtyard. Washing hung from side to side. He could see his own clothes amongst them. He touched them. They were dry. Moving through the washing he approached the door of his mother's apartment, entering the kitchen.

Inessa was seated on a wooden stool, her face bloody, her hands tied. Behind her stood a man he didn't recognize. Without trying to figure out what had happened or who this man was Nesterov strode forward, overwhelmed with anger. He didn't care that the man was wearing a uniform: he'd kill him all the same, whoever he was. He raised his fist. Before he could get close pain engulfed his hand. Looking to the side he saw a woman, perhaps forty years old. She was holding a black truncheon. He'd seen her face before. He remembered now – on the beach, two days ago. In her other hand she held a gun, casually, enjoying her position of power. She gestured to her officer. He stepped forward, throwing a selection of papers onto the floor. Falling around their feet was every document he'd accumulated over the past two months, photos, descriptions, maps – the case file of the murdered children.

— *General Nesterov, you're under arrest.*

Voualsk

7 July

Leo and Raisa got off the train, waiting on the platform, pretending to fix their bags until all the other passengers had moved into the main building. It was late but not yet dark and feeling exposed they climbed off the platform, hurrying into the forest.

Reaching the spot where they'd hidden their belongings, Leo stopped, catching his breath. He stared up at the trees, wondering at his decision to destroy the letter. Had he done his parents a disservice? He understood why they'd wanted to write down their thoughts and feelings: they'd wanted to make their peace. But Raisa had been right about him when she'd said:

> *Is that how you're able to sleep at night, by blanking events from your mind?*

She was more right than she knew.

Raisa touched his arm.

—Are you OK?

She'd asked him what was in the letter. He'd considered lying and telling her it contained information about his family —

personal details that he'd forgotten. But she'd have known he was lying. So, instead, he'd told her the truth that he'd destroyed the letter, ripped it into a hundred pieces, thrown it out of the window. He didn't want to read it. His parents could rest easily believing that they'd unburdened themselves. To his relief she hadn't questioned his decision and hadn't mentioned it since.

Using their hands they dug away at the cover of leaves and loose soil, unearthing their belongings. They took off their city clothes, intending to change back into the trail gear they'd set out in – a necessary part of their cover. Undressed, alone, they paused, naked, staring at each other. Perhaps it was the danger, perhaps it was opportunistic, but Leo wanted her. Uncertain about her feelings for him, he did nothing, waiting, afraid to make the first move, as though they'd never had sex before, as though this was their first time with both of them unsure of the boundaries, unsure what was acceptable and what wasn't. She reached out, touching his hand. That was enough. He pulled her towards him, kissing her. They'd murdered together, deceived together, plotted and planned and lied together. They were criminals, the two of them, them against the world. It was time to consummate this new relationship. If only they could stay here, live here in this exact moment, hidden in the forests, enjoying these feelings forever.

*

They rejoined the forest trail, walking into town. Arriving at Basarov's they entered the main room. Leo was holding his breath, expecting hands to grab his shoulders. But there was no one here, no agents and no officers. They were safe, at least for another day. Basarov was in the kitchen and didn't even turn round when he heard them arrive.

Upstairs, they unlocked their room. A note had been pushed

under the door. Leo put his bags down on the bed. He picked up the note. It was from Nesterov, dated today.

> *Leo, if you're back as planned, meet me tonight in my office at nine. Come alone. Bring all the documents relating to the matter we've been discussing. Leo, it's very important that you're not late.*

Leo checked his watch. He had half an hour.

Same Day

Even back in the militia headquarters, Leo was taking no chances. He'd hidden the papers in official documents. The blinds to Nesterov's office were drawn shut and it was impossible to see in. He checked his watch: he was late, two minutes late. Unable to see how that would matter particularly, he knocked on the door. Almost as soon as he did the door was opened, as though Nesterov had been waiting behind it. Leo was ushered in with a sudden, inexplicable urgency, the door shut behind him.

Nesterov was moving with an uncharacteristic impatience. His desk was covered with documents from the case file. He took hold of Leo by the shoulders and spoke in a hushed, hurried voice.

—Listen very carefully and don't interrupt. I was arrested in Rostov. I was forced to confess. I had no choice. They had my family. I told them everything. I thought I might be able to persuade them to help, persuade them that they should elevate our case to an official level. They reported it back to Moscow. They've accused us of anti-Soviet agitation. They think this is a personal vendetta you have against the State, an act of revenge. They dismissed our findings as an elaborate piece of Western propaganda: they're certain that you and your wife are working as spies. They offered me a choice. They're prepared to leave my family alone if I give them you and all the information we've collected.

Leo's world fell away. Even though he'd known danger was close he hadn't expected it to cut across his path just yet.

—*When?*

—*Right now. The building's surrounded. Agents will enter this room in fifteen minutes, arresting you in this office and collecting every piece of evidence we've amassed. I'm to spend these minutes finding out all the information you discovered in Moscow.*

Leo stepped back, looking at his watch. It was five past nine.

—*Leo, you have to listen to me. There's a way for you to escape. But for this to work don't interrupt, don't ask any questions. I've come up with a plan. You're going to hit me with my gun, knocking me unconscious. You're then going to leave this office, go down one flight of stairs and hide in the offices to the right of the stairway. Leo, are you listening? You need to concentrate. The doors are unlocked. Go into them, don't turn on the lights and lock the doors behind you.*

But Leo wasn't listening – all he could think about was.

—*Raisa?*

—*She's being arrested as we speak. I'm sorry but there's nothing you can do about her. You need to concentrate, Leo, or this is over.*

—*This is over. This was over the moment you told them everything.*

—*They had everything, Leo. They had my work. They had my file. What was I supposed to do? Let them kill my family? They still would've arrested you. Leo, you can get angry with me, or you can escape.*

Leo shook free of Nesterov's grip, pacing the office, his mind trying to catch up. Raisa had been arrested. They'd both known this moment would come but had understood it only as a concept, an idea. They hadn't understood what it would mean. The prospect of never seeing her again made it difficult to breathe.

Their relationship, their relationship reborn, consummated barely two hours ago in the forest, was over.

—*Leo!*

What would she want? She wouldn't want him to get sentimental. She'd want him to succeed, to escape, to listen.

—*Leo!*

—*All right, what's your plan?*

Nesterov continued, recapping the first part:

—*You're going to hit me with my gun, knocking me unconscious. You're then going to leave this office, go down one flight of stairs and hide in the offices to the right of the stairway. Hide in those offices; wait until the agents enter the building. They'll come up to this floor, passing you by. Once they've gone past, you descend to the ground floor, exiting through one of the windows at the back. There's a car parked there. Here are the keys, which you will have stolen from me. You have to leave town, don't look for anyone or stop for anything, just drive. You will have a small advantage. They'll believe that you're on foot, somewhere in the town. By the time they realize you've taken a car, you should be free.*

—*Free to do what?*

—*To solve these crimes.*

—*My trip to Moscow was a washout. The eyewitness refused to talk. I still don't have any more of an idea of who this man is.*

That took Nesterov by surprise.

—*Leo, you can do this, I know it. I believe in you. You need to head to Rostov-on-Don. That's the centre of these crimes. I'm convinced that's where your efforts must be focused. There are theories about who is killing these children. One involves a group of former Nazi—*

Leo interrupted.

—*No, it's the work of an individual, acting alone. He has a job.*

He appears normal. If you're sure the concentration of murders is Rostov then it's likely he lives and works there. His job is the connection between all these locations. His job means that he travels: he kills as he travels. If we can work out his job, then we have the man.

Leo checked his watch. There were only minutes left before he'd have to leave. Nesterov put his fingers on the two towns in question.

—What is the connection between Rostov and Voualsk? There have been no murders east of this town. At least that we know of. That suggests that this is the end point, this is his destination.

Leo agreed.

—Voualsk has the car assembly plant. There are no other significant industries here other than the lumber mills. But there are lots of factories in Rostov.

Nesterov knew both locations better than Leo.

—The car factory and the Rostelmash share close ties.

—What is the Rostelmash?

—A tractor factory, enormous, the biggest in the USSR.

—Do they share components?

—The tyres for the GAZ-20 come from there while engine components are shipped south in exchange.

Could that be the connection? The murders followed the train lines up from the south and across into the west, point to point. Running with this theory, Leo remarked.

—If the car plant sends deliveries to the Rostelmash factory then that factory must employ a tolkach. *Someone travels here to make sure the car plant fulfils its quota obligations.*

—There have only been two child-murders here and they were recent. The factories have been working together for some time.

—The murders in the north of the country have been the most

recent. That means he's just got this job. Or that he's only just been posted along this route. We need the employment records at Rostelmash. If we're right, by cross-referencing those records with the locations of these murders we'll have the man.

They were close. If they weren't being hunted, if they had the freedom to act at their leisure, they could've discovered the killer's name by the end of the week. But they didn't have a week, or the support of the State. They had four minutes. It was eleven past nine. Leo had to leave. He took one document – the list of murders, compiled with dates and locations. That was all he needed. Having folded it into his pocket he moved to the door. Nesterov stopped him. He was holding his gun. Leo took hold of the weapon, delaying for a moment. Nesterov saw this hesitation and remarked:

—Or my family will die.

Leo struck him across the side of his head, splitting the skin and sending him to his knees. Still conscious, he looked up.

—Good luck, now hit me properly.

Leo raised the gun. Nesterov closed his eyes.

Hurrying into the corridor, Leo reached the stairs only to realize he'd forgotten the car keys. They were on the table. He turned around, ran back down the corridor into the office, stepping over Nesterov, grabbing the keys. He was late – nine fifteen, agents were entering the building. Leo was still in the office, exactly where they wanted him. He ran out, down the corridor, down the stairs. He could hear footsteps coming up towards him. Reaching the third floor he darted to the right, grabbing hold of the nearest office door. It was unlocked, as Nesterov had promised. He entered, locking the door behind him just as the agents ran up the stairs.

Leo waited in the gloom. All the blinds had been closed so that no one from outside could see in. He could hear the clump of footsteps. There were at least four agents on this stairway. He was tempted to remain in this room, behind this locked door, in temporary safety. The windows opened out onto the main square. He glanced out. There was a ring of men outside the main entrance. He pulled away from the window. He had to reach the ground floor and the back. He unlocked the door, peering out. The corridor was empty. Shutting the door behind him he moved to the stairway. He could hear an agent's voice below him. Leo ran to the next stairway. He couldn't see or hear anyone. As soon as he began running, shouting broke out on the top floor: they'd found Nesterov.

A second wave of agents entered the building, alerted by the calls of their colleagues. It was too much of a risk going down another flight of steps, and abandoning Nesterov's plan, Leo remained on the first floor. He only had moments of confusion to exploit before the men organized themselves into search teams. Unable to reach the ground floor, he ran along the corridor, entering the toilet, a room facing out onto the back of the building. He opened the window. The window was high up, narrow, barely wide enough to squeeze through. The only way he'd fit was if he clambered head first. Checking outside, he couldn't see any officers. He was maybe five metres above the ground. He pulled his body through the window, hanging above the ground, supported by his feet. There was nothing to grab onto. He'd have to let himself fall, protecting his head with his hands.

He hit the ground with his palms, his wrists snapping back. He heard a shout, looked up. An agent was at the top-floor window. Leo had been spotted. Ignoring the pain in his wrists, he stood up, running towards the side street where the car was meant to be parked. Shots rang out. Puffs of brick dust exploded to the side of his head. He dropped down, crouching, still running. More shots rang out, pinging off the street. He turned the corner out of the line of fire.

The car was there, parked, ready. He clambered in, slotting the key in the ignition. The engine spluttered and died. He tried again. It wouldn't start. He tried again – *please* – this time it started. Putting the car into gear, he pulled out, accelerating, careful not to let the tyres screech. It was crucial that the agents following didn't see the car. He'd be one of the few cars on the streets. Since it was a militia vehicle, hopefully any officers who saw it would presume he was on their side whilst they continued their search on foot.

There was no traffic. Leo was driving too fast, too ragged, heading out of the city. Nesterov was wrong: he couldn't drive all the way to Rostov. For a start it was several hundred kilometres, he didn't have anywhere near enough petrol and he had no way of getting any more. More importantly, once they figured out that he'd taken a car they'd shut down all the roads. He had to get as far away as he could then dump the car, conceal it and slip into the countryside, before boarding a train. As long as they didn't find the abandoned car his chances were much better without it.

He accelerated onto the only major connecting road which led in and out of the town, travelling west. He checked the rear-view mirror. If they were going to organize a comprehensive search of the nearby buildings, believing him to be on foot, then he might have at least an hour or so head start. He increased his speed, reaching the car's top speed of eighty kilometres per hour.

Up ahead there were men standing on the road clustered around a parked car: a militia car. It was a roadblock. They'd taken no chances. If the road west was blocked so was the road heading east. They'd closed down the entire town. His only hope now lay in punching through the roadblock. He'd pick up enough speed, smash into the car positioned across the road. The car would be knocked aside. He'd have to control the impact. With their car damaged, they wouldn't be able to pursue him immediately. It was desperate, shortening his advantage to a matter of minutes.

The agents up ahead began firing. Bullets hit the front of the car, sparking against the metal. A bullet punctured the windscreen. Leo lowered himself behind the steering wheel, no longer able to see the road. The car was in position: he just had to hold steady. Bullets continued smashing through the windscreen. Fragments of glass showered down. He was still on course – braced for the collision.

The car lurched down and to the side. Sitting back up in the seat, Leo tried to maintain control but the car veered left, pulling away from him. The tyres had been shot out. There was nothing he could do. The car flipped onto its side, the window smashing. He was thrown against the door, millimetres from the road, skidding, sparks flaring up. The front smashed into the other car, spinning Leo's car around. It rolled onto the roof, running off the road into the verge. Leo was tossed from the door to the roof where he lay huddled as the car finally came to a stop.

*

Leo opened his eyes. He wasn't sure if he could move and he couldn't muster the strength to find out. He was staring up at the night sky. His thoughts moved slowly. He was no longer in the car. Someone must have dragged him out. A face appeared above him, blocking the stars, looking down at him. Concentrating, Leo focused on the man's face.

It was Vasili.

Rostov-on-Don

Same Day

Aron had been under the impression that a job in the militia might be exciting or at least more exciting than working on a *kolkhoz*. He'd always known it didn't pay very well but the upside was that competition wasn't fierce. When it came to looking for work he'd never been a strong candidate. There was nothing wrong with him. In fact, he'd done well at school. However, he'd been born with a *deformed* upper lip. That's what the doctor had told him – it was *deformed* and there was nothing he could do. It looked as though a portion of his upper lip had been cut away and the remaining bits stitched together so that the lip went up in the middle, revealing a portion of his front teeth. The overall result was a permanent sneer. Although this made no difference to his ability to work it certainly made a difference to his ability to get a job. The militia had seemed like the perfect solution, they were hungry for applicants. They'd bully him, make comments behind his back – he was used to that. He'd put up with it all just as long as he got to use his brain.

Yet here he was, in the middle of the night, sitting in the bushes, getting bitten by bugs, watching a bus shelter for signs of *unusual activity.*

Aron hadn't been told why he was sitting here or what *unusual activity* might possibly mean. As one of the youngest members of the department, only twenty years old, he wondered if this was some kind of initiation ritual – a test of loyalty, to see if he could follow orders. Obedience was valued more than anything else.

So far the only person around was a girl at the nearby bus stop. She was young, maybe fourteen or fifteen, but she was trying to look older. She seemed drunk. Her shirt was unbuttoned. He watched her straighten her skirt and play with her hair. What was she doing at the bus stop? There were no buses until the morning.

A man approached. He was tall, wearing a hat and long coat. His glasses had lenses as thick as glass bottoms. Carrying a smart case, he stood by the timetable, reading it with his finger. As though the girl was some kind of scantily clad spider, waiting in the corner she immediately got up, moving towards him. He continued reading the timetable as the girl circled him, touching his case, his hand, his jacket. The man seemed to ignore these advances until finally he looked away from the timetable, studying the girl. They spoke. Aron couldn't hear what they were saying. The girl disagreed with something, shaking her head. Then she shrugged. They were in agreement. The man turned around and seemed to stare straight at Aron, looking right at the under-growth beside the shelter. Had the man seen him? It didn't seem likely – they were in light, he was in shadow. Both the man and girl began walking towards him, straight towards the place where he was hiding.

Aron was confused, checking his position – he was completely hidden. They couldn't have seen him. Even if they had, why were they walking towards him? They were only metres away. He could hear them talking. He waited, crouched into the undergrowth, only to find that they'd walked straight past him, heading into the trees.

Aron stood up.

—*Stop!*

The man froze, his shoulders hunched up. He turned around. Aron did his best to sound authoritative.

—*What are you two doing?*

The girl, who didn't seem at all afraid or concerned, answered:

—*We were going for a walk. What happened to your lip? It's really ugly.*

Aron flushed with embarrassment. The girl was staring at it with obvious disgust. He paused for a moment, composing himself.

—*You were going to have sex. In a public place; you're a prostitute.*

—*No, we were going for a walk.*

The man added, his voice pathetic, barely audible:

—*No one has done anything wrong. We were just having a conversation.*

—*Let me see your papers.*

The man stepped forward, fumbling for his papers in his jacket. The girl hung back, nonchalant: no doubt she'd been stopped before. She didn't seem fazed. He checked the man's papers. The man was called Andrei. The papers were in order.

—*Open your case.*

Andrei hesitated, sweating profusely. He'd been caught. He'd never imagined this would happen: he'd never imagined his plan would fail. He lifted the case, opening the buckle. The young officer peered in, his hand tentatively searching through. Andrei stared down at his shoes, waiting. When he looked up the officer was holding his knife, a long knife with a serrated blade. Andrei felt close to tears.

—*Why do you carry this?*

—*I travel a lot. Often I eat on trains. I use the knife to cut salami. Cheap, tough salami but my wife refuses to buy any other kind.*

Andrei did use the knife for lunch and dinner. The officer found half a stick of salami. It was cheap and tough. The edge was rough. It had been cut by the same knife.

Aron lifted out a glass jar with a sealed top. The jar was clean and empty.

—*What's this for?*

—*Some of the component parts I collect, as samples, are fragile, some are dirty. This jar is useful for my work. Listen, officer, I know I shouldn't have gone off with this girl. I don't know what came over me. I was here, checking the times for the buses tomorrow and she approached me. You know how it is – with urges. One came over me. But look in the pocket of the case, you'll find my Party membership card.*

Aron found the card. He also found a photograph of the man's wife and two daughters.

—*My daughters. There's no need to take this any further, is there, officer? The girl is the one to blame: I would've been on my way home by now otherwise.*

A decent citizen momentarily corrupted by a drunken girl, a reprobate. This man had been polite: he hadn't stared at Aron's lip or made any disparaging comments. He'd treated him as an equal even though he was older with a better job and a member of the Party. He was the victim. She was the criminal.

Having felt the net close around him, Andrei realized he was almost free. The photograph of his family had proved invaluable on numerous occasions. He sometimes used it to persuade reluctant children that he was a man who could be trusted. He was a father himself. In his trouser pocket he could feel the coarse length of string. Not tonight; he'd have to exercise patience in the future. He could no longer kill in his home town.

Aron was about to let the man go, putting the card and photograph back, when he caught sight of something else in the case: a slip of newspaper folded in half. He pulled it out, opening it up.

Andrei was unable to watch this idiot with his revolting lip touch that piece of paper with his dirty fingers. He could barely stop himself from snatching it from his hands.

—*May I have that back, please?*

For the first time the man's voice had become agitated. Why was this paper so important to him? Aron studied the page. It was a clipping from several years ago, the ink had faded. There was no text, no copy – that had all been cut away so that it was impossible to tell which newspaper it had come from. All that remained was a photograph taken during the Great Patriotic War. It showed the burning wreck of a panzer. Russian soldiers stood with guns triumphantly pointing into the air, dead German soldiers at their feet. It was a victory photo, a propaganda photo. With his *deformed* upper lip Aron understood all too well why this photo had been printed in a newspaper. The Russian soldier at the centre of the photo was a handsome man with a winning smile.

Moscow

10 July

Leo's face was swollen, tender to touch. His right eye remained closed, hidden beneath folds of puffy skin. There was intense pain down the side of his chest as though he'd broken several ribs. He'd been given basic medical assistance at the scene of the crash, but as soon as it had been ascertained that his life wasn't in danger he'd been loaded into a truck under armed guard. On the journey back to Moscow he'd felt each bump in the road like a punch in the gut. Without painkillers on the journey he had passed out several times. His guards had woken him by prodding him with the barrels of their guns, fearful of him dying on their watch. Leo had spent the journey alternating between feverish heat and freezing cold. These injuries, he accepted, were merely the beginning.

The irony of ending up here – secured to a chair in a basement interrogation cell in the Lubyanka – hadn't escaped his attention. A guardian of the State had become its prisoner, a not uncommon reversal of fortunes. This is what it felt like to be an enemy of his country.

The door opened. Leo raised his head. Who was this man with sallow skin and yellow-stained teeth? He was a former colleague, he remembered that much. But he couldn't remember the man's name.

—*You don't remember me?*

—*No.*

—*I'm Dr Zarubin. We've met on a couple of occasions. I visited you when you were ill not so many months ago. I'm sorry to see you in this predicament. I say that not as a criticism of the action being taken against you; that is just and fair. I simply mean that I wish you hadn't done it.*

—*What have I done?*

—*You've betrayed your country.*

The doctor felt Leo's ribs. Each touch caused him to clench his teeth.

—*Your ribs aren't broken, as I was told. They're bruised. No doubt it's painful. But none of your injuries require surgery. I've been ordered to clean up the cuts and change the dressings.*

—*Treatment before torture, a quirk of this place. I once saved a man's life only to bring him here. I should have let Brodsky drown in that river.*

—*I don't know this man of whom you speak.*

Leo fell silent. Anyone could regret their actions once the tables had been turned. He understood, more clearly than ever, that his only chance of redemption had slipped through his fingers. The killer would continue to kill, concealed not by any masterful brilliance but by his country's refusal to admit that such a man even existed, wrapping him in perfect immunity.

The doctor finished patching up Leo's injuries. Such assistance was intended to guarantee full sensitivity to the torture which would follow. Make them better so they could be hurt to a greater extent. The doctor leaned down and whispered into Leo's ear.

—I'm now going to tend to your wife. Your pretty wife, she's tied up next door. Quite helpless, and it's your fault. Everything I'm going to do to her is your fault. I'm going to make her hate the day she ever loved you. I'm going to make her say it aloud.

As though it had been spoken in a foreign language it took a while for Leo to comprehend what was being said to him. He had no grudge against this man. He'd barely recognized him. Why was he threatening Raisa? Leo tried to stand up, lunging for the doctor. But his chair was secured to the floor and he was secured to the chair.

Dr Zarubin pulled back, like a man who'd put his head too close to a lion's cage. He watched Leo strain against his restraints, his veins bulging in his neck, his face red, his eye pathetically swollen. It was intriguing – like watching a fly trapped under a glass. This man didn't understand the nature of his predicament.

Helplessness

The doctor picked up his case and waited for the guard to open the door. He expected Leo to call out after him, perhaps threaten to kill him. But on that front, at least, he was disappointed.

He walked down the basement corridor, a matter of metres, arriving at the adjacent cell. The door was opened. Zarubin entered. Raisa was seated and secured in exactly the same way as her husband. The doctor was excited by the prospect of her recognizing him and recognizing that she should have accepted his offer. If she had, she would've been safe. She was evidently not the skilled survivor he'd taken her for. She had extraordinary beauty, something she'd failed to capitalize on, opting instead for fidelity. Perhaps she believed in an afterlife, a heaven where her loyalty would be rewarded. It had no value here.

Convinced that he'd find her regret stimulating, he expected her to beg:

Help me.

She'd accept any conditions now: he could ask anything of her. He could treat her like filth and she'd willingly accept it and plead for more. She'd submit to him completely. The doctor opened the grate on the wall. Although the grate appeared to be part of a ventilation system, in fact it was designed to carry sound from one cell to another. He wanted Leo to listen to every word.

Raisa stared up at Zarubin, watching as he struck a look of pantomime sadness, no doubt trying to communicate a sense of pity, as if to say:

If only you'd accepted my offer.

He put his case down and began examining her even though she had no injuries.

—*I need to study every part of you. For my report, you understand.*

Raisa had been taken without any fuss. The restaurant had been surrounded: agents had entered and secured her. As she'd been escorted out, Basarov had shouted with predictable malice that she deserved whatever punishment she got. Tied up in the back of a truck, given no information, she had no idea what had happened to Leo until she overheard an officer say they'd got him. She guessed, from the satisfaction in his voice, that Leo had at least attempted to escape.

She tried to remain looking straight ahead as the doctor's hands crept across her body, as though he wasn't there. But she couldn't help stealing glances at him. His knuckles were hairy, his nails perfectly clean and carefully cut. The guard behind her began to laugh, a childish laugh. She concentrated on the idea that her body was out of his reach and no matter what he did, he wouldn't be able to lay a finger on her. It was an impossible idea to sustain. His fingers moved up the inside of her leg with awful and deliberate slowness. She felt tears in her eyes. She blinked them away. Zarubin moved closer: his face close to hers. He kissed her cheek, sucking her skin into his mouth as though about to take a bite.

The door opened. Vasili entered. The doctor pulled back, stood up, stepping back. Vasili was annoyed.

—*She's not injured. There's no need for you to be here.*

—*I was just making sure.*

—*You may leave.*

Zarubin took his case and left. Vasili closed the grate. He crouched down beside Raisa, observing her tears.

—*You're strong. Maybe you think you can hold out. I understand your desire to stay loyal to your husband.*

—*Do you?*

—*You're right. I don't. My point is it would be better for you if you told me everything immediately. You think I'm a monster. But do you know who I learnt that particular line from? Your husband, that's what he used to tell people before they were tortured – some of them in this very room. He meant it sincerely, if that matters.*

Raisa stared at this man's handsome features and wondered, as she had in the train station all those months ago, why he appeared ugly. His eyes were dull, not lifeless or stupid, but cold.

—*I'll tell you everything.*

—*But will that be enough?*

*

Leo should have been conserving his strength until there was an opportunity to act. That moment wasn't now. He'd seen many prisoners waste their energy banging fists against doors, shouting, relentlessly pacing their tiny cells. At the time he'd wondered why they couldn't see the futility of their actions. Now that he was in that same predicament he finally appreciated how they felt. It was as if his body was allergic to this confinement. It had nothing to do with logic or reasoning. He simply couldn't sit and wait and do nothing. Instead, he strained against his restraints until his wrists began to bleed. Some part of him actually believed he might be able to break these chains even though he'd seen a hundred men and women secured to them and not once had they broken. Lit up with the notion of a great escape, he ignored the fact that this kind of hope was as dangerous as any torture they could inflict.

Vasili entered, gesturing for the guard to place a chair opposite Leo. The guard obeyed, positioning it just outside of Leo's reach. Vasili stepped forward, picking up the chair and moving it closer. Their knees were almost touching. He stared at Leo, taking in the way his whole body was straining against his restraints.

—*Relax, your wife is unharmed. She's next door.*

Vasili waved the guard towards the grate. He opened it. Vasili called out:

—*Raisa: say something to your husband. He's worried about you.*

Raisa's voice could be heard like a faint echo:

—*Leo?*

Leo pulled back, relaxing his body. Before Leo could answer the guard slammed the grate shut. Leo looked at Vasili.

—*There's no need to torture either of us. You know how many sessions I've seen. I understand there's no point in holding out. Ask me any question, I'll answer.*

—*But I already know everything. I've read the files you collected. I've spoken to General Nesterov. He was very keen that his children shouldn't grow up in an orphanage. Raisa has confirmed all his information. I only have one question for you. Why?*

Leo didn't understand. But his fight was gone. He just wanted to say whatever it was this man wanted to hear. He spoke like a child addressing a teacher.

—*I'm sorry. I mean no disrespect. I don't understand. You're asking why . . . ?*

—*Why risk the little you had, the little we allowed you to keep, for this fantasy?*

—*You're asking about the murders?*

—*The murders have all been solved.*

Leo didn't reply.

—*You don't believe that, do you? You believe that someone or some group of people are randomly murdering Russian boys and girls up and down this country for no reason at all?*

—*I was wrong. I had a theory. It was wrong. I retract it fully. I'll sign a retraction, a confession, an admission of guilt.*

—*You realize you're guilty of the most serious act of anti-Russian agitation. It feels like Western propaganda, Leo. That, I could understand. If you're working for the West then you're a traitor. Maybe they promised you money, power, the things you had lost. That I could at least understand. Is this the case?*

—*No.*

—*That is what worries me. It means you genuinely believe these murders were connected rather than the actions of perverts and vagrants and drunks and undesirables. To be blunt, it is madness. I've worked with you. I've seen how methodical you are. And if the truth be told, I even admired you. Before, that is, you lost your head over your wife. So when I was told of your new adventures it didn't make sense to me.*

—I had a theory. It was wrong. I don't know what else I can say.

—Why would anyone want to kill these children?

Leo stared at the man opposite him, a man who'd wanted to execute two children for their parents' association with a vet. He would've shot them in the back of the head and thought nothing of it. Yet Vasili had asked this question in earnest.

Why would anyone want to kill these children?

He'd murdered on a scale comparable to the man Leo was hunting, perhaps even greater. And yet he scratched his head over the logic of these crimes. Was it that he couldn't understand why anyone who wanted to kill simply didn't join the MGB or become a Gulag guard? If that was his point then Leo understood it. There were so many legitimate outlets for brutality and murder, why choose an unofficial one? But that wasn't his point.

These children.

Vasili's confusion came from the fact that these crimes were apparently motiveless. It wasn't that the murder of children was unfathomable. But what was the gain? What was the angle? There was no official need to kill these children, no notion of it serving a greater good, no material benefit. That was his objection.

Leo repeated.

—I had a theory. It was wrong.

—Perhaps being expelled from Moscow, from a force you'd loyally served for so many years, was a greater shock than we expected.

You are a proud man, after all. Your sanity has clearly suffered. That is why I'm going to help you, Leo.

Vasili stood up, mulling the situation over. State Security had been ordered, after Stalin's death, to cease all use of violence against arrestees. A creature of survival, Vasili had adapted immediately. And yet here was Leo in his grasp. Could Vasili just walk away and leave him to face his sentencing? Was that enough? Would that satisfy him? He turned towards the door, realizing that his urges towards Leo were now as much a danger to himself as they were to Leo. He could feel his usual caution giving way to something personal, something a little like lust. He found it impossible to resist. He gestured for the guard to approach.

—*Bring Dr Hvostov.*

Even though it was late, Hvostov didn't feel put out by the abrupt call to work. He was curious as to what could be so important. He shook Vasili's hand and listened as the situation was summarized, noting that Vasili referred to Leo as a patient not as a prisoner. He understood that this was necessary to guard against the accusation of physical harm. Having heard in brief the patient's elaborate delusions about a child-killer, the doctor ordered the guard to escort Leo to his treatment room. He was excited about picking away at what lay beneath this outlandish notion.

The room was exactly as Leo remembered it: small and clean, a red leather chair bolted to the white-tiled floor, glass cabinets filled with bottles and powders and pills, labelled with neat white stickers and careful, tidy black handwriting, an array of steel surgical instruments, the smell of disinfectant. He was secured to the same chair Anatoly Brodsky had been secured to; his wrists, ankles and neck were fastened with the same leather straps. Dr Hvostov filled a syringe with camphor oil. Leo's shirt was cut away, a vein was found. Nothing needed to be explained. Leo had seen it all before. He opened his mouth, waiting for the rubber gag.

Vasili stood, trembling with anticipation as he watched the preparations. Hvostov injected Leo with the oil. Seconds passed by, suddenly Leo's eyes rolled back in his head. His body began to shake. It was the moment Vasili had dreamt of, a moment he'd planned in his head a thousand times. Leo looked ridiculous, weak and pathetic.

They waited for the more extreme physical reactions to calm down. Hvostov nodded, approving.

—*See what he says.*

Vasili stepped forward and untied the rubber gag. Leo vomited gobs of saliva onto his lap. His head fell forward, slack.

—*As before, ask simple questions to start off with.*

—*What is your name?*

Leo's head rolled from side to side, more saliva dribbled from his mouth.

—*What is your name?*

No reply.

—*What is your name?*

Leo's lips moved. He said something but Vasili couldn't hear. He moved closer:

—*What is your name?*

His eyes seemed to focus – he looked straight ahead and said:

—*Pavel.*

Same Day

What is your name?
Pavel.

Opening his eyes he saw that he was standing ankle deep in snow, in the middle of a forest, a bright moon above him. His jacket was made of coarse grain sacks, stitched together with care, as though made of the finest leather. He lifted one foot out of the snow. He wasn't wearing shoes; instead, wrapped around each foot were rags and a strip of rubber, tied together with string. His hands were the hands of a child.

Feeling a tug on his jacket he turned around. Standing behind him was a young boy dressed in the same kind of coarse sacks. On his feet were the same kind of strips of rubber and rags tied together. The boy was squinting. Snot ran down from his nose. What was his name? Clumsy and devoted and silly – his name was Andrei.

Behind him a scrawny black-and-white cat began to screech, struggling in the snow, tormented by some unseen force. It was being pulled into the forest. There was string around the cat's paw. Someone was tugging the string, dragging it across the snow. Pavel ran after it. But the cat, still struggling, was being pulled faster and faster. Pavel increased his pace. Looking back he saw that Andrei, unable to keep up, was being left behind.

Suddenly he came to a stop. Standing in front of him, holding the end of the string, was Stepan, his father, not as a young man but as an elderly man, the man he'd said goodbye to in Moscow. Stepan picked up the cat, snapped its neck and dropped it into a large grain sack. Pavel walked up to him.

—*Father?*

—*I'm not your father.*

*

Opening his eyes, he found himself inside the grain sack, his head caked in blood, his mouth as dry as ash. He was being carried, bouncing against a grown man's back. His head hurt so much he felt sick. There was something underneath him. He reached down, touching the dead cat. Exhausted, he closed his eyes.

Feeling the heat of a fire, he awoke. He was no longer in a sack; he'd been emptied onto the mud floor of a farmhouse. Stepan — now a young man, the man in the woods, gaunt and fierce — was sitting beside the fire holding the body of a young boy. Beside him was Anna: she was young again too. The boy in Stepan's arms was part human, part ghost, part skeleton — his skin was loose; his bones protruding, his eyes enormous. Stepan and Anna were crying. Anna stroked the dead boy's hair and finally Stepan whispered the boy's name.

—*Leo.*

This dead boy had been Leo Stepanovich.

Finally Anna turned around, her eyes red, and asked.

—*What is your name?*

He didn't reply. He didn't know his name.

—*Where do you live?*

Yet again he didn't know.

—*What is your father's name?*

His mind was blank.

—*Could you find your way home?*

He didn't know where home was. Anna continued:

—*Do you understand why you are here?*

He shook his head.

—*You were to die, so that he might live. Do you understand?*

He did not. She said:

—*But our son cannot be saved. He died while my husband was hunting. Since he is dead, you're free to go.*

Free to go where? He didn't know where he was. He didn't know where he'd come from. He didn't know anything about himself. His mind was empty.

Anna stood up, walking towards him, offering her hand. He struggled to his feet, weak and dizzy. How long had he been in that sack? How far had he been carried? It had felt like days. If he didn't eat soon he'd die. She gave him a cup of warm water. The first sip made him feel sick, but the second was better. She took him outside where they sat, wrapped up together under several blankets. Exhausted, he fell asleep against her shoulder. When he awoke Stepan had come outside.

—*It's ready.*

Entering the farmhouse, the boy's body was gone. On the fire was a large pot, a bubbling stew. Guided by Anna he sat down close to the heat, accepting the bowl which Stepan filled to the brim. He stared down at the steaming broth: crushed acorns floated on the surface alongside bright white knuckles and strips of flesh. Stepan and Anna watched him. Stepan said:

—*You were to die, so that our son might live. Since he has died, you can live.*

They were offering their own flesh and blood. They were offering their son. He raised the broth to his nose. He hadn't eaten for so long that he began to salivate. Instinct took over and he reached in.

Stepan explained.

—*Tomorrow we begin our journey to Moscow. We cannot survive here any longer. I have an uncle in the city, he could help us. This was to be our last meal before our journey. This meal was to get us to the city. You can come with us. Or you can stay here and try and find your own way home.*

Should he stay here, with no idea of his identity, no idea of where he was? What if he never remembered? What if nothing came back to him? Who would look after him? What would he do? Or should he go with these people. They were kind. They had food. They had a plan, a way to survive.

—*I want to come with you.*

—*You're sure?*

—*Yes.*

—*My name is Stepan. My wife's name is Anna. What is your name?*

He couldn't remember any names. Except for one, the name he'd heard earlier. Could he say that name? Would they be angry with him?

—*My name is Leo.*

11 July

Raisa was shunted forward towards a line of tables, each manned by two officers, one seated checking a stack of documentation while the other frisked the prisoner. No distinctions were made between men and women: they were all searched together, side by side in the same rough fashion. There was no way of knowing which table held your particular documentation. Raisa was pushed to one table, waved to another. She'd been processed so quickly that her paperwork hadn't caught up. Something of an irritation, she was taken aside by the guard accompanying her, the only prisoner with her own escort, bypassing this initial part of the process. These missing papers contained the statement of her crime and her sentence. All around prisoners listened blankly as they were told they were guilty of AKA, KRRD, PSh, SVPsh, KRM, SOE or SVE, indecipherable codes which determined the rest of their lives. Sentences were thrown out with professional indifference:

Five years! Ten years! Twenty-five years!

But she had to excuse these guards their callousness – they were overworked, they had so many people to deal with, so many prisoners to process. As they called out the sentences she observed the same reaction from almost every prisoner: disbelief. Was any of this real? It felt dreamlike, as though they'd been plucked out of the real world and thrown inside an entirely new world where no one was sure of the rules. What laws governed this place? What did people eat? Were they allowed to wash? What did they wear? Did they have any rights? They were newborn with no one to protect them and no one to teach them the rules.

Guided out of the processing room onto the station platform, her arm held by the guard, Raisa didn't board the train. Instead, she waited as all the other prisoners were loaded onto the row of carriages, converted cattle carts used to transport prisoners to the Gulags. The platform, though part of Kazan station, had been constructed so as to be hidden from the view of regular passengers. When Raisa had been moved from the basement of the Lubyanka to the station she'd been transported in a black truck with the words FRUIT & VEGETABLES painted across it. She understood this was no cruel joke on the part of the State but part of the attempt to conceal the scale of arrests. Was there a person alive who didn't know someone who'd been arrested? And yet the pretence of secrecy was zealously maintained, an elaborate charade fooling no one.

At a guess there were several thousand prisoners on the platform. They were being forced into carriages in such a way that it seemed as if the guards were trying to break some record, hundreds being beaten into spaces which, at a glance, should take no more than thirty or forty. But she'd already forgotten – the rules of the old world no longer applied. This was the new world with new rules and space for thirty was space for three hundred. People didn't need air between them. Space was a precious commodity in the new world, one that couldn't be wasted. The logistics of moving people were no different from the logistics of moving grain; pack it in and expect to lose five per cent.

Amongst these people – people of all ages, some in fine tailored clothes, most in tattered rags – there was no sign of her husband. As a matter of routine families were broken up in the Gulags, sent to opposite sides of the country. The system took pride in breaking bonds and ties. The only relationship which mattered was a person's relationship with the State. Raisa had taught that lesson to her students. Presuming that Leo would be sent to another camp she was surprised when her guard stopped her on the platform, ordering her to wait. She'd been made to wait on the platform before, when they'd been banished to Voualsk. This was a particular trait of Vasili, who seemed to delight in witnessing as much of their humiliation as possible. It wasn't enough that they suffer. He wanted a ringside seat.

She saw Vasili coming towards her, leading an older man with a stooped back. Less than five metres away she recognized this man as her husband. She stared at Leo, bewildered at his transformation. He was frail, aged by ten years. What had they done to him? When Vasili let go of him he seemed ready to fall over. Raisa propped him up, staring into his eyes. He recognized her. She placed her hand on his face, feeling his brow:

—*Leo?*

It took him an effort to reply, his mouth shaking as he tried to pronounce the word.

—*Raisa.*

She turned to Vasili, who was watching all of it. She was angry that there were tears in her eyes. He'd want that. She wiped them away. But they wouldn't stop.

Vasili couldn't help feeling disappointed. It wasn't that he didn't have exactly what he'd always wanted. He did, and more. Somehow he'd expected his triumph, and this was the crowning moment of it, to be sweeter. Addressing Raisa, he said:

—It's usual for husbands and wives to be separated. But I thought you might like to take this journey together, a small act of my generosity.

Of course, he meant the words ironically, viciously, but they stuck in his throat and gave him no satisfaction. He was curiously aware of his actions as pathetic. It was the absence of any real opposition. This man who'd been his target for so long was now weak, beaten and broken. Instead of feeling stronger, triumphant, he felt as if some part of him had been damaged. He cut short the speech he'd planned and stared at Leo. What was this feeling? Was it a kind of affection for this man? The idea was ridiculous: he hated him.

Raisa had seen that look before in Vasili. His hatred wasn't professional; it was an obsession, a fixation, as if unrequited love had grown awful, twisted into something ugly. Though she felt no pity for him she supposed that once upon a time there might have been something human inside of him. He gestured at the guard, who shoved them towards the train.

Raisa helped Leo up into the carriage. They were the last prisoners to be loaded in. The door slid shut after them. In the gloom she could feel hundreds of eyes staring at them.

Vasili stood on the platform, his hands behind his back.

—Have arrangements been made?

The guard nodded.

—Neither of them will reach their destination alive.

One Hundred Kilometres East
of Moscow

12 July

Raisa and Leo crouched at the back of the carriage, a position
they'd occupied since boarding the previous day. As the last prisoners on, they'd been forced to make do with the only space left.
The most coveted positions, the rough wooden benches which ran
along the walls at three different heights, had all been taken. On
these benches, which were little more than thirty centimetres
wide, there were up to three people lying side by side, pressed
together as close as if they were having sex. But there was nothing
sexual about this terrified intimacy. The only space Leo and Raisa
had found was near a hole the size of a fist cut out of the floorboards – the toilet for the entire carriage. There was no division,
no partition, no option but to defecate and urinate in full view.
Leo and Raisa were less than a foot from the hole.

Initially, in this stinking darkness, Raisa had felt uncontrollably
angry. The degradation wasn't only unjust, appalling, it was
bizarre – wilfully malicious. If they were going to these camps to
work, why were they being transported as if they were intended
for execution? She'd stopped herself from pursuing this line of

thought: they wouldn't survive like this, fired up with indignation. She had to adapt. She kept reminding herself:

New world, new rules.

She couldn't compare her situation to the past. Prisoners had no entitlements and should have no expectations.

Even without a watch or a view of the world outside, Raisa knew it must be past midday. The steel roof was being cooked by the sun, the weather collaborating with the guards, inflicting a steady punishment, radiating an unrelenting heat on the hundreds of bodies. The train moved with such sluggishness that no breeze came through the small slits in the timber walls. What little breeze there might have been was soaked up by the prisoners lucky enough to sit on the benches.

Forced to let go of her anger, these intolerable temperatures and smells became tolerable. Survival meant adjusting. One of the prisoners had chosen not to accept these new rules. Raisa had no idea exactly when he'd died: a middle-aged man. He'd made no fuss – no one had noticed him or if they had, no one had said anything. Yesterday evening, when the train had come to a stop and everyone had disembarked for their one small cup of water, someone had called out that a man was dead. Passing his body, Raisa suspected that he'd decided this new world was not for him. He'd given up, shut down, turned off, just like a machine – cause of death: hopelessness, uninterested in surviving if this was all there was to survive for. His body was slung off the train, rolling down a bank, out of sight.

Raisa turned to Leo. He'd slept for most of the journey so far, resting against her, childlike. When he was awake he appeared calm, neither uncomfortable nor upset, his mind and thoughts elsewhere; his brow furrowed as though he was trying to make sense of something. She'd searched his body for signs of torture, finding a large bruise on his arm. Around his ankles and wrists there were red strap marks. He'd been tied down. She had no idea what he'd been through, but it was psychological and chemical rather than crude cuts and burns. She'd rubbed his head, held his hand – kissed him. This was all the medicine she was able to offer. She'd fetched his chunk of black bread and single strip of dried salty fish, their only meal so far. The fish, with its small crunchy white bones, had been so crystallized in salt that some prisoners had held it in their hands, desperately hungry and yet agonized by the prospect of eating it without water. Worse than hunger was thirst. Raisa had brushed off as much of the salt as she could before feeding it to Leo in small pieces.

Leo sat up, speaking for the first time since boarding the train, his words barely audible. Raisa leaned closer to him, straining to hear.

—*Oksana was a good mother. She loved me. I left them. I chose not to go back. My little brother always wanted to play cards. I used to say I was too busy.*

—*Who are they, Leo? Who is Oksana? Who is your brother? Who are you talking about?*

—*My mother refused to let them take the church bell.*

—*Anna? You're talking about Anna?*

—*Anna is not my mother.*

Raisa cradled his head, wondering if he'd gone insane. Surveying the carriage, she was conscious that Leo's vulnerability made him an easy target.

Most of the prisoners were too terrified to be of any threat except for the five men in the far corner perched on a high bench. Unlike the other passengers they were fearless, at ease in this world. Raisa guessed that they were professional criminals with sentences for theft or assault, crimes which carried far shorter sentences than the political prisoners around them, the teachers, nurses, doctors, writers and dancers. Imprisonment was their turf, their element. They seemed to understand the rules of this world better than the rules of the other world. This superiority came not only from their evident physical strength; she noted power was conferred on them by the guards. They were spoken to as equals, or if not equals at least as a man might speak to another man. Other prisoners were afraid of them. They made way for them. They were able to leave their bench, use the toilet and fetch their water, all without fear of losing their prized spot. No one dared take their place. They'd already demanded that one man, who they apparently did not know, give them his shoes. When he'd asked why they'd explained, in a matter-of-fact tone, that his shoes had been lost in a wager. Raisa had been thankful that this man didn't question the logic of this:

New rules, new world.

He'd handed over his shoes, receiving a tattered pair in exchange.

The train came to a stop. Calls for water sounded out up and down, from every carriage. These were ignored or imitated, spat back at them:

Water! water! water!

As though the request was somehow repugnant. It seemed as if all the guards were clustering around their carriage. The door was opened, orders shouted out for the prisoners to keep back. The guards called for the five men. They swung down from their bench like jungle animals, pushing through the prisoners, leaving the train.

Something was wrong – Raisa lowered her head, breathing fast. It was not long before she could hear the men return. She waited. Then, slowly, she lifted her head, glimpsing the men as they climbed back into the carriage. All five were staring at her.

Same Day

Raisa took hold of Leo's face.

—*Leo.*

She heard them approaching. There was no way to move through the crowded carriage without pushing a path through the prisoners on the floor.

—*Leo, listen to me, we're in trouble.*

He didn't move, didn't seem to understand, the danger didn't seem to register.

—*Leo, please, I'm begging you.*

It was no good. She stood up, turning to face the approaching men. What else could she do? Leo remained crouched on the floor behind her. Her plan: resist as much as she could.

The leader, and the tallest of the men, stepped forward grabbing her arm. Expecting such a move, Raisa struck him in the eye with her free hand. Her nails, uncut and filthy, jabbed into the skin. She should have ripped his eye out. The thought crossed her mind, but instead all she managed was a gash. The man tossed her to the floor. She landed on prisoners who scuttled out of the way. This wasn't their fight and they weren't going to help. She was on her own. Trying to scramble away from her attackers, Raisa found that she couldn't move. Someone was holding her ankle. More hands grabbed her, lifting her up and flipping her onto her back.

One man dropped to his knees, holding her arms, pinning her down whilst the leader kicked open her legs. In his hand he held a shard of thick, jagged steel, like an enormous tooth.

—*After I fuck you I'm going to fuck you with this*.

He gestured to the steel shard which, Raisa understood, had just been given to him by the guards. Unable to move her body, she turned to Leo. He was gone.

Leo's thoughts had shifted away from the forest, the cat, the village, his brother. His wife was in danger. Struggling to assess the situation, he wondered why he was being ignored. Perhaps these men had been told that he was insensible and posed no threat. Whatever the reason, he'd been able to stand without them reacting. The leader was unbuttoning his trousers. By the time he'd noticed that Leo was standing, there was only an arm's length between them.

The leader sneered and swung around, punching him in the side of the face. Leo didn't block or duck, falling to the floor. Lying on the wooden planks, his lip split, he listened to the sound of the men laughing. Let them laugh. The pain had done him good, focusing him. They were over-confident, untrained – strong but unskilled. Making a deliberate show of being shaky and clumsy, he slowly stood up, keeping his back to the men, an inviting target. He could hear someone moving towards him, someone had taken the bait. Glancing over his shoulder, he saw the leader lunge at him with the steel shard, intending to finish him off.

Leo sidestepped, moving with a speed that took the man by surprise. Before he could recover, Leo punched the man's throat, winding him. The man gasped. Leo caught hold of his hand, twisting the shard free and jabbing the tip into the side of the man's muscular neck. Leo hit the shard again, plunging it all the way in, severing every sinew, vein and artery in its path. He pulled the weapon free and the man collapsed, clasping the wound in his neck.

The nearest member of his gang stepped forward, arms outstretched. Leo allowed the man to grab hold of his neck, in reply pushing the shard into his stomach, through the man's shirt, dragging it sideways. The man was gurgling but Leo kept on dragging the steel, cutting through skin and muscle. Releasing his grip on Leo's neck, the wounded man stood, peering down at his bleeding stomach, as though puzzled by it, before slumping to his knees.

Leo turned to the remaining three men. They'd lost all interest in the struggle. Whatever deal they'd been offered wasn't worth the fight. Maybe all they'd been promised was better rations or easier work at the camp. One of the men, perhaps identifying this as an opportunity for promotion within his gang, took charge.

—*We have no quarrel with you*.

Leo said nothing, his hands covered in blood, the steel shard jutting out of his hand. The men pulled back, leaving their dead and injured. Failure was quickly disowned.

Leo helped Raisa up, hugging her.

—*I'm sorry*.

They were interrupted by the injured man calling for help. The first man, the man with his neck cut open, had already died. But the man with the cut stomach was alive, conscious, clutching the injury. Leo looked down at him, assessing his injury. He would take a long time to die: it would be painful and slow. He deserved no mercy. But on balance it was better for the other prisoners that he should die quickly. No one wanted to listen to his screams. Leo crouched down, locking the man's neck in a grip, choking him.

Leo returned to his wife. She whispered:

—*Those men were ordered to kill us by the guards*.

Considering this, Leo replied:

—*Our only chance is to escape.*

The train was slowing down. When it eventually stopped the guards would open the doors, expecting to find Leo and Raisa dead. When they discovered two of their assassins dead instead, they'd demand to know who'd killed them. Some prisoner would almost certainly speak up, out of fear of torture or desire for reward. It would be more than enough of a pretext for the guards to execute Leo and Raisa.

Leo turned to face the prisoners. There were pregnant mothers, elderly men too old to survive the Gulags, fathers, brothers, sisters — ordinary, unremarkable, the kind of people that he himself had arrested and taken to the Lubyanka. Now he was forced to ask for their help.

—*My name is not important. Before I was arrested I was investigating the murder of over forty children, murders which stretched from the Ural Mountains down to the Black Sea. Boys and girls have been killed. I know that this crime is hard to believe, perhaps even impossible for some of you. But I have seen the bodies for myself and I'm sure they're the work of one man. He doesn't kill these children for money or sex or any reason that I can explain. He'll murder any child, from any town. And he will not stop. My crime was to investigate him. My arrest means he is free to continue killing. No one else is looking for him. My wife and I must escape to stop him. We cannot escape without your help. If you call for the guards, we're dead.*

There was silence. The train was almost at a stop. At any second the doors would slide open, guards would enter, guns at the ready. Who could blame them when faced with the barrel of a gun not to tell the truth? A woman on one of the benches called out:

—*I'm from Rostov. I've heard of such murders. Children with their stomachs cut out. They are blaming them on a group of Western spies who have infiltrated our country.*

Leo replied:

—*I believe the murderer lives and works in your city. But I doubt he's a spy.*

Another woman cried out:

—*When you find him you'll kill him?*

—*Yes.*

The train stopped. The guards could be heard approaching. Leo added:

—*I have no reason to expect your help. But I ask for it all the same.*

Leo and Raisa crouched down among the prisoners. She wrapped her arms around Leo, covering up his bloodstained hands. The doors slid open, sunshine flooded the carriage.

Finding the two bodies, the guards called out for an explanation.

—*Who killed them?*

They were answered with silence. Leo looked over his wife's shoulders at these guards. They were young, indifferent. They'd obey orders but they wouldn't think for themselves. The fact that they hadn't personally killed Leo and Raisa meant that they hadn't been given instructions to do so. It had to be done on the sly, through a proxy. Without explicit authorization they wouldn't act. These guards had no initiative. However, given some slight justification, they might seize the opportunity. Everything depended upon the strangers in this carriage. The guards were shouting, pushing guns into the faces of those nearest them. But the prisoners told them nothing. They selected an elderly couple. They were frail. They'd talk.

—*Who killed these men? What happened here? Speak!*

One of the guards raised his steel-capped boot above her head. She wept. Her husband pleaded. But neither of them replied to their questions. A second guard moved towards Leo. If he made him stand up he'd see the bloodied shirt.

One of the remaining gang, the man who'd told Leo there was no longer any quarrel between them, got down from his bench approaching the guards. No doubt he'd now claim the reward promised to them. The man called out:

—*Leave them alone. I know what happened. I'll tell you.*

The guards stepped away from the elderly couple, stepped away from Leo.

—*Tell us.*

—*They killed each other, because of a card game.*

Leo understood that there was a perverse logic to the gang's refusal to give them up. They were prepared to rape and murder for a small profit. But they were not prepared to snitch, to be a guard's stool pigeon. It was a question of status. If the other *urki*, the members of their criminal fraternity, found out they were selling inmates for perks they would never be forgiven. They would probably be killed.

The guards looked at each other. Unsure of what to do, they decided to do nothing. They were in no rush. The journey to Vtoraya Rechka, on the Pacific coast, would take weeks. There would be plenty of opportunities. They would await further orders. They'd come up with another plan. One of the guards addressed the whole carriage.

—*As a punishment we will not offload these bodies. Soon, in this heat, they will begin to rot and stink and you will all become ill. Perhaps then you will talk.*

Proud of himself, the guard leapt off the carriage. The other guards followed. The door was shut.

After a while the train began to move again. A young man with broken spectacles, peering at Leo through a cracked lens, whispered:

—*How will you escape?*

He had a right to know. Their escape now belonged to everyone in the carriage. They were all in it together. In reply Leo raised the bloody steel shard. The guards had forgotten to take it back.

Two Hundred and Twenty Kilometres East of Moscow

13 July

Leo was lying flat on the floor, his arm squeezed through the small hole used by the prisoners as a toilet. With the steel shard he scratched at the iron nails fastening the plank to the underside of the carriage. None of the nails were accessible from inside: they'd all been hammered in the underside. The only access point was this small hole not much wider than his wrist. Leo had taken the dead man's shirt and cleaned the area as best he could. It was not more than a token effort. To reach the three iron nails he was forced to bring his face down flat against the stinking piss- and shit-sodden wood, retching while blindly groping, guided by touch alone. Splinters dug into his skin. Raisa had offered to do the work instead since her hands and wrists were smaller. While this was true Leo had a longer reach and at full stretch it was just possible to reach each of the three nails.

With a strip of shirt tied around his mouth and nose as limited protection from the stench, he picked at the third and last nail, scraping, cutting at the wood, gouging the timber and giving himself just enough space to wedge the tip under the nail-head and lever it out. It had taken many hours to remove two nails since the work had to be interrupted by any prisoner needing the toilet.

This final nail was proving the hardest. Partly that was due to tiredness – it was late, maybe one or two in the morning – but something else was wrong. Leo could get his fingertip under the nail's head but it wasn't coming loose. It felt crooked, as if it had been banged in at an angle, the body of the nail bent by the blows. It wouldn't pull out. He'd have to dig further into the wood, perhaps all the way through. At this realization, that it would take maybe another hour, a wave of exhaustion came over him. His fingers were bloody and raw, his arm ached – he couldn't get the stink of shit out of his nose. Suddenly the train jolted to the side, he lost concentration, and the steel shard slipped from his fingers, clattering onto the tracks below.

Leo pulled his hand out of the hole. Raisa was beside him.

—*Is it done?*

—*I dropped it. I dropped the shard.*

Furious with his own stupidity at discarding the other nails he no longer had any tools.

Seeing her husband's bloody fingers, Raisa grabbed hold of the plank and tried to lift it. One side of it rose up, fractionally, but not enough to grip underneath it, not enough to pull it free. Leo wiped his hands, looking around for something he might use.

—*I have to scratch through the wood and get to the base of that last nail.*

Raisa had seen every prisoner comprehensively searched before being allowed on the train. She doubted if anyone had metal implements of any kind. Contemplating the problem, her eyes drifted towards the nearest of the dead bodies. The man was lying on his back, his mouth open. She turned to her husband.

—*How long or sharp does it need to be?*

—I've done most of it. I need anything harder than my fingertip.

Raisa stood up, walking to the body of the man who had tried to rape and murder her. With no sense of justice or satisfaction, only a feeling of disgust, she positioned the dead man's jaw so that it faced upwards. She raised her shoe directly above his jaw, hesitating, looking around. Everyone was watching. She closed her eyes, bringing her heel down against his front teeth.

Leo crawled over, feeling the inside of the man's mouth and pulling out a tooth still affixed to a stump of bloody gum, an incisor, not ideal but sharp enough and hard enough to continue the scraping already done. He returned to the hole, lying on his front. Holding the tooth, he squeezed his arm through, finding the remaining nail and continuing to pick away at the wood, pulling off the splinters as they came loose.

The nail was completely exposed. Holding the tooth in the palm of his hand, in case further excavation was necessary, Leo gripped the head of the nail but his fingertips were raw and he was unable to get a fix on it. He pulled his arm out, wiping the sweat and blood off his fingers, wrapping them in a shredded strip of shirt before trying again. Struggling to remain patient, he tugged at the nail, incrementally pulling it free from the plank. That was it: it was done. The third nail had been removed. He checked the wood, feeling for other nails, but there were no more, at least that he could find. He sat up, pulling his arm out of the hole.

Raisa sunk both her hands through the hole, gripping the plank. Leo added his hands. This was the test. They both pulled. The top side of the plank lifted up while the bottom of the plank remained secured. Leo moved over, grabbing the end and lifting it as high as he could. Looking down, he could see the train tracks below the carriage. The plan had worked. Where the plank had lain there was now a gap of about thirty centimetres in width and over a metre in length, barely enough for a person to lower through, but enough all the same.

It would've been possible with the help of the other prisoners to snap the plank. But worried that the sound would alert the guards they decided against this. Leo turned to his audience.

—*I need people to hold this plank up while we drop through the gap, down onto the tracks.*

Several volunteers stood up immediately, coming forward and taking hold of the plank. Leo assessed the space. After they'd squeezed through, they'd fall straight down, directly underneath the train. The distance from the underside of the carriage down to the tracks was perhaps a little over a metre, maybe a metre and a half. The train was travelling slowly but still fast enough for the fall to be dangerous. However, they couldn't wait. They had to go now, whilst the train was moving, during the night. When the train stopped at daybreak, they'd be seen by the guards.

Raisa took hold of Leo's hands.

—*I'll go first.*

Leo shook his head. He'd seen the blueprints to these prisoner transports. They faced one more obstacle: a final trap for prisoners about to attempt exactly this kind of escape.

—*On the underneath of this train, at the very end, the last carriage, there are a series of hooks which hang down. If we fell onto the tracks right now and waited, as the last carriage passed overhead the hooks would snag us, dragging us with the train.*

—*Can't we avoid them? Roll out of the way?*

—*There are hundreds of them, hanging on wires. There's no way we'd slip through. We'd get tangled up in them.*

—*What are we supposed to do? We can't wait till the train stops.*

Leo examined the two dead bodies. Raisa stood beside him, evidently unsure of his intentions. He explained:

—When you drop down to the tracks, I'll throw one of these bodies after you. Hopefully it will land somewhere near you. Wherever it lands, you'll have to crawl to it. Then, once you reach it, lie under it. Position it exactly on top of you. As the last carriage passes overhead the body will get hooked and snagged. But you'll be free.

He dragged the bodies close to the loose plank, adding.

—Do you want me to go first? If it doesn't work then you should stay here. Any other death would be better than being dragged along by this train.

Raisa shook her head.

—It's a good plan. It will work. I'll go first.

As she was ready to climb down, Leo reiterated his instructions:

—The train isn't moving fast. The fall will be painful but not too dangerous, make sure you roll with the impact. I'll throw down one of the bodies. You won't have much time—

—I understand.

—You must collect the body. When you get it, put yourself underneath it. Make sure no part of you is exposed. If even one hook gets into you, you could be dragged along.

—Leo, I understand.

Raisa kissed him. She was shaking.

She squeezed through the gap between the planks. Her feet were dangling above the tracks. She let go of the plank and fell, disappearing from view. Leo grabbed the first body and lowered it through the gap, squeezing it through. The body dropped onto the tracks, out of sight.

*

Raisa had landed awkwardly, bruising her side and tumbling. Disorientated, dazed, she lay still for a moment. Too long, she was wasting time. Leo's carriage was already far away. She could see the body which Leo had thrown down and began to crawl towards it, in the same direction as the train. She glanced behind her. There were only three carriages until the end of the train. But she couldn't see any hooks. Perhaps Leo had been wrong. There were now only two carriages left. Raisa still hadn't reached the body. She stumbled. There was now only one carriage separating her from the end of the train. With only metres before the final carriage passed over her, she saw the hooks – hundreds of them, all attached to fine wires, at different heights. They covered the entire width of the carriage, impossible to avoid.

Raisa got up, crawling again, as fast as she could, reaching the body. It was laying face down, head nearest her. She didn't have time to turn it around so she turned herself around, lifting up the body and crawling under this man, positioning her head under his head. Face to face with her attacker, staring into his dead eyes, she made herself as small as possible.

Suddenly the dead body was wrenched off her. She saw wires all around her, like fishing lines, each one barbed with many jagged hooks. The body lifted up, as though alive, a puppet, tangled up, no longer even touching the tracks. Raisa remained flat on the tracks, perfectly still. She could see the stars above her. Slowly she stood up. No hook had caught her. She watched the train move away. She'd done it. But there was no sign of Leo.

*

As he was larger than Raisa, Leo had figured that he needed the bigger of the two dead men, he'd need more body mass to protect him from the hooks. However, this dead man was so large he didn't fit through the gap in the planks. They'd stripped him in an effort to reduce his width but he was too broad. There was no way to get him through the hole. By this point Raisa had been on the tracks for several minutes.

Desperate, Leo lowered his head though the gap. He could see a body caught at the end of the train. Was it Raisa or the dead man? It was impossible to tell from this distance. He had to hope it was the dead man. Adjusting his plan, he supposed that if he positioned himself correctly he could escape underneath this tangled body. That body would have caught all the hooks in that section. He'd be free to pass underneath it. He said goodbye to the other prisoners, thanked them, and dropped onto the tracks.

Rolling close to the enormous steel wheels, he pulled himself away, facing the end of the train. The body in the wire was rapidly approaching, tangled up on the left-hand side. He positioned himself accordingly. He could do nothing but wait, making himself as small and as flat as possible. The end of the train was nearly over him. He lifted his head up off the ground just long enough to see that it wasn't Raisa. She'd survived. He had to do the same. He lay down flat and closed his eyes.

The dead body brushed over him.

Then, pain – a single stray hook caught his left arm. He opened his eyes. The hook had cut through his shirt, into his flesh. With only a fraction of a second before the wire went taut, pulling him along, he grabbed hold of the hook and tugged it out, taking a clump of skin and flesh with it. He clutched his arm: feeling dizzy as blood seeped from the wound. Staggering up, he saw Raisa hurrying towards him. Ignoring the pain, he put his arms around her.

They were free.

Moscow

Same Day

Vasili wasn't well. He'd done something he'd never done before – he'd taken time off work. Not only was such behaviour potentially dangerous, it was out of character. He'd rather be ill at work than ill at home. He'd managed to rig his accommodation arrangements so that he was, for the most part, able to live alone. He was married, of course; it was unthinkable that a man could remain single. It was his social duty to have children. And he'd followed the rules accordingly, marrying a woman with no opinions, or at least none that she expressed, a woman who'd dutifully given birth to two children – the minimum acceptable if no questions were to be asked. She and the children lived in a family apartment on the outskirts of the city while he occupied an inner-city work address. He'd arranged this ostensibly so that he could have his pick of mistresses. In fact, he partook in extra-marital affairs only very occasionally.

After Leo's exile to the Urals, Vasili had petitioned to move into Leo and Raisa's apartment; apartment 124. He'd got his wish. The first few days had been enjoyable. He'd ordered his wife to go to the *spetztorgi*, the restricted shops, to buy fine food and drink. He'd held a work party in his new apartment, no wives allowed, where his new deputies drank and ate and congratulated him on his success. Some of the men who'd served under Leo now reported to him. Yet despite all these ironies and the delicious reversal of fortune he hadn't enjoyed the party. He felt empty. He no longer had anyone to hate. He no longer had anyone to scheme against. He was no longer irritated by Leo's promotion or efficiency or popularity. There were other men who he competed with but the feeling wasn't the same.

Vasili got out of bed and decided he'd drink himself better. He poured a large measure of vodka and stared at the glass, swishing the liquid from side to side, unable to raise it to his lips. The smell made him feel sick. He put the glass down. Leo was dead. Soon he would receive official notification that the two prisoners had not arrived at their destination. They'd died en route as so many did, after getting into a fight over shoes or clothes or food or whatever. It was the final defeat of a man who'd humiliated him. Leo's very existence had been a kind of perpetual punishment for Vasili. So, then, why did he miss him?

There was a knock. He'd expected the MGB to send round men to authenticate his illness. He walked to the door, opening it, seeing two young officers standing before him.

—*Sir, two prisoners have escaped.*

He could feel the dull ache inside him vanishing as he said the name:

—*Leo?*

The officers nodded. Vasili was feeling better already.

Two Hundred Kilometres South-East of Moscow

Same Day

Half running, half walking, constantly looking behind them — their speed depended on whether fear or exhaustion had the upper hand. The weather was in their favour: weak sunshine and thin cloud, not too hot, at least compared to the inside of that carriage. Leo and Raisa knew from the position of the sun that it was late afternoon but had no way of knowing the exact time. Leo couldn't remember where or how his watch had been lost or if it had been taken. He estimated they had at the most a four-hour head start on their guards. A rough calculation put their speed at eight kilometres an hour whilst the train had been moving not much more than an average of sixteen, putting a distance of some eighty or so kilometres between them. That was a best-case scenario. It was possible the guards might have been alerted to the escape much sooner.

They broke out of woodland into open countryside. Without the cover of trees they were visible for kilometres. They had no choice but to continue, exposed as they were. Seeing a small river at the bottom of an incline they adjusted direction, picking up speed. It was the first water they'd come across. Reaching it they dropped to their knees drinking greedily, cupping their hands, scooping it into their mouths. When this wasn't enough, they submerged their faces. Leo joked:

—*At least we'll die clean*.

The joke had been misjudged. It wasn't enough that they do their best to stop this man. No one would appreciate their attempt. They had to succeed.

Raisa focused on Leo's injury. The gash wasn't closing; it wouldn't stop bleeding, too much of the skin and flesh had been ripped. The strip of shirt they'd tied around it was now soaked with blood. Leo unpeeled the shirt.

—*I can put up with it*.

—*It's leaving a powerful scent for the dogs*.

Raisa stepped out of the river, approaching the nearest tree. A spider's web had been spun between two branches. Very carefully she broke the web with her fingers, transferring it whole and laying it across the ripped flesh of Leo's upper arm. Immediately blood seemed to solidify upon touching the thin silver lines. She worked for several minutes, searching for more webs, finding them, collecting them and layering them, until the injury was criss-crossed with silky threads. By the time she'd finished the bleeding had stopped.

Leo remarked:

—*We should follow this river for as long as possible. The trees are the only cover and the water will hide our smell*.

The water was shallow, knee deep at the deepest point. Not fast enough or powerful enough so that they could float and drift with the current. Instead they had to walk. Hungry, exhausted, Leo knew there was only so long they could keep this up.

While guards were indifferent to whether prisoners lived or

died, escape was unpardonable. It made a mockery not only of the guards but of the entire system. No matter who the prisoners were, no matter how unimportant, their escape made them important. The fact that Leo and Raisa were already classified as high-profile counter-revolutionaries would make their escape a matter of countrywide significance. Once the train had come to a stop and the guards had noticed the dead body caught up in the wire a count would be done of all the prisoners. The escapees' carriage would be identified; questions would be asked. If answers weren't given prisoners might be shot. Leo hoped that someone would be sensible enough to tell the truth immediately. Those men and women had already done more than their share to help them. Even if they confessed there was no guarantee that the guards wouldn't make an example out of the entire carriage.

The hunt would begin along the tracks. They'd use dogs. A pack of trained dogs travelled with every train, kept in far better conditions than the human cargo. If a sufficient distance had been established between their point of escape and the point at which the search began then the beginning of the scent trail would be difficult to find. Considering the fact they'd been on the run for maybe three-quarters of a day without sight of their pursuers Leo could only presume this was the case. It meant Moscow would be notified. The search would be broadened. Trucks and cars would be mobilized – the possible escape area divided up into grids. Planes would scour the countryside. Local military and security organizations would be informed, their efforts coordinated with national organizations. They would be hunted with a zeal that went far beyond professional duty. Rewards and bonuses would be offered. There was no limit to the manpower and machinery that could be thrown after them. He should know. He'd been involved in these hunts himself. And that was their only advantage. Leo knew how their hunts were organized. He'd been trained by the NKVD to operate unseen behind enemy lines and now the enemy lines were his own borders, borders he'd fought to protect. The size of these searches made them heavy handed, difficult to manage. They'd be centralized, vast in sweep but inefficient. Most importantly he hoped they'd target the wrong area. Logically Leo and Raisa should be heading to the nearest border, towards Finland, the Baltic coast. A boat was their best chance of getting out of the country. But they were heading south – through the very heart of Russia, towards the city of Rostov. In this direction there was almost no chance of freedom, no promise of safety at the end.

Walking through the water, moving at a much slower pace, they frequently stumbled and fell; each time it was harder to get up. Not even the adrenaline from being hunted could sustain them. Leo was careful not to let the web wash off his arm, keeping it raised. So far neither of them spoke about their predicament, as though their existence was on too short a lease to even make plans. Leo guessed that they were about two hundred kilometres east of Moscow. They'd been on the train for almost forty-eight hours. Speculatively this put them somewhere near the town of Vladimir. If he was right then they were now travelling in the direction of Ryazan. Ordinarily from this point, travelling by train or car, Rostov was at least a twenty-four-hour journey south. However, they had no money, no food; they were injured, dressed in filthy clothes. They were wanted by every national and local State Security apparatus.

They came to a stop. The river flowed in between two halves of a small village, a collective farm. They stepped out of the water, some five hundred paces up stream from the huddle of houses. It was late, light was fading. Leo said:

—*Some of the villagers will still be working; they'll be on their land. We can sneak in, unnoticed, see if we can find some food.*

—*You want to steal?*

—*We can't buy anything. If they see us, they'll hand us in. There's always a reward for escaped prisoners, far more than these people make in a year.*

—*Leo, you've worked in the Lubyanka for too long. These people have no love of the State.*

—*They need money like everyone else. They're trying to survive like everyone else.*

—*We have hundreds of kilometres to cross. We can't do it alone. We just can't. You must realize that. We have no friends, no money, nothing. We have to convince strangers to help us – we'll have to sell them our cause. That's the only way. That's our only chance.*

—*We're outcasts, harbouring us will get them shot, not just for the individual who helps us but the entire village. State officials wouldn't think twice about sentencing all of them to twenty-five years, deporting the whole population, children included, to a northern encampment.*

—*And that's exactly why they'll help us. You've lost faith in the people of this country because you've been surrounded by the people in power. The State doesn't represent these villages, it doesn't understand them and it doesn't have any interest in them.*

—*Raisa, this is city-dissident talk. It's not relevant to the real world. It would be insanity for them to help us.*

—*You have a short memory, Leo. How did we just escape? We told the inmates of that carriage the truth. They helped us, all of them, several hundred, probably about the number that live in this village. The prisoners in our carriage will almost certainly face some sort of collective punishment for not alerting the guards. What did they do it for? What did you offer them?*

Leo remained silent. Raisa pressed her point.

—*If you steal from these people, you'll be their enemy when we are in fact their friends.*

—*So you want to walk into the centre of the village, as if we were family, and greet them?*

—*That's exactly what we're going to do.*

Side by side, they walked into the centre of the village as if they were returning from work, as if they had a right to be here. Men and women and children gathered around them, surrounding them. Their houses were made of mud and wood. Their farm equipment was forty years out of date. All they had to do was turn them over to the State and they'd be richly rewarded. How could they refuse? These people had nothing.

Encircled by hostile faces, Raisa spoke up.

—*We're prisoners. We've escaped from the train transporting us to the Kolyma region, where we would've died. We're now being hunted. We need your help. We ask for this help not for ourselves. Eventually we'll be caught and killed. We've accepted that. But before we die there is one task we have to perform. Please let us explain why we need your help. If you don't like what we tell you, then you should have nothing to do with us.*

A man stepped forward, in his mid-forties, an air of self-importance about him.

—*As chairman of this* kolkhoz, *it is my duty to point out that it would be in our best interests to turn them over.*

Raisa glanced at the other villagers. Had she been wrong? Had the State already infiltrated these villages, planted their own spies and informers in the management system? A man's voice called out.

—*And what would you do with the reward, hand that over to the State too?*

405

There was laughter. The chairman went red, embarrassed. Relieved, Raisa realized this man was a comic figure, a puppet. He wasn't the real authority. From the back of the crowd an elderly woman spoke out:

—*Feed them.*

As though an oracle had spoken, the debate was over.

They were led into the largest house. In the main room, where food was prepared, they were seated and given cups of water. A fire was stoked. All the while their audience grew until the entire house was crowded. Children filled the spaces in between the adults' legs, staring at Leo and Raisa as children might stare in a zoo. Fresh bread, still warm, was brought from another house. They ate with their wet clothes steaming in front of the fire. When a man apologized for not being able to offer them a new set of clothes, Leo merely nodded, disorientated by their generosity. He could offer them a story; that was it. Finishing his bread and water, he stood up.

Raisa watched the men, women and children as they listened to Leo. He began with the murder of Arkady, the young boy in Moscow, a murder he'd been ordered to cover up. He spoke of his shame at having told the boy's family that it was an accident. He went on to explain why he was expelled from the MGB, sent to Voualsk. He explained his amazement when he'd found another child had been murdered in almost exactly the same way. The audience gasped, as though he was performing some magic trick, when they were told that these murders were being committed across their entire country. Some parents ushered their children out of the house as Leo warned them of what he was about to describe.

Even before Leo had finished his story his audience had formed ideas as to who could've been responsible. None of them supposed these murders were the work of a man with a job, a man with a family. The men in the audience found it hard to believe that this killer couldn't be immediately identified. All of them were certain they'd know he was a monster just by looking him in the eyes. Glancing around the room, Leo realized their perspective on the world had been shaken. He apologized for introducing them to the reality of this killer's existence. In an effort to reassure them he outlined the murderer's movements along the railways, through the major towns. He killed as part of his routine; a routine wouldn't bring him into villages like this.

Even with these assurances, Raisa wondered whether or not these people would any longer be so trusting and welcoming. Would they feed a stranger? Or from now on would they fear that strangers were hiding some evil they couldn't see? The price of this story was the audience's innocence. It wasn't that they hadn't seen brutality and death. But they'd never imagined that the murder of a child could give pleasure.

It was dark outside and Leo had been speaking for some time, well over an hour. He was nearing the end of his story when a child ran into the house.

—*I saw lights on the northern hills. There are trucks. They're coming this way.*

Everyone got to their feet. Reading the faces of those around him Leo knew that there was no chance these trucks could be anything other than the State. He asked:

—*How long do we have?*

Asking that question, he'd already grouped himself with them, presumed a connection when in fact there was none. They could quite easily surrender them and claim their reward. Yet it appeared as if he was the only one in the room even contemplating such an idea. Even the chairman had surrendered to the collective decision to aid them.

Some of the adults hurried out of the house, perhaps to see for themselves. Those remaining quizzed the boy.

—*Which hill?*

—*How many trucks?*

—*How long ago?*

There were three trucks, three sets of headlights. The boy had seen them from the edge of his father's farm. They were coming from the north, several kilometres away. They'd be here in minutes.

There was nowhere to hide in these houses. The villagers had no belongings, no furniture to speak of. And the search would be thorough, brutally so. If there was a hiding place it would be found. Leo knew how much pride was at stake for the guards. Raisa took hold of his arms:

—*We can run. They'll have to search the village first. If they pretend we were never here, we can get ahead, maybe hide in the countryside. It's dark.*

Leo shook his head. Feeling his stomach tense, his thoughts were thrown back to Anatoly Brodsky. This is what he must have felt when he'd turned around to see Leo on the crest of the hill, when he'd realized that the net had closed around him. Leo remembered how that man had paused, staring for a moment, unable to do anything other than contemplate that he'd been caught. On that day he'd run. But there was no way to outrun these guards. They were rested, equipped to hunt – long-range rifles, telescopic sights, flares to light up the sky and dogs to pick up suspicious trails.

Leo turned to the young boy who'd seen the trucks.

—*I need your help.*

Same Day

Nervous, his hands shaking, the boy crouched in the middle of the road in almost complete darkness, a small bag of grain spilled before him. He could hear the trucks approaching, the tyres kicking up dirt: they were only a couple of hundred metres away, coming fast. He closed his eyes, hoping they'd see him. Was it possible they were going too fast to stop in time? There was a screech of brakes. He opened his eyes, turning his head, caught in the beam of powerful headlights. He raised his arms. The trucks lurched to a stop, the metal bumper almost touching the boy's face. The door to the front cabin opened. A soldier called out.

—*What the fuck are you doing?*

—*My bag split.*

—*Get off the road!*

—*My father will kill me if I don't collect it all.*

—*I'll kill you if you don't move.*

The boy wasn't sure what to do. He continued picking at the grains. He heard a metallic click: was that the sound of a gun? He'd never seen a gun: he had no idea what they sounded like. Panicking, he continued picking at the grains, putting them in the bag. They wouldn't shoot him: he was just a boy picking up his father's grain. Then he remembered the stranger's story: children were being killed all the time. Maybe these men were the same. He grabbed as much grain as he could, picked up the bag and ran back towards the village. The trucks followed him, chasing him, beeping their horns, getting him to run faster. He could hear soldiers laughing. He'd never run so fast in his life.

Leo and Raisa were hiding in the only place they could hope the soldiers wouldn't search – underneath their own trucks. While the boy was distracting the soldiers, Leo had sneaked under the second truck, Raisa under the third. Since there was no way of telling how long they'd have to hold on for, perhaps for as long as an hour, Leo had wrapped their hands in ripped shreds of shirt in an attempt to ease the pain.

As the trucks came to a stop, Leo wedged his feet around the axle shaft, his face close to the wooden underside of the truck. The planks strained towards him as the soldiers walked across it, jumping off the back of the truck. Looking down over his toes, he saw one of the men crouch down to tie his bootlaces. All the man had to do was turn around and Leo would be seen and caught. The soldier stood up, hurrying towards one of the houses. Leo hadn't been seen. He repositioned himself so he was able to get a view of the third truck.

Raisa was afraid but mostly she was angry. This plan was smart, that was true, and she hadn't come up with anything better but it depended entirely on their ability to cling on. She wasn't a trained soldier: she hadn't spent years crawling through ditches, climbing over walls. She didn't have the upper-body strength needed to make this work. Already her arms were aching, not just aching, they were hurting. She couldn't imagine how she was going to manage another minute, let alone an entire hour. But she refused to accept that she was going to be the one to get them caught just because she wasn't strong enough, refused to accept the idea that they'd fail because she was weak.

Fighting the pain, silently crying with frustration, she could no longer hold on, she had to lower herself to the ground and rest her arms. However, even with a rest, she'd recover only enough to hold on for another minute or two. The length of time she'd be able to hold herself up would rapidly decrease until she couldn't do it at all. She had to think around this problem. What was the solution that didn't rely on strength? The strips of the shirt – if she couldn't hold on, she'd tie herself on, tie her wrists to the axle shaft. That would be fine as long as the truck was stationary. All the same she'd still have to lower herself to the ground for a couple of minutes while she bound herself. Once on the ground, even still under the truck, the chances of her being seen increased dramatically. She looked sideways, checking right and left, trying to get a sense of where the soldiers were. The driver had remained guarding the vehicle. She could see his boots and smell his cigarette smoke. Actually, his presence suited her just fine. It meant they were unlikely to suspect that anyone could've clambered underneath it. Slowly, carefully, Raisa lowered her legs to the ground, trying not to make a noise. Even the smallest of slips would alert that man to her presence. Unwinding the strips of shirt she fastened her left wrist to the shaft before partially tying her right wrist. She had to finish the knot with her already bound-up hand. Done, secured, pleased with herself, she was about to lift up her feet when she heard a growl. Looking sideways, she found herself staring at a dog.

Leo could see the pack of dogs being held beside the third truck. The man with them wasn't aware of Raisa, not yet. But the dogs were. He could hear the snarling: they were at the perfect eye level. Unable to do anything, he turned his head and saw the boy, the boy who'd helped them on the road. No doubt fascinated by events, he was watching from the inside of his house. Leo lowered himself to the ground, getting a better look. The soldier in charge was about to move off. But one of the dogs in particular was straining at the leash, almost certainly having seen Raisa. Leo turned to the little boy. He'd need his help again. He gestured at the dogs. The boy hurried out of the house. Leo watched – impressed at the boy's cool head – as he moved towards the pack of dogs. Almost immediately all the dogs turned on the boy, barking at him. The soldier called out:

—*Stay in your house.*

The boy reached out, as though to stroke one of the dogs. The soldier laughed:

—*It'll bite your arm off.*

The boy pulled back. The soldier led the dogs away, repeating his order that the boy return to his house. Leo pulled himself back up, pressing himself flat against the underside of the truck. They owed that boy their lives.

Raisa had no idea how long she'd been tied under the truck. It felt like an impossibly long time. She'd listened as the soldiers carried out their search: furniture was kicked over, pots upturned, objects smashed. She'd heard the dogs barking and seen the explosion of light as flares were fired. The soldiers were returning, moving back to the trucks. Orders were being shouted. The dogs were loaded into the back of her truck. They were about to leave.

Excited, she realized the plan had worked. Then the engine started. The axle shuddered. In a couple of seconds it would start spinning. She was still tied to it. She had to get free. But her wrists were bound and it was difficult to untie the knots, her hands were numb, her fingers unresponsive. She was struggling. The last of the soldiers were in the truck. The villagers were crowding round the trucks. Raisa still wasn't free. The trucks were about to drive off. She leaned forward, using her teeth, tugging at the knot. It came undone and she dropped to the ground, landing with a thump on her back, a noise masked by the sound of the engines. The truck drove off. She was in the middle of the road. In the light of the village she'd be seen by the soldiers sitting at the back of the truck. There was nothing she could do.

The villagers moved forward, clustering. As the truck drove off, leaving Raisa on the road, they surrounded her. Looking back the soldiers saw nothing unusual. Raisa was hidden amongst the villagers' legs.

Raisa waited, still on the road, curled up. Finally a man offered his hand. She was safe. She stood up. Leo wasn't there. He wouldn't have risked letting go until the trucks were in the dark. She guessed he was worried about being seen by the driver of the third truck. Perhaps he'd wait until they were turning. But she wasn't worried. He'd know what to do. All of them waited in silence. Raisa took the young boy's hand, the boy who'd helped them. And before long they could hear a man running towards them.

Moscow

Despite the many hundreds of soldiers and agents now searching for the fugitives, Vasili was convinced that none of them would succeed. Although the odds were heavily weighted in the State's favour, they were chasing a man who'd been trained to avoid detection and survive in hostile territory. There was a belief in some quarters that Leo and Raisa must have had assistance, either from treacherous guards or from people waiting at a designated location on the railway line who'd orchestrated the breakout. This had been contradicted by the confessions of the prisoners who'd been travelling in Leo's carriage. They'd declared, under duress, that they'd escaped alone. That wasn't what the guards wanted to hear – it embarrassed them. So far the search had focused on possible approach routes towards the Scandinavian border, the northern coastline and the Baltic Sea. It was taken for granted that Leo would try and cross into another country, probably using a fishing boat. Once in the West he'd connect with senior government figures who'd gladly aid and shelter him in exchange for information. For this reason his capture was considered a matter of the highest urgency. Leo had the potential to inflict untold damage on Soviet Russia.

Vasili dismissed the idea that Leo's escape had been assisted. There was simply no way anyone could have known which train the prisoners would be on. The process of getting them on a Gulag transport had been hurried, improvised and last-minute. He'd pushed it through without the proper paperwork or procedure. The only person who could've helped them escape was him. This meant that there was a chance, no matter how ridiculous the notion, that he'd be blamed. It seemed that Leo had the potential to ruin him after all.

So far none of the search groups had found any trace of them. Neither Leo nor Raisa had any family or friends in that area of the country – they should be alone, in rags, penniless. When he'd last spoken to Leo the man hadn't even known his own name. Evidently he'd regained his wits. Vasili had to figure out where Leo was going: that was the best way to trap him rather than searching the countryside at random. Having failed to recapture his own denounced brother, he must succeed in capturing Leo. He wouldn't survive another failure.

Vasili didn't believe that Leo had any interest in fleeing to the West. Would he return to Moscow? His parents lived here. But his parents couldn't help him and they'd lose their life if he turned up on their doorstep. They were now under armed surveillance. Perhaps he'd want revenge, perhaps he'd turn up to kill Vasili? He mulled over this idea briefly, flattered by it, before rejecting it. He'd never felt anything personal about Leo's dislike of him. There was no way he'd risk his wife's life for an act of revenge. Leo had an agenda and it was rooted in the pages of this captured case file.

Vasili studied the stack of documents accumulated over the past months by both Leo and the local militia officer whom he'd convinced to help him. There were photos of murdered children, witness statements. There were court documents about convicted suspects. During his interrogation Leo had denounced this work. Vasili knew that denunciation was a lie. Leo was a believer and he believed in this fanciful theory. But what exactly did they believe? A single killer was responsible for all these motiveless murders — murders spread over many hundreds of kilometres in over thirty different locations? Aside from the theory itself being bizarre, it meant they could be heading anywhere. Vasili could hardly pick one of these locations and wait. Frustrated, he re-examined the map marked with each alleged murder, numbered chronologically.

44

Vasili's finger tapped the number. He picked up the phone.

—*Bring me Officer Fyodor Andreev.*

Since Vasili had been promoted he'd been rewarded with his own office — a small space, admittedly, but one of which he was immensely proud as if each square metre had been personally conquered during a military campaign. There was a knock on the door. Fyodor Andreev entered, now one of Vasili's subordinates: a youngish man, loyal, hardworking and not too bright, perfect virtues in a subordinate. He was nervous. Vasili smiled, gesturing for Fyodor to sit down.

—*Thank you for coming. I need your help.*

—*Certainly, sir.*

—*You're aware that Leo Demidov is a fugitive?*

—*Yes, sir, I've heard.*

—*What do you know of the reasons behind Leo's arrest?*

—*Nothing.*

—*We believed that he was working for Western governments, collecting information — spying. But that turns out not to be true.*

We were wrong. Leo wouldn't tell us anything during his interrogation. Now, belatedly, I've found out that he was working on this.

Fyodor stood up, staring at the case file on the table. He'd seen these documents before. They'd been taped to Leo's chest. Fyodor was beginning to sweat. He leaned forward, as though examining these papers for the first time, trying to hide the fact that he was trembling. Out of the corner of his eye he could see that Vasili had moved and was now standing beside him, staring down at the pages, as though they were working together, partners. Vasili's finger slid across the map, slowly, reaching Moscow and tapping:

44

Fyodor felt sick. He turned his head to see Vasili's face close to his own.

—*Fyodor, we know Leo came to Moscow recently. I now believe that rather than spying, this journey was in fact part of his investigation. You see, he believes that a murder took place here. Your son was murdered, am I correct?*

—*No, sir. He was killed in an accident. He was cut down by a train.*

—*Leo was sent to deal with the matter?*

—*Yes, but*—

—*And at the time you believed that the boy was murdered, am I right?*

—*At the time, I was upset, it was very difficult . . .*

—*So, when Leo came back to Moscow to investigate, it wasn't your child that he was interested in?*

—*No, sir.*

—*How do you know?*

—*Sir?*

—How do you know what Leo was or wasn't interested in?

Vasili took a seat, glancing at his fingernails, pretending to be hurt.

—Fyodor, you obviously have a very low opinion of me.

—That's not true, sir.

—You must understand that if Leo is right, if there is a child-murderer, then he needs to be caught. I want to help Leo. Fyodor, I have children of my own. It is my duty as a father and as an officer to stop these terrible crimes. This supersedes any personal animosity that exists between Leo and myself. If I wanted Leo dead, I would simply do nothing. At the moment everyone considers both him and his wife to be spies. They will be shot on sight and I fear their investigation will be lost. More children will die. However, if I had all the facts, I might be able to persuade my superiors to call off the man hunt. If I don't, what chance do Leo and Raisa have?

—None.

Vasili nodded, pleased with the confirmation. It was true, then: Leo was convinced that there was one man responsible for all these deaths. Vasili continued.

—My point exactly, they have no money; they're hundreds of kilometres from their destination.

—Where did they escape?

Fyodor's second mistake, revealing that he too believed Leo would be intent on catching this killer. All Vasili needed now was the destination itself. He pointed east of Moscow, the train lines, and watched as Fyodor's eyes moved from that position, across the map, southwards. Leo was heading south. But Vasili still needed a name. Coaxing Fyodor, he remarked:

—The majority of the murders are taking place in the south.

—Just from glancing at this map . . .

Fyodor paused. It was possible to tip Vasili off without incriminating himself. They could then jointly petition their superior officers to change their mind about Leo and Raisa. Fyodor had been looking for a way to help them. This was it: he'd turn them from villains into heroes. When they'd met in Moscow, Leo had mentioned that a militia officer had travelled to Rostov to confirm that the city was the most probable location of the killer. Fyodor pretended to scrutinize the papers.

—*Judging from the concentration of the murders, I'd say the city of Rostov-on-Don. All the early murders were in the south. He must live there or somewhere near there.*

—*Rostov?*

—*What do you think is the best way of convincing our superiors?*

—*I need to understand everything. We'd be taking a great risk, putting our necks on the line. We have to be sure. Show me again, why do you believe this killer lives in the south?*

With Fyodor engrossed in the documents, talking about this and that, Vasili stood up, stepped around the desk, drew his gun and aimed at Fyodor's heart.

South-Eastern Rostov Oblast

14 July

Leo and Raisa were in a crate one metre high and two metres wide: human cargo – contraband – in the process of being smuggled south. After the military had completed their search of the *kolkhoz*, the villagers had taken Leo and Raisa by truck to the nearest town, Ryazan, where they'd introduced them to friends and family. In the stifling heat of a small apartment filled with an audience of nearly thirty and the fog of cheap cigarette smoke, Leo had told the story of their investigation. No one needed any convincing as to the urgency of the objective and no one had any difficulty believing that the militia had proved useless in dealing with the killer. They'd never turned to the militia for help or taken their disputes to the authorities, always depending on each other. This was the same, except at stake were the lives of an unknowable number of children.

Together, as a collective, plans were laid to transport them south. One member of the audience worked as a truck driver shuttling loads between Moscow and towns such as Samara and Kharkov. Kharkov was some three hundred kilometres north of Rostov, half a day's drive. Though it was decided that driving into

Rostov itself was too risky since the driver had no business there, he'd be prepared to take them to the nearby town of Shakhty. He could legitimately pass off this diversion by claiming that he was visiting family. That same family would, after listening to the story, almost certainly agree to help Leo and Raisa travel into the city.

At the very least they had a day and a half in this crate, cooped up in complete darkness. The driver was transporting bananas, luxury exotic goods intended for the *spetztorgi*. Shops for high ranking Party figures, the kind of shops Leo and Raisa once bought their own groceries in. Their crate was positioned at the back of the truck wedged under other crates all filled with precious fruit. It was hot and dry and the journey uncomfortable. There were breaks every three to four hours when the driver would stop, slide off the crates above them, letting his human cargo stretch their legs and relieve themselves by the side of the road.

In complete darkness, with their legs crossed over each other, in opposite corners of the crate, Raisa asked:

—*Do you trust him?*

—*Who?*

—*The driver.*

—*You don't?*

—*I don't know.*

—*You must have some reason for asking?*

—*Of all the people listening to the story he was the only one who didn't have any questions. He didn't seem to engage with it. It didn't shake him as it shook the others. He seems blank to me, practical, unemotional.*

—*He didn't have to help us. And he's not going to be able to betray us and then go back to his friends and family.*

421

—He could make something up. There was a roadblock. We were caught. He tried to help us but there was nothing he could do.

—What do you suggest?

—At the next stop, you could overpower him, tie him up and drive the truck yourself.

—You're serious?

—The only way to be sure, to be absolutely certain, is to take his truck. We'd have his papers. We'd have our lives back in our hands, back under our control. We're helpless like this. We don't know where he's taking us.

—You were the one who taught me to trust in the goodness of strangers.

—This man isn't like the others. He seems ambitious. He spends his entire day transporting luxury items. He must think: I want that, I want those fine textiles, those rare foods. He understands that we're an opportunity. He knows how much he can sell us for. And he knows the price he'll pay for being caught with us.

—I'm hardly the one to say this, Raisa, but you're talking about an innocent man, a man who seems to be risking his life to help us.

—I'm talking about guaranteeing that we reach Rostov.

—Isn't this how it starts? You have a cause you believe in, a cause worth dying for. Soon, it's a cause worth killing for. Soon, it's a cause worth killing innocent people for.

—We wouldn't have to kill him.

—Yes we would, because we couldn't leave him tied up on the roadside. That would be a far greater risk. We either kill him, or trust him. Raisa, this is how things fall apart. We've been fed, sheltered and transported by these people. If we turn on them, execute one of their friends for no reason other than as a precaution, I'd be the same man you despised in Moscow.

Even though he couldn't see her, he knew she was smiling.

—*Were you testing me?*

—*Just making conversation.*

—*Did I pass?*

—*That depends on whether we get to Shakhty or not.*

After a stretch of silence, Raisa asked.

—*What happens once this is over?*

—*I don't know.*

—*The West will want you, Leo. They'll protect you.*

—*I'd never leave this country.*

—*Even if this country is going to kill you?*

—*If you want to defect, I'll do everything I can to get you onto a boat.*

—*What are you going to do? Hide in the hills?*

—*Once that man is dead, once you're safely out of the country, I'm going to turn myself in. I don't want to live in exile, among people that want my information but hate me. I don't want to live as a foreigner. I can't do it. It would mean that everything these people in Moscow have said about me would be true.*

—*And that's the most important thing?*

Raisa sounded hurt. Leo touched her arm.

—*Raisa, I don't understand.*

—*Is it that complicated? I want us to stay together.*

Leo said nothing for a moment. Finally he replied:

—*I can't live as a traitor. I can't do it.*

—*Which means we've got about twenty-four hours left?*

—*I'm sorry.*

—*We should make the most of this time together.*

—*How do we do that?*

—*We tell each other the truth.*

—*The truth?*

—We must have secrets. I know I have some. Don't you? Things you've never told me.

—Yes.

—Then I'll go first. I used to spit in your tea. After I heard about Zoya's arrest, I was convinced you'd reported her. So, for about a week, I spat in your tea.

—You spat in my tea?

—For about a week.

—Why did you stop?

—You didn't seem to care.

—I didn't notice.

—Exactly. OK, your turn.

—Truthfully—

—That's the point of this game.

—I don't think you married me because you were afraid. I think you scouted me out. You made it look like you were scared. You gave me a false name and I pursued you. But I think you targeted me.

—I'm a foreign agent?

—You might know of people working for Western agencies. Maybe you were helping them. Maybe that idea was at the back of your mind when you married me.

—That's not a secret, that's speculation. You have to share secrets – hard facts.

—I found a kopek *among your clothes, the coin could be split it in two – it's a device for smuggling microfilm. Agents use them. No one else would have one.*

—Why didn't you denounce me?

—I couldn't do it.

—Leo, I didn't marry you as a way of getting close to the MGB. I told you the truth before, I was scared.

—And the coin?

—That coin was mine . . .

Her voice drifted off, as though weighing up whether or not to continue.

—I didn't use it to carry microfilm. I used it to carry cyanide paste, when I was a refugee.

Raisa had never spoken about the period after her home had been destroyed, the months on the road – the dark ages of her life. Leo waited, suddenly nervous.

—I'm sure you can imagine the kind of things that happened to women refugees. Soldiers, they had needs, they were risking their lives – they were owed. We were their payment. After one time – and there were several – I hurt so much, I swore if it ever happened again, if it ever looked like happening again, I'd rub that paste across his gums. They could kill me, hang me, but maybe it would make them think twice about doing it to another woman. Anyway, it became my lucky coin because as soon as I started carrying it I never had any problems. Maybe men can sense a woman with cyanide in her pocket. Of course, it didn't cure the injuries I'd sustained. There was no medicine. That's the reason I can't get pregnant, Leo.

Leo stared into the darkness, at the place where he imagined his wife must be. During the war women had been raped during the occupation and then raped again by their liberators. As a soldier he knew such activity had been sanctioned by the State, considered part of the fabric of war and an appropriate reward for a brave soldier. Cyanide had been used by some to take their own lives in the face of impossible horrors. Leo supposed that most men might've checked the woman for a blade or a gun but a coin – that would've slipped their attention. He rubbed the palm of her hand. What else could he do? Apologize? Say he understood? He'd framed that newspaper clipping, hung it on the wall, proud, oblivious to what the war meant to her.

—*Leo, I have another secret. I've fallen in love with you.*

—*I've always loved you.*

—*That's not a secret, Leo. You're three secrets behind.*

Leo kissed her:

—*I have a brother.*

Rostov-on-Don

15 July

Nadya was alone in the house. Her mother and sister had gone to visit their grandmother and although Nadya had initially accompanied them, as they'd approached her grandmother's apartment block she'd feigned a stomach ache and begged to be allowed to return. Her mother had agreed and Nadya had hurried back home. Her plan was simple. She was going to open the basement door and find out why her father spent so long downstairs in what must be a dark cold room. She'd never been down there, not once. She'd walked around the building feeling the damp bricks and imagining what it must be like inside. There were no windows, just a ventilation hole for the stove. It was strictly forbidden, out of bounds, an unbreakable rule of the house.

Her father was on a work trip at the moment. But he'd be back soon, perhaps as early as tomorrow, and she'd heard him talk about improving their home, which included building a new door for the basement. Not the front door, not the door that everyone used and which kept the warmth in. His first priority was the basement door. Admittedly it was flimsy but all the same. Why was it so important? In a couple of days he'd have fitted a new door which she wouldn't be able to open. If she wanted to break in, if she wanted answers to her questions, she had to do it now. The lock was a simple latch. She'd studied it carefully and tested it to see if a knife could be squeezed in between the door and the frame, lifting up the latch. It could.

The latch raised, Nadya pushed the door open. Excited, afraid, she took a step down. She released the door and it swung shut. Some light crept in behind her, under the door and around the sides. Other than that the only light came through the ventilation hole downstairs. Adjusting her eyes to the gloom she reached the bottom of the stairs and surveyed her father's secret room.

A bed, a stove, a small table and a chest – there was nothing mysterious. Disappointed, she snooped around. An old lamp hung on the wall and pinned up beside it were a series of newspaper clippings. She walked towards them. They were all the same: a photograph of a Russian soldier standing beside a burning tank. Some of the photographs had been cropped so that all you could see was the soldier. He was handsome. She didn't recognize him. Puzzled by this collage she picked up a tin plate which had been left on the floor, no doubt for the cats. Turning her attention to the chest, she put her hands on the top and lifted, just a little, just to see if it was locked. The wooden lid was heavy but it wasn't locked. What was inside? She lifted it a little more; suddenly she heard another noise – the front door.

There were heavy footsteps, too heavy for her mother. Her father must have returned early. Light appeared as the door to the basement was opened. Why was he back so soon? Panicking, Nadya lowered the lid, trying not to make a noise, listening to her father's footsteps coming down the stairs. With the lid closed she dropped to her knees and clambered under the bed, squeezing herself into the small space, watching the bottom step. There they were — his big black boots, coming right towards her.

Nadya closed her eyes, expecting when she opened her eyes to see his furious face inches away from her. Instead, the entire bed creaked and sank. He was sitting on it. Opening her eyes she had to scramble out of the way. With the gap between the bed and the floor even smaller she watched as he began to untie his bootlaces. He didn't know she was here. The latch must have locked after she'd shut it. She hadn't been caught, not yet. What was she going to do? Her father could spend hours down here. Her mother would return and be alarmed that Nadya wasn't home. Perhaps they'd think she was missing and go looking for her. If they did she'd be able to sneak upstairs and tell some lie about where she'd been. That was her best hope. Until then she had to remain where she was and keep very quiet.

Her father pulled his socks off and stretched his toes. He stood up, the bed rising with him, and fired up the lamp, which gave out a weak light. He walked towards the chest. Nadya could hear the top of the chest being opened but couldn't see what he'd taken out. He must have left the lid open because she didn't hear it close. What was her father doing? Now he was sitting at one of the chairs, tying something around his foot. It was a strip of rubber. Using string and rags he seemed to be making some kind of home-made shoe.

Aware of something behind her, Nadya turned her head and saw the cat. It had seen her too, its back was arched, its fur stuck out. She didn't belong down here. It knew that much. Scared, she turned to see if her father had noticed. He dropped to his knees, his face appearing in the gap under the bed. She didn't know what to say, didn't dare move. He said nothing, standing up, lifting the entire bed upright, exposing her curled up in a ball.

—Stand up.

She couldn't move her arms, her legs – her body didn't seem to be working.

—Nadya.

Hearing her name, she stood up.

—Step away from the wall.

She obeyed: stepping towards him, her head down, staring at her father's one bare foot and his other foot wrapped in rags. He lowered the bed, putting it back in position.

—Why are you down here?

—I wanted to know what you do.

—Why?

—I want to spend more time with you.

Andrei could feel that urge again – they were alone in the house. She shouldn't have come down here: he'd told her that for her own sake. He was a different person. He was not her father. He stepped away from his daughter until his back was pressed against the wall, as far from her as the room would allow.

—Father?

Andrei raised a finger to his lips.

Control yourself.

But he could not. He took his glasses off, folding them up and putting them in his pocket. When he looked at her again she was nothing more than a blurred outline, no longer his daughter – just a child. Indistinct, fuzzy, any child he chose to imagine.

—Father?

Nadya stood up, walking right up to her father and taking his hand.

—Don't you like spending time with me?

She was too close now, even without his glasses on. He could see her hair, her face. Wiping his brow, he put his glasses back on.

—*Nadya, you have a younger sister – why don't you like playing with her? When I was your age, I spent all my time with my brother.*

—*You have a brother?*

—*Yes.*

—*Where is he?*

Andrei pointed at the wall, the photos of the Russian soldier.

—*What's his name?*

—*Pavel.*

—*Why doesn't he visit us?*

—*He will.*

Rostov Oblast
Eight Kilometres North of
Rostov-on-Don

16 July

They were seated on an *elektrichka*, travelling towards the outskirts of the city, edging closer to their destination – the centre of Rostov-on-Don. The truck driver hadn't betrayed them. He'd taken them through several checkpoints and dropped them at the town of Shakhty where they'd spent the night with the driver's mother-in-law, a woman called Sarra Karlovna, and her family. Sarra, in her fifties, lived with some of her children, including a daughter who was married with three children of her own. Sarra's parents also lived in the apartment, a total of eleven people in three bedrooms; a different generation in each bedroom. For the third time Leo had told the story of his investigation. Unlike the towns in the north they'd already heard of these crimes – the child-murders. According to Sarra there were few people in this oblast who weren't aware of the rumours. Even so, they knew no facts. When confronted with the estimated number of victims the room had fallen silent.

It had never been a question of whether or not they'd agree to help: this extended family had immediately set about making plans. Leo and Raisa had decided to wait until dusk before travelling into the city since there'd be fewer people at the factory at night. There was also a greater chance the killer would be at home. It had also been decided that they shouldn't travel alone. For this reason they were now accompanied by three small children and two energetic grandparents. Leo and Raisa were playing the parts of a mother and father while the real mother and father remained in Shakhty. This semblance of a family was a precautionary measure. If the hunt for them had reached Rostov, if the State had guessed that their objective wasn't to flee the country, then they'd be looking for a man and woman travelling together. It had proved impossible for either of them to change their appearance to any significant degree. They'd both cut their hair short, they'd been given a new set of clothes. Even so, without the family surrounding them, they would've been easy to spot. Raisa had expressed concerns about using the children, worried she was putting them in danger. It had been decided that if something should go wrong, if they were caught, then the grandparents would claim that Leo had threatened them and that they feared for their lives if they didn't help.

The train stopped. Leo glanced out of the window. The station was busy: he could see several uniformed officers patrolling the platform. The seven of them got off the train. Raisa was carrying the smallest child; a young boy. All three children had been instructed to behave boisterously. The older of the two boys understood the nature of the deception and played their part, but the youngest boy was confused and merely stared at Raisa, his lips downturned, sensitive to danger and no doubt wishing he was at home. Only the most observant of officers would suspect that this family was a fraud.

There were guards dotted around the platform and concourse, too many for an ordinary day in an ordinary station. They were looking for someone. Though Leo tried to reassure himself that there were many people being hunted and arrested, his gut told him that they were looking for them. The exit was fifty paces away. Concentrate on that. They were almost there.

Two armed officers stepped in front of them.

—*Where you are travelling from and where are you travelling to?*

For a moment Raisa couldn't speak. The words evaporated. In order not to appear frozen, she moved the young boy from one arm to the other arm and laughed.

—*They get so heavy!*

Leo stepped in.

—*We've just visited her sister. She lives in Shakhty. She's getting married.*

The grandmother added:

—*To a man who's a drunk, I disapprove. I told her not to do it.*

Leo smiled, addressing the grandmother.

—*You want her to marry a man who only drinks water?*

—*That would be better.*

The grandfather nodded before adding.

—*He can drink but why does he have to be so ugly?*

Both grandparents laughed. The officers did not. One of them turned to the little boy.

—*What's his name?*

The question was directed at Raisa. Once again her mind went blank. She couldn't remember. Nothing was coming to her. Plucking a name from her memory.

—*Aleksandr.*

The boy shook his head.

—*My name is Ivan.*

Raisa laughed.

—*I like to tease him. I'm always getting the brothers' names muddled and it drives them mad. This young man I'm carrying is Ivan. That is Mikhail.*

That was the middle child's name. Raisa now remembered that the eldest was called Aleksei. But for her lie to work he would have to pretend his name was Aleksandr.

—*And my eldest boy is called Aleksandr.*

The boy opened his mouth to contradict but the grandfather quickly stepped in and rubbed his head affectionately. Annoyed, the boy shook his head.

—*Don't do that. I'm not a child any more.*

Raisa struggled not to let her relief show. The officers stepped out of their way and she led her imitation family out of the station.

Once they were out of sight of the station they bade farewell to the family, splitting up. Leo and Raisa got into a taxi. They'd already given Sarra's family all the information pertaining to their investigation. If Leo and Raisa failed for whatever reason, if the murders continued, then the family would inherit the investigation. They'd organize others in an attempt to find this man, making sure that if any one group failed there would be another ready to take their place. He mustn't be allowed to survive. Leo appreciated that it was a mob execution, no court, no evidence or trial – an execution based upon circumstantial evidence – and that in trying to exact justice they were forced to imitate the very system they were up against.

Sitting in the back of the taxi, a Volga, almost certainly one produced in Voualsk, neither Leo nor Raisa spoke. They didn't need to. The plan was in place. Leo was going to enter the Rostelmash factory and break into the employment records. He didn't know how exactly, he'd have to improvise. Raisa was going to remain with the taxi, convincing the driver if he became suspicious that all was well. He'd been paid in advance and generously to keep him placid and obedient. Once Leo had found the killer's name and address they'd need the driver to take them to where the killer lived. If the killer wasn't home, if he was travelling, they would try to find out when he'd be back. They'd return to Shakhty, remain with Sarra's family and wait.

The taxi stopped. Raisa touched Leo's hand. He was nervous, his voice barely a whisper.

—*If I'm not back in an hour.*

—*I know.*

Leo got out, shutting the door.

There were guards stationed at the main gates, although they didn't seem to be particularly alert. Judging from the security arrangements, Leo was almost certain no one in the MGB had guessed that this tractor factory was his destination. There was a chance that the front guards had been deliberately reduced in number as a way of luring him in, but he doubted it. They might have guessed that he was heading to Rostov but they hadn't figured out where exactly. Walking around the back, he discovered a point where the wire fencing was sheltered from view by the side of a brick building. He clambered up, straddling the barbed wire, and lowered himself down. He was in.

The factory ran a twenty-four-hour production line. There were shift workers but not many people around. The grounds were vast. Several thousand people must be employed here, Leo reckoned as many as ten thousand – bookkeeping, cleaning, shipments and the production line itself. With the additional split between day- and night-workers he doubted if anyone would recognize him as a stranger. He walked calmly, purposefully, as if he belonged here, making his way towards the largest of the buildings. Two men exited, smoking, heading in the direction of the front gates. Maybe they'd finished for the night. They saw him and paused. Unable to ignore them Leo waved, moving towards them.

—*I'm a* tolkach *working for the car factory in Voualsk. I was meant to arrive much earlier but my train was delayed. Where's the administrative building?*

—*It doesn't have a separate building. The main office is inside, on one of the upper floors. I'll take you there.*

—*I'm sure I'll find it.*

—*I'm not in any rush to get home. I'll take you there.*

Leo smiled. He couldn't refuse. The two men said goodbye to each other and Leo followed his unwanted escort into the main assembly plant.

Stepping inside Leo briefly forgot himself – the sheer size, the high roof, the noise of the machinery – all creating a sense of wonder normally reserved for religious institutions. But, of course, this was the new church, the people's cathedral, and a sense of awe was almost as important as the machines it produced. Leo and this man walked side by side, making idle conversation. Leo was suddenly glad of his escort; it meant no one looked twice at them. All the same, he wondered how he was going to get rid of him.

They took the stairs off the main factory floor, climbing up towards the administrative department. The man said.

—*I don't know how many people are going to be there. They don't normally work night shifts.*

Leo still didn't have a clear idea of what he was going to do next. Could he bluff his way through? It seemed unlikely considering the sensitive information he needed, they wouldn't just give it to him no matter what excuse he came up with. If he'd still had his

State Security identification card, it would've been easy.

They turned a corner. The corridor leading to the office had views over the factory floor. Whatever Leo decided to do he'd be visible to the workers below. The man knocked on the door. Everything now depended on how many people were inside. The door was opened by an older man, a bookkeeper perhaps, dressed in a suit, with sallow skin and a bitter expression.

—*What do you want?*

Leo peered over the bookkeeper's shoulder. The office was empty.

Leo swung around, punching his escort in the stomach, causing him to double up. Before the bookkeeper had time to react Leo had his hand tight around the old man's neck.

—*Do as I say and you'll live, understand?*

He nodded. Leo slowly released his neck.

—*Close all the blinds. And remove your tie.*

Leo pulled the younger man, who was still wheezing inside. He shut the door, locking it behind him. The bookkeeper took off his tie, throwing it to Leo before moving to the windows, shutting out the view over the factory. Using the tie, Leo secured the young man's hands behind his back, all the time keeping his eye on the bookkeeper. He doubted if there was a weapon or alarm in here, there was nothing worth stealing. With the blinds closed the man turned back to Leo.

—*What do you want?*

—*The employment records.*

Baffled but obedient, the man unlocked the filing cabinet. Leo moved forward, standing beside him.

—*Stay there, don't move and keep your hands on top of the cabinet.*

There were thousands and thousands of files, extensive documentation not just for the current work force but for people who'd left. *Tolkachs* weren't supposed to exist, since their necessity implied some fault in distribution and production. It was unlikely they'd be listed under that title.

—*Where are the files on your* tolkachs?

The old man opened up a cabinet, taking out a thick file. The front was marked RESEARCHERS, a cover. As far as Leo could tell there were five *tolkachs* currently on the payroll. Nervous – their entire investigation rested on these documents – he checked the employment history of these men. Where had they been sent and when? If these dates corresponded to the murders he would have found the killer, at least in his own mind. If it was enough of a match he'd go to the man and confront him – he was sure face to face, confronted with his crime, the killer would crack. He ran his finger down the list, comparing it to the dates and places held in his memory. The first list didn't match. Leo paused for a moment, wondering about his own powers of recall. But the three dates he couldn't forget were the murders in Voualsk and the murder in Moscow. This *tolkach* had never been there or anywhere along the Trans-Siberian railway line. Leo opened the second file, ignoring the personal information and moving to the employment record. This person had only started working last month. Leo pushed the files aside, opening the third file. It didn't match. There were only two files left. He flicked to the fourth.

Voualsk, Molotov, Vyatka, Gorky – a row of towns which followed the train line west towards Moscow. Moving south from Moscow, there were the towns of Tula and Orel. Now into the Ukraine, Leo saw the towns of Kharkov and Gorlovka, Zaporoshy and Kramatorsk. In all these towns there had been murders. He shut the file. Before he studied the personal details he'd check the fifth file. Barely able to concentrate he ran his finger down the list.

There were some cross-references but no perfect fit. Leo returned to the fourth file. He flicked to the front page, staring at the small black-and-white photo. The man was wearing glasses. His name was Andrei.

Same Day

Vasili sat on his hotel bed, smoking, dumping ash on the carpet and drinking straight from the bottle. He was under no illusions: if he didn't hand his superior officers the fugitives Leo and Raisa, they would almost certainly look upon the death of Fyodor Andreev with unkind eyes. That had been the deal they'd struck before he'd left Moscow. They'd believe his story about Fyodor working with Leo, they'd believe that when Fyodor had been presented with the truth he'd tried to attack Vasili, only if he brought them Leo. The MGB were embarrassed at their inability to catch this unarmed, penniless married couple who seemed to have melted away. If Vasili could catch them they were prepared to forgive him any sin. Officials were preparing for the fact that Leo was already abroad in the clutches of Western diplomats. Their own foreign agents had been briefed. Photos of Leo and his wife had already been sent out to embassies across the world. Plans to assassinate them were being drawn up. If Vasili could save them the trouble of launching an expensive and diplomatically complicated international man hunt, then his slate would be wiped clean.

He dropped his cigarette stub on the carpet, watched it smoulder for a moment before crushing it under his heel. He'd been in contact with the State Security in Rostov, a ragtag bunch. He'd given them photos. He'd told the officers that they should bear in mind Leo might have grown a beard or cropped his hair short. They might not be travelling as a couple. They might have parted ways. One of them might be dead. Or they might be travelling in a group, assisted by others. Officers should pay little attention to paperwork, all of which Leo knew how to fake. They should detain anyone they considered even remotely suspicious. Vasili would make the final decision as to whether to release them or not. With thirty men in total he'd set up a series of checkpoints and random searches. He'd ordered every officer to log all incidents, no matter how trivial, in order that he'd be able to check them himself. These reports were brought to him, day and night.

There had been nothing so far. Would this prove another opportunity for Leo to humiliate him? Perhaps that idiot Fyodor had been wrong. Maybe Leo was heading somewhere completely different. If that was the case then Vasili was dead.

There was a knock on the door.

—*Come in.*

A red-faced young officer stood to attention holding a sheet of paper. Vasili gestured for him to give it to him.

> *Rostelmash factory. Administrative section.*
> *Two men attacked, employment files stolen.*

Vasili got to his feet.

—*He's here.*

Same Day

They stood side by side, fifty paces from the front door. Leo glanced at his wife. She was unaware of this madness that had descended upon him. He felt giddy: as though he'd ingested some narcotic. He half expected that the feeling would fade and normality would return, there'd be another explanation and that this wouldn't be the house belonging to his little brother.

Andrei Trofimovich Sidorov.

But that was his little brother's name.

Pavel Trofimovich Sidorov.

And that had been his own name, until he'd shed his childhood identity as a reptile sheds its skin. The small photo on the employment file had confirmed it was Andrei. The features were the same – a lost expression. The glasses were new. But that's why he'd been so clumsy, he was short-sighted. His awkward, shy little brother – murderer of at least 44 children. It made no sense and yet it made perfect sense: the string, the ground-up bark, the hunt. Forced to concentrate on the memories he'd banished, Leo recalled teaching his little brother how to make a string snare, he'd told him to gnaw on the bark of trees to suppress hunger. Had those lessons become the template for some kind of psychotic frenzy? Why hadn't Leo made the connections before? No, it was ridiculous to have expected him to. Any number of children had been taught the same lessons and shown how to hunt. Upon seeing the victims these details hadn't registered any deeper into Leo's mind. Or had they? Had he chosen this path or had it chosen him? Had this been the reason he'd been drawn into the investigation when there was every reason to look the other way?

When he'd seen his brother's name printed in black and white Leo had been forced to sit down, staring at the file, checking the dates, checking and rechecking. He'd been in shock, oblivious to the dangers around him. It wasn't until he noticed the bookkeeper sidestepping towards the phone that he snapped back. He'd secured the bookkeeper to a chair, disabled the phone and locked both men in the office, gagging them. He had to get out. He had to pull himself together. But going down the corridor he hadn't even been walking straight, lurching from side to side. He'd felt dizzy. Having made it outside, his thoughts still scrambled, his world still upside down, he'd instinctively turned towards the main gates, too late realizing that it would've been far safer to climb over the fence as he'd done before. But he'd been unable to change direction; the guards had seen him approach. He'd have to walk right past them. He'd begun to sweat. They'd let him go unchallenged. Once in the taxi he'd told the driver the address, ordering him to hurry. He'd been shaking, his legs, his arms – he'd been unable to stop. He'd watched as Raisa had studied the file. She now knew the story of his brother: she knew his first name but not their full name. He'd watched her reaction as she studied the papers. She hadn't put the two together, she hadn't guessed. How could she? He'd been incapable of telling her.

That man is my brother.

There was no way of knowing how many people were inside his brother's house. The other inhabitants posed a problem. They were almost certainly unaware of the nature of this man, this killer, unaware of his crimes – surely part of the reason he murdered away from home. His little brother had created a split identity, his home life and his life as a killer, just as Leo had cleaved his own identity in two, the boy he'd been and the boy he'd become. Leo shook his head: he had to stay focused. He was here to kill this man. The question was how to get past the other occupants. Neither he nor Raisa had a gun. Raisa sensed his hesitation and asked:

—*What's worrying you?*

—*The other occupants of that house.*

—*You saw this man's face. We've seen the photo. You can slip in and kill him while he sleeps.*

—*I can't do that.*

—*Leo, he deserves nothing more.*

—*I have to be sure. I have to talk to him.*

—*He's only going to deny it. The longer you speak to him, the harder it becomes.*

—*That might be true. But I won't kill him in his sleep.*

They'd been given a knife by Sarra. Leo offered it to Raisa.

—*I won't be using this.*

Raisa refused to take it.

—*Leo, this man killed over forty children.*

—*And I will kill him for it.*

—*What if he defends himself? He must have a knife. Maybe even a gun. He might be strong.*

—*He's no fighter. He's clumsy, shy.*

—Leo, how do you know that? Take the knife. How can you kill him with your bare hands?

Leo gave her the knife, pressing the handle into her hand.

—You forget: this is what I was trained to do. Trust me.

It was the first time he'd ever asked for her trust.

—I do.

There was no future for them, no hope of escape, no hope of being together much beyond the events of tonight. Raisa realized that some part of her wanted this man not to be at home, she wanted him to be away on some trip, then they'd have a reason to stay together, evading capture for at least another couple of days, before returning to finish the job. Ashamed of this thought she pushed it aside. How many people had risked their lives so that they might be here? She kissed Leo, willing him to succeed, willing that man dead.

Leo moved towards the house leaving Raisa hidden. The plan was already agreed. She was to remain set back from the house, watching and waiting. If the man tried to escape she'd intercept him. If something went wrong, if Leo failed for whatever reason, she'd make a separate attempt on the man's life.

He reached the door. There was a dim light inside. Did that mean someone was awake? He tentatively pushed on the door, which swung open. Before him was a kitchen area, a table, a stove. The light came from an oil lamp: a flame flickered inside a sooty glass bulb. He stepped into the house, moving through the kitchen into the adjoining space. To his surprise there were only two beds. In one of the beds two young girls slept together. Their mother slept in the second bed. She was alone: there was no sign of Andrei. Was this his brother's family? If so then was it his family too? Was this his sister-in-law? Were these his nieces? No, there might be another family downstairs. He turned. A cat was staring at him, two cool green eyes. Its coat was black and white. Though it was better fed than the cat in the forest, the cat they'd hunted and killed, it was the same colours, the same kind. Leo felt as if he was in a dream, with fragments of the past all around him. The cat squeezed through a second door, going downstairs. Leo followed.

The narrow stairway led down to a basement illuminated by a dim light. The cat descended the stairs and turned out of sight. From the top step most of the room was concealed. All Leo could see was the edge of another bed. It was empty. Was it possible Andrei wasn't home? Leo moved down the stairs, trying not to make any noise.

Reaching the bottom he peered around the corner. A man was seated at a table. He wore thick square glasses, a clean white shirt. He was playing cards. He looked up. Andrei didn't seem surprised. He stood up. From where Leo was standing he could see on the wall behind his brother, as though flowering out of his brother's head, a collage of newspaper clippings taped up, the same photo over and over again, the photo of him — Leo, standing, triumphant, beside the smoking wreck of a panzer, the hero of the Soviet Union, the poster boy of triumph.

—*Pavel, what took you so long?*

His little brother gestured at the empty seat opposite him.

Leo felt powerless to do anything except obey, aware that he was no longer in control of the situation. Far from being alarmed or caught off guard, far from stumbling over his words or even running away, Andrei seemed prepared for this confrontation. In contrast Leo was disorientated, confused: it was hard not to follow his brother's instructions.

Leo sat down. Andrei sat down. Brother opposite brother: reunited after more than twenty years. Andrei asked.

—You knew it would be me from the beginning?

—The beginning?

—From the first body you found?

—No.

—What body did you find first?

—Larisa Petrova, Voualsk.

—A young girl, I remember her.

—And Arkady, Moscow?

—There were several in Moscow.

Several, he used the word so casually. If there were several, then they'd all been covered up.

—Arkady was murdered in February this year, on the railway tracks.

—A small boy?

—He was four years old.

—I remember him too. They were recent. I had perfected my method by then. Yet you still didn't know it was me? The earlier murders weren't as clear. I was nervous. You see, I couldn't be too obvious. It needed to be something only you would recognize. I couldn't just have written my name. I was communicating with you, and only you.

—What are you talking about?

—Brother, I never believed you were dead. I always knew you were alive. And I have only ever had one desire, one ambition . . . to get you back.

Was that anger in Andrei's voice or affection or both emotions together? Had his only ambition been to get him back or get back at him? Andrei smiled, it was a warm smile — wide and honest — like he'd just won at cards.

—Your stupid, clumsy brother was right about one thing. He was right about you. I tried telling Mother that you were alive. But she

wouldn't pay any attention to me. She was sure someone had caught you, killed you. I told her that wasn't true, I told her you'd run away, with our catch. I promised to find you and when I did I wouldn't be angry, I'd forgive you. She wouldn't listen. She went mad. She would forget who I was and pretend that I was you. She'd call me Pavel and ask me to help her, as you used to help her. I would pretend to be you, since that was easier, since that made her happy, but as soon as I made a mistake she'd realize I wasn't you. She'd become furious, she'd hit me and hit me until all her anger was gone. And then she'd mourn for you again. She never stopped crying over you. Everyone has a reason to live. You were hers. But you were mine too. The only difference between us was that I was sure you were alive.

Leo listened, like a child seated in front of an adult in rapt silence as the world was explained. He could no more lift his hands, stand up – do anything – than he could interrupt. Andrei continued:

—*Whilst our mother let herself fall to pieces, I looked after myself. Luckily for me the winter was coming to an end and things slowly got a little better. Only ten people survived from our village, eleven including you. Other villages were completely dead. When the spring came and the snows thawed they stank, entire villages were rotting and diseased. You couldn't go near them. But in the winter they were quiet, peaceful, perfectly still. And all through that time I went hunting through the forest, every night, on my own. I followed tracks. I searched for you and called your name, shouted it out to the trees. But you did not return.*

As though his brain was slowly digesting the words, breaking them down, Leo asked – his voice hesitant:

—*You killed those children because you thought I'd left you?*

—I killed them so you would find me. I killed them to make you come home. I killed them as a way of talking to you. Who else would've understood the clues from our childhood? I knew you'd follow them to me, just as you'd followed the footprints in the snow. You're a hunter, Pavel, the best hunter in the world. I didn't know whether you were militia or not. When I saw that photo of you, I spoke to the staff of Pravda. *I asked for your name. I explained that we'd been separated and that I thought your name was Pavel. They said Pavel wasn't your name and that your details were classified. I begged them to tell me which division you were fighting in. They refused to even answer that. I was a soldier too. Not like you, not a hero, not the elite. But I understood enough to realize you must have been in a special force. I knew from the secrecy regarding your name that there was a strong chance you'd either be in the military or the State Security or the government. I knew you'd be an important person, you couldn't be anything else. You'd have access to the information regarding these murders. Of course, that didn't necessarily matter. If I killed enough children, in enough places, I was sure you'd come across my work, whatever your occupation. I was sure you'd realize it was me.*

Leo leaned forward. His brother seemed so gentle, his reasoning was so careful. Leo asked:

—Brother, what happened to you?

—You mean after the village? The same thing that happened to everyone: I was conscripted into the army. I lost my glasses in battle, stumbled into German hands. I was caught. I surrendered. When I returned to Russia, having been a prisoner of war, I was arrested, interviewed, beaten. They threatened to send me to prison. I told them, how could I be a traitor when I could hardly see? For six months I had no glasses. The world beyond my own nose was a

blur. And every child I saw was you. I should've been executed. But the guards used to laugh at me bumping into things. I used to fall over all the time, just as I did as a child. I survived. I was too stupid and clumsy to be a German spy. They called me names, beat me and let me go. I returned here. Even here I was hated and called a traitor. But none of that bothered me. I had you. I concentrated my life on a single task – bringing you back to me.

—So you started murdering?

—I started in this area first. But after six months I had to consider the fact that you might be anywhere in the country. That's why I got a job as a tolkach, *so that I could travel. I needed to leave the signs spread across the whole of our country, signs for you to follow.*

—Signs? These were children.

—First I killed animals, catching them as we caught that cat. But it didn't work. No one paid any attention. No one cared. No one noticed. One day a child stumbled across me in the forest. He asked what I was doing. I explained I was leaving bait. The boy was the same age as you were when you left me. And I realized that child would make a far better bait. People would notice a dead child. You would understand the significance. Why do you think I killed so many children in the winter months? So you'd follow my tracks through the snow. Didn't you follow my boot prints deep into the forests, just like you followed the cat?

Leo had been listening to his brother's soft voice as if it was a foreign tongue he could barely understand.

—Andrei, you have a family. I saw your children upstairs, children just like the children you've killed. You have two beautiful girls. Can you not understand that what you've done is wrong?

—It was necessary.

—No.

Andrei banged the table with his fists, furious.

—Don't take that tone with me! You have no right to be angry! You never bothered to look for me! You never came back! You knew I was alive and you didn't care! Forget about stupid clumsy Andrei! He's nothing to you! You left me behind with a crazy fucking mother and a village full of rotting bodies! You have no right to judge me!

Leo stared at his brother's face, twisted with anger, suddenly transformed. Was this the face the children saw? What had his brother been through? What impossible horrors? But the time for pity and understanding had long since been passed. Andrei wiped the sweat from his brow.

—It was the only way I could make you find me, the only way I could get your attention. You could've looked for me. But you didn't. You cut me out of your life. You put me out of your mind. The happiest moment of my life was when we caught that cat, together, as a team. When we were together I never felt the world was unfair, even when we had no food, even when it was bitterly cold. But then you went away.

—Andrei, I didn't leave you. I was taken. I was hit over the head by a man in the woods. I was put in a sack and carried away. I would never have left you.

Andrei was shaking his head.

—That's what mother said. But it's a lie. You'd betrayed me.

—I almost died. That man who took me — he was going to kill me. They were going to feed me to their son. But when we arrived at the house, their son had already died. I was concussed. I couldn't even remember my own name. It took me weeks to recover. By that time I was already in Moscow. We'd left the country behind. They had to find food. I remembered you. I remembered

our mother. I remembered our life together. Of course I did. But what was I supposed to do? I had no choice. I had to move on. I'm sorry.

Leo was apologizing.

Andrei picked up the cards and shuffled them.

—You could've looked for me when you were older. You could've made some effort. I haven't changed my name. I would've been easy to find, particularly for a man in power.

That was true, Leo could've found his brother; he could've sought him out. He'd tried to bury the past. And now his brother had murdered his way back into his life.

—Andrei, I spent my whole life trying to forget the past. I grew up afraid to confront my new parents. I was afraid to remind them of the past because I was afraid to remind them of the time when they'd wanted to kill me. I used to wake up every night – sweating, terrified – worried that they might have changed their minds and that they might want to kill me again. I did everything in my power to make them love me. It was about survival.

—You always wanted to do things without me, Pavel. You always wanted to leave me behind.

—Do you know why I've come here?

—You've come to kill me. Why else would a hunter come? After you kill me, I'll be hated and you'll be loved. Just like it has always been.

—Brother, I'm considered a traitor for trying to stop you.

Andrei seemed genuinely surprised.

—Why?

—They've blamed your murders on other people – many inno-cent people have died directly and indirectly from your crimes. Do you understand? Your guilt is an embarrassment to the State.

Andrei's face remained blank. Finally he said:

—*I'll write a confession.*

Another confession: and what would it say?

I – Andrei Sidorov – am a killer.

His brother didn't understand. No one wanted his confession, no one wanted him to be guilty.

—*Andrei, I'm not here to collect your confession. I'm here to make sure you don't kill any more children.*

—*I'm not going to stop you. I've achieved all I set out to achieve. I've been proved right. You've been made to regret not looking for me sooner. If you had, think how many lives would've been saved.*

—*You're insane.*

—*Before you kill me I would like to play one hand of cards. Please, brother, it is the least you can do for me.*

Andrei dealt the cards. Leo looked at them.

—*Please, brother, one game. If you play, I'll let you kill me.*

Leo took up his cards, not because of his brother's promise, but because he needed time to clear his mind. He needed to imagine Andrei was a stranger. They began their game. Concentrating, Andrei appeared perfectly content. There was a noise to the side. Alarmed, Leo turned around. A pretty little girl was standing at the bottom of the stairs, hair dishevelled. She remained on the bottom step, most of her body concealed, a tentative voyeur. Andrei stood up.

—*Nadya, this is my brother, Pavel.*

—*The brother you told me about? The one you told me was coming to visit?*

—*Yes.*

454

Nadya turned to Leo.

—*Are you hungry? Have you travelled far?*

Leo didn't know what to say. Andrei answered instead.

—*You should go back to bed.*

—*I'm awake now. I won't be able to go back to sleep. I'd just lie upstairs listening to you talk. Can't I sit with you? I'd like to meet your brother too. I've never met any of your family. I'd like that very much. Please, Father, please?*

—*Pavel has travelled a long way to find me. We have a lot to talk about.*

Leo had to get rid of the little girl. He was in danger of being entrenched in a family reunion, glasses of vodka, slices of cold meat and questions about his past. He was here to kill.

—*Perhaps we could have some tea, if there's any?*

—*Yes. I know how to make that. Shall I wake Mother?*

Andrei remarked:

—*No. Let her sleep.*

—*I can do it by myself, then.*

—*Yes, do it by yourself.*

She smiled and ran back upstairs.

Excited, Nadya climbed the stairs. Her father's brother was handsome and she could tell that he had many interesting stories to tell. He was a soldier, a hero. He could tell her how to become a fighter pilot. Maybe he was married to a pilot. She opened the door to the living room and gasped. There was a beautiful woman standing in her kitchen. She stood perfectly still, with one hand behind her back, as if a giant hand had reached in through the window and placed her there – a doll in a dolls' house.

Raisa held the knife behind her back, steel pressed against her dress. She'd waited outside for what felt like an impossibly long time. Something must have gone wrong. She'd have to finish this herself. As soon as she'd stepped though the door she realized to her relief that there were very few people in this house. There were two beds, a daughter and mother. Who was this girl in front of her? Where had she come from? She seemed happy and excited. There was no sense of panic or fear. No one had died.

—*My name is Raisa. Is my husband here?*

—*Do you mean Pavel?*

Pavel – why was he calling himself Pavel? Why was he calling himself by his old name?

—*Yes . . .*

—*My name is Nadya. I'm pleased to meet you. I've never met any of my dad's family.*

Raisa kept the knife positioned behind her back. Family – what was this girl talking about?

—*Where is my husband?*

—*Downstairs.*

—*I just want to let him know I'm here.*

Raisa moved to the stairs, placing the knife in front of her so Nadya couldn't see the blade. She pushed open the door.

Walking very slowly, listening to the sound of measured conversation, Raisa descended the stairs. She held the knife in front of her, outstretched, trembling. She reminded herself that the longer she took to kill this man, the more difficult it would become. Reaching the bottom of the stairs she saw her husband playing cards.

*

Vasili ordered his men to circle the house – there was no way anyone could escape. He was accompanied by fifteen officers in total. Many of them were local and he had no relationship with them. Fearful that they'd do things by the book, arrest Leo and his wife, he would have to take matters into his own hands. He'd end this here, making sure he destroyed any evidence which might mitigate in their favour. He moved forward, gun ready. Two men moved with him. He gestured for them to remain where they were.

—*Give me five minutes. Unless I call for you don't enter. Is that clear? If I'm not out in five minutes storm the house, kill everyone.*

*

Raisa's hand was shaking, holding the knife in front of her. She couldn't do it. She couldn't kill this man. He was playing cards with her husband. Leo stepped towards her.

—*I'll do it.*

—*Why are you playing cards with him?*

—*Because he's my brother.*

Upstairs, there were screams. The little girl was screaming. There was the sound of shouting, a man's voice. Before anyone could react Vasili appeared at the bottom of the stairs, his gun raised. He surveyed the scene. He too appeared confused, staring at the cards on the table.

—*You've travelled a long way for a game of cards. I thought you were hunting for a so-called child-killer. Or is this part of your reformed interrogation process?*

Leo had left it too late. There was no way he could kill Andrei now. If he made any sudden movement he'd be shot and Andrei would remain free. Even with his brother's declared reason for killing – their reunion – removed, Leo didn't believe Andrei would be able to stop. Leo had failed. He'd talked when he should've acted. He'd lost sight of the fact that far more people wanted him dead than his brother.

—*Vasili, I need you to listen to me.*

—*On your knees.*

—*Please . . .*

Vasili cocked his gun. Leo dropped to his knees. All he could do was obey, beg, plead, except this was the one man who wouldn't listen, who cared about nothing other than his own personal vendetta.

—*Vasili, this is important—*

Vasili pressed the gun against his head.

—*Raisa, kneel beside your husband, do it now!*

She joined her husband, side by side, in imitation of the executions outside the barn. The gun was moved behind her head. Raisa took hold of his hand, closing her eyes. Leo shouted:

—*No!*

In response Vasili tapped the barrel of the gun against her head, teasing him.

—*Leo . . .*

Vasili's voice trailed off. Raisa's grip tightened around Leo's hand. Seconds passed; there was silence. Nothing happened. Very slowly, Leo turned around.

The serrated blade had entered Vasili's back and exited through his stomach. Andrei stood there, holding the knife. He'd saved his brother. He calmly picked up the knife – he hadn't stumbled or fallen over – and he'd stabbed this man cleanly and quietly, skilfully. Andrei was happy, as happy as he'd been when they'd killed the cat together, as happy as he'd ever been in his life.

Leo stood up, taking the gun from Vasili's hand. Blood snaked from the corner of Vasili's mouth. He was still alive but his eyes were no longer calculating, plans were no longer being formed. He raised a hand, placing it on Leo's shoulder, as if saying goodbye to a friend, before collapsing. This man, whose whole being had been bent on Leo's persecution, was dead. But Leo felt neither relief nor satisfaction. All he could think about was the one task he had left to perform.

Raisa got up, standing beside Leo. Andrei remained where he was. No one did anything. Slowly, Leo raised the gun, taking aim, just above the bridge of his brother's glasses. In the small room there was barely a foot between the barrel of the gun and his brother's head.

A voice cried out:

—*What are you doing?*

Leo turned. Nadya was at the bottom of the stairs. Raisa whispered:

—*Leo, we don't have much time.*

But Leo couldn't do it. Andrei said:

—*Brother, I want you to.*

Raisa reached out, put her hand around Leo's hand. Together they pulled the trigger. The gun fired, recoiled. Andrei's head jerked back and he fell to the floor.

At the sound of the shot, armed officers stormed the house, running down the stairs. Raisa and Leo dropped the gun. The lead officer stared at the body of Vasili. Leo spoke first, his hand shaking. He pointed to Andrei – his little brother.

—*This man was a murderer. Your superior officer died trying to apprehend him.*

Leo picked up the black case. With no idea if his guess would prove correct, he opened it. Inside there was a glass jar lined with paper. He unscrewed the lid, tipping the contents onto the table, onto his game of cards. It was the stomach of his brother's last victim, wrapped in an edition of *Pravda*. Leo added, his voice almost inaudible:

—*Vasili died a hero.*

As the officers moved around the table, examining this gruesome discovery, Leo stepped back. Nadya was staring at him, her father's fury in her eyes.

Moscow

18 July

Leo stood before Major Grachev in the office where he'd refused to denounce his wife. Leo didn't recognize the major. He hadn't heard of him. But he wasn't surprised that someone new was in charge. No one lasted long in the upper echelons of the State Security force and four months had passed since he'd stood here. This time there was no chance that they'd be punished with unsupervised exile or sent to the Gulags. Their executions would happen here, today.

Major Grachev said:

— *Your previous superior was Major Kuzmin, a Beria appointee. Both have been arrested. Your case now falls to me.*

In front of him was the battered case file confiscated in Voualsk. Grachev flicked through the pages, the photographs, the statements, the court transcripts.

— *In that basement we found the remains of three stomachs, two of which had been cooked. They'd been taken from children, although we're still trying to find out who these victims might be. You were right. Andrei Sidorov was a murderer. I've reviewed his background. It seems he was a collaborator with Nazi Germany*

461

and was mistakenly released back into society after the war instead of being correctly processed. That was an unpardonable error on our part. He was a Nazi agent. They sent him back with instructions to take revenge on us for our victory over the Fascists. That revenge has taken the form of these terrible attacks on our children; they targeted the very future of Communism. More than that, it was a propaganda campaign. They wanted our people to believe our society could produce such a monster when in fact he was corrupted and educated by the West, transformed by his time away from home and then returned with a poisoned, foreign heart. I notice that not one of these murders took place before the Great Patriotic War.

He paused, looking at Leo.

—Was this not your thinking?

—That was exactly my thinking, sir.

Grachev offered his hand.

—Your service to your country has been remarkable. I've been instructed to offer you a promotion, a higher grade of position within the State Security organs, there's a clear route to a political role if you should want it. We're in new times, Leo. Our leader Khrushchev considers the problems you faced in your investigation part of the unpardonable excesses of Stalinist rule. Your wife has been released. Since she assisted you in hunting this foreign operative any question of her loyalty has now been answered. Both your records will be wiped clean. Your parents will have their old apartment back. If that is not available, then they will have a better one.

Leo remained silent.

—You have nothing to say?

—That is a very generous offer. And I'm honoured. You understand that I acted without any thought of promotion or power. I merely knew this man had to be stopped.

—I understand.

—But I would like permission to turn down your offer. And instead make a request of my own.

—Go on.

—I want to take charge of a Moscow homicide department. If such a department does not exist I would like to create it.

—What need is there of such a department?

—As you already said yourself, murder will become a weapon against our society. If they cannot spread their propaganda through conventional means, they will use unorthodox means. I believe crime will become a new front in our struggle with the West. They will use it to undermine the harmonious nature of our society. When they do, I want to be there to stop it.

—Go on.

—I would like General Nesterov transferred to Moscow. I would like him to work with me in this new department.

Grachev considered the request, nodding solemnly.

*

Raisa was waiting outside, staring up at the statue of Dzerzhinsky. Leo exited the building and took her hand, a brazen display of affection no doubt scrutinized by those staring out of the Lubyanka. He didn't care. They were safe, at least for the time being. That was long enough; that was as long as anyone could possibly hope for. He glanced up at Dzerzhinsky's statue and realized that he couldn't remember a single thing that man had ever said.

ONE WEEK LATER

Moscow

Leo and Raisa were seated in the director's office of Orphanage 12, located not far from the zoo. Leo glanced at his wife and asked:

—*What's taking so long?*

—*I don't know.*

—*Something's wrong.*

Raisa shook her head:

—*I don't think so.*

—*The director didn't like us very much.*

—*He seemed OK to me.*

—*But what did he think of us?*

—*I don't know.*

—*Do you think he liked us?*

—*It doesn't really matter what he thinks. It matters what they think.*

Leo stood up, restless, saying:

—*He has to sign off on it.*

—*He'll sign the papers. That's not the issue.*

Leo sat down again, nodding.

—*You're right. I'm nervous.*

—*So am I.*

—*How do I look?*

—*You look fine.*

—*Not too formal?*

—*Relax, Leo.*

The door opened. The director, a man in his forties, entered the room.

—*I've found them.*

Leo wondered if that was just a turn of phrase or whether he'd literally searched the building. The man stepped aside. Standing behind him were two young girls, Zoya and Elena, the daughters of Mikhail Zionoviev. It had been several months since they'd witnessed their parents' execution in the snow outside their home. In that time the physical change was dramatic. They'd lost weight, their skin had lost colour. The younger girl, Elena, only four years old, had a shaved head. The elder girl, Zoya, ten years old, had her hair cropped short. They'd almost inevitably been infested with lice.

Leo stood up, Raisa beside him. He turned to the director.

—*Could we have a moment alone?*

The director didn't like the request. But he obliged and retired, shutting the door. Both girls positioned themselves with their backs against the door as far away from them as possible.

—*Zoya, Elena, my name is Leo. Do you remember me?*

No response, no change in their expression. Their eyes were alert, waiting for danger. Zoya took hold of her little sister's hand.

—*This is my wife Raisa. She's a teacher.*

—*Hello, Zoya. Hello, Elena. Why don't you both take a seat? It's much more comfortable sitting down.*

Leo picked up the chairs, putting them down near the girls. Although reluctant to move from the door, they sat down, still holding hands, still saying nothing.

Leo and Raisa crouched so that they were below the children's eye level, still keeping their distance. The girls' fingernails were black – perfect lines of grime – but their hands were otherwise clean. It was obvious that they'd been hastily tidied up before the meeting. Leo began.

—*My wife and I want to offer you a home, our home.*

—*Leo has explained to me the reason you're here. I'm sorry if this is upsetting to talk about, but it's important we say these things now.*

—*Although I tried to stop the murder of your mother and your father, I failed. Maybe you see no difference between me and the officer who committed that terrible crime. But I promise you, I am different.*

Leo faltered. He took a second, regaining his composure:

—*You might feel that by living with us you're being disloyal to your parents. But I believe your parents would want the best for you. And life in these orphanages will offer you nothing. After four months I'm sure you understand that better than anyone.*

Raisa continued:

—*This is a difficult decision we're asking you to make. You're both very young. Unfortunately we live in a time when children are forced to make adult decisions. If you stay here your lives will be tough and they're unlikely to get any easier.*

—*My wife and I want to offer you back your childhood, we want to offer you a chance to enjoy being young. We won't take the place of your parents. No one can replace them. We'll be your guardians. We'll look after you, feed you and give you a home.*

Raisa smiled, adding:

—*We expect nothing in return. You don't have to love us: you don't even have to like us necessarily, although we hope, eventually, you will. You can use us to get out of here.*

Supposing the girls wanted to say no, Leo added:

—*If you say no, we'll try and find another family that will take you, a family that doesn't have connections to your past. If that would be easier for you, you can tell us. The truth is, I cannot fix what happened. However, we can offer you a better future. We do not expect anything in return. You will have each other. You will have your own room. But you will always know me as the man who came to your farm, the man who came to arrest your father. Perhaps that memory will grow smaller over time, but you'll never forget it. That will make our relationship complicated. But I believe, from personal experience, that it can work.*

The girls sat in silence, staring at Leo, staring at Raisa. They'd made no reaction and they hadn't changed position, still sitting on the chairs holding hands. Raisa remarked:

—*You are free to say yes or no. You can ask us to find you a different family. It's entirely up to you.*

Leo stood up.

—*My wife and I will go for a walk. We'll let you talk about it, the two of you, alone. You'll have this room to yourself. Make whatever decision you like. You have no reason to be afraid.*

Leo walked around the girls and opened the door. Raisa stood up and stepped out into the hallway, Leo followed, shutting the door behind them. Together they walked down the corridor, as nervous as they'd ever been in their lives.

*

Back in the office, Zoya gave her little sister a hug.

Acknowledgements

I've been lucky to have the support of a wonderful agent, St John Donald at PFD, who nudged me towards writing this book. For that nudge – and many other things beside – I'm extremely grateful. Thanks also to Georgina Lewis and Alice Dunne for their help along the way. Through the various drafts I had feedback from Sarah Ballard, which was the perfect mix of criticism and encouragement. Finally – and it's clear I owe a lot to PFD – I'd like to thank James Gill for taking on the book once it was finished, only for him to tell me it wasn't finished at all, making me rewrite it again. His enthusiasm at that stage was much needed and much appreciated.

My editors, Suzanne Baboneau at Simon & Schuster UK and Mitch Hoffman at Grand Central Publishing, have been amazing. I've loved working with both of them. Thanks also to Jessica Craig, Jim Rutman and Natalina Sanina. Natalina was kind enough to point out some of the errors I made with regards to Russian names and Russian life in general.

Special mention must go to Bob Bookman at CAA for all his advice and for putting me in contact with Robert Towne. A writing hero of mine, Robert took time to share his thoughts with me on a late draft of the book. Needless to say, they were inspirational.

Outside of the professional sphere, I've had a handful of great readers. Zoe Trodd helped me enormously. Alexandra Arlango and her mother Elizabeth read numerous incarnations of the novel and at each stage offered detailed and invaluable comments. I cannot thank them enough. As it happens, Alexandra, through Qwerty Films – working with Michael Kuhn, Emmeline Yang and Colleen Woodcock – gave me my first break at writing. And it was while researching a screenplay I was writing for them that I stumbled across the real life case of Andrei Chikatilo and the events around it.

Many people assisted with the completion of this book but none more so than Ben Stephenson. I've never been as happy as I have been during these past few years.

Further reading

There would have been no way to write this story without having first read the memoirs, diaries and histories of a number of authors. I've enjoyed the research as much as writing and the body of work on the subjects touched upon in this book is of an awesome quality. What follows is a small selection of these works. I should point out that any liberties with the truth or historical inaccuracies in my novel are purely my own doing.

Janusz Bardach's memoir *Man is Wolf to Man* (co-written by Kathleen Gleeson, Scribner 2003) offers a powerful portrait of trying to survive in the Gulags of Stalinist Russia. On that subject both Anne Applebaum's *Gulag* (Penguin 2004) and Aleksandr Solzhenitsyn *The Gulag Archipelago* (Harvil 2003) have been essential reading.

For general historical background I've found Robert Conquest's

The Harvest of Sorrow (Pimlico 2002), Simon Sebag Montefiore's *Stalin* (Phoenix 2004) and Shelia Fitzpatrick's *Everyday Stalinism* (Oxford University Press 1999) extremely useful.

With regards to Russian police procedure, Anthony Olcott's *Russian Pulp* (Rowman & Littlefield 2001) went into detail not only about the justice system itself but also literary representations of that system. Boris Levytsky's *The Uses of Terror* (Coward, McCann & Geoghergan Inc. 1972) was invaluable when it came to understanding, or at least trying to, the machinations of the MGB. Finally, Robert Cullen's *The Killer Department* (Orion 1993) provided a clear account of the real-life investigation into the crimes of Andrei Chikatilo.

I cannot recommend any of these books highly enough.

Tom Rob Smith – Q&A

How do you write? For example, do you have a favourite time of day to write? Or a favourite place?

I start early. I'm a morning person, I like those early hours. Midday is the worst time for me writing wise – I go for a walk, take a long lunch and then start again around two. I rarely work later than seven in the evening. It adds up to a lot of hours but it never feels particularly tough as a regime.

At the moment I work in a study but I'm not sentimental about it, which is fortunate since it's a rented flat. In fact, I'm about to move, so I'll be working somewhere new in a month or two.

Which book(s) inspired you to become an author?

I don't know if there was any one book. I'm pretty sure it was every book I ever loved. And not just books but also television, film, theatre – I've always liked stories, it's nice to be able to make it my living.

Which other writers do you most admire and why?

The list is long, I wouldn't know where to start – and I'd get nightmares that I'd forgotten someone. Plus, I don't know how meaningful a list it would be anyway: you love different authors for different reasons at different times of the day. Coming up with a list would be like scratching names in fresh cement, I'd be fine with it today, embarrassed by it tomorrow.

What influenced the creation of CHILD 44?

The television series *24* was an influence. I wanted to write a book that was as exciting as *24*, a page-turner in the way that show is compulsive. I buy the DVD box sets. I've watched three or four episodes back to back. I've never watched one episode by itself. I have to force myself to stop and put them aside for at least another day just to make it last. Of course, there are plenty of books like that, books you finish in a day, but I remember very distinctly watching series three of *24* at the beginning of sitting down to write *CHILD 44*.

Without wishing to seem oblique, another big influence was public transport. I used to live in South London and commute to East London: it took an hour with no delays and often it was an hour and a half. There was no way to do that journey without a book, and a certain type of book, a book you could get wrapped up in, a book you could read standing up, a book you'd miss your tube stop for. That was the kind of book I wanted to write. I owe a debt of gratitude to the District line.

Were any of the central characters based on real-life historical figures?

The events surrounding real life serial killer Andrei Chikatilo were the springboard for the novel. But the bungled criminal process, the injustices, the system itself – these were more important than any real life characters in terms of inspiration. Soviet Russia is itself a character in the book – a peculiar blend of horror and absurdity. I've tried to be as close as I can to that.

However, I didn't model the character of my fictional serial killer on the real killer. I took his crimes but not his character. Andrei Chikatilo discovered that other people's pain gave him intense pleasure. That is a very interior, private motivation: one that is essentially unfathomable, indescribable. It belongs to him and no one else. It makes sense to him and no one else. It doesn't give a reader, or me for that matter, any way in. Therefore, there's a risk they'd seem flat, a device, a mere monster, rather than a "real" person. It's ironic since in some ways making the killer dull and flat might have been a more accurate description of the man. Would it have made good reading? I didn't think it would so I've totally rethought his reasoning and, insane though it still is, my killer offers up a warped logic to his crimes, that allows us to get a little closer to him.

What first attracted you to a narrative set in Stalinist Russia?

The story attracted me – the idea of a criminal investigation being hampered by a social theory, the theory that this crime simply could not exist. The story and setting, in that regard, are inextricable. But I didn't suddenly think Stalinist Russia would be a great place to set a novel and go fishing for a story. Having said that, the more research I did, the more I realised what an amazing stretch of history it was and that definitely powered me forward.

Out of all the research, what was the most illuminating or unforgettable piece of information you discovered?

Some facts do stick in your mind, not always because they're the most shocking or the most extreme. I remember reading that Stalin ordered a census of his population, I think in 1937. When the results of census came back, stating that the population was much lower than Stalin desired it to be (because he'd murdered so many people) he had the census takers shot. It was jaw dropping: executing people because he was annoyed the population wasn't higher which was his fault anyway. Stalin then released his own inflated figures, figures he could've just made up in the first place.

What works similar to your own would you recommend to the reader who wanted to find out more?

There's a selected bibliography at the back of the novel. I haven't come across a bad book on the period, the histories, the memoirs, diaries – they're all incredible.

What are you working on now?

The follow up to *CHILD 44*!

What was your favourite childhood book?

I loved Roald Dahl – I must have read everything he wrote. And then there was Tolkein, any adventure stories really, other worlds. I also remember being addicted to a kind of fantasy fiction where you'd read a page and then be forced to make a choice: do you want to go down this tunnel, or climb the ladder. You'd be given different page numbers to turn to and different adventures would unfold depending on the choices you made. I had about forty of those books. You were supposed to follow rules: using a dice to determine if you defeated a monster or not. I'd ignore those rules and cheat my way through. I could never imagine killing myself halfway through a book and starting again. I'd be interested to know if anyone ever did. Anyway, those books must seem quaint now – usurped by computer games where you make those kinds of interactive decisions every single second.

44 Stalinist Statistics

1. In 1919 there were 21 registered concentration camps in Russia.

2. In 1920 there were 107.

3. In 1930 there were 179,000 prisoners in the GULAG system.

4. In 1953, the year of Stalin's death, there were 2,468,524.

5. Number of those prisoners who were pregnant – 6,286.

6. Total number of forced labourers in the USSR – 28.7 million.

7. On 12th November 1938 number of execution warrants signed by Stalin – 3,167.

8. Number of political executions between 1930 & 1953 – 786,098.

9. Number of prisoners carried by the transit GULAG ship *Indigirka* – 1500.

10. Number of life rafts on the ship *Indigirka* – 0.

11. Number of prisoners who died when the ship sunk – 1000.

12. Number of distress messages sent by the crew – 0.

13. Amount of bread given to a GULAG worker in 1940 – 550 grams per day.

14. Amount of coal expected to be dug per day to earn that bread ration – 5.5 tonnes.

15. Amount of bread stolen in the last two quarters of 1946 from 34 camps – 70,000 kilograms.

16. Specified height of a toilet bucket – a *parasha* – in a male prison holding cell – 55 centimetres.

17. Specified height of a toilet bucket in a female prison cell – 30 centimetres.

18. Number of children in a Stalinist orphanage in 1940 – 212.

19. Number of spoons in that same orphanage – 12.

20. Number of plates in that same orphanage – 20.

21. Number of homeless children 1943–45 – 842,144.

22. Number of those children assigned to labour colonies – 52,830.

23. Number of churches in Moscow before the revolution – 460.

24. Number of churches in Moscow by 1st January 1933 – 100.

25. Total number of writers in the Ukraine in 1935 – 240.

26. Number of writers who "disappeared" from the Ukraine – 200.

27. Number of peasants who died during the terror-famine and dekulakization 1930–1933 – 14.5 million.

28. During the deportation of the kulaks in 1933 total death toll in one district in the Poltava Province – 7,113.

29. Of those 7,113 that died, number of children under the age of 18 – 3,549.

30. Number of Soviet children estimated to have died 1932–34 due to famine and execution – 3 to 4 million.

31. Number of minutes a worker needed to be late in order to suffer criminal proceedings – 20.

32. Number of people queuing outside one shop in Leningrad for groceries – 6000.

33. Average living space in Moscow in 1940 per capita head – 4 square metres.

34. In 1938 total distance in kilometres of sewage pipes in Stalingrad – 0.

35. Population of Novosibirsk in 1929 – 150,000.

36. Number of bathhouses for entire population of Novosibirsk – 3.

37. In 1937 percentage of all men aged 30–39 married – 91.

38. In 1937 percentage of all women aged 30–39 married – 82.

39. Amount paid to mothers with seven or more children – 2000 rubles a year.

40. Price of a pair of shoes – 12 rubles.

41. In Moscow oblast number of families registered with 8 children – 2,730.

42. In Moscow oblast number of families registered with 9 or 10 children – 1,032.

43. In Shakhovskoi district number of children in one family – 15.

44. Age at which a child could be executed – 12.

If you enjoyed *Child 44*, don't miss out on
Tom Rob Smith's chilling sequel:

THE SECRET SPEECH

TOM ROB SMITH

ISBN: 978-0-85720-409-7

Turn the page to read an extract …

Seated at his kitchen table, Leo stared at the sheet of paper. Three words were all that remained of the document that had resulted in Suren Moskvin taking his own life:

Under torture, Eikhe

Leo had read the words over and over again, unable to take his eyes off them. Out of context, their effect was none the less hypnotic. Breaking their spell, he pushed the sheet of paper aside and picked up his case, laying it flat on the table. Inside were two classified files. In order to obtain access to them he'd needed clearance. There'd been no difficulty regarding the first file, on Suren Moskvin. However, the second had prompted questions. The second file he'd requested was on Robert Eikhe.

Opening the first set of documents, he felt the weight of this man's past, the number of pages accumulated on him. Moskvin had been a state security officer — a Chekist — just like Leo, for far longer than Leo had served, keeping his job while thousands of officers were shot. Included in the file was a list: the denunciations Moskvin had made throughout his career:

Nestor Iurovsky. Neighbour. Executed
Rozalia Reisner. Friend. 10 years
Iakov Blok. Shopkeeper. 5 years
Karl Uritsky. Colleague. Guard. 10 years

Nineteen years of service, two pages of denunciations and nearly one hundred names – yet he'd only ever given up one family member.

Iona Radek. Cousin. Executed

Leo recognized a technique. The dates of the denunciations were haphazard, many falling in one month and then nothing for several months. The chaotic spacing was deliberate, hiding careful calculation. Denouncing his cousin had almost certainly been strategic. Moskvin needed to make sure it didn't look as if his loyalty to the State stopped at his family. To suffuse his list with credibility the cousin had been sacrificed: protection from the allegation that he only named people who didn't matter to him personally. A consummate survivor, this man was an improbable suicide.

Checking the dates and locations of where Moskvin had worked, Leo sat back in surprise. They'd been colleagues: both of them were employed at the Lubyanka seven years ago. Their paths had never crossed, at least not that he could remember. Leo had been an investigator, making arrests, following suspects. Moskvin had been a guard, transporting prisoners, supervising their detention. Leo had done his utmost to avoid the basement interrogation cells, as if believing the floorboards shielded him from the activities that carried on below, day after day. If Moskvin's suicide was an expression of guilt, what had triggered such extreme feelings after all this time? Leo shut the folder, turning his attention to the second file.

Robert Eikhe's file was thicker, heavier, the front cover stamped CLASSIFIED, the pages bound shut as if to keep something noxious trapped inside. Leo unwound the string. The name seemed familiar. Glancing at the pages he saw that Eikhe had been a party member since 1905 – before the Revolution – at a time when being a member of the Communist Party meant exile or execution. His record was impeccable: a former candidate for the Central Committee Politburo. Despite this, he'd been arrested on 29 April 1938. Plainly, this man was no traitor. Yet Eikhe had confessed: the protocol was in the file, page after page detailing his anti-Soviet activity. Leo had drafted too many pre-prepared confessions not to recognize this as the work of an agent, punctuated with stock phrases – signs of the in-house style, the template to which any person might be forced to sign their name. Flicking forward, Leo found a declaration of innocence written by Eikhe while imprisoned. In contrast to the confession, the prose was human, desperate, pitifully heaping praise on the party, proclaiming love for the State and pointing out with timid modesty the injustice of his arrest. Leo read, hardly able to breathe:

> *Not being able to suffer the tortures to which I was submitted by Ushakov and Nikolayev – especially by the former, who utilized the knowledge that my broken ribs have not properly mended and caused me great pain – I have been forced to accuse myself and others.*

Leo knew what would follow next.

On 4 February 1940 Eikhe had been shot.

*

Raisa stood, watching her husband. Engrossed in classified files, he was oblivious to her presence. This vision of Leo – pale, tense, shoulders hunched over secret documents, the fate of other people in his hands – could have been sliced from their unhappy past. The temptation was to react as she'd done so many times before, to walk away, to avoid and ignore him. The rush of bad memories hit her like a kind of nausea. She fought against the sensation. Leo was not that man any more. She was no longer trapped in that marriage. Walking forward, she reached out, resting a hand on his shoulder, appointing him the man she'd learnt to love.

Leo flinched at her touch. He hadn't noticed his wife enter the room. Caught unawares, he felt exposed. He stood up abruptly, the chair clattering behind him. Eye to eye, he saw her nervousness. He'd never wanted her to feel that way again. He should have explained what he was doing. He'd fallen into old habits, silence and secrets. He put his arms around her. Resting her head on his shoulder he knew she was peering down at the files. He explained:

— *A man killed himself, a former MGB agent.*

— *Someone you knew?*

— *No. Not that I remember.*

— *You have to investigate?*

— *Suicide is treated as—*

— *I mean . . . does it have to be you?*

Raisa wanted him to pass it over, to have nothing to do with the MGB, even indirectly. He pulled back.

— *The case won't take long.*

She nodded, slowly, before changing the subject.

— *The girls are in bed. Are you going to read for them? Maybe you're busy?*

— *No, I'm not busy.*

He put the files back in his briefcase. Passing his wife he leaned in to kiss her, a kiss that she gently blocked with a finger, looking into his eyes. She said nothing, before removing her finger and kissing him – a kiss that felt as if he was making the most unbreakable and sacred of promises.

Entering his bedroom, he placed the files out of sight, an old habit. Changing his mind, he retrieved them, leaving them on the side table for Raisa should she want to read them. He hurried back down the hallway on his way to his daughters' bedroom, trying to smooth the tension from his face. Smiling broadly, he opened the door.

Leo and Raisa had adopted two young sisters. Zoya was now fourteen years old and Elena, seven. Leo moved towards Elena's bed, perching on the edge, picking up a book from the cabinet, a children's story by Yury Strugatsky. He opened the book and began to read aloud. Almost immediately, Zoya interrupted:

— *We've heard this before.*

She waited a moment before adding:

— *We hated it the first time.*

The story concerned a young boy who wanted to be a miner. The boy's father, also a miner, had died in an accident and the boy's mother was fearful of her son continuing in such a dangerous profession. Zoya was right. Leo had read this before. Zoya summarized contemptuously:

— *The son ends up digging more coal than anyone has ever dug before, becomes a national hero and dedicates his prize to the memory of his father.*

Leo shut the book.

— *You're right. It's not very good. But, Zoya, while it's OK for you to say whatever you please in this house, be more careful outside. Expressing critical opinions, even about trivial matters, like a children's story, is dangerous.*

— *You going to arrest me?*

Zoya had never accepted Leo as her guardian. She'd never forgiven him for the death of her parents. Leo didn't refer to himself as their father. And Zoya would call him Leo Demidov, addressing him formally, putting as much distance between them as possible. She took every opportunity to remind him that she was living with him out of practical considerations, using him as a means to an end – providing material comforts for her sister, freeing her from the orphanage.

Even so, she took care that nothing impressed her, not the apartment, not their outings, day trips or meals. As stern as she was beautiful, there was no softness in her appearance. Perpetual unhappiness seemed vitally important to her. There was little Leo could do to encourage her to shrug it off. He hoped that at some point relations would slowly improve. He was still waiting. He would, if necessary, wait for ever.

— *No, Zoya, I don't do that any more. And I never will again.*

Leo reached down, picking up one of the *Detskaya Literatura* journals, printed for children across the country. Before he could start, Zoya cut in:

— *Why don't you make up a story? We'd like that, wouldn't we, Elena?*

When Elena arrived in Moscow she was only four years old, young enough to adapt to the changes in her life. In contrast to her older sister, she made friends and worked hard at school. Susceptible to flattery, she sought her teachers' praise, trying to please everyone, including her new guardians.

Elena became anxious. She understood from the tone of her sister's voice that she was expected to agree. Embarrassed at having to take sides, she merely nodded. Leo, sensing danger, replied:

— *There are plenty of stories we haven't read, I'm sure I can find one we like.*

Zoya wouldn't relent.

— *They're all the same. Tell us something new. Make something up.*

— *I doubt I'd be very good.*

— *You're not even going to try? My father used to make up all kinds of stories. Set it on a remote farm, a farm in winter, with the ground covered in a layer of snow. The nearby river is frozen. It could start like this. Once upon a time there are two young girls, sisters . . .*

— *Zoya, please.*

— *The sisters live with their mother and their father and they're as happy as can be. Until one day a man, in a uniform, came to arrest them and—*

Leo interrupted:

— *Zoya? Please?*

Zoya glanced at her sister and stopped. Elena was crying. Leo stood up.

— *You're both tired. I'll find some better books tomorrow. I promise.*

Leo turned the light off and closed the door. In the hallway, he comforted himself that things would get better, eventually. All Zoya needed was a little more time.

*

Zoya lay in bed, listening to the sound of her sister sleeping – her slow, soft intakes of breath. When they'd lived on the farm with their parents, the four of them shared a small room with thick mud walls, warmed by a wood fire. Zoya would sleep beside Elena under their coarse, hand-stitched blankets. The sound of her little sister sleeping meant safety: it meant their parents were nearby. It didn't belong here, in this apartment, with Leo in the room next door.

Zoya never fell asleep easily. She'd lie in bed for hours, churning thoughts before exhaustion overcame her. She was the only person who cherished the truth: the only person who refused to forget. She eased herself out of bed. Aside from her little sister breathing, the apartment was silent. She crept to the door, her eyes already adjusted to the darkness. She navigated the hallway by keeping her hand on the wall. In the kitchen, street lighting leaked in through the window. Moving nimbly, like a thief, she opened a drawer and took hold of the handle, feeling the weight of the knife.

Pressing the blade flat against her leg, Zoya walked towards Leo's bedroom. Slowly she pushed open the door until there was enough space to sidestep inside. She moved silently over the wooden floor. The curtains were drawn, the room dark, but she knew the layout, where to tread in order to reach Leo, sleeping on the far side.

Standing directly over him, Zoya raised the knife. Although she couldn't see him, her imagination mapped the contours of his body. She wouldn't stab him in the stomach: the blankets might absorb the blade. She'd plunge it through his neck, sinking it as far as she could, before he had a chance to overpower her. Knife outstretched, she pressed down with perfect control. Through the blade she felt his arm, his shoulder – she steered upwards, making small depressions until the knife tip touched directly onto his skin. In position, all she had to do was grip the handle with both hands and push down.

Zoya performed this ritual at irregular intervals, sometimes once a week, sometimes not for a month. The first time was three years ago, shortly after she and her sister moved into this apartment from the orphanage. On that occasion she had every intention of killing him. That same day he'd taken them to the zoo. Neither she nor Elena had been to a zoo, and confronted with exotic animals, creatures that she'd never seen before, she'd forgotten herself. For perhaps no more than five or ten minutes, she'd enjoyed the visit. She'd smiled. He hadn't seen her smile, she was sure of that, but it didn't matter. Watching him together with Raisa, a happy couple, imitating a family, pretending, lying, she understood that they were trying to steal the place of her parents. And she'd let them. On her way home, on the tramcar, her guilt had been so intense she'd thrown up. Leo and Raisa had blamed the sweet snacks and the motion of the tram. That night, feverish, she lay in bed, crying, scratching her legs until they bled. How could she have betrayed the memory of her parents so easily? Leo believed he could win her love with new clothes, rare foods, day trips and chocolate: it was pathetic. She vowed that her lapse would never happen again. There was one way to make sure: she took the knife and resolved to kill him. She stood, as she stood now, ready to murder.

The same memory that had driven her into the room, the memory of her parents, was the reason she hadn't killed him. They wouldn't want this man's blood on her hands. They would want her to look after her sister. Obedient, silently crying, she'd allowed Leo to live. Every now and then she'd come back, creeping in, armed with a knife, not because she'd changed her mind, not for revenge, not to murder, but as a memorial to her parents, as a way of saying she had not forgotten them.

The telephone rang. Startled, Zoya stepped back, the knife slipping from her hand, clattering to the floor. Dropping to her knees she fumbled in the pitch black frantically trying to find it. Leo and Raisa were stirring, the bed straining as they moved. They'd be reaching for the light. Working by touch alone Zoya desperately patted the floorboards. As the telephone rang for the second time she had no choice but to leave the knife behind, hurrying around the bed, running towards the door, slipping through the gap just as the light came on.

*

Leo sat up, his thoughts sluggish with sleep, intermingled dreams and reality – there had been movement, a figure, or perhaps there hadn't. The phone was ringing. It only ever rang because of work. He checked his watch: almost midnight. He glanced at Raisa. She was awake, waiting for him to answer the phone. He mumbled an apology and got up. The door was ajar. Didn't they always close it before they went to sleep? Maybe not, it didn't matter, and he headed into the hallway.

He picked up the receiver. The voice on the other end was urgent, loud.

— *Leo? This is Nikolai.*

Nikolai: the name meant nothing to him. He didn't reply. Correctly interpreting Leo's silence, the man continued:

— *Nikolai, your old boss! Your friend! Leo, don't you remember? I gave you your first assignment! The priest, remember, Leo?*

Leo remembered. He hadn't heard from Nikolai in a long time. This man was of no relevance to his life now and he resented him calling.

— *Nikolai, it's late.*

— *Late? What's happened to you? We didn't start work until about now.*

— *Not any more.*

— *No, not any more.*

Nikolai's voice drifted off, before adding:

— *I need to meet you.*

His words were slurred. He was drunk.

— *Nikolai, why don't you sleep it off and we'll talk tomorrow?*

— *It has to be tonight.*

His voice cracked. He was on the verge of crying.

— *What's going on?*

— *Meet me. Please.*

Leo wanted to say no.

— *Where?*

— *Your offices.*

— *I'll be there in thirty minutes.*

Leo hung up. His annoyance was tempered by unease. Nikolai wouldn't have got back in contact unless he had cause. Returning to the bedroom, Raisa was sitting up. Leo shrugged an explanation.

— *A former colleague. He wants to meet. Says it has to be tonight.*

— *A colleague from when?*

— *From . . .*

Leo didn't need to finish the sentence.

— *Out of nowhere, he calls?*

— *He was drunk. I'll speak to him.*

— *Leo . . . ?*

She didn't finish. Leo nodded.

— *I don't like it either.*

He grabbed his clothes, hastily getting changed. Almost ready to leave, tying his shoelaces, he saw something under the bed, something catching the light. Curious, he moved forward, crouching down. Raisa asked:

— *What?*

It was a large kitchen knife. Near it was a notch in the floor.

— *Leo?*

He should show it to her.

— *It's nothing.*

As Raisa leaned over to look he stood up, hiding the knife behind his back and turning the light off.

In the hallway he laid the blade flat across his palm. He glanced at his daughters' bedroom. He stepped towards the door and gently pushed it open. The room was dark. Both girls were in bed, asleep. In the process of retreat, silently shutting the door, he smiled at the slow, shallow breathing of Elena sleeping. He paused, listening carefully. He couldn't hear any noise coming from Zoya's side of the room. She was holding her breath.

AGENT
6

TOM ROB SMITH

**The heart-racing adventure that began in *Child 44* and
The Secret Speech now reaches its epic conclusion.**

**Leo Demidov's last case forces him to question what we live
for when we've lost the people we love . . .**

Moscow, 1965. Former Secret Service agent Leo Demidov is
forbidden to travel with his wife and daughters to New York as part
of a 'Peace Tour', meant to foster better relations between the two
Cold War enemies. Leo's natural paranoia reaches its peak: Why
have his family been selected? What is being planned?

When Leo's worst fears are realised and a tragic murder destroys
everything he loves, he demands only one thing: that he is
allowed to investigate and find the killer who has struck at the
heart of his family. Crippled by grief, his request denied, Leo
sees no other option than to take matters into his own hands,
thousands of miles from the crime scene.

In a surprising, thrilling story that spans decades and continents –
from the backstreets of 1960s New York to the mountains of
Afghanistan in the 1980s – Leo will stop at nothing as he
hunts the one person who knows the truth: Agent 6.

ISBN 978-1-84737-567-4

COMING 07.07.11